Prai...

THE SOULSEE...

'Powerfully creepy'
Publishers Weekly

'*Cursed* was amazing . . . This is a series I would recommend to
pretty much anyone who's into fantasy and mythology'
Wayfaring Bibliomaniac

'Gripping and tantalisingly sexy'
Holdfast Magazine

'A beautifully written, flowing Urban fantasy with a terrific story
and some really great characters'
Liz Loves Books

'Instantly absorbing . . . will certainly leave a lasting impression'
SciFiNow

'I loved this book. The characters, the atmosphere, the humour, the
romance, it all worked. *Marked* is a wonderful debut for Tingey'
A Fantastical Librarian

'A compelling debut . . . a brisk paranormal tale with outstanding world building,
a large cast of well-drawn characters, and an intricate plot filled with intrigue and
adventure. Reads like a PG-13 version of the Sookie Stackhouse series'
Booklist

'Great fun and a delight to read'
Upcoming4.me

'The kind of story that sucks readers in very quickly and you end up completely
losing track of time while you're reading . . . A fantastic start to this new series'
Feeling Fictional

'I was enthralled. A strong and interesting debut'
Draumr Kópa Blog

'A thrill ride to the very end. The intrigue and action began immediately,
drawing t... I cannot

Essex County Council

3013021372522 8

Praise for

THE SOULSEER CHRONICLES

'Powerfully creepy'
Publishers Weekly

'Great . . . amazing . . . This is a serial world, recommend to
pretty much anyone who's into fantasy and mythology'

Also by Sue Tingey

The Soulseer Chronicles
Marked
Cursed

'A beautifully written, dark, twisted fantasy with terrific story
and some really great characters'
Liz Loves Books

'Insanely absorbing . . . will certainly leave a lasting impression'
SciFiNow

'I loved this book. The characters, the atmosphere, the humour, the
romance; it all worked. Marked is a wonderful debut by Tingey'
A Fantastical Librarian

'A compelling debut . . . a gripping paranormal tale with outstanding world building,
a large cast of well drawn characters, and an intricate plot filled with danger and
adventure. Reads like a PG-13 version of the book . . . Sit back home to the'
Booklist

'Great fun and a delight to read'
Upcoming4.me

'The kind of very slick, quick read . . . it's very quickly and immoderately
losing track of time while you're reading . . . A fantastic start to this new series'
Feeling Fictional

'I was enthralled. A strong and interesting debut'
Dreams Kept Blog

'A thrill ride to the very end. The intrigue and action began immediately
drawing the reader in and keeping their eyes glued to the pages . . . I cannot
wait to see where it goes from here'
Fangirls Read It First

THE SOULSEER CHRONICLES BOOK III

SUE TINGEY

BOUND

Jo Fletcher
BOOKS

First published in Great Britain in 2017 by

Jo Fletcher Books
an imprint of
Quercus Editions Ltd
Carmelite House
50 Victoria Embankment
London EC4Y 0DZ

An Hachette UK company

Copyright © 2017 Sue Tingey

The moral right of Sue Tingey to be
identified as the author of this work has been
asserted in accordance with the Copyright,
Designs and Patents Act, 1988.

All rights reserved. No part of this publication
may be reproduced or transmitted in any form
or by any means, electronic or mechanical,
including photocopy, recording, or any
information storage and retrieval system,
without permission in writing from the publisher.

A CIP catalogue record for this book is available
from the British Library

PB ISBN 978 1 78429 076 4

This book is a work of fiction. Names, characters,
businesses, organizations, places and events are
either the product of the author's imagination
or used fictitiously. Any resemblance to
actual persons, living or dead, events or
locales is entirely coincidental.

10 9 8 7 6 5 4 3 2 1

Typeset by Jouve (UK), Milton Keynes

Printed and bound in Great Britain by Clays Ltd, St Ives plc

For Mum, Dad and Mike
who always encouraged me in everything I ever wanted to do.

I left Jamie cooking supper. Jinx was off somewhere on Bob – getting wine I hoped; we were almost out.

I loved this time of the evening when it was still light enough to walk along the crystal sand beach surrounding our lake. I had about half an hour before sunset, when the two suns would drop from the heavens and sink below the horizon, empurpling the sky before it changed to black.

Pyrites gambolled along beside me chasing the crab-like creatures that scuttled here and there across the sand, sometimes flapping his wings to fly along by my shoulder. He was enjoying this holiday just as much as we were.

Jamie, Jinx and I spent most afternoons making love, and just thinking about that made me shiver.

Of the two, Jamie was the more serious lover – and I would have said the most conventional until a couple of days ago when he'd whisked me up into the sky while Jinx was still sleeping and we'd given the term 'Mile High Club' a whole new meaning.

Jinx, on the other hand, was – as in most things – not serious at all. He loved to nip and suck and lick and kiss – he could turn the most ordinary patch of skin into a full-blown erogenous zone. Not a square inch of me was safe. He was my bad boy, and although he hadn't said as much, if he thought he could get away with tying me up I think he'd be more than happy to give it a go.

I couldn't help but smile remembering earlier this morning, when I'd woken up to the sound of muffled male laughter and puffs of warm liquorice-breath on my face. As soon as I'd opened my eyes, I'd been rewarded with a swipe of Pyrites' tongue: my drakon was more than a little excited to see me awake.

'What is it, boy?' I'd asked, and he'd scrambled off the bed and waited just inside the door puffing white smoke, clearly impatient for me to get up. After yawning and stretching, I'd wrapped a blanket around me before clambering off the bed and padding barefoot across the marble floor to join him, but as soon as I reached him, he'd shot into the next room and out through the open door onto the beach.

The laughter had become louder as I'd followed him; my men were obviously enjoying themselves and I wondered what they were doing that was making Pyrites so eager for me to go outside.

Jamie and Jinx were in the lake, leaving boots and trousers discarded on the jetty. I strolled across the sand and along the wooden walkway to crouch down at the edge. They were ducking and diving and acting more like little boys than daemons who were thousands of years old. But seeing Jinx and Jamie laughing and playing around and generally enjoying each other's company made me happier than I could have possibly imagined. Over the weeks we'd spent together they had become friends, and I was hoping it was more than their love for me that bound them to each other.

I sat down next to their clothes and Pyrites took to the air to dive-bomb them as they swam. All of my men being in playful moods had chased away the spectre of Amaliel Cheriour, the disgraced Court Enforcer and Corrector, if only for a short time.

'Hey!' Jamie shouted upon seeing me. 'Come in!'

I leaned forward and dangled my fingers in the water. 'Brr, too cold,' I told him.

'Come on, it'll be fun.'

I shook my head.

'We can always warm you up afterwards,' Jinx said, and gave me an exaggerated wink which made my heart sing – and him hard to refuse.

'All right,' I said with a smile, 'but no peeking.'

They both covered their faces with splayed fingers, their eyes glinting through the gaps, and I laughed and let the blanket slip to the deck, which earned a wolf-whistle from Jinx. I sat down on the jetty's edge and slid into the water – I'd been right: it was bloody cold!

They swam over to greet me, Jamie with his wings pulled up like a great dorsal fin and Jinx with his tail snaking out behind him, weaving from side to side across the water's surface and steering him like a rudder. Then I was surrounded, and any thoughts of the cold water vanished, for there was nowhere else I'd rather have been.

We swam and we played while Pyrites sped around us, creating waves for us to ride and puffing steam across the surface, which had the double effect of warming our upper bodies and surrounding us in thick white clouds, through which we had to fight to find each other. This started a rather bizarre game of hide and seek, with the finder demanding a forfeit from the one they'd found. Needless to say, neither of them bothered to find each other but ganged up on me. I didn't mind – some of the forfeits were more than a little interesting.

It was just one memorable morning out of many, and as I strolled along the sand I wondered what new joys tomorrow would bring.

Then Pyrites and I rounded an outcrop and any happiness I'd been feeling drained away. A tight feeling of foreboding gripped my chest as I saw Bob plodding along the beach towards us – alone. Something was wrong; I'd never seen him without Jinx. He whinnied upon seeing us, a truly pathetic sound coming from such a huge, fearsome creature.

Pyrites stayed beside me, puffing grey smoke; I clearly wasn't the only one who thought something was amiss. As I began to run towards Bob, panic welled up inside me. Where was Jinx? Why wasn't he with Bob? When we reached him, Bob snorted and stamped his hooves then hung his head, eyes half closed, his wings pressed back tight against his body.

I laid my palm on his neck, struggling to keep the worry from my voice. 'What's the matter, boy?'

He gave another whinny and his flanks quivered; his fear and dejection were almost palpable and I was getting really scared now. Bob was an infernal-eyed powerhouse of a flying machine – I'd always though he looked like he should be ridden by one of the Four Horsemen of the Apocalypse. To see him in such a bad way frightened me more than if he'd come storming down the beach with the aforesaid Horsemen in tow.

'Come on,' I said, leading him towards the villa. Jamie would know what to do. Jamie *always* knew what to do.

When we reached the front step I called out, not wanting to leave the despondent horse. I waited a few moments and called again, 'Jamie!'

I glanced at Bob, and he pushed his snout against my shoulder, a gesture very similar to when Pyrites wanted comfort. My heart was pounding; my fear cranked up another notch. This was so unlike him – he never craved affection; an offhanded pat on the neck or rump from Jinx was about the sum of what he would tolerate.

'What's happened, Bob?' I asked, stroking his silky black forehead. 'What's happened to Jinx?' Because I was pretty sure something had happened – something really bad.

I looked back up at the villa. 'Jamie!' I called again – *where was he?* 'Jamie—!'

—then a searing pain hit me, like something was skewering my brain with a red-hot iron, and with a groan I collapsed to my knees, clutching my head.

'Lucky?' I heard my name, but it sounded like I was being shouted at me through water – no; not water, *blood*. It felt like my ears were thick with blood.

Then hands were on my shoulders and Jamie was on his knees in front of me. 'Lucky – are you all right? What's wrong? Are you hurt?'

'I . . . I—' Then the pain hit me again and I screamed.

'What's wrong? What's happening to her?' I could hear Kayla, but Jamie couldn't; he couldn't hear the dead, not like Jinx and me.

They were both talking at once and although they probably weren't shouting they might as well have been, because each word shot through my head like a bullet.

'Be quiet,' I managed to gasp, 'please – *be quiet*. Please . . .'

Jamie scooped me up into his arms and carried me inside, and every step sent a spike of pain across the front of my head, making my eyes feel like they were being pressed outwards and it was only my tightly-squeezed eyelids keeping them within their sockets. When he laid me down on the bed it was a blessed relief. I felt the bed shift as Pyrites hopped up beside me and snuggled down, his head against my hip. I tried to lift a hand to stroke him, but it felt so heavy, as though a brick was strapped to my wrist.

'Lucky,' Jamie whispered, 'can you talk? Can you tell me what's wrong?'

'Something's happened to Jinx,' I mumbled through lips that felt like they belonged to someone else.

Then another spike of pain shot through my right side just below the ribs, as though I'd been stabbed with something burning-hot. I screamed, and I could hear someone else's screams reverberating inside my skull – Jinx's.

'They're torturing him,' I sobbed, and then whoever it was did something so incredibly awful that my body couldn't stand it and everything turned red and then black.

I was only unconscious for a moment or two, but when I woke I could no longer feel Jinx and I guessed he had passed out too. I still had an ache behind my eyes, but the rest of the pain had receded as if it had been washed away, leaving traces like a tide-mark throughout my body.

I struggled to sit up.

'Lucky, are you all right?' Kayla was sitting on the edge of the bed.

I didn't dare risk nodding. 'Better,' I mumbled.

'What happened?' Jamie asked. 'You said something about Jinx—'

'Bob was on the beach, alone – he looked so lost; so despondent.'

I flopped back against the pillows, too weak to stay upright. 'Someone has Jinx and they're hurting him. *Really* hurting him.'

Kayla gasped, and Jamie's brow crinkled into a puzzled frown. 'Are you sure?'

'Yes . . . No . . . I—' I was finding it hard to think straight. 'Yes. Yes, I don't know how I know; I don't know how I can feel what he's feeling, but I know he's in terrible pain.'

Jamie sank down on the bed next to me, making Kayla shift to one side, otherwise he'd have been more or less sitting on her lap. He ran his hand through his blond curls in an agitated swipe.

I looked up at him. 'Do you think it's—?' I couldn't bear to say his name, let alone believe he might have my Deathbringer in his clutches.

'Amaliel?' he said with a grimace. 'I hope not. I truly hope not.'

'It doesn't bear thinking about,' Kayla added.

'Could he somehow have trapped Jinx?' I forced myself to ask.

'I would have said no,' Jamie said. 'Jinx is nigh-on fireproof – but if you're sure it was Jinx you were feeling . . .' He looked down at me. '*Are* you sure? I mean, how can it be?'

'I heard him scream . . .' The words caught in my throat. 'It was awful.'

'I think you need the rest of your guard. I'd better get Shenanigans and Kerfuffle.'

'And Kubeck,' I reminded him.

He gave a distracted nod.

'How will you get a message to them?' If Jinx had been here he would have sent a raven – the Deathbringer had an affinity with the harbingers of death – but he was gone. If I'd been in my human form I'd have cried at the thought. But I wasn't, I hadn't been human for more than two weeks, since the first time the three of us had made love.

'Maybe tomorrow, if you feel better, we should return to court and we can find them together. We should also go to Baltheza; if Amaliel has truly captured Jinx, then he should know.'

'Rather you than me,' Kayla said. 'He is so not going to be happy about any of this.'

I ignored her. 'If it *is* Amaliel . . . but you and Jinx were both so sure he had no real power,' I said, clutching at straws.

Jamie's expression was grim. 'Maybe we were wrong.'

There was nothing we could do until the morning, so we both picked at the dinner Jamie had cooked, the empty seat at the table stealing away any appetite we may have had. Even Pyrites wasn't interested in eating, and as for poor Bob, he just stood on the beach with his head hanging down, his huge muzzle almost scraping the sand.

We went to bed, though neither of us really slept. Jamie held me in his arms, but that was the sum of it. Making love was the furthest thing from our minds. Without knowing Jinx was safe and well it would have felt wrong.

A couple of times I almost dozed off, but each time I came to with a start and looked about me, hoping I'd find a maroon arm draped about my waist, but I knew in my heart it couldn't be: Jinx was gone.

We set off at first light – Jamie and I were both awake and neither of us could face breakfast. Kayla had been unusually quiet, wafting around from room to room as I collected our things. Jamie had hardly said a word. Although he and Jinx were often at odds with each other – after all, Jinx was the daemon who brought death to my world and Jamie the Guardian who protected it from daemon activity – Jinx's disappearance had hit my angel harder than I could have ever have imagined. I didn't know if it was because he loved me and knew how much I was hurting, or because they were now truly friends, but he was definitely as troubled as I was.

Jamie rode Bob – a first for both of them, but we needed him if Shenanigans, Kerfuffle and Kubeck were to join us. Kayla sat behind me on Pyrites, and even though she said very little throughout the journey, just having her close was comforting.

The countryside below us passed in a blur; for the first time I barely noticed the forests of scarlet and burgundy pines and the lush fields of copper and bronze crops. Even the sight of amethyst rivers meandering below us and the ice-capped mountains shining like crystal in the sunshine didn't fill me with my usual enthusiastic wonder.

And every mile brought us a little closer to the royal palace.

Returning to court was not at the top of my things-to-do list. Officially I was Lord Baltheza's daughter and Kayla's sister. The latter was true – Kayla and I shared the same mother – but I was not truly Baltheza's child, and for this I was eternally grateful. Baltheza was a monster, as far as I was concerned, though his cruel and violent nature hadn't been helped by Amaliel Cheriour feeding him a poison which had been slowly driving him mad – so mad that Amaliel had been able to turn Baltheza against my mother, the woman he allegedly loved and whose ring I now wore, even going so far as to have her tortured and executed. He was recovering now, but I wasn't looking forward to spending even a short time in his company.

My heart sank even further when the fortress surrounding the royal palace came into sight. Although I loved the vibrant little town within the fortress walls, I hated the palace and its occupants; the members of the court were every bit as debauched and cruel as their ruler, and that hatred compounded my gloom so that even the bustle of the town below us couldn't lift my spirits.

It was market day; the streets were packed with carts and brightly coloured stalls and had we been on foot, it would have taken us an age to fight our way through to the palace entrance. We were coming in low enough that I could hear some of the vendors shouting out to potential customers, inviting them to try their wares, and I caught the occasional whiff of musky perfume or the tart aroma of pickled vegetables. A few shoppers looked up as we passed over, but on the whole the daemons crowding the cobblestoned streets paid us no heed, being more interested in procuring bargains.

We carried on over the mêlée and all too soon the grey stone walls and turrets of the gothic castle that was home to Lord Baltheza were right before us.

As much as I hated the palace, it was an impressive sight. Had I been a child I would have thought it a fairytale castle with its ramparts, moat and portcullis; as an adult I knew it was a much darker place, more akin to something out of a horror movie. Only once had I been deep down in the bowels of the castle, to the place where Amaliel Cheriour had plied his trade, and that was one time too many. It was worse than any set someone in Hollywood could have thought up.

We came in to land at the front entrance and Jamie wasted no time in calling over a bored-looking guard – a skinny daemon with a walrus moustache and tusks to match – and sending him to announce our arrival to Baltheza.

Kayla and I climbed down from Pyrites as he began to shrink, and when he was the size of a parrot he alighted on my shoulder so he could enter the palace. Bob was another matter; there was no way we could take him inside the building. Although Baltheza's court was a perverse and strange place, a depressed, winged horse trudging through its passageways would probably be one strangeness too far.

'Will he be all right if we leave him here?' I asked. Usually as soon as Jinx had finished with him he would slap Bob on the rump and the beast would fly off, returning when Jinx called him.

Jamie patted Bob's neck. 'He'll come if we call him,' Jamie said. 'He wants to find Jinx as much as we do.' And with that Bob trotted away, unfurled his wings and launched himself up into the sky.

Baltheza didn't keep us waiting for long. Two guards the size of grizzly bears, if not nearly so attractive, arrived within ten minutes to take us to their leader. They escorted us through the long, gloomy corridors of the palace, the echo of our footsteps sounding too loud in the confined space, and out into a walled garden; coincidently, the place where Jamie and Jinx had last seen Amaliel.

Baltheza was sitting on the low stone wall surrounding the

pond. Unusually, there was no naked slave girl lounging at his feet; apart from two guards standing by the entrance to the garden he was alone.

His back was to us, his beautiful black curls veiling his face as he leaned forward to drop small pieces of bread onto the water's surface, which were immediately swallowed by brightly coloured fishlike creatures. He turned to look up as he heard us approaching.

His nostrils flared and his thin jade lips pressed together. 'Why do I feel I'm about to get more bad news?' he said, looking from me to Jamie. 'It would be nice if, just for once, you came to visit me for the pleasure of my company.'

'Same old Daddy,' Kayla muttered as she dropped down to sit next to him.

Jamie gave a bow and I did the same. 'Lord Baltheza,' Jamie said.

'You're looking well,' he said to me, ignoring Jamie.

I couldn't say the same of him; he was as ugly and frightening as ever. Two thick, disfiguring ridges of puckered skin ran from the bridge of his aristocratically long, narrow nose, across where his eyebrows should be and up into his hairline where they met twisted ram horns. His opalescent white skin shimmered with green and blue, but spots of rose flushed his cheeks: he really wasn't at all happy. Then he fixed me with his truly terrifying eyes, dark orbs of orange dissected by vertical slits of black.

'The Deathbringer has gone missing,' Jamie said without any preamble.

Baltheza froze for a moment. 'Missing?'

'He flew off with Bob yesterday afternoon and never came back, though Bob did – alone.'

Baltheza frowned at us both as he took this in. 'Maybe he was called away on business.'

'I'd know if he had been,' Jamie said. 'When he walks the Overlands I'm made aware of his mission.'

'Hmm,' Baltheza tapped a pointed talon against his lips, still looking at me.

'There's something else,' Jamie said.

Baltheza almost had to drag his eyes away from me to pay attention to Jamie. 'More?'

'We think . . .' Jamie glanced my way. 'We're pretty sure whoever has him is torturing him.'

Baltheza's reptilian eyebrows shot up almost into his hairline. 'Torturing the Deathbringer? Impossible.' Then his eyes narrowed. 'How could you know this? And more importantly, why did you come here – to me?'

Kayla gave sniff. 'Typical of Daddy, it's always me, me, me.'

'We came to you because you're the Lord of the Underlands and we thought this was something you should know,' Jamie said, clearly as exasperated as Kayla.

Baltheza crossed his arms and glared at Jamie. 'You can search the palace; he's not here.'

'We didn't expect him to be.'

Baltheza snorted and started to say something, but I didn't hear him as pain blossomed in my chest and I staggered and fell to one knee. Before I could recover, something punched into my stomach leaving me gasping for breath.

Then I was being picked up and hugged against a hard chest, and it was only when he spoke that I realised it was Baltheza who was holding me.

'What's happening to her?'

'I don't know how, but Lucky's feeling what Jinx is feeling; at least that's what she says.'

Long slender fingers stroked my hair. 'Attacking Lucinda is as good as attacking me.'

'Oh, for goodness' sake!' I heard Kayla mutter in irritation.

'I don't think whoever is doing this knows they're attacking Lucky,' Jamie said – then another spike of pain hit me in between the eyes, Jinx's roar of pain, anger and hate bounced around inside my skull, and although I was still conscious and I could hear him and feel his pain, everything else was a blur of shadows.

This time the torment didn't stop: I'd barely got over one

assault when the next hit me. Had I been totally human I'm sure my heart would have given out, but worse than the pain were Jinx's screams, though he didn't plead or beg for it to stop; I could feel him fighting whoever was doing this to him.

'Can't we give her something?' I heard a voice say. 'Something to knock her out?' Then there was muttering, and the sound of a door opening and closing – then another blast of pain had me whimpering.

'Here, try this.'

Someone lifted my head and a goblet was pressed to my lips. 'Try to drink some, darling,' Kayla said. 'It'll make you feel so much better.'

I forced myself to take a sip. The liquid tasted sweet but with a kick, like a liqueur, leaving a trail of warmth that ran across my tongue, down my throat and into my chest. Then my head began to spin, first in slow, lazy circles, then faster and faster until I thought I might just throw up – and then another spike of pain, this one freezing cold, like I'd been stabbed with a shard of ice, shot through my upper body just above my heart.

But before I could open my mouth to scream the drug did its job and I sank into blessed oblivion.

Two

I awoke to arguing male voices. 'We can't break the connection if we don't know what it is and how it works,' Jamie said.

'Is she connected to you in the same way? I mean, is it the mark that's doing it?'

Vaybian? I struggled to open my eyes, but my eyelids felt like they were weighed down with pennies. I felt a moment of panic – had I died?

'I've never heard of someone who's been marked having this sort of connection,' Jamie said, 'and Lucky's never felt it when either of us were wounded before.'

'Then why now?' Yes, it was definitely Vaybian, Kayla's green-skinned captain and petulant lover.

'Does it really matter?' I heard Kerfuffle say. 'The Deathbringer is in trouble and Mistress Lucky is in pain. We find him and save him, and then we can worry about the whys and wherefores.'

'I agree,' Shenanigans said. 'We have to stop Mistress Lucky's pain.' Present tense! Relief washed over me – I was alive.

'Easier said than done, when we don't know where Jinx is or who's taken him,' Jamie said.

'I wouldn't have believed it possible,' Shenanigans said. 'How could anyone capture the Deathbringer?'

'Irrelevant,' Kerfuffle said in his no-nonsense way. 'We'll worry about that once we've got him back.'

'Since when have you started caring about the Deathbringer's wellbeing?' Vaybian asked.

'Since my mistress' welfare depended upon his,' Kerfuffle said, and I didn't need to have my eyes open to know my smallest guard would be standing with his hands on his hips, his oversized marshmallow head tilted back so he could glare up at Kayla's lover.

I forced my eyelids apart, squinting against the light, and tried to drag myself into a sitting position. I had a dull ache behind my eyes again, but thankfully all the other pains had faded away, leaving only a memory.

'Mistress,' Shenanigans said, hurrying over to my bedside. He was the biggest of my guards at over seven feet tall, and looked like a two-legged, emerald-green rhinoceros. One ivory tusk sprouted from the centre of his forehead and another from the top of his snout above cavernous flared nostrils, and large ivory fangs protruded between thick, rubber-band lips. For all his size, his eyes – currently full of concern – were his smallest feature; tiny buttons mostly hidden within his wrinkly hide. 'How are you feeling?'

'Not so bad now,' I said, giving him a shaky smile.

He didn't look so sure. 'Maybe you should have another draught to make you sleep.'

'That won't help find Jinx.'

Kayla sank down onto the bed next to me. 'Daddy's sent his spies out everywhere, but they've found no trace of him.'

'They didn't find Amaliel either?'

'No, they didn't,' she said, tapping her forefinger against her lips. 'I'm sure we're missing something.'

'Who's she talking to?' Vaybian asked, and I winced. In my befuddled state I'd forgotten I'd been hiding the fact that Kayla was still around. He was jealous enough of our relationship without knowing that, even when dead, she was with me and not him.

'I was talking to Jamie,' I said.

Jamie raised an eyebrow, but very sensibly kept quiet as he sat down next to me. Vaybian wasn't so easily deflected. 'You were talking to someone else – who is it you see?'

'I think you have to tell him,' Kayla said.

'And make him more morose than he already is?' I murmured to her.

'Is it Kayla?' he asked, glancing around the room. 'Is she here? Is my princess here?'

Jamie took hold of my hand, squeezed my fingers and gave me an encouraging smile. 'It's time he knew.'

'*Knew?*' Vaybian asked, his expectant expression enough to tell me what I had to do, even though I really didn't want to be dealing with this right now.

'When Kayla died, the last thing she said was that she'd never leave me,' I told him.

'She's here now?'

I gave a small nod then wished I hadn't as I saw sparkles and felt slightly sick.

Jamie moved closer, hugging me to him. 'You should rest,' he said.

'How can I rest when I know Jinx is out there somewhere all alone?'

'If he were out there all alone, there wouldn't be a problem,' Kerfuffle pointed out.

'You know what she means,' Shenanigans told his small friend, giving me an apologetic smile.

'How is she?' Vaybian asked, totally focused on what mattered to him and ignoring everything else, as usual. Though I supposed I couldn't blame him – finding out the love of his life was still around after he thought she was gone for ever would have focused his attention.

Baltheza had asked exactly the same thing when he had realised I could still see my friend even in death and Vaybian repeating the question did nothing to improve Kayla's temper. She glared at him, even though he couldn't see it. 'Why is it people keep asking how I am when it's pretty bloody obvious? I'm *dead*, Vaybian.'

'Oh, you know,' I said. I wasn't sure I wanted to say she was pissed off with him for asking something so amazingly stupid. 'Kayla is Kayla; she hasn't changed any now she's dead.' I looked at her and smiled. 'Though she has re-grown her hair and snakes,' I added as an afterthought. Before Amaliel had ruthlessly slit her throat, he'd tortured her by shearing off the vipers and her beautiful scarlet and emerald locks, which was not a good way for Vaybian to remember her.

To my surprise, Vaybian's expression softened into a gentle smile. 'Where is she?'

I nodded to where she was sitting and winced. I really had to stop doing that.

'Tell her I miss her,' he said.

'You just did.'

'I wish I could see her again.'

'Maybe one day,' I told him, but didn't add that it would most likely be the day that he died; he didn't need to hear that.

Kerfuffle abruptly crossed to the door and was reaching for it even as we heard the first rap of knuckles against wood. He opened the door and to my complete and utter surprise Baltheza swept in. Never before had he come to me; I was always summoned to appear before him.

Jamie got up from the bed and all my guard bowed, but they could have been as invisible as Kayla. He strode past them to me and sat on the edge of the bed, in the spot Jamie had just vacated.

'I didn't expect to find you awake. How are you feeling?'

'A little weak.'

When he peered at my face and gently brushed the hair back from my brow to take a better look at me I had to fight to hide my shudder of revulsion.

'You look a little better.' He glanced up at Jamie. 'Any more attacks?'

'Lucky's only just awakened.'

He returned his attention to me. 'I've had my spies combing the Underlands, but wherever Amaliel is, he's hidden from me.'

'Any news on Jinx?' I asked.

He gave a sniff, not hiding his dislike; the mannerism reminded me of Kayla. 'The Deathbringer was last seen in the small village north of the lake where you were staying, where he bought bread, cheese and three bottles of red wine. The bag containing the items was found less than twenty yards from the shop. It looked as if he'd been picking flowers when he was taken – most strange.'

'If he was that close to the village, didn't anyone hear or see anything?' Jamie asked.

Baltheza glanced up at him. 'Not that they're saying – although I can't see any reason why they'd lie about it. The young woman who served him was apparently well-smitten by the Deathbringer; she said they'd shared a word or two before he left. My agents said she was visibly upset at the thought that something might have happened to him.'

'How does he do it?' I heard Kerfuffle mutter. 'The most feared daemon in the Underlands and yet he's probably had more women than I've had hot dinners.'

'And of those you've had quite a few,' Shenanigans finished for him – then seeing me looking their way, both started paying their footwear a lot of attention.

If Baltheza heard, he ignored the two daemons. 'As disconcerting as I find all this, I'm more concerned about your wellbeing than his,' he said.

'You are?'

'I've lost Kayla and her mother, for ever; I don't want to lose you as well.'

'Not so long ago you wanted Lucky executed for treason,' Jamie pointed out, which was most unlike him – he usually treated Baltheza with all the caution due a highly volatile, venomous snake.

Baltheza waved his comment aside with an aristocratic flick of the wrist. 'I was fed lies about her by someone we now know to be untrustworthy and dangerous. It won't happen again. Now' – he got to his feet – 'I'll leave you to rest, but if there's anything you think I can do to help, tell me.' He bent down and kissed my cheek before striding across the room and pausing as he reached the door. 'Guardian, a word alone, if I may.'

Jamie glanced at me, then followed Baltheza out into the hallway.

As the door closed, my guards exchanged puzzled glances. 'What in the name of Beelzebub,' Vaybian muttered, 'was that all about?'

Kayla shifted on the bed so she was right beside me. 'Daddy is acting a little strangely. It's almost as though he actually cares for you. Most odd.'

'He cared for *you*,' I said. 'When we told him you were dead he was very upset.' I looked around the room. 'Where's Kubeck?' I asked, suddenly noticing my newest guard's absence.

'Down in the Chambers of Rectification,' Kerfuffle said.

'What?' I said, pulling the covers back and swinging my legs out of the bed. Bad move – the room gave a very unpleasant lurch.

'No, no, mistress,' Shenanigans said, throwing Kerfuffle an exasperated look, 'he's searching through Amaliel's stuff, in case we missed anything last time.'

I dragged my legs back up onto the bed and slumped against the pillows. 'I don't know what he's likely to find that would be helpful.'

'Anything, something, nothing,' Shenanigans said. 'I think he just wanted to keep busy and he knew there was nothing else he could do for you here.'

The door swung open and Jamie returned, his expression perplexed.

'Well?' Kerfuffle asked.

Jamie pushed the door closed behind him and ran a hand through his hair in agitation. 'Just when I think Baltheza can't possibly surprise me any more, he manages to do just that.'

'He's not acting crazy again?' Kerfuffle asked.

'No,' Jamie said. 'Here's the thing; he's genuinely upset that Lucky's in so much pain. He's also concerned by Jinx's disappearance and its significance. For once he's acting like a responsible monarch and worrying about what effect this could have on his people.'

My guards stood in silence for a few moments.

'I must admit he's treating you in a way that he never treated me,' Kayla said. 'Quite often he would say words of concern about my wellbeing, but they were just that – words. There was never any sincerity.' She tapped her lips with her forefinger. 'It makes me wonder how long Amaliel had been drugging him.'

I repeated this to Jamie. He thought on it for a moment. 'Amaliel had been poisoning his mind for years – maybe, towards the end, he wanted to hurry up the process. Maybe he had an end-game in mind.'

'Amaliel did say he'd suspected I was the Soulseer from the moment I was born. Maybe that was when he started to plan?'

'No,' Kayla said, her expression grim, 'it must have been going on long before then.'

'Baltheza is going to have Henri questioned,' Jamie said.

'Even though he's a horrible little shit I wouldn't wish that on anyone,' Kerfuffle said with a shudder. There was muttered agreement from the rest of my guard.

'Maybe we should speak to Henri first,' Vaybian suggested. 'Once Baltheza's been at him he'll be good for nothing.'

'He hasn't got Amaliel to do his dirty work now,' Shenanigans pointed out.

'That's what I mean,' Vaybian said, his lips twisting in distaste. 'If Baltheza's in charge of Henri's questioning he'll go too far, probably leave him as nothing more than a gibbering wreck, then we'll get nothing of value out of him.'

'That's if he doesn't kill him outright,' Kerfuffle added.

'They have a point,' Kayla said with a sigh. 'Daddy has never had much finesse when it comes to the extraction of information.'

'I doubt Henri will tell us anything,' Jamie said. 'He hates Lucky with a passion.'

'Well,' I said, pushing back the covers and swinging my legs out of the bed again, this time a little more gently, 'unless we try, we'll never know.'

'Where do you think you're going?' Jamie said.

'To see Henri.'

'No way—'

'Yes way: if anyone knows what Amaliel's plans are, it'll be Henri.'

'And Henri has no reason to be loyal to Amaliel,' Shenanigans added. 'He hung Henri out to dry.'

'Exactly,' I said. 'He may have revenge on his mind.'

'Lucky, if he's feeling vengeful towards anyone it's going to be you,' Jamie pointed out.

'That's true,' Kerfuffle said, and Shenanigans gave a grunt of agreement.

'You stabbed him, mistress, and Pyrites burned him, scarring him terribly,' Shenanigans reminded me.

'And Henri le Dent was always vain about his looks,' Kerfuffle added.

'They have a point,' Kayla said.

'Then there's the small matter of cutting off his hand,' Vaybian said with a snort of laughter, and Kayla giggled.

'I stabbed him to save my life,' I said, though why I thought I should justify my actions I didn't know, 'and I cut off his hand to save Pyrites from getting his throat cut.' Hearing his name, my drakon rubbed his head against my legs. 'Anyway, there's no harm in trying.'

'Let me do it,' Jamie said. 'You don't want to go down into that terrible place again.'

'Jamie, you can't protect me from everything,' I said in exasperation. 'I need to be *doing* something – anything – to stop myself going mad with worry.'

Jamie dipped his head in acquiescence, but I could tell he wasn't happy about it.

They followed me out of the room and to the dark stone staircase that led to the Chambers of Rectification. As we descended, I began to wish I'd taken Jamie's offer and let him deal with Henri. Each downward step brought a little more fear to my heart and by the time we reached the cell-lined corridor which led to the torture chamber, I had to grit my teeth to stop them chattering.

'You don't have to do this, you know,' Jamie said.

'We can attend to this matter for you, mistress,' Shenanigans added.

'Probably best if you let us attend to this for you,' Kerfuffle mumbled and by his grim frown and stony eyes I knew why none of them wanted me there; they didn't think I'd have the stomach for what might have to be done to get the information we needed out of Daltas' former assassin.

At one time they would've been right. Now I wasn't so certain. Someone – and I was pretty sure it was Amaliel – was torturing Jinx, one of the two men I loved, and I knew I was prepared to do whatever it took to save him and get him home safe to me.

We stopped at a cell halfway along the corridor. 'Are you sure you want to do this?' Jamie asked.

I took a deep breath. 'Let's get on with it.'

Jamie drew back the bolts unlocking the door. 'I'll go in first, you follow with Pyrites, and you three,' he said to Shenanigans, Kerfuffle and Vaybian, 'come in behind us and watch our backs.'

Pyrites grew a bit until he was the size of a mastiff. If Henri was scared of any of us it was my drakon – he had good reason to be; Pyrites did not like him one little bit and would happily finish off roasting him given half the chance.

'Right,' Jamie said, 'let's do this.'

He pushed open the door and walked inside. I was right behind him, Pyrites and Kayla by my side, and the others crowded in after us and closed the door.

Henri was sitting on the floor in the far corner, his knees bunched up to his chest. He looked up with fearful eyes, but upon seeing us his misshapen lips twisted into a sneer and he straightened his legs out in front of him, displaying a stained shirt and grubby breeches.

'And to what do I owe this pleasure?' he asked.

'We've come to talk about Amaliel,' Jamie said.

'And why would I want to talk to *you* about *him*?'

'He deserted you. He left you here to suffer. You help us find him and we may be able to get you out of your present predicament.'

'Not to mention prevent you from receiving a visit from Lord Baltheza, who also wants to know Amaliel's whereabouts and won't be quite as restrained in his methods of extracting the information,' Vaybian said.

Henri's eyes flicked from Jamie's face to mine and back again and he licked his lips, clearly rattled. 'I don't know where Amaliel is. As you pointed out – he left me.'

'What were his plans? He must have spoken to you of his intentions,' Jamie said.

'What would I know? He didn't tell me he planned to leave me, that was for sure.'

'He must have said something about what he was planning.'

'I know it was all about the Sicarii.'

'What about the Sicarii?'

'He was going to make them into an unbeatable force, depose Baltheza and take over the Underlands.'

'With you by his side?'

Henri gave a snort. 'That was what he said, but as you can see, he lied.'

'Then help us find him,' I said.

Henri glared up at me, and I knew Jamie was right: Henri's animosity towards me was tangible. His eyes glittered with hatred and when he spoke his voice dripped with venom.

'Why don't you ask your *human* friend, Philip? After all, it was he whom Amaliel saved – but I suppose if you've lost Amaliel, you've probably lost the human as well,' Henri said with a smirk.

'You are such a little shit,' Kayla said, glaring down at him.

'We know exactly where Philip Conrad is,' Jamie told him.

'Then go and ask *him* what Amaliel intends.'

I glanced at Jamie; his expression was far from angelic. 'Hard to ask a dead man to tell tales.'

If Henri was surprised by this news he didn't show it. 'I thought *she* was the Soulseer.'

Jamie and I looked at each other, and Jamie began to smile. 'Thank you, Henri,' he said, 'you've been *very* helpful.'

'I have?' Henri said with a confused frown.

'You're right: if you can't – or *won't* – help us, I'm sure Philip will. Amaliel slaughtered him, so I guess his longing for revenge will be greater than yours. Although I would have thought an impending visit from an angry Lord Baltheza would be enough to loosen your tongue.'

Henri licked his lips again and I'm sure I saw a flicker of fear in his eyes. 'I have nothing to say – I've told you all I know. Amaliel didn't share any confidences with me. I swear it, *I swear it . . .*'

'It's not me you've got to convince,' Jamie said with a dark smile, and as if on cue, the sound of footsteps echoed along the stone corridor outside. 'Goodbye, Henri. I doubt we'll meet again – at least, not in this life. As for the hereafter, I somehow think our paths will be different ones.'

He swung around towards the door and gestured for me to leave first.

'Wait, wait,' Henri cried, all his haughty indifference gone. 'Give me time to think.'

Jamie glanced back over his shoulder. 'Time's just run out.'

'The Soulseer!' Henri almost screamed. 'The Soulseer, Deathbringer and the Guardian – Amaliel called you "the Trinity". He said if you were his, nothing could stop him; he would rule supreme. And if he couldn't tame you, he'd kill you – with the three of you gone, there'd be no one to stop him from becoming Lord of the Underlands.'

'Not enough and too late,' Jamie said.

We walked out of the door and Shenanigans slammed it shut behind us.

We met Baltheza and four of his guards in the corridor. His nostrils flared, but he said nothing until we stopped before him.

'Learn anything useful?' he asked.

'Nothing we hadn't surmised already,' Jamie said. 'Amaliel seems to think he can use Lucky, Jinx and me to fulfil his ambitions.'

'How?'

'I can see how he could use the Deathbringer, but I'd have thought Lucky would be a danger to any plans he might have. He curses the dead to remain bound to this world, while Lucky sees them on their way.'

Baltheza shrugged off his burgundy velvet jacket, folded it and handed it to one of the guards, then rolled up the lace cuffs of his very white shirt. I watched in morbid fascination. His glowing orange eyes met mine.

'Don't feel any pity for Henri,' he told me. 'If it were you waiting in that chamber he wouldn't feel an ounce of it for you.'

I managed a small nod; I couldn't find the words to speak. He gave me an affectionate smile before looking back at Jamie. 'I'll let you know if I learn anything of interest.'

'We're travelling to Dark Mountain,' Jamie told him.

'Explain.'

'It's where the human, Philip Conrad, met his end. Amaliel cursed him, and although he's now released from the curse, he's bound to the mountain's caverns forever – unless Lucky helps him pass. As he was in Amaliel's company for some time he might know something of his plans.'

'Will he tell you if he does?'

'He has no reason to love Amaliel.' Jamie gave him a grim smile. 'And we will give him an incentive to tell us what he knows.'

Baltheza frowned. 'Incentive?'

'To remain alone, bound to Dark Mountain for ever, or to pass onto the place where he deserves to be.'

'Ah. In his position it is perhaps his good fortune that he has been so bound.'

'Funnily enough, I doubt he sees it that way – but it's worth a try.'

We stood aside to let Baltheza and his men pass. 'Let me know how you get on,' Baltheza ordered as he reached the cell door.

'Lord Baltheza,' Jamie murmured, bowing, with my other guards following suit.

One of his guards stepped forward and opened the cell door and Baltheza entered, followed by his men. The door slammed shut behind them and we started to walk away. As I climbed the first step of the staircase out of the dungeons, Henri began to scream.

I hesitated, but Jamie placed a hand under my elbow and urged me on. I didn't resist him.

Back at our chambers we made ready for our trip. It wasn't something I was looking forward to. Dark Mountain had once been the home of the Sicarii, a sect of assassins who cursed their victims, forcing them to remain tied to this world so the assassins could feed on their torment. The mountain itself was actually a huge shard of ruby that had erupted out of the ground. It towered over the landscape — it should have been beautiful, but stacked high around its base were the mouldering bones of the thousands of daemons the Sicarii had sacrificed over the years. It was as close to Hell as I ever wanted to be.

'Do you think it's even worth trying to speak to the human?' Kerfuffle asked. 'From what you've told us he's probably just as unlikely to want to help.'

'We didn't exactly part on the best of terms,' Jamie admitted, 'but we have to start somewhere.'

'I just wish it wasn't there,' I said, probably reflecting what everyone else was feeling. 'Has Kubeck come up with anything yet?'

'Not yet,' Shenanigans said, 'but there's still a mass of scrolls, books and other documents for him to wade through.'

'We told him to stay here and keep on searching while we go to Dark Mountain,' Kerfuffle said.

'I hope that meets with your approval, mistress,' Shenanigans added.

'It can't hurt,' I replied, but it was all taking too long. I wanted to find Jinx *now*. I wanted him safe and back with me.

'Lucky, we will find him,' Jamie said, as usual knowing what I was thinking. He took my hand and held it within his, but even that didn't give me the sense of wellbeing that it usually did. It was as though a big part of me was missing.

Three

When we reached the courtyard outside the palace we found Bob surrounded by fearful guards. We hadn't called him; he knew he was needed, but he was still unhappy, stomping his huge hooves and snorting puffs of steam at any who ventured too close.

The guards were visibly relieved to see us – whether they were scared of Bob because of his association with the Deathbringer or because he was frightening in his own right I wasn't sure, but scared they were.

'Vaybian, you and Kerfuffle ride Bob. Lucky and Shenanigans can ride on Pyrites,' Jamie said.

'May I make a suggestion?' Vaybian interrupted as we all went to our steeds.

Jamie stopped and folded his arms, a *what now?* expression hardening his face; no doubt he expected more of Vaybian's moaning. 'Go on.'

'Would it not be more sensible for the lady to fly with you? If she has another of her fits whilst on the back of the drakon she might well fall.'

Jamie and I exchanged a glance.

'I would not let my mistress fall,' Shenanigans said with a scowl.

If Vaybian was worried by the huge daemon's disgruntled expression he didn't show it. 'I doubt you would *intentionally*, but what if you did? Are you willing to take the risk? In fact, why are we bothering to do this at all? The human won't help us – if anything, he will relish our predicament.'

'We have to—' I started to say, but before I could finish, Vaybian was proved right on at least one thing as a lightning bolt of pain hit me right between the eyes and I doubled over, clutching my head. Then it happened again and I couldn't hold back the scream.

Someone held on to me, supporting me – I assumed it was Jamie – but then another spike of agony pierced my brain and I bucked in his arms, almost falling. As the pain subsided I could feel something warm trickling down my upper lip and I could taste blood in my mouth. I didn't have time to figure out what this meant, for I was hit by another bolt of pain and my world turned crimson.

Jamie must have carried me back to our room, but I wasn't aware of it; I was too consumed by pain and Jinx's screams bouncing around inside my skull.

'Give her some of the draught,' a voice said, and then a phial was pressed to my lips and a dribble of warming liquid trickled down my throat. There were a few more moments of excruciating pain and then everything went black.

I awoke to flickering candlelight. I was lying on the bed covered by a blanket with Pyrites stretched out beside me. The others were sprawled out across the room. By the smell of it, they had just eaten, but even the thought of food made my throat close up.

Kayla was sitting on the end of the bed, knees pulled up under her chin and as soon as she realised I was awake she moved along the mattress to sit beside me.

'How are you feeling?'

I waggled a hand from side to side. 'So, so.'

Vaybian looked up upon hearing my voice and without any preamble, spoke to the room, his eyes fixed on me. 'The fits are getting worse. We shouldn't risk taking my lady's sister to Dark Mountain.'

'As she's the only one of us who can see the dead there'd be little point going without her,' Kerfuffle said.

I considered this for a moment – I could see Vaybian's point, but Kerfuffle was right, I had to go – and more than that, I *needed* to go. I had to find Jinx.

As I stretched and pushed myself up into a sitting position,

Jamie came instantly to my side. Kayla got out of his way to go and sit next to Vaybian. 'You must see that I have to go – our only possible lead is in that mountain. There's no alternative; without Jinx I'm the only one who can see and hear Philip.'

'I'm concerned for your safety; we all are.'

'There must be some way for me to get there safely.'

He wrapped his arms around me and kissed the top of my head. 'We've been worried about you,' he told me. 'Even unconscious, you've been crying out in pain.'

'How long did it go on for?' I asked.

'About three hours,' Kerfuffle said, and seeing Jamie's expression, he frowned at him saying, '*What?*'

'Can you manage something to eat?' Shenanigans quickly asked, trying to change the subject.

I shook my head. The thought of Jinx being tortured for three solid hours made me feel too sick to even think of trying to eat.

Jamie studied my face, then gently stroked my cheek with his thumb. 'If we do as Vaybian said and you fly with me, maybe you'd be safe. The trouble is, we have no idea when the next fit will strike, or how long it'll last.'

'And are you sure you're strong enough? Not only to travel, but to face Philip?' Kayla added. 'That's probably going to be pretty miserable in itself.'

'I must go,' I repeated.

'Great idea,' Vaybian sneered. 'If we'd set off five minutes earlier this morning you would have been splattered all over the countryside.'

'Not if Jamie had been holding me. And anyway, *I* have to question Philip.'

'Lucky, it could be a total waste of time – time we probably don't have,' Jamie said.

'But what if it isn't? What if Philip does know something that might help?'

'How about I go?' Kayla butted in. She sat down on the bed next to me. Of course; I'd forgotten Kayla was *really* dead, so she too could see and hear him. She smiled as she saw the understanding dawn on my face. 'Besides, we have something in common: we were both tortured and murdered by Amaliel. I'll probably have more luck in talking him around than you.'

I really wanted to be there, to be doing something, anything other than just sitting around waiting, but she did have a point. 'You're right: we didn't part on the best of terms and you might just be able to talk him into helping us.'

'What?' Jamie asked.

'Kayla says she'll go and talk to Philip,' I explained.

'Actually, that isn't such a bad idea,' Jamie admitted.

I had to cool my heels waiting for Kayla to return – she promised me it wouldn't take long, as she wasn't constrained by distance; as an ethereal body she could go wherever she pleased in not much more than a blink of an eye. All the same, the time she was gone felt like an eternity to me.

Rather than mope, I put my mind to other things, such as whether Baltheza had managed to learn something from Henri. I guessed he hadn't, he'd have soon told us if he had. It was becoming increasingly obvious that Amaliel didn't trust a soul; I had a suspicion that if we did learn anything from anyone, it would be because Amaliel wanted us to.

It was more likely that Kubeck would find some answers before Baltheza did; I was counting on him.

'I'll go and get him, mistress,' Kerfuffle volunteered when I'd voiced this opinion. It wasn't long before he reappeared with the huge daemon in tow.

Kubeck was almost as big as Shenanigans, though more human to look at apart from a short tusk between his eyebrows. He was an unarguably handsome daemon, muscular and broad, with semi-glazed terracotta skin and sandy Grecian curls. I had saved him from a horrible death by execution, which meant he was mine, body and soul, to do with what I wanted, until death us did part. I chose to use him as one of my guard, and he appeared to be happy enough in his new employ – it was certainly better than the alternative.

'Kubeck has news,' Kerfuffle said as he marched through the door.

'It may be nothing,' he said, giving me a bashful smile.

'But it may be something,' Kerfuffle said, plonking a couple of flagons on the low table in the middle of the room.

I gave them a weary smile as I sank down next to it. 'What have you found, Kubeck?'

'This.' He pulled a large folded piece of parchment from his jerkin and handed it to me.

I spread the yellowing document out across my lap, the aged skin crackling beneath my fingertips. My guards clustered around me and Kerfuffle sucked in a gasp. 'This is not good,' he said, 'not good at all.'

I had to agree with him.

'What is it?' Vaybian asked, leaning over the table to take a look.

'It's a map,' Kubeck said.

'A map?' Vaybian repeated. 'Of where? I don't recognise these places.'

'You wouldn't,' I told him. 'It's a map of the Overlands.'

Jamie sucked in air through his teeth. 'Although I sort of thought Amaliel might have crossed over into the world of humans, I'd hoped I was mistaken. That he has Jinx makes me fear for humanity.'

'What do you mean?' I asked.

'He threatened to go to your world to collect the souls of the dead.'

'You said he couldn't – you said he didn't have the power,' I said in alarm.

'He hasn't, but sadly, Jinx has.'

'Fuck!' I said, as the penny dropped. Then, 'Jinx *wouldn't*.'

'He's been doing it for millennia.'

'Yes, but only when necessary. Only when he has to.'

Jamie ran a hand through his hair. 'It's true that Jinx only takes death to your world to maintain the balance – but what if he went rogue? Think what would happen then.'

I crossed my arms and said stubbornly, 'He *wouldn't*. He hates what he has to do.'

'Yet still he does it.'

'It's his job, his mission, if you like. That's what he told me. That's what *you* told me.'

'It's true,' Jamie said, albeit a bit reluctantly, 'both he and I are governed by certain laws. But what I'm trying to say is, if he's being tortured, if he's being put under duress, then maybe, just maybe, Amaliel can make him do something he would never have done before.'

And it slowly dawned on me that Jamie might be right. I had never felt as miserable as I did then. If let loose in my world, Jinx would be the ultimate weapon of mass destruction, and that would give Amaliel exactly what he wanted: hundreds, thousands, maybe even millions of souls. If he followed in Jinx's wake cursing the dying as he had in this world, tying the dead to the Overlands so he and his cult of Sicarii could feed on them . . . It didn't bear thinking about.

Then another thought hit me. 'But Amaliel knows that the living can't travel to the other side,' I said. 'That was his objective before. Now he knows it's impossible, what would be the point in collecting more souls?'

Jamie's face twisted into an angry frown. 'To be cruel, to torture and to cause pain?'

'He must be insane to do something so wicked.'

'He is,' Jamie said simply, 'and he's linked to the Sicarii, who've been around for a very long time, and like any cult, their rituals have become obsessions. It's like humans praying to their gods. People do it, even though time and again their prayers aren't answered – they carry on because it's what they *believe*.'

'Believing in God is hardly the same as cursing the dying—'

'Maybe not, but it's still as pointless.'

'You can argue about it all day,' Kerfuffle interrupted, clearly irritated, 'but even if Amaliel is doomed to failure it's not going to stop him from trying.' He gestured to Kubeck. 'Show them what else you found.'

Kubeck delved into the pocket of his jerkin and pulled out a small, hide-covered book. 'He writes in some sort of code, which I couldn't make head nor tail of, but towards the back there are some sketches I recognised.' He flicked through the book and handed it to me.

Jamie dropped down next to me to peer at the page. It was covered with pictures of little oblong cages on chains.

'You recognise these?' Jamie said, looking up at Kubeck.

The huge daemon nodded, his expression grim.

'What are they?' I asked.

Kubeck moved closer and glanced around, as though worried he'd be overheard. My other guards read his body language too and closed in around us. This was somehow very important, and I had to suppress a shiver as a full battalion of Royal Marines marched right over my grave.

'I've seen such drawings before,' Kubeck told us, 'in my uncle's workshop.'

'Kubeck's uncle is a gold and silversmith,' Shenanigans explained.

'I remember,' I said, but I was confused by the sudden change of direction. 'What does jewellery have to do with anything?'

Kubeck moved even closer and crouched down in front of us. 'About five or six months ago Amaliel Cheriour swept into the smithy demanding to see Uncle Davna. My cousin took him out back and they were squirrelled away with my uncle for a couple of hours or more.' Kubeck rubbed his chin. 'When Amaliel left, I could tell my uncle was worried. He shut up shop for the rest of the day and went home. Simion, my cousin, was another matter. He was excited and strutting around the place like he was suddenly a very important person.'

'Did you ask him what Amaliel wanted?' Kerfuffle asked.

Kubeck gave a half-smile. 'Of course I did – we all did. The court's Chief Enforcer and Corrector visiting our little workshop was . . .' He shook his head as though he couldn't quite believe what he was about to say. 'It was exciting, if a trifle scary.'

'It's the sort of excitement I could do without,' Kerfuffle murmured.

'You, my friend, are quite right,' Kubeck agreed. 'Simion was full of himself for days; at least when we got to see him. He spent most of his time locked away in my uncle's workroom. About two months later we had another visit from Amaliel, and when he left he was carrying a red leather-bound box. It was clear that my uncle and Simion had been making something very special for him, but neither of them would talk about it – my uncle was scared, but Simion would tap the side of his nose with his foreclaw and wink. Of course I knew what would happen. Simion had a liking for grog, but unlike the rest of us he couldn't hold it. One night he had one too many and it all came tumbling out: he and Uncle had made Amaliel four crystal phials, to be worn in intricately designed golden baskets hung from golden chains. Four phials, four baskets and four chains.'

'Not good, not good,' Kerfuffle said.

'No, not good at all. When Simion woke up the following morning and realised he'd let the drakon out of the cage he was terrified. He knew it was only a matter of time before Amaliel found out he'd flapped his tongue. Sure enough, within the week he was arrested for treason and executed.'

'And when you tried to clear his name you were arrested too?' Jamie said.

Kubeck nodded.

'Gentlemen please,' I said, 'can we get back to the point: what's the relevance of this jewellery?'

Kubeck's eyes were worried when they met mine. 'A very long time ago there was a daemon princess who, rumour had it, murdered her lovers when she had no further use for them and retained their spirits in small glass phials which she wore upon a chain about her neck.'

'Necrodyti,' Kerfuffle said.

'Pardon?'

'Her name was Necrodyti.'

'That's the one,' Kubeck agreed. 'We believe that the trinkets Amaliel asked my uncle to make were for the same purpose.'

'I knew Amaliel was evil, but I never imagined he used the dark arts,' Kerfuffle said. 'I'm surprised your uncle and cousin agreed to make them.'

'Would you deny anything to the Court Enforcer and Corrector?' Kubeck said.

'True enough,' Kerfuffle said.

'Anyway, before I was arrested I learned something even more interesting.' He leaned in and lowered his voice to a whisper. 'My uncle, distraught over the loss of his son, told me that this wasn't the first time; Amaliel had come to him once before, a quarter-century ago.'

'To make crystal phials?' Shenanigans asked, his voice hushed, as though he too thought someone might be listening.

Kubeck's head bobbed. 'One amethyst phial. He told my uncle it was for a very special lady, and Uncle Davna didn't think he meant as a gift.'

There was a knock on the door, stopping our discussion dead: four guards were standing outside to escort Jamie and me to Baltheza's private chambers. Kayla hadn't yet returned, which was weighing heavy on my mind, and I really could have done without having to talk to her father; I nearly always felt emotionally drained after one of our conversations.

'I wonder what he wants now,' Jamie said.

'Let's hope it's good news,' I said, though I seriously doubted it.

'I wouldn't wager on it,' Jamie said with a snort.

'Jamie, this is taking far too long.'

'Jinx is strong and he's obviously fighting Amaliel.'

'But what if Amaliel does break him?' I asked.

'He won't,' Jamie said.

I hoped he was right. I couldn't bear to think of what Amaliel might be doing to Jinx. On a previous occasion Baltheza had boasted that his chief executioner could reduce a daemon to barely more than a beating heart and the poor creature would still live; he could make a victim scream until his lungs bled without causing any permanent damage. That's probably what he would do to Jinx if we were right and he wanted Jinx alive and under his control.

Baltheza was standing by the huge fireplace that dominated the back wall of his chamber. He glanced up briefly as Jamie and I entered, but then resumed his study of the flaming logs as they crackled and spat. We stopped halfway across the room and stood waiting; he would get to the point eventually, I was quite sure.

'Did the human tell you anything worthy of note?' he asked, when I'd almost thought he'd forgotten we were there.

'No,' I said, and explained how I'd had another attack as we were about to leave, though I had a suspicion he already knew this. Why he insisted on playing these games I had no idea. 'Did you have better luck with Henri?' I asked.

Baltheza abruptly swung around to face us. 'Mr le Dent was amazingly uncommunicative, at least of anything that mattered.'

'We do have some news,' Jamie said, in an unusually tentative tone for him.

Baltheza's nostrils flared. 'Why do I think I am about to hear something I'd rather I didn't?'

'We think Amaliel may have set his sights on the Overlands.'

Baltheza's forked tongue flickered across his lips. 'If this is so, it is the worst of possibilities.'

'We have to find him,' I said.

'Do you think you will?' Baltheza looked from me to Jamie.

'We have to,' Jamie told him. 'If we don't it won't just be the Overlands that will be at risk.'

Baltheza drew in a deep breath and slowly exhaled. 'Then I suggest you head for the human world sooner rather than later.' His attention switched to me, his blazing orange eyes staring into mine. 'And how are you bearing up, Lucinda?'

'All right, I suppose,' I lied.

He considered me for a few heartbeats longer. 'Guardian,' he said, his eyes remaining locked with mine, 'see to it that Lucinda returns to our world safe and sound. She may not be my daughter by blood, but she's all I have left.'

'My Lord,' Jamie said, bowing, and with that Baltheza turned back to the fire and we were dismissed.

'It's most odd how he's suddenly taken a shine to you,' Jamie commented as we started along the corridor.

'I'm not sure whether I should be relieved or—' I started, but it turned into a scream as a welt of burning pain seared my back. '*Ahhh—!*' I groaned as I collapsed against the wall.

Jamie grabbed my arm to stop me sliding to the floor as another red-hot poker burned into my back and an image from the past flashed into my head: Amaliel, pressing a long glowing iron rod against Vaybian's body. And I knew without a shadow of a doubt that was what he was doing to Jinx; he was branding him with red-hot irons.

I was screaming loud enough that the whole palace could probably hear me, and as Jamie scooped me into his arms I heard a door slam and then Baltheza's voice and a cool hand taking mine as Jamie hurried along the passageway to our chamber.

Five times Amaliel branded Jinx. Five times I felt his skin blister and burn as if it was mine and, as he pressed the final poker again his flesh, I heard Amaliel whisper as clear as if he was in the room with me, 'You will be bound to me – fight it as much as you want, but you will be mine.'

Jinx gasped, 'Never!' and for a split-second I rejoiced that he still had the strength to fight him, but it was to be only one moment of celebration. Amaliel's expression of displeasure was swift and he pressed the tip of another glowing iron into Jinx, starting just above his right hip and then going through flesh and muscle until it came out the other side.

I didn't pass out, as such, though I might have been delirious, for reality merged with a dreamlike state where I tumbled from one nightmare to another. At least, I hoped they were nightmares; at the time they were incredibly real.

I heard voices talking in hushed whispers. 'Stop it!' I cried. 'Stop your vile plotting and scheming.' Then my head was lifted and they dripped more of the sleep-bringing liqueur between my lips and at last I slept.

They were still talking in quiet voices when I awoke, though my mind was no longer so befuddled that I thought they were whispering about me – well, maybe they were, but if so I was certain it was in a good way.

'You may be her guard but you're also her lover – that, my friend, gives you the right to have some say in the matter – not to mention that you're the Guardian,' Vaybian said.

Okay – maybe not so much in a good way. I kept my eyes closed – not because I wanted to snoop, but listening to Vaybian wasn't helping my thumping head any.

'I can just imagine you standing up to the Lady Kayla like that,' Kerfuffle muttered.

'Him and whose army?' Kayla said with a huff – she was back, thank Heavens.

'What did you say, little sprite?' Vaybian said.

'You heard. And call me a sprite again and I'll kick you in the bollocks so hard you'll find it hard to swallow.'

It was no good. If I didn't open my eyes and let them know I was awake open warfare was likely to break out.

'How long was I out this time?' I managed to ask, though I felt like I was gargling with broken glass.

'A couple of hours,' Jamie said from beside me.

'We need to get moving,' I told him, and tried to sit up, but I felt so weak I had to rest a couple of seconds before I tried again.

'Lucky, you were muttering in your sleep. Can you remember what happened during this attack?'

I could, but I really didn't want to talk about it. 'More torture,' I said shortly.

'You said something like "never bind him". What did you mean?'

I thought for a moment; trying to remember. The pain I had felt was a mere reflection of what was happening to Jinx. When his ended, my pain went away; Jinx wouldn't be so fortunate. He would be left in agony.

'Amaliel said – and I'm sure it was Amaliel – "you will be bound to me however much you might fight me" or something like that.'

Kerfuffle and Shenanigans came to stand behind Jamie.

Jamie asked, 'The pain you were feeling – what was it like?'

'It was a burn: Amaliel was branding Jinx – pressing red hot pokers across his back and shoulders. Then when Jinx told Amaliel he'd never succeed, he pressed the point through his side and out his back, just here,' I said, pointing to the flesh above my hip.

'These brands,' Jamie asked, 'were they just randomly placed?'

'What do you mean?'

'Were they random – like, just lines across his back – or did they form a pattern?'

I chewed on my lip and after a moment, said slowly, 'The first one was diagonally across my back from my left shoulder to my waist above my right hip. The second started in the same place but went down to almost the base of my spine.'

'And the next started where the second ended and went up to your right shoulder?'

'Yes – how did you know?' Jamie stood up and began to pace. 'What?'

'Amaliel's branding him with a pentagram,' Shenanigans said.

'An inverted pentagram,' Kerfuffle added.

'What does that mean?'

'The inverted pentagram is believed by some to be a symbol of the triumph of evil over the spirit.'

'In other words, Amaliel is trying to bind Jinx's spirit; he's trying to control him,' Jamie said.

'But we already thought this – how does this change anything?'

Shenanigans and Kerfuffle exchanged a worried look and Pyrites hopped up onto the bed and lay with his chin resting just above my hip.

'If Jinx is bound by Amaliel, he will lose all free will. Amaliel will be able to make Jinx do the most terrible things, and Jinx will be unable to stop himself.'

I stared at Jamie as the full implications of this sank in. 'It will destroy him,' I whispered, and my voice broke. Jinx might be the Deathbringer, but he hated cruelty and suffering. If Amaliel forced him to bring destruction to the human world it would be a greater torture than anything physical that might be done to him. 'We have to stop him.'

'The Deathbringer is strong, mistress,' Shenanigans said. 'He will fight Amaliel.'

'But if he faltered, for even a second,' Kerfuffle said, 'he would be lost.'

'We have to find him before it's too late,' Shenanigans said, and all my guards looked at Jamie.

An unreadable expression passed across his face, which turned into a determined frown. 'I'm going to have to go somewhere for a few hours.' He turned to the rest of my guards. 'Stay here with Lucky and don't let her out of your sight.'

'Where are you going?' I asked, alarmed that he was leaving me too. 'What happens if you go missing?' I was beginning to panic. 'What happens if you never come back?'

Kayla quickly shuffled out of the way as he crossed the room to drop down on the bed beside me and take me by the hand. 'I'll be back before you know it,' he said, 'but there's somewhere I must go. A place where I might find help.'

Then he kissed me and I clung to him, not wanting to let go. I didn't want him to leave me. I needed him with me, but if he really did know of someone who might be able to lead us to Jinx I had no choice. I needed both my men.

'I'll be back soon,' he whispered into my hair and then kissed me again before getting to his feet and when he walked out of the room it was like some of the light went with him, leaving me in a darker, colder place.

Then I remembered – I hadn't even told him Kayla was back . . .

Four

There was a despondent tension in the air, my guards' moods reflecting my own. However, the practicalities of life soon took over. Shenanigans and Kerfuffle decided we should prepare to leave so we would be ready when Jamie returned, so Kerfuffle went off with Kubeck to get provisions. Shenanigans and Vaybian stood by the door, and Pyrites stayed next to me on the bed, ready to roast any would-be intruder.

When Kerfuffle and Kubeck returned weighed down with baskets and boxes – did they think we'd starve in the Overlands? – I asked Kayla to tell us what had happened to her. I was desperately hoping for some good news at last, but she hadn't been able to find Philip at Dark Mountain.

'I searched everywhere,' she told me, 'but he was gone.'

'Could he have been hiding?' I asked.

'I promise you, I searched every inch of that terrible place and he wasn't there.' Her forehead creased into a puzzled frown. 'There was one thing that was really odd, though: his body was gone too – the two dead Sicarii were still there, but Philip's wasn't.'

I passed this piece of information on to the others, but they were just as nonplussed. My mind was in turmoil: I was desperate to get to the Overlands to start looking for Jinx – if he was even there; I was concerned about Jamie, and where he might be; I was puzzled by the disappearance of Philip's body and spirit, and what this might mean – and so I couldn't settle. I worried, paced and worried some more, driving my daemon guards to distraction with my constant fidgeting.

'Can I run you a bath, mistress?' Shenanigans asked, making me quite sure they'd all had enough of me.

'How can I have a bath at a time like this?'

'There's nothing much we can do until the Guardian returns,' Kerfuffle said. 'After all, the Overlands are under his jurisdiction.'

'I know, but—'

'Mistress?' Shenanigans asked.

'All right. Thank you, Shenanigans. I think I will have that bath,' I agreed, if only to keep him happy.

'Don't fill it, just in case,' Kerfuffle said. 'We wouldn't want you drowning if you have another turn.'

Once Shenanigans had half-filled the bathtub and Pyrites had warmed the water, I left them polishing their weaponry. Pyrites took up position guarding the bathroom door, so at least I'd have some semblance of privacy.

I sank down into the huge black stone bath that glittered and shone like the night sky and closed my eyes, trying not to think about anything at all, but as soon as I pushed one worrying thought from my mind it was instantly filled by another.

I caught a whiff of something slightly bad over the floral bath salts I had swirled into the water and it briefly crossed my mind that maybe I should get someone to look at the rather antiquated dae-mon plumbing, but then my mind turned to my Deathbringer.

'Where are you, Jinx?' I murmured to myself, and it was almost as if saying his name had summoned him, for an explosion of pain shot through me, jerking my body rigid.

My muscles had barely begun to relax when another agonising spike of flame burst inside me, followed by another, and then another. As I clung to the edge of the bath I thanked God that Shenanigans had only partly filled it. Another blast of pain had me screwing my eyes shut, but as I hauled myself up the slippery sur-face, I suddenly felt hands encircle my ankles and tug hard, wrenching the bath's rim from my grasp.

I slid beneath the surface, the back of my head smashing against the marble, and when I gasped I sucked in water. For a moment I floundered, my hand hitting stone, then another spasm hit me and I knew I was sinking. Above me I saw a shadow and a hand reach-ing out towards me: I was going to be saved, someone was going help me – but I was wrong. I felt a pressure upon my forehead, pushing me down. The shadow loomed over me, filling my fast-fading vision.

I heard Jinx scream my name, and he began to sob – somehow, he knew I was dying. Then there was another voice, and I could hear Kayla shouting through the burble of the water filling my ears.

'Help, please somebody help—!' But there was no one there who could hear her; only Jinx and I could hear the dead.

Everything turned to black, but I could still feel Jinx. Overwhelming anguish blotted out any pain he was feeling, and then it was like he stopped feeling anything at all. Was he dying too? As darkness took me, I heard the whispered words, 'You're mine now, Deathbringer, all mine—'

—and Jinx was gone.

I felt like I was floating – maybe I was; didn't the drowned float to the surface eventually? Darkness was replaced by golden light: the light I'd seen welcoming the dead to the other side. Then I was walking into the light, and I could hear music and laughter and all the worry washed away from me, to be replaced by contented happiness. Two figures walked through the light towards me: two men – no, angels, like Jamie.

'Felicitations, Soulseer,' one said, and they both smiled.

'It is good to see you again,' said the other, 'but sadly for us, as we will miss your company, it's not yet your time.'

'I'm dead,' I said.

They both shook their heads, still smiling. 'You have much work to do. Both your worlds are under threat and only the Trinity can save them.'

'But Jinx is . . .' I paused. What was Jinx?

'Lost,' said the first angel, 'and only you and his brother can find him again.'

They gestured for me to return the way I'd come and walked with me back towards the darkness.

'Can't I stay?'

'What about the Deathbringer? What about the Guardian? Do you want to leave them so soon?'

He was right; I didn't. Then I was falling, falling, falling, and darkness surrounded me.

'Do something, please do something,' I heard Kayla crying and there was a splash and I was being lifted.

I could see shadows above me, and cold stone on my back.

'It's too late,' I heard Vaybian say.

'No!' Kerfuffle shouted at him and then there was pressure on my chest and lips against mine, forcing air into my lungs, then more pressure on my chest. I felt so cold. And why was it I could see only shadows?

'Lucky, *please* wake up,' Kayla said, 'please, darling, please.'

'Look at her,' Vaybian said again. 'You're wasting your time.'

'If you can't say or do anything useful just get the fuck out of here,' Kerfuffle growled.

'Come on, mistress, come on,' I heard Shenanigans say as someone pumped on my chest so hard I thought something might break.

Why wouldn't they leave me alone? I just wanted to go to sleep. I wanted to go back to the warm, golden light. Wait ... No, I couldn't go back – there was a reason I couldn't go back. What was it? Jinx ... Jamie ... And suddenly I was scared I would never see them again. I was scared I'd lost them both for ever.

'Come on, Lucky, come *on*,' Kayla was sobbing.

Suddenly my chest felt like it was about to explode and I began to choke ... I rolled over and began to cough up bathwater until my chest felt like it was on fire.

Then someone was wrapping me in a blanket and I was being carried and laid down on something soft and warm and I must have slept.

Once again I woke to the sound of murmuring voices, and I so wished they'd shut up. I felt awful. My lungs and throat felt raw and every breath hurt my battered and bruised chest as it rose and fell; I could hear wheezing as I gingerly sucked in air.

I opened one eye – and quickly closed it again. *Too bright*. I tried again; this time peering through my eyelashes, gradually letting the light filter through until I was brave enough to open them fully. It wasn't actually particularly bright at all. The room was full of the soft glow of torches and lamplight. There was no electricity in the Underlands and thankfully, no fluorescent or halogen lighting.

'Mistress Lucky is awake,' I heard Kubeck say, and the bed was suddenly surrounded by all of my guards except Jamie.

'How are you feeling, mistress?' Shenanigans asked.

'Like I've done ten rounds with Mike Tyson,' I replied, my voice coming out as a croaking rasp.

'Who?' Kerfuffle asked.

'Never mind.' I couldn't be bothered to explain; my throat and head hurt too much. 'How long—?'

'Have you been unconscious?' Kerfuffle finished for me.

I gave a tiny nod, but it still hurt like shit.

'It's coming up to lunchtime,' he told me. So I'd been out since the previous evening.

'Here.' Shenanigans handed me a goblet. 'This will ease your throat.'

I took a sip. The draught tasted a bit like honey and lemon, sweet but at the same time tart. He was right, it did make swallowing a little easier.

I risked trying to say a few words. 'How did you realise—?' then wished I hadn't.

'That you were in trouble?' Kerfuffle again finished for me.

'Umm.'

'Kubeck,' Kerfuffle said. 'We were sitting talking and suddenly he got up and went to the bathroom door and started calling you.'

All eyes turned to Kubeck. His terracotta complexion took on a rust-coloured glow. 'I just had this feeling,' he said, 'like cold fingers touching the back of my neck.'

'I was calling them,' Kayla said, plonking herself down beside me, 'but they couldn't hear me. So I tried touching them, but none of them could feel me . . .'

'Except Kubeck,' I murmured, remembering the first time I'd seen him, just before he was due to be executed. He had felt the touch of the spirits inhabiting the great hall and I'd thought then that he was a sensitive.

'He shuddered at my touch – I was screaming at him to go to you and somehow he got the message.' Kayla let out a ragged sigh. 'You almost drowned.'

'Thank you, Kubeck,' I said, and his cheeks took on an even richer glow – and then a horrible thought occurred to me and my face flushed scarlet. I'd been in the bath; I'd been naked when they'd hauled me out and started to try and revive me.

I think they must have all seen from my horrified expression where my mind was going, as they all started to talk at once.

'I'll just go and—'

'We'd better—'

'Perhaps we should—?'

They all trotted off and busied themselves getting lunch, while Pyrites put his head on my lap and looked up at me with his beautiful multicoloured eyes. I gave his scales a scratch, and was rewarded with a puff of smoke and a purr from deep at the back of his throat.

Kayla started to giggle. 'I think they're probably as embarrassed as you are.'

I scowled at her.

'They did cover you up as soon as they got you breathing again, but I think saving your life was more on their minds than you being buck-naked.'

'I suppose . . .' I wondered if I'd ever be able to look any of them in the eye again. Though I guessed Kayla was right; they were probably just as embarrassed – not that nudity worried daemons, they don't have the same hang-ups as humans – it was more because I was their mistress.

Then something occurred to me. 'Kayla, when I was drowning I thought I saw someone else in the room with me before you went for help.'

She gave me a funny look. 'Who?'

'I don't know – I thought they were going to help me, but they pushed me under.'

'A hallucination. No one else but me was there, until I went to get the others.'

I pinched the bridge of my nose. 'Hallucination? It must have been, because who else could it have been?'

'I wonder where Jamie is?' Kayla said, changing the subject, which instantly started me worrying about something a lot more important than my guards seeing my naked body.

Then the door opened, and a little bit of light came back into my life: Jamie had returned. Unfortunately, his expression wasn't as happy as I would have liked – but when he hurried to my side I realised why.

'Are you all right?' he asked, pulling me so tightly against him I couldn't have replied had I wanted to. 'I met Kerfuffle in the hallway – he said you almost drowned.' Then he loosened his grip a little to look down at me.

I gave him a wan smile and he pulled me close again. 'I should never have left you,' he said, kissing my head. 'I should have taken you with me.'

'Why didn't you?' I rasped.

'You sound terrible.'

'Thanks.'

'What happened?'

'Amaliel,' I whispered. 'I heard him tell Jinx he was his.'

Jamie gave a shake of his head. 'He'll never break Jinx.'

'But what if he binds him?'

We both sat in silence thinking about it, neither wanting to meet the other's eye. Then something occurred to me and I suddenly felt almost as cold as when I thought I was dying.

'Jamie, Jinx thinks I'm dead,' I told him. 'I was drowning and I heard him scream my name and then . . . then I thought maybe he was dying too because suddenly he wasn't feeling anything at all.'

Jamie's expression was bleak. 'If Jinx thinks you're dead . . . If *I* thought you were dead . . .' He gripped hold of my hand. 'If I was in Jinx's position and thought you were dead I might not have the strength to keep on fighting.'

I felt sick with worry. If Amaliel had really broken Jinx and bound his spirit, my world was in serious danger – it might no longer be my home, but I still cared about what happened to it and the billions of people who lived there. Then there was Jinx – I couldn't bear to think of him so badly damaged that he would be forced to do Amaliel's bidding. If Amaliel had managed to do that to him, would he ever be able to recover? If he killed innocent people, I wasn't even sure he could.

'I still don't understand how Amaliel captured Jinx,' I said. 'It doesn't make any sense.'

Shenanigans gave a little cough. 'Ah, well, we think we may have solved that one,' he said.

Kubeck stepped towards us, Amaliel's little book open in his hand. 'I thought I'd have another try at working out Amaliel's code,' he said. 'I wasn't having much luck, until I found this.'

Jamie took the book from him and scanned the page. 'No, no, no! This cannot be—'

'What?' I asked in alarm and he handed the book to me. Five words were scrawled across the paper: '*Malake ha-Mawet Jin Xanthe* – what does this mean?'

Jamie's complexion was ashen. He got up and started to pace.

'It's the Deathbringer's name,' Kerfuffle said.

I could tell this was important, but I was none the wiser.

Jamie saw my confusion. 'When a human summons a daemon, they have no control unless they have his or her *full* daemonic name, and we do not give them out lightly. No one other than Jinx would know it – even I didn't know . . .' Jamie stopped his pacing and stared into the air.

'Well obviously someone *does* know his name,' Vaybian said, equally grim. 'I wonder who *that* could be?'

And *I* wondered what exactly he was getting at.

Jamie's expression said it all. 'You know nothing,' he snapped, but Vaybian just shrugged.

Kerfuffle and Shenanigans looked at each other, then, ever practical, started handing around plates piled with food.

I wanted to ask Jamie for an explanation, but Shenanigans had already started to tell him about Philip's disappearance. He had no answers either.

'So we've still got to go to the Overlands?' Kerfuffle's mouth was full of bread and cheese.

'Isn't it a job for the Guardians?' Vaybian said, and he couldn't quite hide a sneer as Jamie favoured him with another very dark look.

'It's probably for the best if they don't get involved,' Shenanigans said. There was something about the tone of his voice, the worried look that he cast my way, that made me nervous.

I opened my mouth, but Jamie turned to face me, his eyes meeting mine, and for a moment they were all I could see. 'There's nothing to worry about, Lucky. Everything's going to be all right.'

'Yes,' I said. 'Of course it—' No, it wouldn't! What was I thinking? In a flash I knew *exactly* what I was thinking: I was thinking *whatever Jamie wanted me to.*

I jumped to my feet. 'What did you do? What did you just do?'

'Do? I didn't do anything. Sit down and have something to eat. Low blood sugar is making you cranky.'

'Cranky! I'll give you bloody cranky! You were *mesmerising* me!' Then it began to all fall in place. 'You've done this before – this is how you got me to invite you into my home.'

'What are you talking about?'

'I *knew* it – I knew you'd done something, but I just couldn't believe it. I *trusted* you.'

'Actually, you didn't trust him at all,' Kayla pointed out. 'He lied to you all the time.'

'Keep out of this, Kayla; I still haven't forgotten about all the lies *you* told me.'

'That was different—'

I ignored her and turned on Jamie again. 'What is it you're hiding from me this time? I know there's something.'

Jamie glared at Vaybian. 'I'm *never* going to forgive you for this.' His voice was low and dangerous.

'Do you think I care? Anyway, I have a feeling it's not you who needs to do the forgiving.' He looked pointedly at me.

'I just don't want you to worry unnecessarily,' Jamie started. 'You've been through a lot—'

'You've just told me one of the men I love is about to be forced to single-handedly destroy my world and *now* you say you don't want me to worry? Bollocks! You're talking absolute *bollocks*.' I pulled away from him and rounded on Vaybian. 'What did you mean about the Guardians getting involved?'

'Ask your lover,' Vaybian said.

'You are such an arse sometimes,' Kayla said, and I was sorry he couldn't hear her.

I turned to Shenanigans. He at least would tell me the truth. 'What did you mean about it probably being better the Guardians didn't get involved?'

His lips turned down and he glanced at Jamie then at me.

'It's all right,' Jamie said, 'I'll tell her.'

He took me by the hand and led me away from the others. I went with him, but it wasn't with good grace.

'Sit, please,' he said.

'I'm not a bloody dog.' I glared at him for a few moments, then sank down on the bed.

He dropped down beside me. 'Lucky, you know I would never deliberately hurt you—'

'Every time I think I know you, every time I think I can really trust you, you either lie to me or keep things from me,' I whispered. 'Now you've started messing with my head.'

'I thought Daltas was a manipulative shit, but at least he never mind-fucked me,' Kayla muttered.

I rounded on her. 'You stay out of this,' I cried. 'This is between Jamie and me.'

'All right, all right, don't get your knickers in a twist!' She wafted off to sit next to Vaybian, who was looking entirely too pleased with himself.

'Has she gone?' Jamie asked.

'Yes,' I said. 'Just tell me how it really is. Exactly how much trouble are we really in?'

'You know who I am? *What* I am?'

'You're the Guardian – you said you were like the border patrol between the Overlands and Underlands.'

'I maintain the equilibrium. If there's daemon interference in the Overlands, I find out who, what, where and why, then I sort it out.'

'I get it.'

'I don't do all this alone. I have what you might call assistants.'

'Jinx told me: you're *the* Guardian, but there're others.'

Jamie tried to take hold of my hand, but I snatched it away and crossed my arms. His expression was so troubled it was seriously scaring me.

'My role – the role of the Guardians as a collective – is to ensure the Overlands are kept safe from daemon activity. If Amaliel intends using Jinx as a weapon against mankind, the other Guardians and I will have no choice but to do our job.'

'Jamie—'

'We'll have to go to the Overlands, find Jinx and stop him.'

'That's exactly what we're *intending* to do,' I told him. 'We're going to find him, stop him and make him better again.'

'We might not have the time, though. Lucky, if Jinx, one of the most powerful of all daemons, unleashes himself upon the Overlands, my kind will have only one objective: to stop him, *whatever* the cost. We won't be going to the Overlands to *save* him – we'll be going there to *destroy* him.'

'No . . .' I could barely speak.

'We can't risk a whole world of humans for one daemon—'

'I thought we – the three of us – we were meant to be . . . I thought we belonged together—'

'We were and we did, but if what we believe is true, we have to do what's right.'

'Even if it means killing Jinx?'

'What is it you don't understand?' Jamie asked, looking at me as if I was the one being unreasonable. 'Jinx has the potential to wipe out every single man, woman and child in the Overlands in a matter of . . . I don't know – months, weeks, maybe even days; this has never happened before. Think of the worst apocalyptic scenario you've ever read about, the most terrifying movie you've ever seen – *that* is a pale imitation of what will happen to your world if Jinx goes rogue.'

'Now you start calling the Overlands *my* world,' I said as a wave of despondency swept over me. Jamie was right: we did have to stop Jinx before he did any damage, for once done, it could never be undone. Then there was what it would do to Jinx: if he killed hundreds or thousands of people, would he want to live even if we could save him?

'We leave now,' I said getting to my feet. 'We leave now and we find him before it's too late.'

'We have forty-eight hours,' Jamie said.

'*What?*'

'And that's only if he doesn't do anything before then.'

'What are you talking about?' I said, staring down at him.

My other guards were all openly watching us now. Jamie stood. 'We've been given forty-eight hours.'

'Given by *whom*?'

He gave me one of those patient looks that drive me so mad. 'By the Veteribus: those who set me and Jinx our tasks.'

'Is that where you've been?'

He hesitated, then said, 'Yes.'

'You mean you've been telling tales to your boss about Jinx?'

His cheeks flushed pink. 'It wasn't like that—'

'So what was it like, Jamie?'

'I thought they could help us find him.'

'And have they?'

His shoulders slumped. 'No,' he admitted. 'I should never have approached them.'

'Great,' I said, 'so what happens if we don't get him back within forty-eight hours?'

'The Guardians and I take over.'

'Whoa! You mean we could be on the verge of saving Jinx and all because the clock ticks a few minutes over your deadline, you and your mates will swoop in and kill him?'

'I'll be with you – *helping* you.'

'Right, so how exactly will that work? When our forty-eight hours are up, whose side will you be on then?'

'It's not about *sides*, Lucky – it's about doing what's right.'

'So it'll be right to kill Jinx simply because the clock's ticked a few extra tocks, even though at that point he mightn't have done anything wrong? *I don't think so*,' I added. 'Is *this* why you tried to mesmerise me? Because you knew I would never agree to this?'

'There's nothing for you to agree to,' Jamie said, his expression grim and uncompromising. 'It's been decided.'

'Not by me it hasn't.'

'You have no say in it.'

'Oh *fuck*,' I heard one of my guards murmur.

I swung around to face them. 'Right,' I said, '*I'm* going to the Overlands to find Jinx. You can come or not; it's up to you.'

Kerfuffle and Shenanigans exchanged a look, as if they were having some unspoken conversation. Kerfuffle bobbed his head and Shenanigans turned to me. 'We will accompany you to the Overlands, mistress,' he said.

'I must admit the Deathbringer has grown on me over the past few weeks,' Kerfuffle added.

'I too will join you on this venture,' Kubeck said.

'Why not?' Vaybian said. 'If I hang around here for too long Baltheza will probably get it into his head to have me executed for something.'

'I'll come,' Kayla said. 'It'll be nice to go back and see some of our old haunts again – if you'll excuse the expression.'

Pyrites pushed his head up under my hand and purred. 'Sorry, boy,' I said reluctantly, 'but I don't think I can take even a very small drakon into my world.'

'Don't you worry about Pyrites,' Shenanigans said. 'He can fit in just the same as we can.'

'And what about me?' Jamie asked.

'What about you?'

'Do you trust me to come with you to help find Jinx?'

'It depends what you intend to do to him once we find him.'

Jamie looked deeply into my eyes. 'I love you—' he started.

'You sure have picked your moment to tell me that,' I muttered.

He continued, 'I love you, and because I love you, I swear that I'll not harm Jinx if he can be stopped before he hurts anyone.'

'Even if our forty-eight hours are up?'

'Even then, if we can find him before the other Guardians and stop him.'

'Will the other Guardians be looking for him?'

'Not yet, but if I haven't brought him back in two days, they will.'

'What about Amaliel?' Shenanigans asked. 'What if we find him first?'

'He dies,' Jamie said, 'and *that* is not negotiable.'

'That's fine by me,' I said.

'If he was on fire I wouldn't piss on him to put him out,' Kerfuffle said.

'At least that's something we're all agreed on,' Vaybian said as Pyrites puffed very warm grey smoke.

'Can you still feel Jinx?' Kayla asked me as we started collecting our things together.

'Not since I nearly drowned.'

'It's strange you should be connected to him in such a way.'

'I can't explain it either,' I muttered.

'There's not much here that we can take with us,' I heard Jamie say, distracting me.

'No weapons?' Vaybian asked.

'If you started wandering around the Overlands with that' — Kerfuffle indicated Vaybian's sword — 'strapped to your hips, you'd pretty quickly end up arrested or dead.'

'Then what do we use to defend ourselves?'

'We'll worry about that when we get there,' Shenanigans said. 'Humans on the whole won't be a problem. It's Amaliel and his Sicarii we need to worry about.'

'And the Deathbringer,' Kerfuffle said. 'If he's dancing to Amaliel's tune we may well all be mouldering corpses within moments of our first encounter.'

'Jinx wouldn't hurt us,' I said, but the sympathetic looks I was getting suggested they thought differently.

'How are we going to do this?' Vaybian asked.

'Have you ever been to the Overlands before?' Kerfuffle asked, and when Vaybian shook his head, 'it's probably best you follow us. Do what we do and you'll be fine.'

'I didn't think daemons could travel between the worlds without being called,' I said.

'I gained access years ago, and Shenanigans was given access by Lady Kayla. The Guardian can go wherever he likes, it's part of his job. So when he gets to the Overlands, he will call for Vaybian, Kubeck and Pyrites, and we will cross with them to show them the way.'

'It will take a bit of time,' Shenanigans said. 'Lesser daemons can only travel to the Overlands in pairs, and only so many in any one duration.'

'It's a precaution against a daemon attack on the Overlands,' Kerfuffle explained.

I supposed it made sense, but it was wasting time we didn't have. 'I bet Amaliel has managed to spirit a load of his freaky followers over there,' I grumbled.

'But he's probably been planning this for a very long time,' Kerfuffle pointed out.

'Right,' Jamie said, 'let's get going.' He marched over to the huge walk-in wardrobe and pulled open the door. Gone were all the beautiful dresses of silk and velvet, the endless rows of shoes and boots. Instead, the door framed pitch-black nothingness, and it looked as scary as hell.

'I'll never get used to this,' I said as Jamie wrapped an arm around me.

'Ready?' he said, and although I had nowhere near forgiven him I couldn't deny that when he held me, I always felt safe.

'As I ever will be,' I replied, and he stepped into the darkness and we were falling with the wind whistling past our ears until we were standing outside in the gloom of an inclement afternoon with rain pattering down on our faces.

'It's always raining when I arrive in your world,' Jamie said with a shake of his wings, then they were gone and he was wearing jeans and hoodie. 'Go inside – I'll be just a moment.'

I looked around me, surprised by the familiar surroundings: the front garden of my little cottage. If this was unexpected, the yellow and black police tape draped across my front door had me totally flummoxed.

'What the—?'

'Probably best to leave that be,' Jamie said as I reached out to touch the fluttering plastic.

With a sigh I bent down to search for my spare key. The police obviously hadn't discovered it: my fingertips found the square piece of slate that marked the spot and used it to scrape the earth away and, to my relief, I heard the crackle of the plastic bag and felt its weight. I pulled it from the soil.

I opened the front door and ducked under the tape, then held my breath as I clicked on the light. At least I hadn't been disconnected.

'Home sweet home,' I heard a voice say behind me and I spun round.

'Kayla? How did you get here so quickly?'

'I just followed you – I guess now I really am a ghost, the usual rules don't apply. What's happened here?' She squinted at the small table in the hall. There were dirty grey smudges on the varnish.

'You've seen enough telly—'

'Fingerprint powder?'

'I would say so.'

More grey dust marked the kitchen worktops and table; a cupboard had been left slightly ajar, a drawer not quite closed.

'I hope you haven't got a criminal record,' I called to Jamie as he appeared in the doorway.

'Someone obviously missed you.'

'I'd rather they hadn't – now I've probably got a lot of explaining to do.'

'Not if no one realises you're back.'

I opened the fridge door – and slammed it shut, wrinkling my nose at the stench of rotting food. Luckily Kerfuffle and Kubeck had brought supplies.

'If we have to buy more provisions and petrol over the next few days, we'll need money, so I'll have to use my credit card . . .'

'If the police haven't taken it,' Kayla said.

She had a point, but like the hidden key, I had an emergency card stashed away, just in case I was ever robbed or mugged. I liked to be prepared for all eventualities.

I padded upstairs to my office, and stopped dead in the doorway. 'Oh crap!'

'Problem?' Jamie appeared at the bottom of the stairs.

'They've only gone and taken my PC and laptop,' I called back.

'Will you need them?'

'I was going to google me to find out if I've been mentioned in the news or anything. And I was going to look for unnatural natural disasters . . .'

'If you can find your credit card, maybe you should get a new laptop.'

'I'm not made of money—'

'And they've probably stopped all your cards anyway, or put a watch on them,' Kayla supplied.

'Not if they don't know I've got it,' I said, pulling out the bottom drawer of my desk and running my fingers along the underside. 'Here we go!' And hey presto, I had a card.

I ran downstairs to find Jamie. 'Remember, you can probably only get away with using it once, so buy what you have to, and then try drawing out cash.'

'Don't worry about it.'

'I don't want you getting yourself arrested.'

'He'll be all right,' Kayla said with a sniff. 'There's a reason he can mesmerise people.'

Within an hour my kitchen was overflowing with daemons. Shenanigans and Kubeck were so big they took up most of the space – and neither Jamie nor Vaybian were what I'd call small. Despite the circumstances, I had to stifle a slightly hysterical giggle as I looked at them all. If the police had walked in at that moment, they'd've had a blue fit, and doubtless arrested everyone on sight.

'What?' Jamie asked. He at least *looked* human.

'I was just thinking what the police would say if they walked in and saw you all!'

'I think you should make that all of *us*, mistress,' Shenanigans said, and I looked down to see that my hands were still shimmering pink.

I lifted a strand of my mahogany and aubergine hair and gave him a rueful smile. 'You're right. I think I'd have more to explain than just having disappeared for a few weeks.'

'You've got to *think* yourself human,' Jamie said.

'What do you mean?'

'Concentrate on looking like you did before: you covered yourself in a disguise without even knowing you were doing it, so it shouldn't be difficult to do so again.'

I took a deep breath, closed my eyes and tried to think of how I had once looked. Even after such a short time it was hard. The human me had shoulder-length dark chestnut hair, and that me definitely didn't have violet and garnet eyes, just boring old hazel. Pointed maroon fingernails were also a no-no – although they'd probably pass as manicured if I needed them to. It suddenly occurred to me that I didn't really want to be that person any more. I quite liked the daemon me.

I heard Jamie chuckle, and when my eyes snapped open he was grinning at me. 'It shouldn't be that hard.'

I didn't need to look in a mirror to know I hadn't changed. 'Won't I need my daemon strength if we're to take on Amaliel?'

'Now you know what you are and what you're capable of, I think you'll find your human persona will just be a façade, like when Shenanigans and Kerfuffle change.'

'It's easy, mistress,' Shenanigans said, the air about him shimmered and gone were my two daemon friends. Instead, I was looking at a tall man of about six foot four in a dark suit looking like a Mafioso hit man and a short elderly gentleman, similarly dressed, who could have been his diminutive crime lord boss.

'They make you look underdressed,' I remarked to Jamie.

'Whatever makes them feel comfortable.'

'You have a go,' Kerfuffle said to Kubeck.

Kubeck looked him up and down, then with a slight disturbance of air he too shrank to a more reasonable six foot or so. His skin took on a slightly olive tinge, while his hair, which remained short and curly, turned chestnut. He too was dressed in a dark suit, white shirt and black tie.

'Your turn,' Kerfuffle said to Vaybian.

'This I must see,' Kayla giggled, and I had to admit I was interested to see how her green captain would look in human form.

The result wasn't half bad. Obviously he was no longer green, and he'd lost the twisted ivory horn from just above his hairline, but otherwise he was pretty much the same: his hair, tied in a ponytail, was now a long, glossy black and his skin was tanned. He looked a bit like a Native American and had opted for the more casual option of jeans, T-shirt and a hoodie.

'Wow,' Kayla said as she slowly circled him, licking her lips like the cat who got the cream.

'Where's Pyrites?' I asked, suddenly noticing my little drakon was missing, then I felt something warm and furry rub up against my legs. 'Pyrites?' Crouching down, I found a small black, white and tan Jack Russell terrier. Pyrites hopped onto his back legs and dropped his paws onto my knee. I picked him up and he turned in my arms to give my face a good licking. His unreserved love made me feel a damn sight better than I had been.

'Pyrites,' Jamie said, and my drakon swivelled to look at him, 'you're here to guard Lucky – and under *no circumstances* are you to take to wing during the hours of daylight. Do you understand?' Pyrites made a grumbling sound, and when he said firmly, '*I mean it!*' my drakon barked.

Jamie obviously took this as a yes. Then his attention turned to Shenanigans and Kerfuffle. 'And remember, no humans are to be harmed.'

'What are you looking at us for?' Kerfuffle grumbled, glowering up at Jamie.

'You know very well why.'

My smallest guard grunted. 'We have been charged with protecting Mistress Lucky and protect her we will and you'd be lying if you said you'd have it any other way.'

Jamie's own frown softened. 'All right, but only use reasonable force.'

Neither guard replied. Jamie obviously took that as a yes as well, as he smiled at me and said, 'If you give me the card I'll go and get some petrol and any other stuff we might need.'

'All right,' I said, and told him my PIN number. 'I think we probably have enough food for the moment.'

'Oh, there's another thing,' Jamie added. 'You're not overly attached to your car, are you?'

I gave him a puzzled look. 'Why?'

'We're going to need something bigger.' He gestured around the room at the others.

'I guess not,' I said with a sigh. 'All the paperwork is in the filing cabinet in my office – under "V" for "vehicles".'

'Right, I'll just pop upstairs, then we'll be off.'

I couldn't help but think what an odd pair Jamie and Kerfuffle looked as they walked down the path to where my car was parked.

Then I panicked — would it be there? My keys had been on the hallway table, but what if the police had taken it?

They didn't immediately return, so I was hopeful they'd found it. Back in the kitchen, Shenanigans had already emptied most of the contents of my fridge into a bin bag being held open by an unsmiling Vaybian, and Kubeck was scrubbing the worktops.

I left them to it and wandered out into the hall to check the answering machine. There were only six missed messages: two from Philip Conrad's office and four from the police; the last was the day before yesterday, so the search must have happened some time over the last forty-eight hours. There was nothing of interest in the pile of post the police had kindly stacked on the hallway table, but several envelopes had been opened, so they might have taken some away with them. Most of my important correspondence came by e-mail these days and I wasn't going to be able to check my account any time soon, there was no point worrying about it. Rather than sit and wait and slowly go mad, I fetched a duster and some furniture polish and started cleaning up.

'Shouldn't you leave that?' Kayla asked as I set to work in the living room.

'It looks terrible.'

'The police will notice if they come back.'

I pulled a face at her. 'I think it's a bloody disgrace that they didn't clean up after themselves in the first place.'

I had more or less finished by the time Jamie and Kerfuffle returned, laden down with carrier bags; Shenanigans was preparing a quick meal.

'Here,' Jamie said, handing me a newspaper, 'I thought you might like to see this.'

I sat down at the kitchen table and unfolded the paper to find my own face staring up at me from the front page. It was the picture from the back cover of my last book, and not the most flattering. My publisher had wanted me to have a serious, academic demeanour, but I just looked stern and school-marmish.

The piece wasn't very long, but it explained the police tape: it turned out no one had seen fit to report Philip or his two goons missing for more than two weeks, and bearing in mind his wife had been murdered and his daughter abducted, that made no sense at all. It did explain Jamie's emphatic instructions to Shenanigans and Kerfuffle; I never did find out what they'd done to Philip's bodyguards. When someone finally did report him missing, the police discovered that the last time he and his companions had been seen was at a golf club with a mysterious woman and three other men. Further investigations by the boys in blue led them to the dinner I'd had with him at The Riverview – but by the time they'd discovered this, I'd already returned to the Underlands.

When I turned the page to read the rest of the story, I found out why no one had reported him missing: he'd told his staff he was going on holiday for a couple of weeks, no doubt to enjoy whatever he had been promised for betraying me, so no one took his disappearance seriously until he didn't show up at his office for what was in fact eighteen days after he'd been taken.

At first the police had wanted to question me because I was probably the last person to see Philip before he'd disappeared; now, according to the report, I was a possible victim to whatever fate had befallen Philip.

'This is a bit of a mess,' I said when I finished reading.

'I think it's best if we move on from here first thing tomorrow,' Jamie said. 'The last thing we need right now is for you to be taken in for questioning. It would waste time we don't have.'

'We've already wasted several hours,' I said, starting to panic all over again: we'd been cleaning and shopping while we were counting down to Jinx's possible demise.

'No, we've been preparing.' Jamie gestured with his head to Kerfuffle who trotted off, only to return with a couple more bags from the hall. 'This will help us keep an eye on news of any natural or unnatural disasters, plagues or pestilence,' Jamie said, taking a box out of the bag and placing it on the table in front of me: a tablet. I'd always wanted one, but I'd thought it a luxury I could do without.

He dug out six smaller boxes: new mobile phones. 'So we can keep in touch if we need to separate,' he told us.

'But—' Shenanigans started to say.

'No buts; when in the Overlands we do what they do.'

'We got on well enough without this newfangled technology before,' Kerfuffle grumbled.

'Before your most recent visit to protect Lucky, when was the last time you visited the Overlands?'

Kerfuffle frowned at him.

'Did they even have cars?'

'It wasn't *that* long ago . . .'

'Well, things have moved on, and if you don't think Amaliel and his people will be using today's technology, you'll be mistaken. Remember, he's been using a human conduit, and if he or she is anything like Philip Conrad, they're going to be pretty powerful.'

With that happy thought in mind, we put all the devices on charge and sat down to dinner. There wasn't much room around my kitchen table, so we moved into the living room and sat on the floor like we would have done at home – which shocked me: I was thinking of *the Underlands* as home now.

'Hadn't you better try to at least look human?' Jamie said to me. 'Just in case someone comes to the door?'

I closed my eyes and tried to remember what I'd looked like before. 'It's not working.'

'Try harder,' Jamie said with a laugh.

I wrinkled my brow and concentrated very, very hard.

'It's still not working,' I grumbled.

'You're still not trying,' he said in a singsong voice.

I gritted my teeth, and the picture of me on the front page flashed into my head, the air about me gave a little quiver and with a shudder I felt myself change. I looked down at my hands. Yep: all human.

'What now?' I asked.

'We get a couple of hours' sleep and set off before it gets light. The fewer people who see us leave the village the better.'

'Did you manage to get us a bigger car?' I said suddenly; I'd completely forgotten about that, until the memory popped into my head of poor Shenanigans folding himself almost double to get in the back of my little Ford Fiesta.

'Yep. It's probably not your usual cup of tea, but it'll do for the time being.' Jamie gave me what he obviously thought was a winsome smile, and Kerfuffle started to giggle, which was a disconcerting sound at the best of times. 'You've still got a Ford.'

'Will it be big enough?'

He nodded. 'For all of us, and Jinx when we get him back.'

'We will get him back, won't—?' And once again I was struggling to breathe – it felt like I was drowning in the bath again. I was gasping for air, but my mouth was opening and nothing was happening.

'Lucky!'

'Mistress, what's wrong?'

I got up onto my knees, my hands to my throat, still unable to catch my breath. I could sense Jinx was still trying to fight Amaliel, but his mind was in turmoil. I could feel his desperation, his panic, his fear that he had no control. He couldn't draw breath, not because he was choking or being smothered, but because Amaliel wasn't allowing him to breathe. He was showing Jinx how powerless he was, even over his own bodily functions.

Then as we both slipped into unconsciousness, Jinx gasped a word, an image flashed into my head and we could both breathe again.

Five

When I opened my eyes I was still on my knees. Jamie's face was filled with fearful worry.

'Lucky?' he said, reaching for me.

'I think I know where he is,' I said, 'or at least where he's going.'

'The woman's crazed,' Vaybian said.

'I'm going to give him such a smack in a moment,' Kayla snarled.

'Go on,' Jamie said, ignoring Vaybian.

'Before he passed out he showed me an image: a pyramid.'

'He's in Egypt?'

'It was weird, though. I saw chariots and . . .' I thought for a moment about exactly what I had seen. 'It was like the buildings were still under construction.'

'Was it a memory?' Jamie asked. 'Maybe from the last time he was there?'

'I don't know,' I said. 'He whispered the word "Exodus".'

'"Exodus"?' Jamie and Kayla said together. Jamie looked particularly thoughtful. 'Do you have a Bible?' he said.

'I thought you didn't do religion?' I said.

'I don't, but humans used to have the tendency to turn any unusual event, particularly if it was catastrophic, into one of religious significance. Your Bible is full of such events, and the Book of Exodus particularly so. If my memory is correct, the ten plagues of Egypt appear in Exodus.'

'But it was only a story,' Kerfuffle said.

Jamie shook his head. 'Some of it was probably based on historical facts. It might not have happened exactly as the Bible said, and the events could have been hundreds of years apart, but it wasn't like today, when something happens thousands of miles away and the rest of the world knows about it within moments.'

'These plagues,' I said, knowing my question would probably get me an answer I really didn't want, 'was it Jinx last time? The plague of locusts, the rivers turning to blood, the deaths of the firstborn?'

'It was before my time,' Jamie said, 'but some of it, yes, maybe. The locusts are a possibility, but I doubt he would have turned the rivers to blood – too theatrical for our Jinx. As for the killing of the firstborn' – he blew out through pursed lips – 'I don't think so. That's far more Amaliel's style than Jinx's.'

'But he could try and make Jinx do that sort of thing?' I asked.

'If Amaliel has gone to the trouble of binding Jinx, he's done it for a reason, and whatever that is I would say it doesn't bode well for humanity. Though if Jinx is still fighting him, that's something, at least.'

'Do you think Amaliel is trying to make people think he's some sort of god?' Kerfuffle asked.

'Why would he?' Kubeck asked.

'To get a human following, perhaps,' Kerfuffle said.

'You mean like starting a Sicarii sect here in the Overlands?' said Shenanigans.

'Possibly,' Kerfuffle said.

'Damnation,' Shenanigans said, which was nowhere near close to the profanity that'd sprung into my mind.

This was terrible. Amaliel had been successfully running the Sicarii in the Underlands for who knew how long; I doubted it would be particularly difficult to persuade a group of fanatics to follow him here, especially if he'd brought a few of his creepy daemon followers with him. All he needed to do was find any old group of would-be Satanists and they'd be hanging onto his every word.

'I don't think we can afford to wait for morning,' I said with a sigh.

'But where would we start, mistress?' Shenanigans asked. 'The Overlands is a huge place.'

'The ten plagues were in Egypt,' I said. 'Do you think he could be there?'

Jamie took a deep breath and raised his eyes to mine. 'I suspect Jinx was trying to send you a message: I doubt if he knows where he is, but he would know what Amaliel is trying to make him do.'

'No, it wasn't like before,' I said, my voice cracking. 'Jinx wasn't sending me a message; he thinks I'm dead. I think Amaliel is close to doing it, Jamie. I think he's close to binding Jinx – or at least, Jinx thinks he is.'

'Well, whether he meant to or not, you've been given a clue to Amaliel's intentions,' Jamie said.

'What are you thinking?' Kerfuffle asked him.

'Jinx knows the score; he knows the other Guardians and I will be coming for him. He'll hang on as long as he can.'

For that, I had no answer. Plagues of locusts and rivers of blood were bad enough, but if Amaliel made Jinx kill every firstborn in the whole world? I didn't think I could live with it if we didn't somehow save him in time.

As soon as the tablet and phones were charged, we set off. Since Philip had been approached in London – well, that's if he'd been telling the truth about that – we thought we'd start there. And we thought it logical that if Amaliel planned to do something awful, he'd do it in a major city where millions would be affected.

It was still dark when we left the cottage.

'Wow, it is big, isn't it?' I said, looking at the dark red eight-seater MPV Jamie had procured for us.

'You don't have to drive,' he replied.

I hesitated for a moment. A few months ago if he'd suggested I even drive to London, let alone in such a huge vehicle, I'd have had an anxiety attack. I'd loathed driving . . . but now, I realised I'd changed.

'I'll drive,' I heard myself say, and held out my hand for the keys.

'You hate driving.'

'That was then,' I told him, 'but if you want a go, you can take over when we reach the M25.'

'Still scared of driving on motorways?' Jamie couldn't quite hide the superior amusement in his voice.

'No,' I snapped, 'but I'll very likely be distracted by the number of dead I'll see – there's a reason they call it the road to Hell.'

He had the grace to look slightly ashamed of himself, but even so, I could see he didn't want to hand over the keys – he *really* liked to drive, and I couldn't be bothered to argue. I didn't need to be any angrier with him than I already was.

So I climbed into the front passenger seat, and Pyrites jumped onto my lap. Neither Vaybian not Kubeck had been in a car before, and despite our morose moods, Vaybian's wide-eyed, tight-lipped expression as we hurtled down the country lanes did make me crack a small smile. When we hit the motorway, I glanced back at him. I thought his knuckles were about to shatter, he was holding onto the armrests so tight.

Shenanigans and Kerfuffle sat comfortably in the back row. The MPV might not have been my normal choice of transport, but it was perfect for me and my guards – even Shenanigans had enough legroom.

'Where do we start once we get to London?' I asked after a while.

'Maybe we should pay a visit to Philip Conrad's offices? They probably have a record of who he met and where. The police got the information about his meetings with you from somewhere.' Jamie glanced across at me. 'Can you think of anything Philip ever said to you that might lead us to whomever was using him?'

'He told me so many lies, so who knows?'

'Think about it.'

I concentrated on remembering all that Philip had told me. 'Originally he told me he'd been to see a bokor in South London to ask for help in finding his daughter, but that was a lie, part of the story to make me feel sorry for him. Later, at the golf course, he told me he'd met a man at a party who had introduced him to the bokor.'

'What did he tell you about this man?'

'The bokor?'

'No, the man who introduced them.'

I thought back, trying to remember: it was right after Philip had been telling me about this man that the pond we'd been sitting by had erupted upwards in a blood-red fountain and the daemon Argon had appeared to carry me away with him; understandably what had happened just beforehand had blurred into insignificance, until now.

'He said he was waiting for his coat when he and this man – I think he said he was an American – got talking.'

'An American?'

'Hmm.' I visualised me and Philip walking up to the walled garden and Philip pulling open the gate as he spoke, and suddenly recalled his words. Out loud, I said, '*I'd never seen the man before – I would have remembered him if I had. He was tall and slim and looked a bit like a young Barack Obama. He even had a slight American accent.*'

'Did he have a name?' Jamie asked.

I remembered us sitting down on the bench. 'His name was Joseph.'

'And it was this man who introduced him to the bokor?'

'Well, that's what he said, but who knows – the man could lie for England.' I nearly added 'a bit like you really', but bit my tongue; no good would come of me sniping at him.

'If Philip met this man, there'd be a note of it in his office diary.'

'I'm not sure I'd want anything in *my* diary to suggest I was going to meet with a bokor,' Kayla said over my shoulder.

'Philip said this Joseph was in Britain on business, that he was meeting a man who could make him a major player. I suppose that's how he sucked Philip in. I suspect he made it all sound quite legitimate to start with.'

Jamie kept his eyes on the road. 'That's the way it usually works: choose your subject, preferably someone ambitious and greedy, then gradually reel them in until they're in so deep they can't – or don't want to – get out.'

I got goosebumps as I remembered Philip dangling from Lord

Argon's talons. 'I still can't understand how anyone would be so stupid. Making deals with daemons is only ever going to end in tears.'

I heard chuckling from behind me, and Kerfuffle began to giggle. 'What?'

'If you haven't noticed, every single one of us in this vehicle is a daemon – including you,' Jamie pointed out with a smile.

'Half-daemon,' I said quickly. 'I'm *half*-daemon!' But he was right, of course. 'What I *meant* was, if you make a deal with that sort of daemon.'

'Like if you make a deal with *that* sort of human: a crime lord, a drug dealer, a corrupt businessman,' Jamie said.

He was right. human or daemon, there was good or bad in all of them. Fortunately for me, I was in with the good crowd – although if Jinx unleashed his powers upon this world, there'd be some who might not see it that way.

We had some good luck to start with, hitting the M25 before it got too busy; even so there were plenty of cars out and about, and lots of huge lorries lumbering along. It was growing light, but the misty, murky morning was doing nothing to lift my mood. I was impatient as well as anxious and the journey felt like it was taking for ever. I watched the road ahead as Jamie changed lanes expertly, with the confidence of a man who'd been driving all his life. It was strange, really; I had *belonged* to this world, and I had never driven with such assurance.

Then a small blue family car swerved in front of us in a last-minute manoeuvre, making me flinch and Jamie brake.

'Is there nothing you can do for them?' Kayla asked from over my shoulder.

I watched the blue car and its four occupants speed off into the distance: sad casualties of the M25. They'd no idea that they had died. No doubt they would be driving around and around the motorway for ever . . .

I shook my head as the car vanished into the distance. 'Not

unless we catch them up.' But it was too late, they were long gone already.

Then a thought occurred to me and I turned to Jamie. 'How can you see the dead of this world but you still can't see Kayla?'

'I suppose because she's a spirit from our world? Sorry, I don't know all the answers.'

We went back to staring silently at the road ahead, until he said, 'Time to dig out your mobile and google Philip Conrad to find out where his offices are.'

A few taps on the screen later and I had the address and a map of the location in Docklands.

The building was exactly what I'd expected: swanky, with a car park out front. Jamie pulled into the only empty space – it didn't come as any surprise to see a plaque on the wall telling us the parking bay was for the exclusive use of Mr Philip Conrad.

'It's probably best you stay here,' he told me.

'Why?' I could feel myself bristling.

'Because they'll almost certainly recognise you from the newspapers,' he said. 'Also, I'm quite sure what I'm about to do is illegal.'

'What are you about to do?' I asked in alarm.

'Impersonate a police officer.'

'Jamie, policemen don't wear jeans and hoodies, at least not when the—' I didn't get to finish as the air around us rippled and Jamie was suddenly dressed in a navy suit, white shirt and navy and grey silk tie.

'Wait here,' he said, opening the door and climbing out. 'I won't be long.' With that he slammed the door shut and walked across the car park.

'He scrubs up well, doesn't he?' Kayla commented as we watched him stride up the steps to the main entrance.

'Hmm,' I said, but my attention had shifted from his receding back to the two construction workers he'd glanced at as he passed them on the steps. One was pouring tea from a flask into a mug his mate was holding as they laughed and chatted. I undid my seatbelt and reached for the door handle.

'Mistress, where are you going?' Kubeck asked.

'The Guardian said for you to stay here,' Vaybian added unnecessarily.

'There's something I have to do,' I said, opening the door. I could hear my guards beginning to argue, but I ignored them, shifted Pyrites onto Jamie's seat and hopped out.

One of the workmen saw me coming and pushed back his hard hat. Even in death he was still very good-looking: dark hair curled upon his brow and his dark blue eyes twinkled. He nudged his friend. 'Things are looking up,' he said with a soft Irish burr.

His friend glanced my way and his smile widened. 'Well, hello, pet – what can we be doing for you this fine day?'

A Geordie and an Irishman, both a long way from home, and sorely missed, I'd bet. 'Why are you still here?' I asked.

They exchanged a puzzled look. 'What do you mean?'

'The construction's finished.'

They both peered up at me as if I was mad – and then looked back over their shoulders at the building rising up behind them. Their expressions became confused as it slowly dawned on them that they were no longer on a construction site.

'What the hell . . .?' the Geordie lad said, getting to his feet.

His mate joined him. 'How can this be?'

'What's the last thing you remember?' I asked.

'Remember?' The Irishman looked puzzled.

'The last day you worked – what do you remember about it?'

They exchanged a glance. 'Last night, it was raining,' the Geordie said.

'It's always bloody raining,' the other guy said, laughing. 'It hardly ever bloody stops.'

'That wasn't last night,' I told them, gesturing up at the building.

'I don't understand,' the Geordie boy said. 'We were running *way* behind schedule – last night there wasn't even a roof on it, was there, Sean?'

'That's why we were still working, long after we should have finished for the night.' His laughing blue eyes lost some of their sparkle and a frown creased the middle of his forehead. 'We were working late and . . .' His head jerked around to look at his friend. 'Fuck! There was an accident—'

'Accident?' his friend said, and I could see the realisation slowly dawning on them both that all was not quite as it should be.

'You slipped, and I grabbed for you and . . .' His eyes met mine. 'I tried to hold onto him, but he began to slip, and as I tried to drag him back I fell too.' He looked down at his body and held up his hands as though seeing them for the first time. His body wasn't solid; there was a translucence to it.

I gave them an encouraging smile. I might not have been able to help the family on the motorway, but I could do something for these two men. I closed my eyes for a moment and concentrated on opening the gateway to the other side, praying it would work the same way in this world as it did in the Underlands. The air grew heavy and it felt stormy, the atmosphere crackling with electricity. I opened my eyes and a bright speck of light appeared just below them on the steps, a narrow rod of gold spearing down onto the brickwork. The dot became a split and the rod became a swathe, then the split became a tear and the tear opened up into a hole filled with glowing light.

'Oh sweet baby Jesus,' the Geordie lad whispered, taking a step back.

'There's no need to be afraid.'

'What's happening?' he asked, his eyes flicking to me, then the light and back again.

'It's time for you to leave.'

He started to shake his head as he stumbled away from the light. 'This isn't right. This isn't right.'

The Irish guy, Sean, tentatively stretched out his hand, allowing the light to caress his fingertips. 'It's warm,' he said wonderingly.

'Get away from it – it's not natural—'

Sean looked at me. 'We're dead, aren't we?'

'I'm sorry.'

He looked down at his feet, concentrating, trying to take it in. 'How did I not know? I saw him fall — I felt myself fall.'

'Maybe you just didn't want to believe it,' I told him.

His attention turned back to the light. 'Is this the way?'

'Yes,' I told him. A huge lump was forming in my throat.

Sean reached up, took off his hard hat and threw it to the ground, his lips curling into a broad smile. 'Come on, Jacky, lad. Can't you hear the angels?'

Jack still didn't look so sure, but his friend stepped into the light and began to laugh as he turned a full circle, bathing in the golden rays. 'Come on,' he said, reaching out his hand.

Jack took a step towards him, then another; his expression of fear slipping away until he too stood in the golden light. He took hold of his friend's outstretched fingers. I could hear laughter and voices calling to them from beyond the gateway and the two men took that final step and crossed over to the other side. Glowing figures surrounded them, welcoming them home, and for a moment the entrance glowed as bright as the midday sun.

Then with a crack it sprang shut and was gone.

Kayla appeared by my side. 'Do you think daemons and humans go to the same place?'

'It looked and sounded the same, but I don't suppose we'll really know until it's our turn.'

She stood there for a moment looking at where the gateway had been. Her expression was a little wistful.

'You can go you know,' I told her. 'I'll help you cross if you want.'

'No,' she said, with a toss of her scarlet and emerald curls, 'I'll not leave you — at least not until I know you have your Deathbringer back safe where he belongs.'

'That could take a long time,' I said, my shoulders sagging with the enormity of the task ahead. 'He could be absolutely anywhere.'

Kayla tapped her bottom lip with her forefinger. 'It's true that Amaliel isn't likely to make it easy for you.'

'Kayla, what am I going to do? What if I can't find him in time?'

'You'll find him.'

'But what if we don't? What if he's already started to kill people?'

'Let's hope Amaliel is going for dramatic effect and doesn't start straight off with the Black Death and the like; he'll go for plagues of bugs, boils, storms and tempests, most likely.'

'That'll be bad enough – a plague of locusts in the right place could destroy a country's economy.'

'I doubt Amaliel is interested in economies; he wants souls.'

I got back into the car to wait for Jamie. I really hoped he had some good news.

Six

Jamie was gone for such a long time I started to wonder if the people in Philip's office had smelled a rat and called the police. The building wasn't surrounded by police cars, which did give me some cause to hope that this wasn't so, but you could never tell. What if police officers were already inside asking questions when he bowled in? I glanced around at the other cars in the car park: two BMWs, an Audi, a Mini and a VW. None of them were obvious police cars – but did detectives use their own? On the telly they did.

Then the glass door swung open and Jamie came striding out, a manila folder tucked under his arm. He climbed in and handed me the folder

'Well?'

He put the key in the ignition and smiled, showing teeth. 'I have a surname for Joseph and the address of the company he supposedly works for.'

'What's all this?' I asked, holding up the folder.

'Philip's secretary was very helpful. She photocopied several pieces of correspondence between Philip and Joseph and all the newspaper cuttings from when Philip's wife was murdered and his daughter disappeared. She also copied all his diary entries for around those dates and in the run-up to his meeting you.'

'Anything interesting?'

Jamie started the engine. 'I have the address of Philip's London apartment and a key to get in.'

'How did you get a key?'

'I asked for it.'

'And she *gave* it to you?'

Jamie smiled at the windscreen as he negotiated his way out of the car park and onto the street. 'I told you she was very helpful.'

'How come she had a key anyway?'

Jamie glanced my way and smirked.

'I always said Philip was a shit,' Kayla said from behind me. I looked back over my shoulder, puzzled, and she rolled her eyes. 'You are so naïve at times.'

Then the penny dropped. 'Philip was having an affair with his secretary?'

'Not so much of an affair as he was using her for sex whenever he was in town and his wife wasn't.'

'Was she stupid or what?' Kayla grumbled.

'Anyway, she was rather disgruntled about how he treated her,' Jamie added. 'Especially when she heard about you.'

'Not totally stupid, then,' Kayla commented.

'Me?' I said, ignoring her.

'The police think you and he were in a relationship.'

'*What?* I only saw the man three times before he was whisked off to the Underlands—'

'Your name was in his diary several times more than that – the police apparently decided the entries were evidence of meetings between the two of you, but looking at them, I think they were doodles.'

'Doodles?' My head was beginning to ache.

'When he was on the phone – probably talking to Joseph, or his other contact.'

'*What* other contact?'

Jamie gestured at the file. 'It's all in there. When we get to Philip's flat we can try to make some sense of it all. I think it may be a good place to start.'

I opened the folder and flicked through a few pages before tucking it into the side pocket. I've never been able to read in cars without getting travel-sick; the last thing I wanted was to have to ask Jamie to stop the car so I could throw up.

I stroked Pyrites' ears and let my mind wander as I stared out at the streets flashing by. He was happy enough sitting on my lap, though it was a little strange stroking fur rather than scales. I noticed that whenever we passed someone walking a dog he followed it with his eyes until it was out of sight.

I did wonder what he was going to do when he needed to eat – maybe he'd be able to make do on what we could give him until we returned home. He couldn't really grow to his full size and fly across the English countryside – Jamie was right; that *would* cause a stir.

Then I thought of Jinx, wondering where he was now. Last time I'd connected to him he had felt so bereft, so scared. I couldn't imagine Jinx being afraid of anything, but he had been: he was as scared of what Amaliel was liable to make him do as I was. If Amaliel made him carry out some terrible atrocity, Jinx would never forgive himself. Even worse, he would have signed his own death warrant: Jamie's Guardians would hunt him down. Even if we could find him first, I wasn't sure Jamie and I could protect him – in fact, I wasn't convinced Jamie would even try. He had his job, and he'd made it quite clear he would do it.

I glanced across at him, watching his face as he concentrated on driving. I loved him and Jinx with all my heart, and I didn't want to choose, but if Jinx was in danger and Jamie was that danger, then I would have to. Jamie must have felt my eyes upon him for he smiled and keeping his eyes on the road, reached across and squeezed my hand.

'We will find him,' he said very quietly.

My fingers squeezed his and I forced my lips to smile back.

Philip's apartment was only about fifteen minutes away from his offices. It overlooked the Thames and must have cost a fortune. Not for the first time I wondered how a man who was so obviously wealthy had managed to get himself entangled in something so crazy and potentially lethal. What with bokors and daemons, he'd been meeting with some seriously scary people. I did wonder about this man called Joseph: was he just like Philip, a greedy individual who had been enticed by promises of power and riches? Or was he the instigator? Of course, he might even be a daemon himself.

The apartment block, like Philip's offices, was an ultra-modern vision of stainless steel and plate-glass. There was a keypad to gain entry, but that wasn't a problem; Philip's secretary had been helpful in the extreme – which made me wonder whether Jamie had used his mesmerising skills on her, which got me feeling angry again. I reined it in. I had more important things to worry about for the moment.

Philip had the penthouse suite – *of course he did!* – and in the lift I found myself getting even more irritated with him. As he was dead, this was just as stupid as getting angry with Jamie. The man was a total shit – shame I hadn't realised it a whole lot earlier.

As we stepped out of the lift I heard a sound in the hallway, and when I looked around, the door to the fire escape was slowly swinging shut. As Philip's was the only apartment on this floor I wondered who could have been up here. I touched Kerfuffle's arm and put a finger to my lips and pointed to the door. He gave a nod of understanding and hurried along the corridor and through the door as Jamie crossed to Philip's flat.

Kerfuffle returned a moment later. 'No one there,' he told me.

There was police tape across the door to Philip's flat and I imagined the rest of the high-class residents in the block must have been less than impressed, being questioned about their neighbour's activities. But Jamie was already inside, so Pyrites, Kayla and I hurried after him. The lift wasn't big enough for us all – it wasn't much bigger than a large toilet cubicle – so the others were following us, all except for Kubeck, who was keeping watch in the lobby. If anyone looked like they were interested in the penthouse flat, he'd let us know.

'We're looking for anything that might be at all useful,' Jamie said, gesturing around.

I handed Jamie the manila folder and suggested, 'You said you had an address for Joseph?'

'His office, allegedly. I'll ring now.'

While he tapped the number into his mobile I began to look around the flat, wrinkling my nose at the slightly unpleasant odour in the air, like something had gone off.

'Hello, I'd like to speak to Joseph Babel please,' I heard Jamie say as I wandered around the living room.

It was beautifully decorated in monochromatic shades of black, white and grey, but too bland for my taste. The small kitchen was the same: white wall tiles patterned with black and silver bands and gleaming black worktops. The stainless steel oven, fridge and dishwasher shone. The black and white floor tiles also sparkled, and I just knew Philip had to have had a cleaner coming in.

'This is – nice,' Kayla said, screwing up her nose.

'A bit too nice,' I whispered and walked back into the living room.

'Oh, that's a shame. I don't suppose you have a contact number for him? It is rather important. Thank you. Goodbye . . . *Shit!*' Jamie said and dropped the phone into his pocket.

'No luck?'

'Joseph Babel was only based there temporarily while he was in England. Apparently, he returned to the States several weeks ago.'

The door opened and the rest of my guards came trooping in.

Jamie looked round. 'You took your time.'

'A woman on the ground floor questioned our identities,' Shenanigans said.

'Nosy bint,' Kerfuffle added.

'What did you tell her?' I asked in alarm.

'That we understood the penthouse suite was for sale.'

'What did she say?' Shenanigans and Kerfuffle looked like they could have Mafia connections, which meant she'd probably tag Vaybian as a pimp or drug dealer.

'She said once we'd finished looking around, perhaps we'd like to pop in and have a cup of tea,' Shenanigans said.

Jamie gave a snort of laughter and Kayla started to giggle. 'It takes all sorts, I suppose!'

'While I start on the rest of these numbers,' Jamie said, holding up the file, 'Shenanigans and Kerfuffle, you search the living room, and Vaybian can take the kitchen.'

'And I'll make a start in the bedroom,' I said, and headed for the door, Pyrites trotting along beside me.

'Did the man have no bloody imagination at all?' Kayla said as we walked into yet another pretentious monochrome designer room: light grey walls, white ceiling and black lacquered wardrobes and cupboards. The bedlinen was shiny black satin banded with silver, completing the elegant but stark décor.

'I suppose it matched his black heart,' Kayla commented.

I slid open the door to the first wardrobe. 'I told you he was vain the first time we met him,' I said, running my fingers over the sleeves of a dozen suits.

'You should check the pockets,' Kayla suggested.

I pulled a face. 'Nah, Philip wouldn't put anything in his pockets – it would ruin the line.'

'He might have been vain, but a man has to put his bits and pieces somewhere,' she pointed out. Then she laughed. 'Although he'd obviously been putting his in a few places he shouldn't!' That did get me to crack a small smile, and she said gently, 'It will be all right, you know. Jinx is tough.'

'I'm not so sure, Kayla. He's hurting like you wouldn't believe.'

'Because he thinks he's lost you.'

'If that's meant to make me feel better, it doesn't – it makes me more scared for him.'

'This connection between the two of you is strange . . .'

'We used to have something similar,' I said with a sad smile. 'When I first arrived at court I could feel you – it was like we were somehow bound together.'

'Blood!' she said.

'Jamie said being blood-related didn't mean we'd automatically have that kind of connection—'

'No, I didn't mean that. I meant *actual* blood: you and I were connected by blood.'

'I don't understand.'

'When I first came to you I wasn't sure how long I was going to stay, so I shared blood with you so I'd always know if you needed me.'

'What do you mean, *shared blood*?' I shuddered, imagining some sort of vampiric ceremony, but she held up her thumb.

'Like blood-brothers: I just pricked your thumb and mine and pressed them together so our blood became one.'

So Kayla had always known I wasn't a blue-blood, like true daemon royalty – but now wasn't the time for *that* particular conversation.

I stared at her for a moment, then lifted my right hand: there between my middle and forefinger was the tiny white scar where the arrow that had erupted out of Jinx's chest had nicked me. 'You're right: that's exactly how Jinx and I are linked. When I escaped from Amaliel, Jinx knew without me telling him that I had been hurt. At the time, neither of us had thought much about it . . .'

So that was one mystery solved. I started going through Philip's pockets, but it was clear most of the suits had been recently dry-cleaned and by the time I was halfway through them I suspected my first opinion was correct: I'd not found a single thing.

'This is hopeless,' I said to Pyrites, who was watching me with interest.

He padded forward and stuck his nose in the closet, running it along the line of clothing. A couple of times he drew it back out and sneezed – dry-cleaning fluid getting up his nose? – then a few jackets from the end, he began to snuffle in earnest. He pushed his way into the wardrobe and began to paw at a silver-grey suit that probably cost as much as my old Fiesta.

'He's got the scent of something,' Kayla said.

As I grabbed the hanger and pulled it out of the wardrobe, Pyrites whined, the air shimmered and he was a drakon again, albeit a small one. He puffed grey smoke, made a grumbling sound from deep inside his chest and grew a few sizes more.

'What's got him all worked up?' Jamie asked as he strolled into the room.

'Not sure,' I said, holding the suit at arm's length and looking it up and down.

I checked the right-hand pocket of the jacket and then the left – nothing. Nothing in the top pocket either. I pulled the jacket open by the lapels, one side at a time. No right-hand inner pocket, but in the left side, *bingo!* I could feel the edge of a piece of card. I caught it between my fingertips and pulled it out. Pyrites growled and made the strange paddling motion with his front feet he did whenever he was excited or anxious.

'It's a business card, that's all,' I told him.

Pyrites growled and puffed grey smoke again.

'I think it must be more than that,' Jamie said.

It was plain white with navy print and read 'Gabriel Derne'. There was a mobile phone number. 'It's nothing special,' I said, handing it to Jamie.

He took it between his thumb and forefinger. He examined both sides, then breathed out through pursed lips. 'Well, this explains a lot.'

'It does?'

He passed his left hand over the card and held it out to me. 'Look again.'

I peered down at the card. 'I don't see . . .' Then I turned it over. On the back were some very faint symbols. 'What do they mean?'

'I think I mentioned that I spent quite a lot of time in the Overlands in the twenties, thirties and forties.'

'That's when you learned to drive.'

He nodded. 'There was a lot of interest in Satanism then, which included calling on daemons.'

'People actually did that?'

'"fraid so.'

'Why?'

'Oh, for all sorts of reasons. Power, wealth, just to see if they could – and sometimes for darker motives.'

'I should think calling up daemons for any reason was pretty dark,' I said.

'Some humans were pretty dark,' Kayla chipped in, 'especially during that period.'

'Sometimes they called upon a daemon to collect a soul.'

'Like when Lord Argon came to collect me?'

'Exactly. The Satanist or devil-worshiper or whoever would call upon a daemon to collect the soul of an adversary.'

'In other words: *kill them*,' Kayla interrupted.

'To identify the victim to the daemon they used to "pass the runes": a piece of paper inscribed with a daemon-summoning curse was given to the victim, who was usually none the wiser.'

'But Philip wasn't the intended victim – I was.'

Jamie ran his hand through his hair. 'I think what we have here is a variation upon a theme. Passing the runes is a practice fraught with danger.' He tapped the front of the card with his fingernail. 'This Gabriel Derne was probably a conduit between the daemon and Philip, as Philip was between him and you. Once a daemon is called to collect a soul they get mighty pissed off if they have to return empty-handed, and in that case, the soul of the person who passed the runes in the first place becomes forfeit.'

'But Philip never passed me any runes!'

'Did he give you a business card?'

'Oh shit,' I muttered. Of course he did, the conniving, manipulative, lying bastard.

'Whoever called upon the daemon put at least two layers between him and it.'

'So we need to find this Gabriel Derne?'

'I suspect he was being used by Joseph Babel, but it wouldn't hurt. He might help us find him.'

'I thought you said he'd returned to the States.'

'No, the woman I spoke to said he'd returned to the States. If Amaliel is here, I suspect his human ally is too.'

'Guardian,' Vaybian said from the doorway, 'Kubeck just called: two men in suits are on the way up in the small box.'

'Pyrites!' But I didn't need to say anything else; with a shiver, my drakon had changed into a rather large German shepherd.

'What if they're police?' I asked, worried.

'Let me deal with it.' Jamie pocketed the business card and walked through to the living room. 'You carry on searching the bedroom,' he called over his shoulder as an afterthought.

'Yes, sir,' I muttered to myself, sitting down on the bed next to a set of drawers.

I heard the front door open and close, then, 'Who the fuck are you?'

'This is going well,' Kayla said, wafting through to the other room, no doubt to join in the fun.

I let them get on with it. If they were the police, I was the last person they should see: I'd probably go straight from potential victim to the top of Britain's 'most wanted' list. I still couldn't believe they thought I was having an affair with Philip.

I pulled open the top drawer of the bedside cabinet and rummaged through the contents. There wasn't much to see: some loose change, a packet of condoms – bloody man – and other bits and pieces. Then right at the back, I noticed the corner of something black, the edge of a notebook or diary, maybe. I stretched my fingers and pulled out a smart notebook bound in black leather with gold-edged pages.

It had gone very quiet in the room next door, although I could hear a low murmur that sounded like Jamie. I flicked open the cover of the notebook and as I did so, the stone in my mother's ring must have caught the light as it appeared to flare green. But before I could think on it for more than a moment, all hell broke loose. There was an almighty roar from the living room and Pyrites went bounding off. I considered hiding under the bed, but if they were policemen next door, that would make me look guilty, and if they were daemons – and judging by the commotion they probably were – they would find me wherever I hid.

There was a crash and the sound of breaking furniture, then the air quite literally rippled out towards me, as if a boulder had been dropped in a lake, and I felt myself change.

I shoved the notebook in my jacket pocket and ran to the

doorway: everyone had reverted to their daemon selves. I had seen our visitors before: they'd held me still while Amaliel cut off the tip of my finger. Just looking at them made the mutilated finger throb.

They were not just built like sumo wrestlers but dressed like them too, wearing only small leather loincloths. Their glistening orangey skin looked like they'd overdone it with the fake tan; their long black hair was slicked back and braided. That is where any similarity to humans ended: one had the face of a hawk, with a beak, round eyes and a smattering of feathers on his cheeks and where his eyebrows should have been. The other had a flattened stump for a nose, huge nostrils and small black beads for eyes.

Hawkman was holding Kerfuffle above his head and was heading for the window. Shenanigans, Jamie and Vaybian were being kept back by Pigface, who was twirling two double-edged scythes with a skill I would have found awe-inspiring if I hadn't been so afraid for my friends.

I could do nothing for my three guards facing Pigface's deadly steel, but I was buggered if I was going to let Kerfuffle be thrown out of the window of a fourth-floor penthouse.

'Pyrites!' I shouted as I bounded towards Hawkman, and my drakon shot up into the air and flew towards the struggling Kerfuffle. Pigface glared at me as I ran past, but he had his hands full with my other guards.

Hawkman had drawn back his arms over his head, ready to throw my diminutive guard at the window, but as I let out a yell, Pyrites swooped down and grabbed Kerfuffle by his belt. Hawkman spun around as Pyrites sped away, Kerfuffle hanging from his claws, but I was too pumped to stop: I jumped over the smoked glass coffee table, drew up my legs and executed a perfect jump front kick, hitting Hawkman smack-bang in the middle of the chest.

He was caught off-guard, and propelled backwards towards the window – too late, I realised this was probably not a good thing – I wasn't bothered at the thought of him going through the window and ending up splattered all over the pavement, but I didn't want to go with him – I was only half-daemon, after all.

He hit the glass with an almighty thump, the window shuddered and, with a sound like the crack of a whip, fractures radiated out across the pane. The glass bowed behind him, but it must have been safety glass because it held, and he came back at me with a punch to my stomach that sent me sprawling backwards.

I really hoped I wouldn't land on the coffee table; Jamie having to pick glass out of my backside would do nothing for my dignity. Fortunately for me, I smacked into what felt like a brick wall – until it collapsed beneath me and I found myself lying in a crumpled heap on top of a gurgling daemon.

I struggled to sit up, and to my consternation found my hands slick with something sticky. 'Oh God—'

'Lucky!' Jamie cried. 'Are you all right? Are you hurt?'

I lifted my hands. They were covered in blood – jade-coloured blood. 'No, I don't think so. I'm probably a lot better than him anyway . . .' I got up off the fallen daemon.

His gurgling turned to gulping, then to wheezing, then silence. Jamie rolled him over as his eyes flickered shut: the point of one of his own wickedly sharp scythes had pierced his throat; the other had sliced into the artery in his thigh.

His heart gave one final shaky beat, his head flopped to one side and it was all over. For a brief moment a dark stain coloured the air above him, fluttering like an injured bird, and then it was gone. I glanced at Jamie, wondering if he'd seen it, but I didn't think he had. It was my gift – or curse, whatever – not his.

Hawkman staggered to his friend's side and dropped to his knees, all the fight gone from him.

'I knew it was a mistake not to bring the swords,' Vaybian commented, holding his arm and trying to staunch the blood trickling through his fingers.

'Here, let me look at that,' Kerfuffle offered.

Kayla sat down next to Vaybian while Kerfuffle saw to his

wound. 'It's not serious,' she told me, 'although it probably hurts like shit.'

Jamie gave Hawkman a few moments to grieve for his friend, then went straight in. 'Where's Amaliel?'

'Fuck off.'

'You will tell me.'

The daemon looked him up and down from where he was kneeling beside his friend. 'I don't think so.'

'Do you want to end up like your friend?'

'It's better than what Amaliel will do to me if I told you where to find him.'

'If we find him, you'll be safe.'

'If you find him, you'll be dead – or worse.'

'It's only a matter of time before we find out where he's hiding.'

'Then you won't be needing my help.'

Jamie crossed his arms and scowled down on him. 'If you don't help us I *will* kill you.'

The daemon gave a snort of laughter. 'Here – let me help you with that,' he said, and before we had a chance to stop him, he grabbed the scythe protruding from his friend's throat and sliced it across his own.

'No,' I shouted, '*no!*' and I fell to my knees, grabbing his arms and holding him upright. 'Don't you bloody well dare!' A strange tingling sensation ran down my arms and into my fingertips.

Hawkman stared at me with triumph in his eyes – then the triumph turned to panic. He wasn't dying – at least not yet.

Jamie gazed down on him. 'She is the Soulseer, with the power to see a soul on its way – *or not*. Amaliel isn't the only one who can bind a soul for all eternity.'

'No,' Hawkman whispered, looking this way and that as though searching for some way to escape.

'Oh yes,' Jamie said, crouching down beside him. 'Tell us what you know, and she'll let you pass. Refuse, and you'll spend all eternity in this place – or maybe somewhere worse.'

'Please, lady—'

'Where is Amaliel?' I asked. 'And even more importantly, where is the Deathbringer?'

'If I tell you, he'll—'

'He can't kill you,' Jamie interrupted, 'you're already dead. He can't curse or bind you to this world, for once she releases you your soul will be gone.'

'You're sure?' he said, looking from me to Jamie and back again.

'Absolutely.'

The daemon glanced down at his dead friend. 'If I tell you, you'll let me leave?'

'Yes,' I said.

He lifted his hand to his slit throat. 'The High Celebrant of this world has acquired a place that was once holy to mortals: it's there that they will bind the Deathbringer in Blue Fire and conduct the ceremony to bind his soul.'

'Where is this place?' Jamie asked.

'It's on the outskirts of a village south of this city. I can tell you no more than that.'

'A name – give me a name.'

His beak clicked a few times and he cocked his head to one side as if thinking. 'Saint Bartholomew the Martyr,' he said at last.

'The name of the village.'

'I don't know. Truly, I don't know.'

Jamie stood staring down at him for several seconds. 'All right,' he said eventually, 'you can let him go now.'

I released his arms, hoping that if I was no longer touching him, that would do the trick, but nothing happened.

'You promised, you promised,' the daemon said.

'It takes a moment,' I said, giving Jamie a panicked look.

'Do what you usually do,' Jamie whispered, so I got to my feet, closed my eyes and thought of the gateway.

A few more seconds passed. Nothing. I opened one eye, hoping against hope a pinprick of light had appeared. No such luck.

'Please let this daemon move on,' I said inside my head.

Still nothing.

'Jamie, nothing's happening.'

'Be patient and it'll—'

He was interrupted by an ear-splitting crack like a clap of thunder, and a black void appeared behind Hawkman.

Jamie grabbed my arm and pulled me back a step. 'You can see it?' I asked.

'Oh yes.'

Hawkman's eyes jerked from me to Jamie and back again. 'What's happening? What's wrong?' Then he flopped forward, and the daemon's spirit knelt there staring down at his recently vacated body.

Black tendrils of smoke crept out of the void, gradually solidifying as they crept up on the kneeling daemon.

'Oh dear, oh dear, oh dear,' I heard Kerfuffle say. 'I wouldn't want to be in his boots.'

'He's not wearing any,' Shenanigans pointed out.

'I was speaking figuratively,' Kerfuffle explained.

Hawkman finally realised something was going on behind him. He glanced over his shoulder just as the first tendril slithered around his ankle and he leaped to his feet, but he was too late: the oily black tentacle had shot up his leg and was wrapping itself around him. A second grasped hold of his other foot and within moments he was covered by glutinous strands that began to weld together, enveloping him in a shiny second skin. As they reached his throat he began to scream, but no sooner had he opened his beak than the disgusting stuff slid inside his open mouth, cutting off his shrieking. Within seconds he was completely covered, until he was nothing more than an elongated black blob. More tendrils oozed out of the hole and began to drag the struggling daemon towards the gateway. Then he reached the void, and with one final tug from the tendrils, he fell inside and the opening shrank shut with a final phlegmy slap.

'Well, that was . . . different,' Vaybian said.

'His friend might have got off lightly,' Jamie said.

'I don't think so,' I said. 'They've probably ended up in the same place – but I get the impression that if a soul doesn't leave immediately it has to be collected.'

'I think I might just stay where I am,' Kayla said with a grimace.

'You're destined for the better place,' I told her.

'You don't know that.'

'Yes, I do,' I said, and I was sure I was right. Someone who had protected a small child from anyone who might harm her couldn't be considered bad enough to be dragged off to the terrible place where Hawkman was going.

I went to wash the blood off my hands, leaving Jamie tapping away on the iPad. I assumed he was searching for references to Saint Bartholomew. When I came back, he was sitting on the sofa with the others crowded around him, looking over his shoulder at what he was doing.

'So, if you put in a name of someone or something, the information comes instantly to hand?' Vaybian asked.

'Pretty much,' Jamie told him.

'I thought humans didn't practice magic?'

Jamie chuckled. 'Most don't, but this isn't magic, it's what humans call "technology" or "tech".'

'Seems like magic to me,' Kerfuffle grumbled. 'Why pass the runes when you can find someone by tapping their name in to a slab of . . . What's it made of anyway?'

'Plastic and other components, mostly human inventions.'

'Any luck on Saint Bartholomew?' I asked, dropping down beside him. Pyrites, back to being a Jack Russell, hopped up and dropped his head onto my lap. Jamie and Shenanigans looked human again, but Vaybian was still green and neither Kerfuffle nor I had changed either.

'I think so,' Jamie said, looking up. 'I can find only one church of that name, in a place called Sussex – it's south of here.'

'Right then: that's where we head next.'

'Let's hope he wasn't lying,' Kerfuffle said. I looked up at him and he shrugged. 'Just saying.'

Jamie got to his feet. 'Well, it's all we've got at the moment—'
He stopped as his mobile began to ring. 'Kubeck?' His expression
turned to a frown. 'On our way down now.' He pocketed the
phone. 'We have company,' he told us, making for the door.

'What sort of company?' I asked.

'Men wearing brown suits.'

'Sicarii?'

'I suspect so – who on earth wears *brown suits* these days?' Which
was a fair comment.

'Probably best we take the stairs,' Shenanigans suggested, so I
scooped Pyrites up into my arms and hurried after the others to
the white door marked *Fire Exit*.

Jamie peered down the stairwell. 'They're not on their way up.'

'Kubeck is probably distracting them.' Shenanigans started
down the stairs.

'Did he say how many?' Vaybian asked.

'No,' Jamie replied, 'just that they'd pulled up in a vehicle similar to ours.'

'So possibly as many as seven or eight?'

'Possibly.'

There was still no sign of them when we reached the ground
floor. Jamie led the way, followed by Vaybian, Shenanigans and
Kayla, who always wafted ahead when anything exciting was
happening. Kerfuffle and Pyrites stayed with me.

I could see only four Sicarii; they had reverted to daemon form
and were dressed in flowing robes. Three were obviously unconscious and piled in an untidy heap on one side of the entrance lobby,
another, clad in grey, was hanging from Kubeck's meaty fist.

'Is this it?' Jamie asked.

Kubeck gave us a toothy smile. 'Yes. I thought you might want
this one conscious.'

'Put me down, you bag of pus,' the Sicarii hissed.

Kubeck gave him a hearty shake. 'That was very rude.' He was
still smiling.

'If you don't put me down this instant I'll make you sorry—'

Kubeck gave him another shake, and something black and crusty fell out of the Sicarii's hood and drifted to the floor.

'That is so disgusting,' Kayla commented, and I murmured my agreement.

I had seen what was generally hidden beneath a Sicarii's robes, and it was more than gross: the creature's desiccated, ash-grey flesh was encrusted with blackened patches of mould as well as open pus-filled wounds. Even the thought of what else the robes might be concealing made me feel queasy.

'I am not the one who should be concerned about my welfare,' Kubeck said, shaking him again. 'There are several here, myself included, who would be more than happy to snuff out your miserable existence.'

Jamie crossed the lobby to stand beside Kubeck. 'I'm in a hurry,' he said to the Sicarii, 'and have very little patience. Answer my questions the first time I ask and I may well let you keep your life. If not, you won't see another minute.'

'Do with me what you will, but I will not betray my brothers.'

'Then you will die.'

'And I will sit at my master's right hand in the afterlife—'

'You obviously weren't at the temple when the Soulseer opened the gateway to the other side,' Jamie said.

Kerfuffle giggled. 'They certainly didn't see that coming.'

'You cannot intimidate me,' the Sicarii said, but there was a hint of something in his tone that made me think we probably could.

'Shall I open the gateway and see what happens?' I suggested, sauntering over to stand beside Jamie.

'You need souls waiting to pass before you can call upon the other side,' the Sicarii said, but he didn't sound so sure.

I gave him a sunny smile. 'Let's see, shall we?'

'I am not afraid to die – my Lord Astaroth will—'

Jamie burst out laughing. '*Lord Astaroth?* Please don't tell me you've let Amaliel feed you that old rubbish.'

Kerfuffle giggled again, and Shenanigans and Vaybian joined in the laughter. 'The Sicarii are as deluded as Amaliel,' Vaybian said.

'Oh no,' Jamie said, 'Amaliel isn't deluded, he's very clever, and *very* manipulative. He's got the Sicarii eating out of the palm of his hand, believing every single lie he tells them.'

'Why would he lie to us? We are his people.'

'I'm betting not a single one of the Sicarii who were at the temple the day Lucky opened the gateway is alive today,' Jamie said.

'You know none escaped – you and Deathbringer slaughtered them.'

'What?' I said. 'They never did!'

'Amaliel couldn't let his followers find out what really happens to them when they die – if they did, they would probably choose to leave,' Jamie explained. 'So everyone who saw what happened had to be disposed of.'

'Also, there's the small matter of him lying to them about being able to cross over to the other side and return unharmed,' Kayla added, 'which we know is impossible.'

'When we have collected enough souls, we will never die,' the Sicarii said firmly.

'You know what,' Kerfuffle said, 'why don't we just kill him? It's daemons like him who give us all a bad name.' Shenanigans and Kubeck agreed loudly.

'Tell me Amaliel's intentions,' Jamie said.

'Go fuck yourself—'

Jamie grabbed the Sicarii and gave him a really hard shake, and more debris floated to the floor.

'Not too hard,' Kerfuffle warned, 'he might just fall apart.'

'For daemons who reckon they're going to live for ever, they don't strike me as particularly healthy,' Kayla commented.

'Last chance,' Jamie said. 'What are Amaliel's intentions?'

'What do you think?' the creature sneered. 'If it isn't blatantly obvious you must have shit for brains.'

With that, Vaybian stalked across to Jamie, pulled a knife from the side of his boot and stabbed it straight into the Sicarii's throat.

'What th—?' Jamie stared at Vaybian as gouts of blood the colour and consistency of tar oozed down the front of the Sicarii's robe.

Vaybian calmly wiped the blade on the Sicarii's robe. 'He wasn't going to tell us anything, and we have enough problems to be dealing with. Besides, we know where we're headed.'

Jamie lowered the Sicarii to the floor. 'We could have made him talk.'

'And say what? We know what Amaliel wants, we know how he's going to get it. We even know where they're hiding out.'

'I could have made him confirm it.'

'And in the meantime we could lose the Deathbringer and any hope for this world and possibly ours. We have no time for this.'

'Since when have you cared one way or another?' Kerfuffle said.

'If you recall, little man, the Sicarii abducted my princess, and slaughtered my friends, then Amaliel tortured and murdered Kayla: I would see every one of their heads bleeding on spikes for eternity if I had my way.'

'So it's about revenge?'

'No, it's about making sure my world isn't ruled by monsters. The Guardian and Deathbringer are the best daemons for making sure it doesn't happen.'

'Unless Jinx turns rogue,' Jamie said, his voice almost a whisper.

'Let us hope for all our sakes that we get to him in time,' Vaybian said, and began moving towards the door.

'What do you want to do with them?' Kubeck asked, gesturing at the heap of comatose brown-robed minions.

'I suppose dowsing them in oil and putting a flame to them would be out of the question?' Kerfuffle muttered.

'As satisfying as that might be,' Jamie said, 'I think it best to leave them here. Then when they wake they can . . .' Jamie smiled. '*We* can follow them.'

'But we know where Amaliel is,' I argued.

'We *think* we know. If they lead us to this church, we will know for certain.'

'They may not be going back to the church,' Shenanigans said. 'They may have some other part to play.'

'In which case, wouldn't it be a good idea if we knew what it was?'

'How about if we split up,' Kerfuffle said. 'Two of us wait here and follow the Sicarii while the rest go to the church?'

'They came by an automotive vehicle,' Shenanigans pointed out, 'and only Mistress Lucky and the Guardian can drive.'

'It can't be that difficult,' Vaybian said.

'Hah!' I murmured.

'Besides we have only one vehicle,' Kerfuffle added.

'I can wait and go with them; they can't see me so I can hitch a ride,' Kayla said. 'I know where you're heading, so if they go somewhere else, I can find you and tell you.'

'You'll be able to find us?' I was scared that I might lose her.

'My darling, I will always be able to find you. You're like a beacon, not only to me but to all the dead. You'll find that out if you stay in one place for any length of time.'

'But I didn't see one spirit at the cottage, and I was there all the time—'

'Because I warded it. That's why you were never bothered by spooks wherever we lived . . . I warded the buildings. I couldn't do anything about the school; the twins were already there.'

'Lucky,' Jamie made a 'time's rolling on' gesture, 'we have to make a decision and then get moving. The clock's ticking for Jinx.'

I told them Kayla's suggestion, and Jamie grinned. 'That's a brilliant idea,' he said.

'I'm not just a pretty face, you know,' Kayla replied.

'My princess will be able to find us again?' Vaybian sounded concerned.

'She tells me yes.'

'Good. Although I can never see her, knowing she's close at hand is a comfort to me.'

Seven

Kubeck and Shenanigans dragged the dead Sicarii leader into the stairwell, leaving a swathe of black slime coating the shiny lobby tiles. We had to hope nobody decided to take a look before Jamie's Guardians came to clear the body away – they'd get the surprise of their lives if they did. When we left, Kayla was sitting on the heap of brown-robed minions.

'So when a daemon dies in the human world, the Guardians know?' I asked Jamie.

'We can hardly have humans finding dead daemons lying about the place – imagine the fuss they'd make!'

It didn't bear thinking about, so I changed the subject. 'Why's Sicarii blood black?' Jamie's brow creased. After a moment he said, 'I think it's because they're rotten – their evil is putrefying them even as they live.'

'Yuck!'

Those of us who hadn't already, changed back to human form before heading back to the car – we didn't need anyone seeing us like that – while Jamie set up the satnav. The others watched with interest and scepticism in equal measures.

'Do they not have maps in this world?' Vaybian asked.

'Yes, but we don't have a map of Sussex, whereas we do have this gadget,' Jamie pointed out.

'You love all this technology, don't you?' I said.

Jamie glanced up from the keyboard. 'It's funny, I never miss it when I'm at home, but here I use it every chance I get.' He grinned at me. 'And yes, I enjoy it.'

'Probably just as well, as I bet Amaliel's got access to all manner of hi-tech gadgetry.'

'Expensive tech,' Jamie added. 'No doubt the humans he's involved with will be rich and powerful.'

'So why would they risk everything to make a deal with what is, to all intents and purposes, the Devil?'

'The more wealthy and powerful some people are, the more they want; that's what makes the Overlands such a fascinating place to some daemonkind.'

'Too busy and too densely populated,' Kerfuffle grumbled. 'I'd rather be home.'

'If we find the Deathbringer today, we could be home before supper,' Jamie said.

'Or dead.'

Jamie glanced back over his shoulder at the scowling daemon. 'It's being so happy that keeps you going.'

Kerfuffle's expression softened. 'That's what the Deathbringer always used to say,' he said, and we all fell silent.

As we drove through the grey streets of greater London, the sun at last showed its face, making the city look like a whole different place. I could see Kerfuffle's point: in some places the streets were so crowded you couldn't see the shop windows through the sea of bodies – Heaven knows what he'd think of New York or Beijing or New Delhi!

The busy streets and tall buildings gave way to leafier suburban areas, and within an hour or so I saw the first sign for Brighton: we would soon be entering Sussex.

We left the A22 and long stretches of woodland gave way to small villages with quaint tearooms, old-fashioned butchers and picturesque pubs. On any other occasion I'd have been begging Jamie to stop so we could go antiquing, or try the local beer, but today, it all passed me by in a blur. I hadn't been able to feel Jinx for a long time, and I was scared of what this might mean.

'Ten more minutes and we should be there,' Jamie said at last, and those ten minutes felt like the longest of my life. The road went on and on for ever through a corridor of gnarled trees whose branches had intertwined above us, blocking out the sun. It might have been my overwrought imagination, but the place felt dark and evil.

Jamie slowed to a crawl.

'What are you doing?' I asked.

'I'm wondering whether we should park up and walk into the village.'

'We're probably going to need a quick getaway,' Shenanigans said.

'And we don't know what sort of state the Deathbringer's going to be in,' Kerfuffle added. 'We don't want to have to run for it while carrying him.'

'Of course, it may be that he'll fight us and we have to take him by force,' Vaybian added unhelpfully.

'Don't say that,' I whispered. 'Please, don't say that.' I didn't want to think about it, but if he'd lost free will, he wouldn't be able to stop himself.

'Mistress, you must be prepared for the worst,' Kerfuffle said, his voice unusually soft and gentle, 'then anything better than that won't be a disappointment. If we can get him back to the Underlands, we will at least have a chance of repairing the damage.'

'Kerfuffle's right,' Jamie told me. 'We get Jinx back home, then we can worry about getting him better.'

I looked down at my clenched fists – my human clenched fists – resting on Pyrites' back, and took a deep breath. 'I am going to kill Amaliel.' I looked up at Jamie. 'You do know that, don't you?'

'You look after Jinx. Leave the killing to us.'

'We'll see.'

He patted my leg, then announced, 'Right, here we go then!' and put his foot down.

The road ahead narrowed. It was flanked on either side by huge wooden gates standing open, as though at night they barred entry to the village. Two wooden posts supported a sign welcoming us to Chalfont Saint Bartholomew's and urging us to drive safely. Jamie slowed down as we passed through the gates and into a hedge-lined lane that curled up a slight gradient before straightening out into a street lined with centuries-old cottages made of white plaster and black beams. There was a bow-fronted village shop, the leaded windows filled with old-fashioned jars of sweets and racks of pipes and tins of tobacco. The glass panes were streaked and dusty, and despite the time of day the shop was in darkness.

'It's like we've stepped back two hundred years,' I murmured, half to myself.

The street was too narrow for parking and was devoid of cars, which added to the effect. I suspected Kerfuffle felt right at home.

We didn't see a single person: no flicker of curtains, nor face at a window of any of the small cottages we drove slowly by.

'It's like a ghost town.' Jamie's voice was hushed.

There were a few more houses set back from the road, then a huge dirty white building with a forecourt for parking – and still not one car. Black patches of mould clung to the grey walls, reminiscent of Sicarii skin; had I not known this village was our destination, I knew I would have felt it in my bones. I could sense the death all around us. With a shiver, I changed.

'Lucky?' Jamie whispered.

'There's no one living in this place.' The voice wasn't mine – or maybe it was, maybe it was the Soulseer's.

'What do you think's happened to them?' Kubeck asked.

'Amaliel's happened to them,' Jamie said with a bitter twist of the lips.

We didn't see a single living creature, not a cat or dog, not even a bird to be seen on the rooftops, or in the sky overhead.

Vaybian leaned forward between the two front seats to look up ahead. 'This is unnatural,' he said. 'There is a wrongness about this place.'

'Aye, there is,' Kubeck said to murmurs of agreement from Kerfuffle and Shenanigans in the back.

'Look – up ahead on the right,' I said, pointing.

'Saint Bartholomew's,' Jamie said, and slowed the car to a crawl.

We gazed over the grey stone walls surrounding the churchyard and cemetery. 'It can't be unconsecrated, surely,' I said. 'Not if there's still a graveyard.'

'Consecrated, unconsecrated . . . it matters not to daemonkind. I told you before: just because man calls a place a temple, it doesn't make it sacred in our eyes,' Jamie said.

'But what about a Satanist's?'

He gave a humourless laugh. 'It would probably add some piquancy for men who worship the Fallen One.'

I looked at Jamie. 'The Fallen One? I thought you said there was no such thing as God or the Devil.'

'I keep telling you: gods, devils, daemons, angels – these are all names humans give to creatures they don't understand.'

'But "the Fallen One"?' I said in exasperation. 'That sounds like you believe in such a being yourself.'

'This I've got to hear,' Vaybian muttered.

'I suggest you shut up. I have in no way, shape or form forgiven you for your actions earlier.'

Vaybian gave a snort of humourless laughter. 'Just because you don't like me saying something doesn't mean it doesn't need to be said.' He moved a little in his seat so he could look me in the face. 'The Fallen One was once a Guardian.'

'*The* Guardian,' Kerfuffle corrected.

'Just as the Deathbringer may turn now, this Guardian went rogue,' Vaybian went on.

'It is he who humankind call the Devil,' Shenanigans finished.

'A fallen angel,' I whispered to myself. In some crazy way it all began to make sense.

'As much as I would like to sit here and discuss human theology, there are more pressing matters to attend to, like finding Jinx,' Jamie said, and he swerved the car and mounted the kerb with a bump.

'Double yellow lines,' I said.

'You see a traffic warden?'

I very sensibly kept quiet. Jamie was not at all happy, but then neither was I. I was pretty sure there was no one living left in the village, which meant either Amaliel and Jinx had already gone, or—

But that was something I couldn't possibly think about.

We all clambered out and as soon as Pyrites' paws touched the ground, he started to grow, his white and tan fur darkening to black and gold until he was a rather large Rottweiler – and in a moment of sheer psychobabble it crossed my mind that I really should get him a collar and lead; preferably a flexible collar . . .

He pushed his furry head up under my hand and gave a low rumble in his chest. My drakon wasn't very happy either.

We gathered outside the gateway to the church. One of the double gates was hanging ajar on rusted hinges beneath a greying wooden lych gate that had seen better days. Tiles were missing from the ridged roof, their shattered remains scattered at our feet.

Jamie pulled the gate open; the bottom bar scraped the concrete, the rasping sound grating in the silence. He gestured for me to go first then followed, the others close behind us. We were all uneasy; it was too deathly quiet for us to be anything but.

We stopped halfway along the paved path to look up at the imposing, once-beautiful church, incongruously large for the size of the village that surrounded it. Someone very wealthy and pious must have lived here all those centuries ago.

'Come on,' Jamie said, 'let's get this over with.'

'We're unarmed,' Vaybian said.

'There's no one here but the dead,' I told him, and even they were conspicuous by their absence: not a single spirit loitered in the graveyard and I had seen none in the streets as we'd driven through. If Amaliel had used the church for his unholy rites, he hadn't seen fit to curse the dying to bind their souls to this place – but then, he probably had other things on his mind. Like breaking Jinx.

Jamie led the way, waiting at the door until we had all crowded into the vestibule.

'Ready?'

I crossed my arms and hugged myself; I had a very bad feeling about this.

Jamie leaned forward, turned the ringed door handle and pushed. The door swung open without a sound. It was cold inside, our breath clouding the air, and our footsteps echoed as we walked into the church.

'Shit,' Jamie muttered.

Amaliel and his freaks had been here, and as in the Sicarii temple at Dark Rock, he had left us his calling card. I walked down the central aisle between the rows of wooden pews with Pyrites by my side, Jamie at my left shoulder and my guards close behind us. I reached back to find Jamie's hand and his fingers curled around mine and squeezed.

Now we knew what had happened to the local residents. They had been dead for a while – I didn't know exactly what had been done to them, but now they looked like they'd been mummified: dirty-brown desiccated skin stretched taut over their skulls, pulling their lips back to show teeth as if they were laughing at some hideous joke.

Their bodies sat upright in the pews, young and old alike, hymn books on laps and in some cases even pressed between fingers, sightless eyes staring straight ahead.

I couldn't take it in. I knew I should feel something, but I was numb to it, like my heart had been frozen.

The village priest was positioned at the lectern, as though taking the service, peering down at an open Bible. I wondered how they'd managed to keep him standing, but then decided I'd rather not know.

The altar was covered with a black silky material, embroidered with a silver pentacle within which there was the head of a goat – the Goat of Mendes. Anyone who'd ever read a Dennis Wheatley novel knew what that was. Silver candlesticks holding the obligatory black candles flanked a silver chalice. It was all such a cliché – clichéd and sick.

As well as the ridiculous Satanic paraphernalia, *the scene* was dominated by a black inverted cross: because that was what it was – a set piece. Amaliel's set piece.

I guessed the young woman was probably about my age, although it was hard to tell. She had been dead for a day or so; her skin had paled to the colour of marble and her lips had taken on a lilac hue, but she hadn't yet begun to visibly decompose. Her rich chestnut hair hung from her head in a glossy curtain, the only colour in that dreadful tableau except for the blood. There was plenty of that.

Gore-encrusted spikes protruded from her ankles; they had pounded them into her, smashing through bone; her wrists were a similar bloody mess.

'Not a good way to die,' Vaybian said.

'Poor, poor girl,' I said, glancing at Jamie. His expression was strange.

'Is it just me' – Jamie asked – 'or does she remind you of someone?'

Shenanigans and Kerfuffle both gave grim nods.

'Aye, she does,' Kubeck said.

'She looks like you, mistress,' Kerfuffle said.

Jamie squeezed my hand. 'If you weren't here with me now, I would have thought it was you.'

I squinted at the girl's face. I couldn't see it myself. 'Is it some sort of message to me personally, do you think? Like, "interfere in my business and you'll die horribly"?'

'Could be – or it could have been for Jinx's benefit.'

'Jinx already thinks I'm dead,' I said, and my voice cracked. I took a deep breath and breathed out again slowly. Breaking down now would help no one, least of all Jinx. As for this poor girl – well, she was past anything we could do for her.

'Lucky—' When I turned my head Kayla was gliding down the aisle towards us, clearly agitated. 'The three Sicarii from the apartment will be here in about five minutes and they have reinforcements.'

'How could they have got here so quickly?' I asked. 'They were out stone cold when we left.'

'Another two cars turned up a minute or so after you left. They scraped our friends off the floor and came straight here – they're expecting to find you here. I would have come sooner, but I wanted to hear their plans.'

'Which are?'

'Capture you and Jamie, if they can, and kill the rest – but if it comes to it, Jamie's as expendable as the others; it's you they want.'

'Two carloads of Sicarii are on their way,' I told my guard, 'and they have no intention of taking us all alive – only me.' I glanced up at the dead girl. 'And I'd rather they didn't.'

'Fight or flee?' Vaybian asked.

'As you've pointed out several times, we have no weapons,' Jamie said.

'Do they?' I asked Kayla.

'They have at least three humans with them and they have guns.'

'They have guns,' I said out loud.

'Guns can't kill us unless they get a point-blank head-shot,' Jamie said.

'Though it'll probably hurt like you wouldn't believe,' Kerfuffle grumbled.

The slamming of car doors out on the street told us we'd run out of time.

'Is there another way out?' Kubeck asked, and we all started past the altar towards a door to the left.

Kerfuffle got there first and started rattling the ringed door handle. He gave it a hefty tug. 'It's locked.' He pulled again, and I heard something give.

'Leave it,' Jamie said, turning back the way we'd come. 'There's no time.'

The sound of running feet echoed through the entrance and several brown- and grey-robed figures appeared at the far end of the church, followed by some men in suits: humans.

Jamie and my guards stepped forward to put themselves between the Sicarii and me. The air shimmered, and they all reverted to daemons. Pyrites gave a roar and in an instant was all drakon and the size of an elephant. The Sicarii came to an abrupt halt and Jamie began to laugh.

'We don't need weapons: we have real fire power!'

And with that Pyrites let out a blast of flame that set two rows of pews alight.

The Sicarii stood their ground, but the men in suits didn't look so sure; two of them pulled out guns, but Pyrites gave another blast, setting fire to more pews, and they started backing away.

A grey-robed figure glided to the front. 'Give us the woman and we will let you leave unharmed.'

'Leave now and you won't end up as drakon chow,' Jamie said.

'Roasted drakon chow,' Kerfuffle added.

'Bringing a drakon into the world of humans is breaking the law,' the Sicarii hissed.

'And capturing and torturing the Deathbringer for personal gain isn't?'

'Match-point,' Kayla said with a smirk.

'We will have the woman.'

Pyrites let out a low, deep growl that rumbled in his chest and made the ground beneath our feet vibrate.

'Willing to try and take her?' Jamie said, laying a hand on Pyrites' flank.

My drakon puffed black smoke. He, Vaybian and I had been attacked by the Sicarii once before: they had shot him with arrows covered in Drakon Bane, rendering him unconscious and allowing them to abduct me and Vaybian. Judging by the black smoke and rumbling, he wasn't about to forgive and forget; I was betting his growling would translate as, 'Come on, make my day.'

'We will have her: maybe not this time, but she will be ours,' the Sicarii said, and with a jerk of his head indicated to the others that they should leave.

They began to back away, not wanting to take their eyes off my drakon, who sat down on his haunches, threw back his head and let out a roar that shook the building. The men in suits lost their nerve and made a run for it.

'Don't for one minute think this is over,' the Sicarii in grey said, as he too backed down the aisle.

Pyrites dropped down onto his front claws and gave another long low rumble; the end of his tail was twitching back and forth. He took a step forward. Suddenly the Sicarii started to hurry, but he stumbled – and even I was taken by surprise when Pyrites suddenly let loose a prolonged stream of flame which engulfed the retreating figure, turning him into a heap of hissing and popping fat within a moment. The rest of the brown-robed minions ran for their lives.

'Game, set and match, methinks,' Kayla quipped with a smile.

I didn't quite know what to say. Pyrites was usually so calm and gentle that his actions had shocked me somewhat – although he was only doing his job, protecting me.

'Good lad,' Kerfuffle told him, slapping him on the front leg.

Pyrites gave a snort and with a shimmer was once again a small, hairy Jack Russell. I crouched down and scooped him up. As soon as he was in my arms he was all wagging tail and licky tongue.

'Yes,' I told him, 'you are a *good* boy.'

Eight

By the time we got outside, the other vehicles had gone. Kayla had disappeared with the Sicarii and their human friends, and we could only hope they would take her to wherever Amaliel was keeping Jinx. She was our best chance; if we gave chase they'd probably stay well away from Amaliel's latest hideout. I had hoped we would find some clue at the church, but there was nothing and I was rapidly becoming more agitated. That I'd changed back to my human form without even trying was telling.

'Even if they don't take Kayla to Amaliel, she may learn something from them that'll help,' Jamie said, but I could tell the lack of progress was getting to him, too.

'Maybe if the drakon had only roasted the Sicarii a bit we could have questioned him,' Vaybian said.

Kerfuffle was shaking his head. 'He wouldn't have told us anything we wanted to hear. He would have been like the other one. Anyway, it does them good to know we're not frightened to end their miserable lives.'

'We don't even know what direction they went in,' I said.

Jamie glanced at me as he buckled up his seatbelt. 'I didn't hear them turn around, so straight ahead, I suspect.' He reached over and put his hand on mine. 'We will find him, Lucky.'

'It's taking too long.'

'Check online for natural disasters – if there haven't been any, I'm betting it's because Jinx isn't as bound as Amaliel would like him to be.'

'I guess,' I said with a sigh.

I checked the internet and Twitter, but there was no breaking news – at least, not the sort that could be anything to do with Jinx. A US senator had been caught with his trousers down and a minister had resigned from the cabinet over similar allegations, but no plagues, hurricanes or tsunamis had occurred, and I thanked the Lord for that at least. Then something occurred to me.

'Why do you think Amaliel's pet daemons were at Philip's apartment?'

Jamie took his eyes off the road ahead and glanced at me. 'And the Sicarii, too.'

'Do you think they came to search for something?' Vaybian asked.

'I'm hungry,' Shenanigans piped up. 'Is anyone else hungry?'

'How can you eat at a time like this?' I snapped.

'Sorry, mistress.'

I screwed my eyes shut for a second. *Damn.* 'No, it's me who should be sorry. Of course we should eat. I'm just . . .' I trailed off, too miserable to put what I was feeling into words.

'We understand, mistress,' Shenanigans said, to a chorus of agreement – although I noticed that Vaybian kept quiet.

As Jamie drove my mind kept returning to Jinx, where he might be and what Amaliel might be doing to him. I tried to push him out of my head and think of other things – like, why had Pigface and Hawkman been at Philip's flat? It was clear they hadn't been expecting to find us there; even from the bedroom I'd heard one of them cursing in surprise when my guards showed themselves. I'd heard it from *the bedroom* . . . where I had just made a discovery, something I'd completely forgotten about in all the drama.

As I reached for my jacket, Jamie asked, 'Are you cold? I can turn up the heating—'

'No, I found something back at Philip's apartment – I'd completely forgotten until now.' I pulled the slim leather-bound book out of my inside pocket.

'What is it?' Jamie asked, and Pyrites sat up on my lap as Vaybian and Kubeck moved forward in their seats to peer over my shoulder.

'It could just be a diary,' I said, hoping against all hope that it might be something more. I flicked open the cover.

It wasn't a diary but a faint-lined notebook, and each page was headed with a date in what I assumed was Philip's neat handwriting in navy ink – not ballpoint or rollerball, but proper fountain pen ink.

It started eighteen months ago, and Philip was so excited he'd started the journal the very next day.

OMG what a night! And to think I very nearly stayed at home.

He wrote about what started off as a very boring party – until he met a slim young man who called himself Joseph; the way he wrote was almost word for word how he had told me the story: an exchange shared between two men idly waiting for their coats, which rapidly became something else entirely. That Joseph was charismatic fairly leaped off the page; the Philip I'd met wasn't the type to get star-struck, but that's the way he came across.

They exchanged business cards before parting, and Joseph promised Philip he would be in touch. *I think we can do business together,* he had said. Gabriel Derne was mentioned – an afterthought at the end of the first two pages: *a weaselly, little man who was totally outclassed by someone like Joseph Babel.* Philip had taken his card, but in his journal it was clear he wouldn't be calling him anytime soon.

Joseph had waited three days before he'd phoned; they'd met for lunch and reading the journal, I could see how Joseph had reeled him in, oh so slowly, teasing him with talk about important contacts and big players and billion-dollar deals like most people talked about a normal day at the office. They had lunch again a few days later, then dinner a day or so after that.

Joseph left Philip to stew for almost a week before inviting him to a cocktail party; Philip probably hadn't realised it then, but this was the turning point. He was introduced to a woman called Persephone Kore – and just as he'd banged on and on about Joseph, now he started raving about another new friend: she was beautiful, she was classy, she was funny, interesting, blah de blah de blah.

Almost as an afterthought, Philip mentioned Gabriel Derne again, and this bit made me sit up: he too had been a guest at this party, and he appeared to be a close friend of Ms Kore. So maybe this Gabriel wasn't quite so far down the food chain as we'd thought. Surprisingly enough, there was no mention of a bokor – maybe he was another of Philip's lies?

'Anything interesting?' Jamie asked.

I shut the journal and leaned back in my seat; I was feeling decidedly queasy.

'Are you all right? You look rather pale.'

'I get carsick if I read for too long,' I mumbled, winding the window down.

'Perhaps we should stop and get something to eat,' Jamie suggested.

'Urgh . . .' I didn't want to think about food or drink, or anything else, for that matter, but Jamie pulled up outside a pub in a village not too far from the coast.

The pub was an old inn complete with smoke-darkened oak beams and an inglenook fireplace. The ceiling was low enough that even in their human guise, Shenanigans and Kubeck had to bow their heads; Jamie's curls skimmed the beams by a whisper. The only other customers were two old boys sitting at a corner table playing draughts, and two burly guys propping up the copper-covered bar and making small talk with the barmaid, a tall, curvy blonde with a slight West Country burr to her accent.

'And what can I do for you, my lovelies?' I heard her say to Jamie and Vaybian as the rest of us took up position around a long table by the window.

Jamie obviously said something she found amusing as she started to laugh, and Jamie and Vaybian joined in. She may have been enjoying their company, but her other companions were giving Jamie and Vaybian very dark looks indeed. I wasn't surprised; my angel and Kayla's daemon were very handsome in human form – which made me wonder what Jinx would look like without his horns and tail and distinctive maroon skin. Maybe he'd be like Vaybian, have a Native American appearance. I looked away; thinking about Jinx wasn't improving my appetite.

'Go and sit down. I'll come over and take your drinks order while you decide what you want to eat,' the barmaid told Vaybian.

Jamie sank down on the bench next to me and handed out the menus. 'I think you could probably do with a brandy,' he said, and I guessed I must be looking a little green about the gills, although I was beginning to feel a bit better.

'A sparkling water will be fine,' I told him, so he proceeded to order me a dry white wine, which was irritating beyond words. Even if he sometimes knew what I wanted better than I did myself, I didn't need him making my decisions for me.

Kerfuffle convinced the rest of my guards that they would probably like a pint of cider or one of the various beers they had on offer, and happily ordered for them all.

'So, what have you discovered in Philip's journal?' Jamie asked as soon as the barmaid disappeared to get our drinks.

'I'm beginning to think our perception of Joseph's and Gabriel's roles in all of this may be slightly off-kilter. There's a woman involved.'

'Isn't there always,' Vaybian muttered.

I ignored him. 'Joseph strung Philip along, whetted his appetite with tales of mega-deals and "players", then invited him to a party where he was introduced to a woman called Persephone Kore.'

'Whoa,' Jamie said.

'Persephone Kore?' Kerfuffle wrinkled his nose, as though there was a rather nasty smell in the air. 'Oh, please.'

'Humans aren't always the most inventive of creatures,' Shenanigans said.

'Explain?' I said.

'In human mythology—' Jamie started.

'Greek,' Kerfuffle interrupted.

'Yes, Greek,' Jamie agreed. 'Persephone was the Queen of the Underworld; she was also known as Kore.'

'So it's an alias,' I said.

Jamie nodded. 'I would guess that she's Amaliel's human

contact here: some sort of witch or Satanist, probably, or maybe even the bokor, although I thought they were usually male.'

'How would she have hooked up with Amaliel and his schemes?'

'She and her Satanist buddies probably tried to call up a daemon and Amaliel slipped into this world at their invitation.'

'Wonderful,' I said.

'Here you go, my lovelies,' the barmaid said as she handed out the drinks. 'Ready to order?'

The others went for full-blown meals, but I stuck to a chicken Caesar salad – at least I could surreptitiously feed Pyrites the meat. As soon as she walked off again, we got straight back to business.

'Do you think this Persephone's the one we should be looking for?' I asked, then tapped my finger on Philip's journal. 'Maybe I should get on with reading this; it might give us a few more clues.'

'I think that's a good idea,' Jamie said.

'I bet the human fucked her,' Vaybian said.

'You think?' I asked. From what I'd read so far, Persephone hadn't seemed the type to stoop to Philip's level.

Vaybian gave me one of his 'you cannot be serious' looks and I wondered whether Kayla had used me as her excuse for staying away from him for twenty-five years. He certainly irritated the hell out of me.

I pulled the book out and flicked through the pages to where I'd left off. 'Philip was enamoured with her at their first meeting, that's for sure. He goes on and on about her for almost a page and a half.'

I started to read again, leaving the boys chatting amongst themselves. After the party Persephone had invited Philip to join her at her country estate the following weekend. *Country estate?* Now that was interesting. To Philip's surprise, she'd suggested he bring his wife and daughter, and when he'd asked how she knew he was married, she'd replied that she made it her business to know everything she could about men who interested her and that encouraged Philip to go off on another several-paragraph rave about how fantastic this woman was, and laughably, how the feeling was possibly mutual: she had apparently held his hand longer than necessary when they parted and given him a lingering, *meaningful* look.

'Oh, *puh-lease*,' I muttered to myself.

Turned out, when he mentioned the weekend to his wife, to his disappointment she had agreed to go – it was obvious that if he could have put her off, he would have. Then at the last moment, Angela came down with a stomach virus and Philip got his wish.

Typical Philip: their daughter gets sick and he goes off on a jolly for the weekend.

The next few paragraphs were pretty repellent, not much better than a teenage boy's fantasies, then he got back to what *actually* happened. He drove himself down to Persephone's country residence in Sussex – *now we're getting somewhere, but where in Sussex, Philip? Tell me something useful, why don't you?* She wasn't there to greet him when he arrived Friday evening, but he was placated by the news that it was because she was detained with a very important foreign client she was assisting on a specialist project. I knew exactly who the foreign client was; I guessed I was probably the project.

I read on, frustrated by all his wittering on about the wretched woman, and how huge the estate was, and how the house must have twenty or more bedrooms, and OMG there's an indoor and outdoor pool, and a jacuzzi that could take a whole rugby team . . .

The food arrived and with some relief, I closed the journal and pushed it to one side. I was finding it a depressing read. I had refused to listen to Jamie when he'd warned me about Philip; I had insisted that his betrayal of me was all about trying to save his daughter, that although what he had done was wrong, he had done it for the best of reasons. When Amaliel slaughtered him, I'd begun to realise the truth, but even then a part of me wanted to believe that it was only because of his time in the Underlands that he had behaved so badly. The journal told me how wrong I was: the man had always been an egotistical prick who thought only of himself. He barely mentioned his wife and daughter, and when he did, it was usually to complain about them; he showed no ounce of concern for Angela; in fact, he was *pleased* that her illness meant he got what he'd wanted all along.

I picked at my food, slipping most of the chicken to Pyrites – he usually preferred his meat hot, of course, but he didn't complain. If we had to stay in the Overlands for any length of time, I'd have to work out how to feed him – we really couldn't have a fire-breathing drakon hunting above the English countryside. That would definitely scare the natives.

I pushed my lunch aside, took a slurp of wine and opened up the journal again.

Philip's previous disappointment was more than compensated for when he found that he was one of a very select group of Persephone's friends invited to what turned out to be an intimate dinner that Friday evening; the rest of her houseguests wouldn't be arriving until the following day. Joseph and Gabriel were present, together with two young women he instantly dismissed as nothing more than eye-candy for the two men. *Bloody man!*

When Philip had asked whether her 'business associate' would be joining them, Persephone apparently laughed 'like chiming bells' – *yuk!* – and said he'd be meeting her client soon enough. Philip ruminated on this for several lines, thinking it strange that such an important client wouldn't be joining them for what was obviously a private dinner, but he was soon back onto his favourite subject: himself. He was absolutely convinced Persephone was lusting after his body.

'Dickhead,' I muttered.

Jamie glanced my way. 'Pardon?'

'Philip,' I told him, 'a complete dickhead.'

'I won't say I told you so.'

'Huh.' I went back to the journal, hoping for some clue of where in Sussex this country estate was.

By the time the boys had finished eating and Jamie had paid our bill with my credit card – that was still working, at least – I'd made it through Philip's first evening at the estate and the morning of the following day. For the first time I sensed disquiet in Philip's writing.

He was surprised by some of the other guests, not at all the type of person he was expecting Persephone to be associating with. There were a couple of older ladies he charmingly described: 'They looked like two of the three witches from Macbeth: one was at least a hundred and ten, totally blind, and with very few teeth. The other was stick-thin and walked ramrod-straight – she had to be going on ninety. They spent the whole morning cackling and braying – I'm surprised they had the strength to be so raucous.'

Another strange couple, a man and a woman so covered with tattoos that he couldn't see an inch of naked skin between the two of them. They had so many piercings he wondered how they'd get through a metal detector.

And there was a tall, gaunt man with a ritually scarred face who could have been an African tribesman. *Is he the bokor?* I wondered.

'Still nothing?' Jamie asked as we walked to the car.

'Only that this Persephone character has some sort of huge country pile in Sussex and has the strangest of friends.'

'Philip still enamoured?'

'He was up until dinner Saturday evening. I finished where he was just about to get showered and dressed.'

'He was writing it all down in real time?'

'Sometimes the morning after, but the weekend I'm reading now, he's had a quick scribble here and there.'

'For someone who only just started to keep a journal he seems a bit obsessive.'

'He's certainly obsessive about himself.'

Jamie opened the door and I clambered inside. 'Where to now?' I asked as Pyrites hopped up onto my lap.

'Until Kayla returns with some news, all we've got is the journal, so maybe we should just sit here while you read on.'

'Jamie, we don't have the time to sit around! We've used up almost twenty-four of our forty-eight hours—'

'But there haven't been any plagues or pestilence, so we still *have* time, which is better than the alternative.'

'I guess.' I opened the journal and started skimming every

page, desperately hoping something would catch my eye – and
something did: just a few pages after I'd stopped reading, Philip's
neat navy recollections came to an abrupt end.

I peered down at his last few words, a feeling of foreboding
stealing over me. His last entry read, OMG, *what have I done?*
What the fuck have I done?

I went back and read the pages that led up to Philip's exclama-
tion, but they told me nothing at all: he'd gone down to dinner,
chatted with a few of the guests at pre-dinner drinks, was most
gratified to find he'd been seated next to Persephone, and spent
most of the evening chatting to her.

At ten-thirty Persephone had announced 'an entertainment'.
Philip wrote, 'We've all been told to retire to our rooms to freshen
up and be back downstairs by eleven-fifteen.' He was in a frenzy
of anticipation. I guessed it was after the aforesaid 'entertainment'
that Philip had returned to write his last ever entry. I had a sneaky
suspicion Amaliel had something to do with it.

Jamie and my guards were all of the same opinion: Philip had
belatedly realised he'd sold his soul. So now our only chance was
if Kayla had found out anything useful.

'Why isn't she back yet?' I muttered.

'Lucky,' Jamie said, 'Kayla's dead – what else can possibly happen to her?'

'I can't help it. If Jinx—' I gasped, and felt like I'd been struck
blind for a moment, as all I could see was black . . .

Then I was kneeling in front of a figure wearing a long black
hooded robe and a honeyed feminine voice was saying, 'Why not
give in? The pain will stop. Give in, and you can begin to live
again. Give in, and I'll free you from all torment.'

Jinx groaned, and when I looked down I saw maroon arms
wrapped around his upper body; maroon thighs and knees. I was
surrounded by blue light – someone had mentioned blue light
earlier.

'Deathbringer, let me bring you peace,' the woman said, and

she let the robe slip down her body to pool around her feet on the grey stone floor.

I could see her long tanned legs, but Jinx wouldn't look up; in fact, he hunched down further, his long hair loose and forming a veil between him and her.

'Look at me,' she said.

His head moved from side to side. 'No,' he gasped. '*No.*'

'Your lover is dead. What harm could there be to take a little solace from me?'

He groaned again, and I joined him.

She scooped up the robe, her own long black hair hiding her face as she bent. 'You may not come to me willingly now, but tomorrow or the next day you will, and then I will have you crawl across broken glass before I let you have a taste of me.'

Jinx shivered, and I heard Kayla calling, 'Lucky, Lucky! Wake up! I know where Amaliel is – I know where he's keeping Jinx.'

Nine

My eyes snapped open and I was back in the car and Kayla was repeating, 'Lucky, I know where Jinx is.' She was peering at me between the driver and passenger seats.

'He's with that dreadful woman,' I said.

'What?' both Jamie and Kayla said.

'Kayla's back,' I told Jamie.

'By "that dreadful woman", I assume you mean Persephone?' Jamie said.

'How do you know about her?' Kayla asked.

'Philip's journal; I found it at his flat.'

'What are you talking about?' Jamie asked.

'I was talking to Kayla,' I said, a little more sharply than I'd intended. 'I just had another vision.'

'Of Jinx?'

'He's in a bad way, and he's surrounded by blue light. Someone mentioned it before.'

'Blue Fire,' Jamie said. He looked away and ran his hand through his hair, which was enough to tell me it was bad news. 'This Persephone must be the real deal if she's bound Jinx to this world with a binding spell. Blue Fire is as effective as any cage.'

'But you said that *Amaliel* was trying to bind Jinx?'

'A different thing altogether: she has bound Jinx's body by incarcerating him in Blue Fire. Amaliel was trying to bind Jinx's spirit, to take away his free will.'

'Either one alone is bad enough, but both together is not good news.'

'I wondered how they could possibly torture the Deathbringer without risking death itself,' Vaybian said.

I looked at him.

'If he's trapped within the fire, they can reach in with iron and steel to inflict the torture without him being able to touch them.'

'You all knew this – why didn't you tell me?' I said, staring at each of them in turn.

'We didn't want to worry you, Mistress,' Shenanigans said.

'Anyway, Amaliel's daemon could have been lying,' Kerfuffle added. 'I've not heard of a human being able to conjure Blue Fire for' – the little daemon blew through pursed lips – 'oh, a century or more.'

'Crowley,' Jamie supplied, 'just under a century ago, although that might have been rumour.'

'If anyone could've, it probably would've been him,' Kerfuffle agreed.

'Well, if you saw it with your own eyes, I guess it must be true,' Jamie said.

'It is true,' Kayla told me. 'I saw him too, but I don't think he could see me. He was in too much . . .' She looked at my face and stuttered to a stop.

'Too much what?'

She hesitated, but seeing my 'don't shit with me' look, decided it wasn't worth trying to hide anything. 'He was in pain, but you already knew that.'

'So much pain he couldn't see you?'

'I'm not sure, but it could've had something to do with the Blue Fire. It's powerful stuff.'

'Right,' I said, 'so we know Jinx is alive, we know he's hurt-ing and we know he still has some free will. Can you lead us to where he is?'

'Yes,' Kayla said, sounding determined, 'I know exactly where he is.' She hesitated. 'You're not going to like this: I've been there before.'

'Where?'

'This Persephone's place.'

'When could you possibly have been there before?'

Her expression was grim. 'You know I told you I slipped into this world when some group of weirdos tried calling up a dae-mon?' She didn't wait for me to reply. 'Well, they were using the same country pile – I don't think I'll ever forget it. It was my first sight of the Overlands.'

'You're joking?' I said, that sinking feeling telling me she wasn't.

'I wish I was, because there was a familiar face there too.'

'What's happening?' Jamie asked, but I shushed him; I needed Kayla's story first.

'There was a ritually scarred man who could be the bokor Philip told you about . . .'

I let out the deep breath I was holding. 'You sort of gave the impression that after your appearance, their Satanist days were over . . .'

'Obviously I was wrong.'

'Do you think they were trying to call up Amaliel, but got you instead?' I asked at last.

'If they were calling Amaliel they would have had to know his daemon name – but I know they didn't close the doorway between the worlds. They were too afraid after I came through, and those who still could, ran . . . Amaliel may well have slipped through behind me, and that would explain his link to the scar-faced man.'

'He promised the remaining Satanists power.'

'And probably revenge.'

After I explained what Kayla had discovered, there were a lot of very glum faces, and Kerfuffle started muttering, 'Not good, not good at all' until Vaybian told him to shut up; Jamie had to step in to stop fists flying.

There was some argument about what we should do once we reached the place, which was on the borders of Ashdown Forest, remote enough that no one would particularly notice the comings and goings of Satanists and devil worshipers – or daemons, for that matter.

'We can't just go marching straight in and demand that they hand over the Deathbringer,' Kerfuffle said.

'And there's the small matter of Amaliel wanting to capture Mistress Lucky,' Shenanigans pointed out.

'And the Guardian, if at all possible,' Kerfuffle added.

'Well, we as sure as hell can't just do nothing,' I said. 'If Amaliel does manage to take away Jinx's free will we'll all be in trouble.'

'Maybe we should let the Guardians deal with this,' Vaybian suggested.

'No,' I said, crossing my arms. 'That is not an option.'

'It may not be an option you want to consider, but that doesn't mean it isn't one,' Vaybian said.

'Lucky, I know you don't want to hear this, but Vaybian may be right,' Kayla said.

'No.'

'The place is overrun with Sicarii, not to mention this Persephone woman's followers – and then there's Amaliel; he's slipperier than a barrel-full of eels.'

'I cannot just give up on Jinx. He wouldn't give up on me.'

'It's strange that he can't feel you when he could before,' Jamie said. 'I wonder why that is?'

'He thinks I'm dead – maybe he's not allowing himself to feel anything much.'

'I don't understand this connection,' Vaybian said. 'How are you connected to him but not the Guardian?'

I instantly knew where Jamie's mind would be going: he'd think it was because I loved Jinx more than I did him, which was one hundred per cent *not true*. I might be angry with him, but that didn't stop me loving him; that was one of the other reasons I was feeling so shitty.

'Blood,' I told him, then told them what Kayla had told me.

'That explains a lot,' Jamie said, and he did look a little happier for knowing the reason.

'How many men does Amaliel have at his beck and call?' I asked Kayla.

'More than thirty Sicarii: twelve grey and another twenty or so of their disciples. Then there are Persephone's people: she has her own coven of thirteen, including her, then hired help, about ten or so.'

'Hired help?'

'Thugs mainly.'

Jamie was worried; he kept giving me sideways looks as he drove, his forehead creased into a frown. I loved him more than was good for me, and I was pretty sure he loved me too, but he had responsibilities to his world and the Overlands. I understood that, I really did. Unfortunately, it meant when it came to Jinx, his loyalties would be divided. And on top of everything, it looked like we'd totally underestimated Amaliel: we knew he had what was left of his Sicarii followers, but we'd never imagined he'd have a human army of Satanists and thugs ... which could cause Jamie yet another problem. He was meant to *protect* human life, but Persephone and her followers were probably just as dangerous as Amaliel and the Sicarii.

The name Ashdown Forest was a bit of a misnomer: the road was flanked by heath, not forest, and in some places I could see for miles across the bracken and grasses before any trees came into sight. It had a desolate beauty; if Pyrites had really been a dog I could have walked him for hours. Oh, for the ordinary life – then I thought of life without Jamie and Jinx, and I knew I could never do ordinary again.

Kayla directed us down a narrow lane which ended abruptly in a T-junction at a high arched gate surrounded on either side by six-foot-high brick walls. A brass plaque on the wall identified it as Demeter House.

'Not much of an imagination this one,' Kerfuffle said. 'Demeter was Persephone's mother.'

I twisted around. 'Was there – *is* there – such a person?'

'Greek mythology, that's all.'

'How do you know so much about it?'

'I've been going back and forth between the lands for a *very* long time,' was all he said.

I sat back in my seat and immediately spotted the security camera above the gate. I didn't want us drawing attention to ourselves quite yet, so I directed Jamie to turn left and keep driving. The lane followed the wall of the estate for a good few hundred yards before red brick was replaced by a tall, dark green hedge, the boundary to a neighbouring farm and stable block.

'What do we do now?' Kubeck asked.

'Turn around and see what's along the other way,' Jamie said, and executed a very neat three-point turn.

'If they've got someone monitoring the camera they might notice us coming back for a second look,' I said.

'They'll assume we're lost tourists,' Jamie said.

'No, if they're a bunch of Satanists planning world domination, they'll be suspicious as hell. Anyway, they'll know we're coming.'

'I doubt they'll believe we've found them so quickly.'

'Amaliel will,' I said.

As we drove back along the lane we came face to face with a Jaguar, and had to pull onto the verge to let it pass. A few minutes behind it was a limousine, and when I peered through the side window, I saw a very old woman with milky blue eyes sitting in the back. Her lips were curled into an almost manic grin, which did nothing to calm me.

'What day is it today?' I asked, trying to get my thoughts in order.

'Monday, I believe,' Jamie replied.

And at last I had something to smile about. 'Persephone's house-guests are going home!' And as if to prove the point, we pulled aside to let another flashy car pass by.

'Most of these people might be like Philip, with jobs and families to get to,' Jamie said, his own smile returning.

'So, maybe she won't have such an army until next weekend?' It was a lot to assume, but I knew how we could check. 'Kayla, can you go and take a look? Try and get a rough idea of who's staying and who's going?' She gave me a grin and was gone.

We reached the gate as it was opening to let another couple of vehicles out, but we just drove past and continued along the lane the other way.

Jamie stopped when he found a convenient lay-by and swivelled around to face us all.

'Walls and hedges won't keep us out,' he started, 'but Amaliel will know that.'

'Once the humans have left he'll have his Sicarii patrolling,' Vaybian said.

'There'll still be some humans,' I told them. 'A huge place like this doesn't run itself, and there'll probably be a few guests who don't have jobs or families to take them home.'

'I'm willing to bet Joseph and Gabriel won't be going anywhere,' Jamie said.

'Who do you think we really have to worry about,' I asked, 'other than Amaliel?'

Jamie thought for a minute. 'Persephone could be the one with power, or she might just be part of the honey pot they used to entice Philip. Joseph used the promise of wealth, power and success, and she used sex.'

'It could be she has no real power at all,' Kerfuffle said. 'It could be Amaliel who conjured up the Blue Fire.'

'He's more than capable, I'm sure,' Shenanigans added.

'Uncle Davna was pretty sure Amaliel was going to use some kind of dark magic to hold and imprison souls within the crystals,' Kubeck said, 'but Blue Fire . . .?'

'Who do you think the other crystals and cages were for?' I asked.

But none of us could begin to guess.

It started to rain: a light patter on the roof of the car which gradually crescendoed until we had to raise our voices to make ourselves heard. The light had almost gone, though much earlier than it should for the time of year, and the wind was buffeting the van back and forth as the rain lashed down against the window screen, making it almost impossible to see outside.

There were five phials in all: one made a very long time ago, and now four more. If there had been three, I would have thought it had something to do with Jamie, Jinx and me – but four?

'Do you think he could really do it – trap a person's soul in a crystal, I mean?' I asked, though I'm not sure Vaybian and Kubeck heard me in the back over the downpour.

'The question isn't really "could he",' Jamie said, 'but why *would* he? It makes no sense at all.'

'It would if he's planning to try and trap you and Mistress Lucky?' Shenanigans leaned between our seats so he could be heard.

'Trap you, kill you, then imprison your souls,' Kerfuffle added. 'But why *four*?'

'Five,' Jamie said, correcting me, 'if you count the original one he had made.'

Amaliel had had it made for a *special lady*. 'What lady?' I muttered. An unrequited love? Is that why she ended up hanging in a bottle on the end of a chain? I doubted he was capable of love – although I would probably have said the same of Baltheza once, when he had certainly demonstrated considerable affection for Kayla, and for me.

Thinking of that made me wonder where the hell Kayla had got to. She'd been gone far longer than I would have expected for a quick count-up of our adversaries.

'Do you think Kayla's all right?' I wondered aloud.

'Kayla's fine,' Jamie replied.

'We don't know that.'

'She's a spirit: no one can see her but you and Jinx. She's probably eavesdropping and trying to get an idea of their plans. She'll be fine.'

'I hope you're right.'

He reached across and took my hand and gently rubbed his thumb back and forth across mine. 'I am, trust me.'

I looked up into his very blue eyes and wished with all my heart that I could, but as much as I loved him, trust was an issue between us – he must have guessed what I was thinking, for his expression grew sad and his movements faltered for a second.

'I would never deliberately hurt you, Lucky: you *must* believe me.'

'What about Jinx?' I asked him.

'If I can help you save him, I will. I've told you that.'

'But if you can't?'

'I will do whatever I can, but I can't risk the lives of every man, woman and child on this planet for one daemon – in your heart, you know he wouldn't want me to.'

I did know it; I just didn't want to accept it. How could I live without my death daemon? But how could I live without my angel? Because if Jamie did have to destroy Jinx, I doubted I'd ever be able to forgive him. That might not be a rational way to feel, I knew that, but I didn't have any control over it, any more than my love for the pair of them: I shouldn't love two men, but I did, and there was nothing I could do about it.

Jamie continued to stroke my hand, and in a moment of pure melancholy I wondered if he knew it might be one of the last times he would touch me in such a familiar way. The clock was ticking and we were running out of time: for Jinx, and for Jamie and me. I looked at the rest of my friends sitting in the gloom and wished that Jamie and I were alone.

My human eyes filled with tears, and I blinked them away. I was getting maudlin, and that was no help to anyone. 'If Kayla isn't back within ten minutes, I'm going to risk going over the wall and trying to find Jinx myself.'

'Are you mad?' Jamie said.

'I can't sit here doing nothing. If Jinx is to have any future – if you and I are to have any future – I have to do something. Don't you see that?'

He looked me in the eyes as if trying to reach into my soul. 'Yes,' he whispered, 'I do.'

There was a cough from behind us, and Vaybian called out over the deluge of the storm, 'If you want my opinion, you, Guardian, have become too humanised.'

'Well, I don't,' Jamie snapped.

Vaybian got up and leaned over the seat between Shenanigans

and Kerfuffle, and Kubeck shuffled forward too, so everyone could hear. 'We are daemonkind,' he said. 'We are supernatural beings in the human world – or are all the stories untrue?'

Shenanigans and Kerfuffle exchanged a look and Kerfuffle gave one of his disconcerting giggles as Shenanigan's face lit up in one of his toothy smiles.

'Humans are no match for us,' Kerfuffle said.

'Aren't you forgetting something?' Jamie said; by his tone he was clearly disgruntled by Vaybian's accusation. 'As well as the humans there are at least thirty Sicarii, who, if I'm not mistaken, are just as supernatural as us.'

'Of whom ten are not much better than rotting corpses,' Vaybian said with a sneer. 'Punch one hard enough and your fist would probably go right through it.'

'They are falling to bits,' I agreed, turning to Jamie.

He was frowning. 'Do you know something, Vaybian?' he said after moment of contemplation, 'I'll take back all I've ever said about you having shit for brains.'

'In which case I'll take back all I've ever said about you being a pompous know-it-all,' Vaybian said generously.

There was a moment's tense silence, then they both began to laugh. 'Touché,' Jamie said, and all at once the atmosphere between my guards was the best it had been since we'd arrived in the Overlands.

'So,' Kubeck said, 'are we going in?'

'Yes,' Jamie said, 'we're going in.'

BOUND

Ten

It was still pouring hard, which Vaybian – the only real soldier amongst us even if it had been a long time ago – assured us was a good thing. 'Being on lookout in foul weather wearies even the most vigilant of guards,' he explained, 'and the Sicarii are assassins, not soldiers.'

We got out, changing instantly from human to daemon. I had to admit, it felt good to be daemon again.

Pyrites changed from a small dog to a slightly larger drakon and trotted along beside me, his head beneath my hand.

'Maybe it would be an idea if Pyrites took a quick flight over the grounds to see what's about?' Shenanigans suggested.

'Not as a drakon, though,' Jamie reminded him.

Pyrites puffed steam and in a flurry of feathers he changed into a bird that looked a lot like a large hawk.

'Do a quick flight around the estate and then the building,' Jamie suggested. 'We'll meet you just inside the boundary where the wall turns to hedge.'

Pyrites gave a bob of his head, then flew up into the stormy sky and disappeared over the hedgerow. As soon as he was gone we moved off, keeping as quiet as possible. I hoped we didn't meet any humans coming along the lane – a bunch of daemons jogging silently down the road would definitely be hard to explain.

I thought Jamie would have to fly us all over the wall, but Vaybian jumped up and over in one bound, quickly followed by Shenanigans and Kubeck. Kerfuffle need a leg-up from Jamie, but jumped down the other side with no trouble.

'Alone at last,' Jamie said to me, and although I let him draw me into his arms and hug me close, I couldn't relax against him. Too much had happened between us, and I was still dealing with how he'd deliberately manipulated me.

'Lucky,' Jamie said, and I could hear the hurt in his voice, 'whatever happens, know this: I love you, and I will do so for all eternity. If this should all turn out badly, remember that I do, because it is, and always will be, the truth.'

'I love you too,' I whispered, 'but how can I trust you after everything you've done?'

He gave me a gentle smile. 'I know, and I'm so very sorry — I can't tell you *how* sorry.' He brushed his fingers against my cheek, and with a flap of wings carried me over the wall to join the others.

They had taken shelter under a huge old oak tree; we were still getting wet, but at least we were out of the wind. More importantly, we could see the dark silhouette of the manor house looming in the distance. In my imagination it looked like some sleeping monolithic beast: evil, and black of heart.

We waited for Pyrites, my eyes constantly searching the sky, though I doubted I would be able to make him out in the torrential rain. The tension in the group as we stood there in silence was palpable. We needed to be ready for an all-out fight, we all knew it, but we needed to be stealthy too. This was probably the best chance we were going to get.

We didn't have to wait long for Pyrites, who landed softly with a flap of wings and instantly changed back into a drakon.

'Many people about?' Shenanigans whispered.

Pyrites shook his head and pawed the ground three times.

'Three Sicarii?'

He bobbed his head.

Vaybian whispered, 'They'll be disciples, brown Sicarii — the grey aren't going to be standing outside in the pouring rain.'

'Right,' Jamie said, 'let's get on with it. No harming the humans, but the Sicarii are fair game. Once they're incapacitated, take their weapons.'

The rain was still torrential and it was hard to see as we ran across the lawn, our feet sinking into the soaking-wet grass. Lights brightened some of the windows ahead of us, but they cast little glow in the murky night, and there was no moon to be seen through the stormclouds blackening the sky.

We slowed as we neared the building and Jamie gestured at Pyrites, who took off without bothering to change shape, earning a tut from Jamie, though I doubted even the sharpest-eyed daemon could have seen him through the pounding rain, let alone humans.

He did a quick loop, and when he returned he pawed the ground twice and jerked his head towards the right of the stone steps leading up to the entrance.

Jamie held up two fingers and Pyrites bobbed his head. Then he held up three with a questioning look and my drakon shook his head.

Jamie moved in close to whisper in my ear, 'Stay here with Kerfuffle and Shenanigans.' Then he pointed at Vaybian, Kubeck and Pyrites, and gestured for them to follow him. I guessed they were going for the Sicarii. Within a few paces they had melted into the darkness.

The rain was at last beginning to ease, but I was horribly aware that once we did get inside the mansion, anyone wanting to find us would only have to follow the trail of soggy footprints.

Then a vivid flash of lightning lit up the sky – it only lasted a second, but that was long enough for me to see Kubeck and Vaybian dragging two brown bundles into the bushes beside the front door.

Shenanigans gestured for us to move, and we started off across the lawn.

As we got closer to the building I began to feel a little strange: even though I was soaking wet, the hair at the back of my neck was prickling and I could feel the fine hair on my arms standing on end like I was full of static electricity.

'I don't like this,' Kerfuffle mumbled, 'someone is using unnatural forces.'

Then a shadow appeared in front of us and Shenanigans pushed me behind him. 'It's me,' I heard Jamie say. 'This way.'

He led us around the side of the house, to where the grass beneath our feet changed to stone, and opened a door and we were soon sneaking inside and out of the rain. The minute the door shut behind us it became pitch-black. I fumbled in my pocket for my phone, drew it out and covered it with my jacket, then flicked on the torch, keeping the beam swaddled in cloth.

We were in a small anteroom with coats hanging from hooks on the wall and several pairs of Wellington boots lined up beneath them. Three or four large, multicoloured golf umbrellas stood in a ceramic pot in the corner, and it occurred to me if we left this way, I would be able to snaffle some of their wet-weather gear. Then I realised that we might not manage to leave this place at all, and even if we did, we'd probably be fighting our way out and not worrying about another drenching.

'Did you feel that outside?' Shenanigans whispered.

Jamie looked grim. 'Someone's messing with things they really shouldn't.'

'Amaliel?'

'Not sure.' He moved swiftly across the lobby to another door and reached for the handle. 'Light off. Stay close.'

I switched the torch off as he twisted the handle. The door opened into a wood-panelled corridor illuminated by shaded wall-sconce lamps. Jamie pointed at a door across the hall, made a silent dash for it and put his ear against the wood, listening for a moment before slowly turning the handle. He peered inside, then gestured for us to follow him.

Vaybian made the run next, then Kubeck. Pyrites shrank to tiny and accompanied me, with Kerfuffle and Shenanigans close behind.

There was another door at the end of the corridor leading into a wood-panelled square hall with a staircase on the right going up. The narrow corridor behind it was redolent with the scent of cooking vegetables and roasting meat; no one had to tell me where that went. Those smells also meant we didn't have long; the place would soon be bustling with people heading to the dining room for dinner.

My heart was pounding as I followed Kubeck through the next door. I was no good at this creeping-about stuff; I was sure that any moment we would be confronted by a crowd of robed figures. The long, narrow room had a table that would probably seat thirty, although tonight there were just ten places set, highly polished silver cutlery laid out upon an impossibly white tablecloth. Crystal vases full of brightly coloured and perfumed flowers decorated its length.

'This probably isn't the best place for us to be,' Vaybian hissed at Jamie, who ignored him and hurried past the table to the door at the other end.

He opened the door a crack and peered outside, then quickly pulled it closed and held up four fingers. As we crept to the door, Jamie pointed at himself, then at Vaybian, Kubeck and Shenanigans, and the three daemons nodded and positioned themselves directly behind him. Jamie lifted his hand again, and on the silent count of three, he pulled the door open and they slipped through it.

There were some muffled gasps, a grunt and a thud, then silence.

Kerfuffle peered outside and turned to me with a grin and a thumbs-up.

So four down, only twenty-odd to go. If they kept picking them off a few at a time, we might just do it, I thought.

Jamie dragged his victim back into the room by the scruff of his neck and looked around for somewhere to hide him. The only possibility was under the table, the end that wasn't set for dinner. It wasn't ideal, but we were short of time. Vaybian stuffed his brown-robed minion underneath; I noticed a newly acquired dagger pushed through his belt. Shenanigans had a short knife grasped in his right hand and Kubeck had an axe. I kept an anxious lookout as they kicked the bodies out of sight.

It felt like forever, but it was done in moments, and then we were following Jamie into a large dark reception room. My eyes were instantly drawn to the huge fireplace at the other end of the room where several large logs hissed and spat as they burned; in other circumstances I would have happily curled up on one of the low leather couches flanking the fire to warm my bones and dry my sodden clothes.

But Jamie didn't even pause; he strode straight across the room and peered out through the crack between the slightly ajar double doors. He signalled with his fingers and once again, Vaybian, Shenanigans and Kubeck fell in beside him, while Pyrites and Kerfuffle flanked me, ready for any trouble.

One, two, three, and Jamie had the doors open and was through. I moved up to the door, wanting to see, but Kerfuffle gave a slight shake of his head, as if he knew what I was thinking, and I leaned back against the wall.

This time I could hear the sound of fighting – a couple of clashes, steel against steel, some thuds as bodies hit the floor or bounced off walls; a barely formed cry cut off abruptly, ending as a death-rattle – but the struggle was short-lived.

In my head I kept repeating the mantra, *It's them or us* . . . but could I actually kill someone? I didn't know. Then a little voice in my head reminded me, *you would have killed Henri if someone hadn't stopped you.* The voice was right: I would have killed Henri, and if I could, I would kill Amaliel. As for that witch Persephone, human or not, if she had damaged my Deathbringer, at the very least, I would seriously damage her.

Eleven

This time they stacked the bodies in a nearby anteroom. Jamie had procured a sword and Shenanigans handed Kerfuffle a dagger. Kubeck had stuffed the axe into his belt and now held a gleaming blade.

That meant they were all armed but me – I started gesticulating, and Shenanigans immediately got what I meant and disappeared into the anteroom, returning shortly afterwards with another short dagger. As I wrapped my fingers around the hilt, he briefly enclosed my hand within his and squeezed, giving me an encouraging nod.

I thought of Kayla then, and again wondered where she was before my thoughts returned to Jinx. I closed my eyes and started breathing deeply: *he will be all right; he will be all right*. And suddenly I felt something deep inside my head, between my eyes, but right at the back, like something was moving in the centre of my brain, awakening and stretching.

A hand rested on my shoulder – and the feeling was gone.

I opened my eyes to see Jamie's concerned face peering at mine. 'I'm fine,' I mouthed, but he didn't look convinced.

'Guardian, we can't stay here,' Vaybian interrupted before Jamie could speak.

Jamie looked around us. There were stairs going upwards, but the guest rooms would be up there, so that was the last place we should go. He pointed at a room across the hallway, Vaybian strode across the tiled floor, put his ear against the door and, after a couple of heartbeats, turned the doorknob and pushed it open a crack, checked again, then went through, a moment later reappearing in the doorway and gesturing for us to join him.

It took a moment for my eyes to adjust, but when they did

I realised we were in a small reception room; maybe the lady of the manor met with tradesmen here. There were four rather uncomfortable-looking chairs, a low table under the window and an empty fireplace. Insipid watercolours decorated the panelled walls and the carpet was a plain functional brown. It was perfect for us: it was clearly rarely used.

We'd been through most of the ground floor now, and still hadn't seen any sign of Jinx.

Shenanigans risked a whisper. 'Has the Lady Kayla returned?'

'Not yet,' I said, suppressing that worry.

'Without her, we can only guess where the Deathbringer may be,' Kubeck pointed out.

'Aren't you concerned for her?' Vaybian asked me with an ill-concealed glare.

'Actually yes; yes, I am, Vaybian, thanks for asking.' I must have sounded really pissed off, because he looked away first.

'Lucky, when you're in Jinx's head, what is it you see?' Jamie asked. 'Do you remember anything that might give us a clue to where they were? We don't really want to have to search the whole bloody house to find him.'

'Let's think about it: he'd have to be locked up somewhere,' Kerfuffle said, 'and probably away from the guests, so no sounds disturb them.'

'Lucky, think very hard. What did you see?'

I closed my eyes and tried to remember every detail. 'He was on his knees, surrounded by the blue light. She wanted him to look up at her, but he lowered his head.'

'Did you see this Persephone?' Kerfuffle asked.

'Not above the knees.' I suddenly remembered something: 'The floor was made of grey stone slabs.'

'A dungeon?' Vaybian asked.

'This house isn't old enough to have a dungeon,' Kerfuffle pointed out.

'But it might have a wine cellar,' I said, opening my eyes.

'So we look for a flight of stairs going down,' Jamie said.

'It'll probably be near the kitchen – maybe behind those stairs we passed on the way in?'

'Sounds logical.' Jamie put a hand on my arm. 'Lucky, this is the perfect place for you all to wait. I'll check it out, see if there is a wine cellar or a basement and whether Jinx is in it, and if I can't get him out on my own, I'll come and get back-up.'

'No, you can't go in alone – what happens if you end up trapped in Blue Fire? How would we know?'

'She has a point, Guardian,' Vaybian said. 'If you and the Deathbringer both turned rogue, the Lands as we know them would be lost for ever.'

'I would not turn rogue.'

'You don't know that,' I said. 'You told me it happened to a Guardian once before.'

'A very, very long time ago.'

'But this is happening *now*; it's happening to Jinx *now*. It could just as easily happen to you *now*!' I could hear my voice rising and I fought to control it. 'We stick together.'

'There're too many of us.'

'Then you and I go.'

'Great, so if you get caught, Amaliel not only has the Deathbringer, he has the Guardian and the Soulseer as well. Why don't you just go and join them for dinner? Then you'll at least have a hearty last meal before he kills you and puts you in one of his nasty glass phials,' Vaybian said.

'It would be a little foolhardy,' said Shenanigans, ever the diplomat.

'A *little* foolhardy?' Vaybian sneered, turning on Shenanigans. 'A *little* foolhardy? It would be totally moronic.'

I crossed my arms and glared at him. 'If you can't say anything useful . . .'

'Useful? Why bother? You only listen to what you want to hear. We all have to tread around on drakon eggs rather than upset you. We all know it's a waste of time even trying to rescue the Deathbringer, but no one dares tell you.'

'Vaybian,' Jamie cautioned.

Vaybian gave him a disdainful look, which suddenly softened and his shoulders slumped. 'Tell her, Guardian. If you truly love her, tell her. It's better she knows now, then at least if we do find him she will have a chance to say her goodbyes.'

'Tell me *what*? What is it you're keeping from me now?'

Jamie folded his arms and looked down at the floor.

'Mistress,' Shenanigans said, 'if what we think is true, if the Deathbringer has been bound to this world by Blue Fire and his spirit bound through ritual by Amaliel, then when he is released from the Blue Fire there will be nothing left of the daemon you knew.'

'He will be like a wild, feral beast whose only desire is to please the master who controls him,' Kubeck added.

'He will no longer know you.'

I sank down onto one of the chairs. 'Is this true?' I asked, looking up at Jamie.

His expression said it all and I had to look away. 'I had hoped not, but each of your visions has told me differently. You have seen the Blue Fire, you have felt his emptiness.'

'He's still fighting them.'

'Is he?'

I clutched my hands together in my lap and Pyrites put a claw on my knee and whimpered.

'Good boy.' My voice cracking, I laid my hand on his head – my *human* hand. A very human tear splashed down upon it.

Jamie crouched down in front of me. 'I am so sorry.'

'He's fighting them, Jamie. He is still fighting them.'

'Lucky, don't—'

'Jamie,' I said, looking him in the eyes, 'he is still fighting them. I saw.'

'You saw him on his knees cowering away from this human woman – Persephone,' Vaybian said, his voice surprisingly gentle.

'He wasn't cowering.' My shoulders started to shake. 'She was trying to seduce him. Amaliel hasn't broken him with torture so she was trying to seduce him.'

Jamie exchanged a glance with Vaybian and got to his feet. 'We don't dare risk it,' I heard Vaybian mutter beneath his breath.

Jamie gestured and all my guard moved away from me and gathered in a tight group. Only Pyrites stayed by my side, staring up at me with his beautiful multicoloured eyes.

I leaned down and whispered in my drakon's ear, 'I have to try to save him, Pyrites. You understand, don't you?'

Pyrites puffed white smoke and nuzzled my neck.

'Can you keep them here? Just long enough for me to get downstairs?'

Pyrites bobbed his head and trotted off to stand between me and my guards, then began to grow. Once he was blocking them from view he glanced my way and blinked his eyes. I blew him a kiss, jumped to my feet and before they'd fully realised what was happening I was out through the door and hurrying across the entrance hall to the dining room.

I heard raised voices coming from the room behind me, and a low growl from Pyrites. I closed the dining room door behind me, then I was off and running.

When I reached the back staircase close to the kitchen I found a door beneath it that could only open onto a downward staircase. I couldn't hang about; I could hear voices coming from the kitchen and it wouldn't be long before this area became a hive of activity. I put my hand on the doorknob and turned it. The door was locked.

'Shit,' I muttered to myself. It was a wine cellar; of course it would be locked, even if it didn't have a death daemon in residence.

I couldn't let a locked door stop me now. I gripped the handle and twisted it as hard as I could, daemon strength coursed through me and with a metallic clunk, something *gave*. I pushed, and the door opened with a crack.

I listened for a second; no one was coming running at the sound of the lock breaking, so I eased it open and stepped inside. I heard a door open somewhere, and the chatter of voices and clinking of glasses spilled out of it, as what sounded like several people hurried towards the dining room. *Shit!* My guards wouldn't be able to catch up with me now. I really was on my own.

I pulled out my phone and flicked on the torch again, but the dusty white light barely reached the last steps of the narrow enclosed staircase. I padded down as quietly as I could. I suspected there would be at least two Sicarii guarding the door at the bottom, and I wasn't at all sure how I would deal with them – but deal with them I would. I had to.

I hesitated on the last step. I put the phone away and pulled the purloined dagger from my belt, holding it gripped in my right hand the way Jamie and Jinx had taught me. I let my eyes adjust to the darkness, then I reached down, turned the door handle and let the door slowly swing open into more darkness—

—where there were no guards . . .

Why were there no guards?

At the risk of flattening the battery I switched on my phone torch again: I *was* in a wine cellar. I could make out a few racks against the walls, but not much in the way of wine. Some wooden boxes were heaped in one corner and a couple of broken chairs in another. At the far end of the cellar I could see the outline of yet another door. I was certain I'd find what I was looking for behind this one.

But why were there no guards?

For the first time, I began to wonder if maybe there was no longer a need for them: perhaps Jinx had succumbed and was now Amaliel's. Worse still, maybe he was *Persephone's* . . . and God help me, I found myself hoping that if he *had* succumbed, it was to the daemon. If he was hers, I would just curl up and die.

I stopped and rested my forehead and the palm of my hand against the wood, closed my eyes and listened. *Silence.* The handle turned without a sound. I pushed the door open and was greeted with a soft glow of light, which jumped and flared like it was aflame, colouring the stone walls and floor with a pale blue iridescence.

A figure was sitting in the centre of the flickering light, arms wrapped around legs and head on knees, but it wasn't my Deathbringer. As I walked across the stone slabs, Kayla raised her head and upon seeing me, jumped to her feet.

'Am I relieved to see you!'

'What are you doing in there?'

'That bitch Persephone could see me – she pretended she couldn't – and trapped me here.'

'She *saw* you? She couldn't have——'

'Well, she did,' Kayla said with a pout. 'Nasty, evil harpy.'

'Was Jinx here?' I said, walking around her and studying the blue tube of flickering light in which she was encased.

'How do you think I got myself into this mess? She released Jinx from the Blue Fire and made it wrap around me.'

'She *released* Jinx?'

Kayla's lips pressed together into a look I knew all too well. 'Lucky, I'm sorry. I know you love him so very much, but I think it's too late for him.'

'Never——!'

'Where are the others?' she asked, very sensibly changing the subject.

I fought back my fear for them. 'Upstairs. They got trapped on the wrong side of the dining room – look, I'll explain later. Do you know where Jinx is?'

'You're not going to like this.'

I knew what she was going to say, but I wouldn't let myself believe it, even when she started, 'She was petting him like he was her little lapdog. She says he's going to give her guests a taster, show what he can do, but not before she has a taste of him herself. Though if it's any consolation, I think she was saying it for my benefit, as he grimaced every time she touched him.'

'So there's still a chance?' I said, grasping onto that tiniest bit of hope.

Kayla plastered a plastic smile on her face. 'We won't know until you see him, will we? If he sees you and realises you're alive, it could make all the difference.'

'How am I going to get you out of this?' I said, gesturing at the column of blue light.

'I have no idea, though I hope you can. I think she and Amaliel have something rather nasty planned for me.'

I thought about the crystal phials. I had a feeling I knew what that might be.

I circled her again. 'There must be a way,' I murmured to myself. After all, I was meant to be able to look after and protect the dead, wasn't I? I closed my eyes and rubbed the bridge of my nose. I daren't open the gateway to the other side in case I'd be freeing Kayla from her prison, only to make her pass through to the other side before she was ready.

Then I felt that strange sensation again in the centre of my head: something like a waking creature, something living inside my brain – which was rather a disgusting thought.

'What's the matter?'

'What?' I said, opening my eyes.

'You wrinkled your nose like you'd smelled something really horrid.'

'I . . .' The strange sensation in my head was growing: what had started off as a gentle tickle was becoming an insistent pressure. I began to feel warm, despite my wet clothing, almost as though I was sinking into a nice hot bath, and when I looked down I could see a soft golden glow cocooning my body. I lifted my hands, my mother's ring shone bright and light flared out from my fingers. As if by instinct I pointed towards Kayla. The golden glow flowed from me and surrounded the column of Blue Fire.

'What the hell?' Kayla whispered as with a hiss and a shower of sparkles, the blue iridescence disintegrated into a million shimmering pieces which turned into raindrops as they hit the stone floor, surrounding her in a glassy puddle. For a moment the surface of the floor glimmered like it was covered with quicksilver, then it flowed away, the streams disappearing into the cracks between the paving slabs until it was gone.

'What did you do?' she asked.

'I have no idea,' I said, 'but I'm not about to complain. Can you take me to Jinx?'

'You'll have to sneak past a whole load of Sicarii, and if you get that far, you'll have to get him away from her – and I don't think she'll be prepared to give him up that easily.'

'Well,' I said, 'neither am I, and he was mine first.'

The hallway was no longer the quiet, deserted place it had been only a few minutes before: servants were hurrying back and forth bearing trays of glasses and bottles of champagne and wine. We waited for a lull in the proceedings so I could scurry through the hall and up the back staircase; I was hoping Persephone's guests would be using the huge main staircase at the front of the house.

'Do you know which room is Persephone's?' I asked Kayla as I hurried up the first few steps.

'I think so, but . . . Oh ho!' Kayla went to grab my arm and of course her fingers slipped right through me. In any case my eyes were already following her wide-eyed stare. A bunch of disciples had appeared at the top of the staircase, and when I swung around, more were waiting for us at the bottom. At their fore was a figure clad in black flowing robes: Amaliel Cheriour. I would recognise those burning red eyes anywhere.

'Here's a lesson you should learn, Soulseer: never use power in a place of power – it gives your presence away as clearly as if you had screamed out your name.'

And as claws grabbed hold of my forearms, I whispered to Kayla, 'Find Jamie—'

Only as they dragged me away did I remember that she might find him, but she couldn't tell him.

I was on my own.

Twelve

Claws dug into my arms as they marched me back down the stairs, across the hall and into the dining room. Two of the Sicarii hurried forward to open the door to the reception room with a flourish.

Amaliel stood to one side and gestured towards me with his candlewax-white hand. 'I told you she would come. I told you if no other, *she* would come.'

I could feel Jinx as soon as I stepped into the room – at least, I *thought* I could – but I couldn't see him. Inside, I prayed I was wrong: for if it was Jinx I was feeling, if this was how *he* was feeling, this cold dark emptiness, then I feared Kayla was right, and he was lost to me.

Even so, my eyes couldn't help but be drawn to the woman dominating the room. Persephone was everything I expected her to be: tall, voluptuous, beautiful. Her long, lush black hair streaked with ripples of aubergine and gold had been piled in the sort of 'careless' topknot that had probably taken her maid an hour or more to perfect. Her eyebrows were symmetrical black arches, her cheekbones high, her cheeks slightly concave and her plump lips a glossy red. Her dress was a figure-hugging scarlet lace over black that fell to just below the calf, and her stilettos were a matching patent red, and so high they would have given me a nosebleed, if I hadn't broken both my ankles first. Playing the vamp suited her – or did I mean tramp? I knew which word I preferred.

She was scrutinising me over a glass of champagne, her lips curled into an amused smile – the sort of smile I wanted to slap off her smug, arrogant face. She and Vaybian were made for each other.

'Well,' she said, sounding like a member of the British upper classes, 'how nice to meet you at last.' She took a step to one side and the breath caught in my throat.

It was Jinx – I *knew* it was Jinx – but he was far removed from the daemon I'd first met in the moonlit stable yard all those months ago. Gone were the smiling eyes and lips twitching with laughter, gone the sleek, confident daemon. He was still wearing his trade-mark leather trousers and boots, but that was about where the similarities ended. His upper body, usually bare, was now covered by a calf-length black leather coat. His shoulders were slumped, his head was bowed and his beautiful dark maroon hair, which he usually wore in a long braid hanging down to his hips, was loose and falling like a shroud around his face.

Persephone laid a hand on his shoulder and his body quivered like a frightened young colt.

I looked straight into her eyes. Jamie always said my face was an open book. On this occasion I guessed he was right, as her amused smile slipped a little on seeing my expression – '*You are so fucking dead*' was about the sum of it – and her hand dropped from Jinx's shoulder.

Amaliel glided to her side as she said, 'She doesn't look like much, does she?' She took a rather unladylike slurp from her champagne. 'Are you sure she's the Soulseer?'

'I have seen her in action.'

'She looks human.'

'As you know only too well, my dear, looks can be deceptive.'

'Hmm. Well, I suggest you get on with doing whatever it is you want to do to her so we can get down to the important business.'

'Patience, my dear. You promised these good people here a demonstration of the Deathbringer's power and I suggest this might be a good time to give them one.' His glowing eyes met mine. 'Sadly for you, I no longer have any need to keep you alive – in fact, you and your wretched Guardian have become a positive liability.'

Persephone's lips curled into a smile. 'I've been so looking for-ward to this,' she said, and smiled brightly at her guests.

I paid them a cursory glance: a youngish man who did actually resemble Obama was standing next to a smaller, weaselly-looking man – Joseph and Gabriel, I presumed. Two girls, both with bleach-blonde hair and rather vacant faces stood slightly away from them – the eye-candy Philip had been so dismissive of in his journal? I almost moved on, but something made me glance back. They were clearly nervous – and then I realised that they were *scared*. That was interesting: so who were they scared of? Persephone? Amaliel? I could understand why they might be scared of him. Maybe even Jinx, though he didn't look all that scary at the minute. Scared, yes, but not scary.

Two older men stood at Persephone's left; one was tall, well dressed and dapper; the other was slightly shorter and just as well dressed, but the suit was a smidgen too tight, the buttons straining over his portly belly. Investors? Or members of the coven, maybe? They certainly didn't look like hired muscle.

A tall, thin man stood slightly apart from them in the corner: the scar-faced African. There was something about his eyes that made me shiver: was he the bokor? In the subdued lighting the darkness appeared to wrap itself around his gaunt frame. I saw a movement behind him; there was someone else lurking in the shadows.

'I did promise you all a demonstration, that's true,' Persephone said, dragging my attention back to her. Once again she laid her hand on Jinx's shoulder. 'Jinx, my love.' She gave me a nasty look. 'I want you to do something to prove how much you love me.'

His head turned slightly towards her; his first movement other than the shiver since I'd entered the room.

'This woman,' she said, pointing at me, 'means us harm. She means to hurt us. I want you to make her rot: make her rot before our eyes.'

Amaliel looked at her. 'Are you sure he's up to it? I was thinking of a bloodier end—'

She slipped her arm through his – that was unexpected; surely to God they couldn't be—? No, that didn't bear thinking about; the very idea made my skin crawl.

'You wanted her dead and so she shall be. Does it matter how he does it?'

He gave a happy gurgle. 'Very well – if you don't think it's too soon.'

She slipped her arm from his and moved closer to Jinx, reaching up to run her fingers through his hair. 'I keep telling you, it takes a woman like me to get a job like this done. He's mine, and I will prove it to you.'

'Lord Amaliel,' the bokor interrupted, his voice dark and deep, like liquid chocolate, 'why not pit your pet against hers?'

Amaliel began to chuckle. 'An interesting idea – what do you think, my dear?'

Persephone cast a look of irritation in the African's direction. 'Let me deal with this. *Please*.'

His red eyes blazing, Amaliel regarded her from beneath his cowl, still gurgling away happily. I'd never known him so cheerful. 'Very well, my dear. Do your worst.'

From behind the bokor there was a strangled gasp. The African muttered something in what sounded like French, but I couldn't tear my eyes away from Jinx. He loved me, he would never hurt me – would he?

She took hold of Jinx's chin and tilted his head back so he was looking in my direction. 'Make her rot,' she said, and what I saw in his eyes scared me more than Amaliel, Persephone or a hundred Sicarii ever could.

His lips drew back into a snarl and for the first time I realised what the others had meant: he was no longer my Jinx. *He'd gone feral.*

Persephone gestured to the Sicarii who were holding me to let go, and they didn't need telling twice; as soon as they released my arms they hurried out of harm's way as Jinx stalked towards me.

I stood my ground for maybe two seconds, staring into his eyes, *willing* him to recognise me, but there was nothing there other than a burning desire to do his mistress' will. I took a step back, then another, and I heard Persephone and her male guests start to laugh. The girls were silent.

'Not so brave now, Soulseer,' the vile woman called.

Jinx reached out, the hands that had once caressed me so lovingly now twisted into claws—

—then the door at the other end of the room burst open with an almighty crash and I saw Jamie framed in the doorway, my guards by his side. Amaliel shouted, and the Sicarii surged forward to greet them, but Jinx wasn't so easily distracted: he didn't look back, he didn't falter; he just kept on coming, and as the sound of fighting filled the other end of the room, I knew I had no one to save me but myself. I backed away a few steps, then turned and ran. I needed to get the door to the dining room open before Jinx reached me.

I threw it open and ran full-pelt past the long table to the door at the other end, but Jinx was running too; I could hear his footsteps behind me.

'Please God, please God,' I prayed as I struggled with the handle. *They can't have locked it, they just couldn't!* They hadn't; it was my own panic that was going to get me killed. I threw the door open and tried to pull it closed behind me, but I was too late; Jinx's fingers had already curled around the wood and were wrenching it from my grasp.

With a shriek I hared along the passageway, into the small lobby and to the back door.

As I ran through I grabbed a coat off one of the hooks on the wall and threw it behind me, hoping to hamper his progress; I grabbed another, but this one snagged for a second – a second I didn't have. In desperation, I grabbed for an umbrella and yanked the ceramic pot into Jinx's path. I didn't dare look back to see if I'd succeeded in slowing him down but flung open the door and leaped outside, the umbrella still in my hand. It might just help as a weapon to keep some distance between us.

If anything, the rain was coming down even harder than before, and I was facing away from the house and the light, so it was almost impossible to see. I had no idea where I was going – or what I would do when I got there; the only thing on my mind was keeping Jinx away from me. He'd told me before that the merest touch of his hand could bring death if he so chose, and if he was intent on carrying out his mistress' will, I could do very little to stop him.

The sodden grass really hampered my progress: I was running as fast as I could, but I kept slipping, and it was pure luck that I didn't go down. Then I saw shadows rising up out of the dark ahead of me: a line of trees; I had no idea if they'd be my saviours or my undoing. Maybe if I got in amongst them I could hide out, at least until help came – *if* it came.

Arms and legs pumping, I ran for my life, not daring to look back. I was almost at the treeline: they would slow me down, but they might also give me shelter. Above the pounding rain I could hear him coming after me; I was sure of it. Then I heard a grunt, and hoping that meant he'd fallen, I made one final push and suddenly I was in amongst the tall trunks.

I had to slow down to a trot, and even then I was at risk of getting an eye put out by a low branch, but it couldn't be helped, and he was as much at risk as I. Then I had an idea and I held up the umbrella in front of my head, so if I walked into anything at least it wouldn't be with my face, and this gave me the confidence to hurry along a little faster. Where I was hurrying to, I had no idea; I could have been running into a whole load more trouble.

Then ahead of me I could see a little light through the trees, from the lamps along the drive – if I could get there, maybe I could escape.

I was just beginning to think I'd made it when a shadow peeled away from a large tree ahead of me. I immediately turned to run back, but too late: hands grabbed my shoulders, pulling me backwards, and then strong arms wrapped around me, pulling me tight against him.

I struggled and kicked and stamped, but it was hopeless. When

I managed to land a heel on his foot he gave a grunt, but then he lifted me up so I was inches above the ground and floundering in midair.

He swung me around and pushed me face-first against a tree, his front pressed into my back. It occurred to me I should be dead – why wasn't I a rotting corpse? She had ordered him to make me rot . . . so maybe he wasn't quite as much hers as she thought?

'Jinx,' I said firmly, 'let go. If you put me down, I promise not to run.'

The right side of his face rested on mine and he breathed in deeply, like he was smelling me. Then I felt something hard pressed against my backside and I started to struggle again.

'Let go of me, Jinx, let go of me, *right now.*'

With a snarl he pulled me away from the tree and threw me down onto the ground, so hard I hit the earth with a thump that had me seeing stars. He sat astride me and grabbing hold of my wrists, held them up above my head. Too late, I remembered the knife tucked into my belt, but I couldn't reach it – I didn't know if I'd be able to use it on Jinx even if I could.

His long hair hung down, framing his face and pooling around mine, drops of rain running down and mingling with those already wetting my face. I wanted to cry with fear, anger and frustration. I knew I would kill that bloody woman, if it was the last thing I ever did.

'Jinx, stop it,' I screamed at him, but he had only one thing on his mind and it wasn't killing me – at least, not at that very moment.

He hovered above me and I began to struggle again, but it was like trying to shift an immovable force; I was making no impression at all – and then he looked down at my face. I've no idea what he could see in the dark, but he suddenly froze, and the hands about my wrists loosened a bit. That was all I needed: I wrenched my right hand out of his and punched him really hard in the groin.

He crumpled as I scrambled backwards away from him and jumped to my feet, but he staggered up and came straight at me. Shaking, I pulled my dagger out from beneath my jacket. The

Sicarii had been so confident, they hadn't bothered to search me for weapons – I wasn't sure whether I was glad or not. I was pulling a dagger on my lover, hating that I should need to.

'Stay back,' I said, holding the blade out in front of me.

He took a step towards me.

'I mean it, Jinx.'

Then another.

'Don't make me do it,' I said.

I saw a flash of white through the dark as he snarled. I took a pace back.

'Please, Jinx, I don't want to hurt you.'

I held the dagger low and upwards: '*Fight dirty*,' Jinx had told me, '*there's no honour or rules when you're threatened*.'

He was inhumanly fast, brushing the dagger aside with an ease that was embarrassing, then his hands reached out as if to cup my face, and the little worm inside my head reared up and *screamed*.

Something weird happened: deep inside my head there was a movement, like the flick of the tail of an angry drakon. My hand snapped open, palm down, my fingers extending. There was a crack like lightning and a flash of white light – and Jinx flew through the air, smashed through the branches of the tree he'd had me pinned up against and landed on the ground in a tangle of limbs and broken bits of tree.

I stood there, shaking and terrified: what in all Hells had just happened? *What had I done?* Had I killed one of the two men I thought I loved more than life itself? I obviously hadn't loved him that much, not when it came down to him or me.

No, I hadn't chosen my life over his. How could I have lived if he had raped me? Death would be easier than that.

I picked up my dagger and crept towards him. It was too dark to see if he was moving, but I couldn't hear any movement. When I finally stood over him I wasn't sure what to do next. I didn't want to wake him up, that was for sure, but I had to know if he was alive. I prodded him with the toe of my boot. *Nothing.* I gave him another harder prod, but he stayed still as death.

I clenched my fists and took a few deep breaths. He was not dead. He was the Deathbringer; he was stunned, that was all.

I crouched down beside him. He was lying on his side, facing down and covered by a sodden sheet of hair. I strained to hear if he was breathing, but it was impossible with the constant pouring rain through the tree canopies above. I moved a little closer, but it was no good; I couldn't hear a thing.

The sensible thing to do would be to step away and wait until Jamie and the others turned up. If they turned up. Then another terrible thought occurred to me: what if I had saved Jinx, only to get Jamie and my guards slaughtered by Amaliel and his unholy rabble?

I hugged myself tight, shaking, and I wasn't sure if it was from the cold, my fear, or the aftermath of what I'd done to Jinx, and what he had been about to do to me. It was probably all of it.

Above the rain I heard voices, then I saw lights approaching through the trees: flashlights. My guards didn't have flashlights. I prodded Jinx really hard with the hilt of my dagger, but there was still nothing. The lights were getting closer: did I stay and try and fight them off? If I knew I could call up this strange new power at will, there would have been no question, but I didn't: the little creature inside my head was now annoyingly silent.

Then I heard Persephone yelling like the harpy she was: 'Gabriel, if your fucking little daemons don't find him I will castrate each and every one of them with a very rusty knife – you included!' I heard a gurgling, wet laugh too: Amaliel.

Persephone I could cope with, but I didn't want to face Amaliel.

I reached out and stroked the hair away from Jinx's forehead. 'I'll come back for you,' I whispered. 'I'll find you and bring you home.' I leaned forward and kissed his cheek – not much of a kiss, my lips were so cold I could hardly feel them, but it was the best I could do. I ran my fingers across his lips.

I had wasted more time than I should. I jumped to my feet and hurried away into the darkness.

The sound of Persephone's nagging faded as I put some distance between us – then I heard the crack of a twig behind me. I ducked

behind a tree, held my breath and listened. There was nothing for
a moment or two and I exhaled – and then came heavy footfalls,
and the shuffling of wet leaves. I pushed back against the tree as
fear washed through me, as primaeval as a child's terror of the
dark. There was something following me, and it was neither daemon nor human: I could *feel* it.

It was getting closer, but I didn't dare look. I pressed back against
the tree, so hard I would have imprints of the bark on my skin – then
it lurched into view: a hunched figure, almost a caricature of a man.
If it turned its head to the right, just a fraction, it would see me.

I didn't dare move; I *couldn't* move.

Then a deep, dark brown voice called, 'Viens à moi, mon enfant!'

The creature stopped and made a mewling sound. I prayed it
would turn to the left.

It did, and I caught a whiff of something putrid – and with it came
a memory: I had smelled something similar at Philip's flat – and suddenly I remembered the closing fire door. What would we have
found in Philip's apartment if we had been a few minutes earlier?

I pushed myself even closer against the tree as it turned until it
was facing back the way it had come. It made a strange noise, a
crooning sound from the back of its throat, and began to shuffle
away. It was trying to say something.

Then it made the noise again, and I began to shake so hard that
I'd have sworn the leaves above me began to rustle.

'*Luuuucckyyyyy,*' it cried. '*Luuuuccckkyyy!*'

My fear for Jamie and my guards kept me going, and somehow I
managed to find the wall at the edge of the property. What if I had
lost all of them – what if Jamie was trapped in Blue Fire, or even
worse, in one of Amaliel's creepy little glass phials? What if that
creature, whatever it was, had started tracking me again?

I had just stepped out into the open to follow the wall around to
the place where it met the hedge when I saw headlights coming
down the drive, moving away from the house. I darted back into
the trees and waited: there was a limousine of some sort heading

up a procession of SUVs, and they were all far too close to where I was hiding.

I heard other vehicles coming across the lawn. They drew closer to the light and I saw two Land Rovers – so that's how Amaliel and his Sicarii minions had got to us so quickly.

They slithered to a stop parallel to the drive and the doors flew open. Four or five disciples appeared from the Land Rovers and ran to the vehicles on the drive. I thought I saw a hooded figure in black heading for one of the limos.

The internal lights went on – maybe someone checking a map or setting up the satnav? – and I spotted Persephone in the back, next to Amaliel. The man I assumed was Joseph had turned around in the front seat and was talking to them; it was clear from that glimpse of her face that she wasn't receiving good news.

The gate swung open before they reached it and her car shot through, followed by the rest of her entourage. In the second vehicle I caught a glimpse of the scar-faced man and another hunched figure, but it sped by so quickly I couldn't be sure and in no time at all, they were gone. I couldn't help but think of rats leaving the sinking ship, as no one even bothered to shut the gate.

Then it occurred to me that I hadn't seen Jinx: he hadn't been in that front car with Persephone and Amaliel, and I'd not seen a figure being carried by the Sicarii. Would Amaliel and Persephone risk him being in the same vehicle? She might; he was her prized possession, her lapdog, her little killing machine of a pet, and I doubted having almost lost him once, she'd trust him to another's care. *So where was he?*

He could have been lying down in one of the other cars, of course, but I didn't think so: I'd noticed back at the house that Persephone and Amaliel were the only ones who'd stood anywhere close to Jinx; everyone else had been careful to keep some distance away from him.

Then a horrible thought occurred to me: perhaps I *had* killed him. I swung around and started to run back through the wood, praying the creature the bokor had sent after me had gone with them.

I'd lost my umbrella at some point during my fight with Jinx so I held up one arm in front of my face and hoped for the best. I had to try and find the others as well – Persephone and Amaliel leaving in a hurry made me hope we'd scored a victory, although I had no idea how.

I suddenly realised that it was so dark, I could walk straight past Jinx's unconscious body without even knowing it – there were no landmarks; it'd been just one large tree amongst many other large trees. And if I used the phone, I would be lit up like a Christmas tree for anyone to spot; worse still, I might walk straight into the abomination that had been stalking me.

I slowed down to a trudge. If I didn't come across his body soon, I'd go and find Jamie. As I plodded along, peering through the tree trunks, I realised I was seeing a bit more: in fact, there was a soft glow of light creeping through the trees, although I knew it couldn't yet be dawn – Persephone and her guests had only just been getting ready for dinner.

I stared across the grounds to the house in the distance and felt the hair stand up on my arms and legs.

'Wow,' I said. 'Oh wow—'

The house was bathed in a pale golden light: it looked too soft and warm and comforting to be a bad kind of light. Then I saw my angel walking out of the glowing haze, my other guards behind him, and I felt my lips curl up into a smile. They were safe. *Oh my God, they were safe . . .*

I was about to raise my hand and cry out when more people stepped out of the light: Guardian angels.

Jamie had called in the cavalry.

Any pleasure I felt at seeing Jamie was gone: he had *promised* he would help me find Jinx and protect him as long as he hadn't started killing people and now he had reneged on that promise.

'Jamie, how could you?' I muttered to myself. 'How bloody *could* you?'

Now I had no choice; I would have to find Jinx myself, and

keep him safe – and hope that I could do so without him killing me first. Maybe without Persephone there and pulling his strings, I would have a chance.

I swung around and hurried back among the trees. I couldn't have been seen, or someone would have waved or shouted out.

One thing about the appearance of the angels did help: I now had light to see by. I knew I had to make the most of it, as I had no idea how long it would last – I didn't even know what was causing it. If I hadn't known differently, I'd have thought it was celestial light sent down from above to assist His heavenly angels.

I picked up speed, muttering, 'Jinx, where the Hell are you?'

Then I saw a strip of colour on the ground directly ahead of me: the umbrella. I dropped it when he first grabbed me from behind, so if he hadn't been found, he should've been somewhere around here. A snapped branch hung limply ahead of me, and there were more broken-off branches a few feet beyond that. I cautiously followed the arboreal carnage, but still there was no Jinx.

They must have found him and stashed him in one of their cars . . . perhaps they'd realised Jamie's reinforcements were coming; that's why they'd been in such a hurry to get away. I didn't know what the Guardians would do to the humans, but Amaliel and his Sicarii would be in for a rough ride.

I heard voices, now calling – 'Lucky——!' That was Jamie.

'Mistress, where are you?' Shenanigans, I guessed.

'Soulseer?' That chorus could only have come from Jamie's Guardians.

I glanced at the pile of broken branches and my shoulders sagged. Amaliel and Persephone must have found Jinx so there wasn't any point in me hiding. But I still didn't know what to do; help from the Guardians was help I could well do without.

There was only one thing for it: I would have to find my guard and regroup, see if they would still support me in my search for Jinx. If Jamie wasn't willing to help me, well, I'd have to go it alone. Was this a rift that could ever be healed? I wasn't sure.

I trudged back towards the lawn, and now I could see them

stretched out in a line against the glowing backdrop, Jamie slightly in front of the others, with my guard on his right and the Guardians on his left. I was about to step out and call his name when a figure glided to his side and rested a hand on his arm. She tilted her head to smile up at him, and when he glanced down at her I saw her lips move, and whatever she said eased his worried frown.

Even from a distance I could see she was stunning; from her golden-haired beauty I guessed she must be from the same gene pool as the Guardians, although if she had wings, I couldn't see them. She was tall and slim, her long hair swept to one side and flowing over her right shoulder almost to her waist. Her white dress was straight out of a Greek tragedy: soft material draping her body and falling to her ankles, clinging in all the right places and cinched around her narrow waist with a belt of gold.

Who the hell are you?

Another Guardian pushed past the others to join her and what could have been irritation flickered across her face as he distracted her from Jamie. I watched her for a moment or two longer. I'd taken an instant dislike to her – hardly fair, but there was something about her that had my hackles rising. I'd just have to hope that when we were formally introduced she'd prove my first impression wrong.

I pulled back my shoulders and held my head high. 'Here goes nothing,' I muttered, but before I could take that final step a hand clamped over my mouth, a leather-covered arm snaked around my waist and as I began to struggle, I heard the word '*sleep*' ripple through my head. All my strength slipped away and my legs gave out as darkness engulfed me.

Thirteen

I awoke to the comforting smell of fresh hay. *This is nice.* I was warm and cosy, and I could feel the weight of an arm wrapped around my front and a body pressed up against my back. I gave a contented sigh and snuggled back against him.

Then I began to wonder: why were we laying on a bed of hay? I opened one eye and looked down. A leather-clad arm was wrapped around me. *What the fuck?*

My eyes followed the line of the arm to the maroon hand holding the coat around us. *Oh shit!*

I was sure the sound of my racing heart would wake him, that he would feel its thudding against his chest pressed so tightly against my back. *Keep calm*, I told myself. *Keep calm!* And I willed myself to relax.

It was early morning, I could tell that much. The stable, if that was where we were, was slowly filling with the grey light of an overcast morning. Birds were singing out their dawn chorus.

To test the water, I gave a little wriggle, like I was moving in my sleep. Jinx's response was to hug me tighter, pressing his body so close to my back it was like we were moulded together. A few days ago I would have felt like I was in Heaven; now I was more scared than I could believe.

I very carefully ran my hand down to my belt. To my surprise I still had my dagger – then again, why worry about a blade when I could quite literally blow him off his feet? It was something I was going to have to practise if I ever got out of this bloody mess.

Still, I'd wanted to find Jinx and now I had.

Despite my fear, exhaustion got the better of me and I drifted back into a dreamless sleep.

*

I woke with a start to find myself on my own and wrapped in a rough blanket pulled up to my chin. I kept my eyes closed and once again tried to calm my hammering heart. This time I was well aware of my predicament, though the lack of Jinx scared me almost as much as when he had been holding me in his tight embrace.

The blanket smelled familiar and when I took a surreptitious sniff I realised it smelled like Bob. So I *was* in a stable, possibly the one next to the manor.

I opened one eye a crack, then the other. Jinx was sitting with his back against the side of the stall, his arms hugging his knees. His green and gold eyes were glittering with an intensity that was almost bestial: he looked like a feral creature – but for all his glowering anger, he was also afraid; I could feel it.

He wasn't the only one. I was too terrified to move and he looked like he was wound up so tight that if I did, he'd be on me in a moment. He'd been holding me close, and now he was keeping his distance: what on earth was going on inside his head? Was he permanently broken? *He couldn't be.* My Jinx was strong and I would fix him. I *would* fix him. *If he doesn't kill you first*, said a small voice in my head that sounded remarkably like Kerfuffle.

The sound of birdsong was interrupted by the growl of an engine and the rumble of tyres on tarmac, and Jinx was instantly on his feet and pulling me up onto mine. I heard a car door opening, followed by the creak of a gate. He released my arm to take hold of my hand, then hurried me out of the stall and through the stable to a door at the back.

Horses peered at us as we passed, snuffling and snorting, and one gave a low whinny, probably wondering who we were and more importantly, why we weren't providing breakfast. Jinx opened the door and poked his head out. Seeing the coast was clear, he ushered me outside and followed behind, but we hadn't taken more than a few steps before he grasped hold of my hand again.

The stable yard was bounded by a tall wooden fence; he helped me over it and then started off across the open field in front of us – but I paused.

'Jinx,' I started, and he turned with a frown and tugged on my hand.

'Where are we going? I have no intention of becoming a rotting corpse, or being trapped in Blue Fire, or in one of Amaliel's horrible little glass jars.'

'Hunt us,' he said.

'Who's hunting us?' Stupid question really; everyone was bloody hunting us, but I wanted to know who *he* was worried about.

'Come,' he said, pulling on my hand again.

I didn't want to lose him, but I did want to know his intentions – especially after Amaliel had made it quite clear I was no longer needed. 'Where are you taking me?' I repeated.

He grabbed hold of my hand again. 'Somewhere safe.' A confused expression passed over his face and he stared at me. 'I . . . I will recognise the place when we get there,' he said at last.

'Jinx, do you know who I am? Do you recognise me?'

'I . . .' His voice trailed off. 'I don't remember.'

I really wanted to find out what was going on in his head, but we didn't have time for this; we had to get away. Although the day was damp and overcast, at least it wasn't raining – but the ground underfoot was still sodden, and in no time at all my boots and the bottoms of my jeans were soaked through.

Wherever possible, Jinx kept close to the hedgerows or within the tree line, which was just as well as we had one more problem to deal with: I was hiding behind my human persona, but Jinx was just about as daemonic a daemon as he could possibly be – being maroon was one thing, but horns and a tail? I had no idea how I'd explain them away if we met anyone. I supposed I should be grateful his tail at least was covered by the coat.

After a couple of grim hours – my feet were sore and soaking wet, and any attempts to talk had been rebuffed – we reached a road to a village, and judging by the number of cars I'd been hearing in the distance, it was fairly busy.

'We have to find somewhere to lay low until it gets dark,' I told Jinx.

'Why?'

I looked at him in open-mouthed amazement. 'What do you mean, "why"? It's pretty damn obvious, I'd have thought.'

He gave me a puzzled look.

'Have you looked in a mirror recently?'

He looked down at himself.

'Jinx, you have horns and a tail and your skin is a rather fetching maroon.'

'So?'

'You'll scare people.'

'Good.'

'No, *not* good: you scare people and they'll phone the police and then we'll get arrested.'

'I'll be arrested for being a different colour?'

'You'll be arrested because no one will know what else to do with you.'

'I'll not let them arrest us.'

'That's actually sort of what I'm afraid of,' I muttered to myself.

'Come.'

'Jinx.'

'Now,' he said, holding out his hand to me. This wasn't a request; it was an order.

I let him take my hand; I was too scared not to. I had seen Jinx look at others this way, and I'd prayed he would never look at me with these cold, dangerous eyes. And now he was, and his expression made me fear for my life.

It had started to rain again, and despite the discomfort, I was relieved: anyone we met would be hurrying to get out of the weather, not be paying us any attention. Jinx pulled up his collar and walked with his head down, his long hair veiling his face.

Of course, he could do nothing about the horns, but from experience I knew often people only saw what they expected to see. And I was proven correct, as we walked the entire length of the village and out the other side without anyone paying us the slightest attention.

My relief evaporated about a mile further along the road, when

I heard a vehicle coming behind us that was travelling far too slowly, even for a winding country lane. Some kind of sixth sense kicked in, and I was immediately wary.

I wasn't the only one.

'Come,' Jinx said. Throwing his arm around my waist, he leaped effortlessly up and over the tall hedge. We crouched down on the other side and peered through the tangle of branches. I could see two men in grey suits sitting in the front of the SUV that drove past at a snail's pace, and four or five other men dressed in brown sitting in the back.

Jinx let out a hiss and his lips twisted into a snarl, which answered one of my questions: he clearly didn't want to be taken by them either. I wondered whether it would have been a different matter if the beautiful but loathsome Persephone had been with them? I hoped not, but I wasn't counting any chickens; she had certainly had him in her thrall back at the mansion – although I still didn't know why I wasn't a rotting corpse yet.

When the vehicle had gone he stood up and looked around us. 'Come,' he said, taking my hand again and starting across the field.

'Where are we going? Do you even know?'

'Shut up.'

'Jinx . . .'

He spun around, his hand grabbed my chin and forcing my head back so he was looking directly into my eyes, he growled, 'I said, *shut the fuck up.*'

That did the trick. I pressed my lips tightly together and concentrated on not wetting myself – which immediately made me fixate on the growing pressure on my bladder.

I let him drag me a few yards further, then tried, 'Jinx—'

He glared in my direction, but I wasn't about to give up. 'Look, I'm not trying to be difficult, honestly I'm not, but I really do need a piss stop.' That was the term he always used when we travelled.

He gave me a disgusted look. 'Go on,' he said, indicating a nearby hedge.

'You are joking?'

'You want to piss or not?'

'Can you at least turn your back?'

He shrugged, his message clear: *you either do or you don't – why should I care?*

I stalked over to the hedge. 'Turn your back.'

He folded his arms.

'Please.'

'You run, I'll hurt. Understand?'

'Yes.'

He gave a snort and turned his back on me. It was the best I could hope for, and when I had finished he still had his back to me, so I hoped he hadn't taken any crafty peeks – and then I thought, *What the hell am I bothered about?* Jinx had seen every inch of me naked – and with my life in the balance, surely my modesty was the least of my worries.

When I rejoined him he gave me a sideways look before taking my hand, and we were off again.

This time we kept to the fields, and when we came to main roads, we walked with our heads down. We really had to get Jinx another coat: he looked like a maroon Alice Cooper, instantly recognisable to anyone searching for us.

We came to a main road leading to a small town, but Jinx didn't look particularly bothered. I kept glancing up at his face: he was staring straight ahead, and after a while I began to worry; it was like he'd shut down and was working on autopilot.

'Jinx,' I said, touching his sleeve with my free hand, 'Jinx, shouldn't we get off the main road?'

He didn't hear me. 'Jinx?' This time I thumped his arm hard.

His eyelids fluttered, and it looked like he had to force himself to look my way.

'Shouldn't we get off this road?'

He blinked a couple of times and stared at my face as though he not only didn't recognise me, but had no idea why he was clutching onto my hand so tightly.

'I . . .' He closed his eyes, and when they opened, he was back:

not my Jinx, the feral Jinx – but that was better than the vacant creature who'd been plodding along beside me.

'Need to get off the road,' he said, looking around us.

At last. 'Up there,' I pointed, 'there's a turning.'

We picked up pace, as from behind us there came the sound of sirens. We exchanged a look and without a word we both started to run.

I had a feeling someone had just upped the stakes.

We'd almost made it to the corner when two police cars came screaming along the road and squealed to a halt, one blocking the pathway ahead and the other the road behind us.

Policemen leaped out of both cars, all wearing protective body gear and holding guns. *For Heaven's sake: guns?* This was East Sussex, not bloody Miami!

'Put your hands on your heads and get down on your knees,' one shouted, and when we didn't move – I was frozen in disbelief – they all started to shout at once.

We still didn't move, and Jinx was almost vibrating with arrogance and indignation.

'Get down on my knees, to *you*?' Jinx said, his eyes glittering. 'You want *me* to get down on my knees to *you*?'

Oh bugger! It was all going to kick off now. 'Jinx, keep calm,' I whispered. 'These men are police officers, and we don't want any nastiness.'

'Get down on your knees – now!' And eight pistols pointed our way.

'Officers,' I said, 'I think there's been some kind of mistake—'

'Move away from him, Miss!'

I frowned at the officer. 'Excuse me?'

'Move away from him,' the policeman repeated.

'Show me your ID,' I said.

Their expressions were incredulous. 'You cannot be serious,' one said.

'Since when do British police officers carry guns?' I asked. 'You could be anyone!'

'We're wearing uniforms and we've got two bleeding marked police cars – is she insane?' one of them said.

'We're an armed response unit, Miss,' one of the older officers told me.

'No,' I said, 'I'm sure you'd have specially marked cars if you were.'

The eight men looked at me aghast.

'I think the fact that there are *eight* of us pointing *loaded guns* at you would be enough for you to get down on your knees and do as you're told.'

'I will not get down on my knees to mere humans,' Jinx said.

'What the hell is he talking about?'

'And look at him: why is he in fancy dress?'

'He's probably ISIS or something,' another said. 'They must be dangerous, otherwise the Guv wouldn't've sent us.'

'I'm telling you for the last time: put your hands on your heads and get down on your knees.'

'Sorry, that's not going to happen,' I said, clutching Jinx's arm, more terrified of what he might do than getting shot.

The policemen exchanged exasperated looks. This obviously wasn't one of the responses covered in their manual.

'I will count to three, and if you don't capitulate we will have no alternative but to use ultimate force.'

'Like, shoot two unarmed persons in cold blood? That'll look good on the *Ten o'Clock News*.'

'Now look here,' one started to say, but he was interrupted by the whine of more sirens in the distance.

'Jinx, we have to get out of here,' I said urgently. 'Can't you make them sleep?'

He gave me a puzzled frown.

'Jinx! Can you remember how to freeze people in time?'

The sirens were almost upon us, and from the expression on my Deathbringer's face I might as well have been speaking a foreign language.

It was too late – two more cars screeched to a halt behind us:

Jaguars, with blue flashing lights behind the front grids. I grabbed Jinx's hand. If they contained police officers, I was Coco the Clown.

Three men climbed out of each car, and when one ran round to the back of the second to open the door I wasn't at all surprised to see Persephone uncoil herself from the back seat and slither out.

'We'll take it from here, gentlemen,' she said, strutting around to stand in front of us.

'Excuse me, ma'am, but could you identify yourself?' the older cop said.

'Of course,' she said, and turned around to face him. There was a popping sound and a dark red hole appeared in the centre of his forehead.

My mouth dropped open: she had just shot *a policeman*! Before the other policemen, who were standing there equally stunned, had any chance to react, they were shot down in a hail of automatic gunfire from the two men who had climbed unnoticed out of the cars: Joseph and Gabriel.

'Jinx, darling,' Persephone said, smiling and holding out a hand towards him, 'we've been looking everywhere for you.'

I gave him a sideways glance, not daring to take my eyes off her little gun, which was now pointed straight at me.

He shivered.

'Jinx, darling, come here. Come to Persephone.'

His eyes dropped to the gun, and then to me. He moved slightly, still holding my hand, so he was standing between us.

'Jinx, come here.' She was still smiling, but it had become a little fixed.

He didn't move a muscle.

'Do you want to be punished? Do you want me to punish you?' Her voice was still silky-soft, but the colour highlighting her cheekbones gave away her anger.

Jinx's hand tightened on mine.

'You nasty, evil, *manipulative* bitch,' I said.

'You still here?' She glanced at me, then her attention returned to Jinx. 'I seem to remember I gave you a job to do. I suggest you get on and do it.'

'Not here,' a voice said, and Amaliel, swathed in his usual black hooded robe, was gliding towards us.

'I want her dead.'

'And so she will be, but not here, not now. We are too exposed. Anyway, there are certain rituals I'd like to take place.'

And the drawings of the little gold cages skittered through my head.

Persephone's lips curled into a sneer. 'Are they as important as ruling this world?'

'Well, my dear, you will have your Deathbringer, and I will have my Soulseer.'

'What about the Guardian?'

'If you want him you can have him,' Amaliel said, 'I have no use for him whatsoever.'

'So you say . . .'

Amaliel stiffened, then slowly turned to her. 'Do not for one minute forget who I am and what I have done for you: to do so would be the last mistake you will ever make.'

Her smile became more placatory. 'I won't. Really, I won't.'

This was cheering me up a mite: discord in Team Persephone? I liked this a lot, but the sound of more sirens and a helicopter in the distance put an abrupt end to their squabbling.

'We have to go,' Joseph said to Persephone. 'If we're found here now, it'll be game over.'

Her nose wrinkled with distaste and she swung around and stalked back to her car, calling over her shoulder, 'Jinx will come with me. You take the girl.'

'Go on then,' Gabriel said to Jinx, and, hanging the automatic weapon over his shoulder, grabbed hold of my wrist and, with the other hand, snatched the dagger from my belt and threw it to the ground.

Jinx still had hold of my hand, so I felt the sudden surge of power. 'Jinx!' I screamed, but it was too late.

The skin on Gabriel's face began to bubble and blacken. He let go of my wrist to grab for his throat as blood trickled out between his lips, then from his ears and even from his eyes, forming bloody trails down his cheeks.

The other men backed away, doing nothing to help him, even those I guessed were Sicarii. Gabriel sank to his knees still clutching his throat, and with a flick of his wrist, Jinx sent another surge of power radiating out from him, knocking some of the men off their feet.

There was a *rat-a-tat-a-tat* of automatic gunfire and Jinx staggered slightly. I looked around to see one of the humans leaning against a police car, his gun still raised.

'*No!*' I screamed, and the beast inside my head screamed too. It was almost as if Jinx and I were standing in the eye of a hurricane while the world went spinning around us. A police car flipped up on its end, and bodies went tumbling over and over as they flew away from us. There was a roaring in my ears and a pressure inside my head as my inner daemon yelled out her displeasure.

Then the wind dropped, the earth stood still and an eerie silence surrounded us. There were wrecked cars all around us, and broken bodies, some human, some definitely daemon. Jinx had hold of my hand so tightly I was in danger of losing all feeling in my fingers.

Someone began to moan and twisted metal began to creak. Once again I could hear sirens and helicopters in the distance.

'Come on,' I said to Jinx, 'we've got to go.'

He didn't move a muscle.

'Jinx?' I said, looking up at him.

He had his free hand clutched to his stomach and I could see blood seeping between his fingers and dripping to the ground in a steady patter.

'Oh my God—'

'He won't be helping us,' he said, and started towards the side road we'd been making for when we'd been surrounded.

We passed the human with the gun. He was lying in a crumpled heap with his neck bent at a very peculiar angle. I looked away. *I had killed him.* I had taken a human life. Would Jamie and his Guardians be hunting me down now?

I glanced at Jinx and realised I didn't care. I'd always been the good girl; I'd always played by the rules – and look where it'd got me.

I heard a voice cry out behind us, 'They're getting away, you fools – *stop them!*'

Persephone. Why couldn't she have been one of the broken bodies? But that would have been too much to hope for.

We started to run, and a couple of the Sicarii who were still standing came shambling after us, but the whine of sirens and the pounding of rotor blades was getting closer and they quickly gave up. I heard car doors slam: Persephone's Jag had been the furthest away from us, and it had remained on all four wheels, so she wouldn't even have to face the music for the deaths of the policemen. I suspected the blame for that would somehow end up planted squarely on our shoulders; they had been trying to arrest us for a reason, after all.

The helicopter was getting dangerously close. I didn't want us to be seen running away from a crime scene – if they spotted us there would be no hiding from them, not with all their technology.

'We have to get under cover,' I said urgently, and as if to make the point I heard a car turn into the road behind us. Persephone and Amaliel weren't about to give up so easily.

Nor was I. The road curved to the left then came to a T-junction with a boarded-up pub on one corner and a post box on the other. Straight ahead was a six-foot-high hedge.

'Can you jump it?'

Jinx's reply was to throw his arm around me, run straight at the hedge and jump. We cleared it by a good foot, but when we landed he went down on one knee, pulling me down with him and almost pitching forward. I shuffled around so I was facing him and pulled open his coat. It was worse than I thought. A line of bullet holes that would have probably cut a human in half ran across his stomach from above his right hip to just below the left side of his ribcage.

'They will heal,' he said, but he didn't look so good.

'We need to find somewhere to hide out.'

He nodded, and fell straight into my arms. We weren't going anywhere. I pulled him as far under the overgrown hedge as I could, so we wouldn't be obvious from above, but I could hear the purr of an idling engine from the road behind us where Persephone's Jaguar had stopped.

'They can't have gone far,' I heard her say. 'You two, check that pub. Break in if you have to.'

'The Deathbringer is injured,' a Sicarii hissed.

'Idiots.'

'It was your human who fired upon him,' Amaliel said. It sounded like they were all standing in the road.

After a bit we heard footsteps, and someone snarled, 'Nothing.'

'We can't hang about here any longer,' Persephone snapped, 'the police will be all over the place.' And with that, one car door slammed, then the other; the engine growled and the car pulled away.

We'd had a reprieve, but it wouldn't be for long. The police would soon be combing the area, and when it got dark I was sure Persephone and Amaliel would be back with reinforcements. I had a decision to make: did Jinx and I try to go it alone, or did I risk trying to get help from Jamie?

I pulled the mobile phone from my pocket. It had been vibrating on and off all morning, but I'd ignored it. There were half a dozen missed calls, a couple of texts and the battery was almost done for, so it was now or never.

I scrolled through the contacts, my finger hovering over Jamie's name: I so wanted to hear his voice – but I couldn't trust him, not with Jinx's life. And who exactly was that woman I'd seen him with? All my senses were telling me that I couldn't trust her. So who could I trust? They would no doubt all be together, so if I called one of them, the rest would know. There was only one person I *knew* I could trust to keep my secret; I had to hope he would understand.

I need your help – please don't tell the others – particularly not Jamie.

I stared down at the message, almost deleted it . . . but pressed send before I changed my mind. Then there was nothing I could do but sit and wait.

I could still hear sirens, and a chopper passed overhead several times, but it didn't start circling, so I didn't think we'd been spotted. I hoped they wouldn't bring in police dogs. I didn't want them meeting sticky ends should Jinx wake up.

As Persephone had predicted, it hadn't taken too long for the police to search the road. They stopped about where Persephone and Amaliel had stood and had a similar conversation.

'The bastards can't have gone far.'

'Well, they're certainly not here.'

'Nothing adds up.'

'Eight of ours are dead: eight of ours who were *fully armed* with weapons drawn. Two cars are flipped onto their roofs – and everyone's denying all knowledge of why they were even here!'

'I don't care about the whys or wherefores, I just want to find the bastards who did this.'

'I was just saying——'

'Well, don't.'

'Guv, Hawkins, Davis and Brent are searching the pub, but there's nothing else here. These hedges are harder than prison walls to get through – and anyway, there's no broken branches or anything: we've checked three miles in either direction, both sides of the road. We have to face it, they've gone. It's the middle of fucking nowhere – they must've had a vehicle.'

'They must have had a fucking tank, the amount of damage they've done.'

'Then why did they stop?' and the conversation rumbled on as they walked back the way they'd come.

Jinx's wounds stopped bleeding about an hour after he'd been shot and I swear I could see them beginning to heal – although they still looked really nasty.

I kept checking my phone, but there was nothing: if he didn't contact me soon it would be too late; I'd have run out of battery. Maybe he didn't understand how to use the thing properly – Jamie and I had given all my daemon guards a lesson, but it had been pretty cursory. Perhaps he was in an area with no signal – or maybe he just couldn't get away.

Then, just when I'd given up all hope, my mobile finally pinged.

Are you well? Is the DB with you? Where are you?

Yes – yes – not sure. Near deserted pub called

—I had to think for a second; what the hell had it been called?

the Wheatsheaf near a place called Chelwood Gate

I pressed send.

I need to tell the G

No!

Without his help, how can I help you?

Shenanigans was right: I should never have involved him – but who else was there?

I had started to tap in a reply when a hand gripped my wrist.

'What are you doing?' Jinx growled.

'I'm trying to get help.'

He snatched the mobile from my hand.

'*No!*' I shouted as he flung the phone across the field. I watched it arc in the air and fall. 'We need help,' I said, attempting to stand, but he pulled me back down.

'No.'

'You're hurt.'

'I'm healing.'

'You don't remember me – I doubt you even remember your own name.'

'Jinx – you call me Jinx.'

'Do you remember me?'

He gave me a nasty look. 'If you were important to me, I would.'

He might as well have stabbed me in the heart; the pain those few words caused me couldn't have made me feel any worse.

Although he was no longer *my* Jinx he must have seen something in my expression that made him pause. 'You are special to me?'

'Apparently not . . .' I said, my heart breaking into a million pieces. 'Apparently not as much as you are to me.' I turned away from him.

He took hold of my chin and cocked his head to one side, a gesture so familiar to me that it made me want to weep. He sometimes looked so much like one of the ravens he sent forth as spies for him. Even as my heart was being torn asunder, I wondered if it was the same here.

I would never have believed the day would come when I wished we could return to the Underlands and never come back to the world that used to be my home – but that was exactly how I felt right now. The Overlands was as strange and alien to me as the moon.

'Tell me your name,' he said.

I shook my head. 'You either remember it or you don't.'

A hand closed about mine. 'I will try,' he said.

Fourteen

After I heard the slam of the pub door, the receding sound of loud disgruntled voices and boots on tarmac was replaced by birdsong and the occasional bleating of sheep in an adjoining field. To add to our misery, it began to rain again; a gentle patter fast turned into a steady drumbeat.

I'd had enough. I stood up and made myself a tiny eye-sized small gap in the hedge. The road ahead was empty. I could see blue flashing lights still colouring the sky beyond the distant hedgerows: the police would have more than enough to do at the crime scene. It was interesting – this lot of policemen were as surprised as I'd been that the men who'd stopped us had been carrying guns; it looked like Persephone really did have friends in very high places.

'We have to get under cover,' I told Jinx, and with a lot of effort, he clambered to his feet, pointedly ignoring my hand – although he took it soon enough when he was standing.

'I think we should chance hiding out in the pub for a few hours, at least until it gets dark. They've searched it once, so I doubt they'll search it again.' I was hoping this was true; I was also hoping Shenanigans might somehow find us, and I was beginning to not really care overmuch whether he brought Jamie with him or not. I'd cross that bridge when I came to it.

Jinx had stopped answering me again, and I was worried he'd shut down like he had before. Could I ever fix what they had done to him? I had to push those negative thoughts out of my head; they were too unbearable to contemplate.

We had to walk a lot further than I'd wanted before we found a way to double back to the pub, by which time the rain was falling in stair-rods, turning the tarmac oil-slick black. The pub really was called the Wheatsheaf, so I'd at least got that right, although I had no idea how near Chelwood Gate was; I'd seen a signpost for it, but it could have been miles away.

The Sicarii and the police had both broken into the pub through the back door, and neither of them had done a very good job of securing it afterwards, which was lucky for us. Once inside, I could see why. The place had been gutted, and it was obvious from the mess of polystyrene cups, fast-food containers and beer cans that the local kids had been hanging out here for a while.

The windows were all boarded up, so it was dark and gloomy inside – I did try the light switch, hoping for a miracle, but we were all out of those.

I left Jinx sitting on the bottom step of the staircase while I went up to investigate. I found a living room with a kitchenette; the sink was still there, but the water was turned off. There were two bedrooms, both stripped to bare floorboards, but there was an old mattress and sleeping bag in one, so someone had obviously been using it, sleeping rough, maybe, or getting down and dirty . . . the phrase 'beggars can't be choosers' came to mind and vanished just as quickly: there was no way on earth I was going to sleep there! The very thought made my skin crawl.

By the makeshift bed was an old shoebox, an empty water bottle and a flame-blackened jam jar with a stub of a candle in it, which I appropriated.

Then I found the bathroom. I took one look and turned away, gagging. Some people were just plain *disgusting*.

I trudged back down the stairs: we had shelter from the rain and that was the sum of it – but there was nowhere else available, so it would have to do. I doubted Jinx would care; he didn't care about anything very much any more – me included.

But Jinx was no longer on the bottom step where I'd left him. He wasn't in the bar, either – then I noticed the trapdoor to the beer cellar was open, and shuddered. I really didn't want to have to go down there into the pitch-black. I hesitated at the top and called, 'Jinx, are you down there?'

Silence.

I crouched down and peered into the blackness. 'Jinx? Hello?'

More silence.

'Bloody man,' I muttered. I stood up and looked at my candle in its jar. Without matches it was as useless as the disconnected electricity. There was nothing around me, but I remembered the shoebox next to the mattress – maybe I'd get lucky.

I hurried back upstairs to the bedroom and examined the box. I took a deep breath and slowly exhaled. I *really* didn't want to go poking around in someone else's stuff . . . I gritted my teeth and lifted the lid.

The good news: it was doubtful the recent occupant was a druggie – underneath an unopened packet of condoms were four candles and a Swiss Army penknife, all of which I pocketed, and – praise be to Jesus Christ and all his apostles! – a box of matches. I was almost too scared to pick it up, just in case it was empty, but when I shook it, it rattled. Then that little voice in my head suggested, *I bet he was one of those arseholes who put the dead ones back in the box*. I slid the box open: half full, and even in the dim light I could see every single one was unused.

I hurried back downstairs and paused at the top of the cellar steps to light a candle, then carefully made my way down, flinching as the wood beneath my feet creaked. I made it down to the bottom with no mishaps and held up the candle to take a look around. The flickering light revealed a stack of crates in one corner, and a few sagging cardboard boxes. I slowly swung around, lifting the candle so the light could penetrate the furthest recesses. Jinx was sitting wedged into the corner at the far end, legs pulled up in front of him, his forehead resting on his knees and his arms wrapped around them, like he was trying to make himself as small as possible.

'Jinx?'

His arms pulled his legs in even closer.

'Jinx, what's wrong?' I hurried over and dropped down beside him. I reached out to touch his shoulder – it must have been a reflection of the candle's flame, because the green stone in my mother's ring appeared to glow for a moment.

Jinx groaned and slowly raised his head. 'She's calling to me,' he said, and I didn't have to ask who 'she' was.

'Can she find us here?'

'She—' He grimaced and pressed a hand against his temple. 'She won't let me go. She hurts—' He groaned through gritted teeth.

'There must be *something* we can do.' I remembered the terrible pains I'd felt in my head before – I had assumed Amaliel had been torturing him, but perhaps it had been her?

He cried out again and stumbled to his feet.

I hurried back to the stairs, dripped some wax on a step halfway up and stuck the candle to it so I had my hands free. I wanted to help him, but how? He jerked upright, his head pulled back, arms dead straight and extended behind him, and the air grew thick – my ears felt like they were full of cotton wool. I reached a hand out towards him – and the stone in my ring glowed with some sort of inner light as blue flames sprang from the cellar floor and began to creep up my Deathbringer's body.

How was she doing that? She wasn't even here, but she was enclosing him in Blue Fire? 'Oh no, you bloody don't!' I swore as my inner daemon flexed her muscles and roared, and I roared with her as I *changed*.

Just as before, golden light flowed from my body and flew out from my fingers, smashing into the blue light encircling his body. As soon as it touched the Blue Fire, it flared up in a great sheet of flame. After a moment it fizzled and died, leaving a black stain on the ground around his feet.

Jinx fell to one knee, but when he looked up his eyes were glowing with life and he managed a bit of a smile. 'Tell me your name.'

'I told you, you either know me or you don't,' I said, crossing my arms.

'I think I might like to, very much,' he said, looking me up and down, taking in my daemonic appearance.

My heart gave a little leap.

'She won't give up,' he said.

'Nor will I,' I told him. 'That's why I'm here.'

'We have to leave.'

'It's not dark yet.'

'We can't be here then; she is so much more powerful during the hours of darkness.'

'So she's the real deal?'

He took my hand and led me towards the stairs. 'She is not of this world.'

I stopped, pulling him to a halt. 'What do you mean? She's *daemon*?'

His forehead creased. 'I have no words.'

If that was true, we were in deeper trouble than any of us had thought. I stuffed the candles and matches back in my pocket and as we headed for the back door, I heard something hit the floor with a metallic clatter. Then it happened again, and I dropped to my knees and started feeling around for whatever it was. The only thing I could find was a little lump of metal.

I held it out to Jinx – just as he flinched, and I pulled aside his coat to see another bullet pushing out through his skin. The puckered pink hole pulled together and closed, leaving a small wrinkled depression.

'Better out than in, I suppose,' I told him.

While we'd been in the pub, the bad weather had closed in and the sky was a mass of black clouds. It felt like the gods were conspiring against us – and just to confirm it, the moment we stepped outside, the wind began to howl, thunder rumbled and lightning flashed across the sky.

'Are you sure this is a good idea?' I paused at the back door.

'She knows where we are. We must keep moving.'

'Will she be able to follow us?'

His expression grew bleak. 'Probably.'

We walked out of the pub with no idea where we were going, but Jinx said firmly, 'We go right.'

'Any reason why?'

'The left-hand path is always favoured by evil.'

The memory of all those Dennis Wheatley novels resurfaced. 'Yes, let's go right.'

This time he put his arm around me as we walked – I'd've liked to think it was because he wanted to hold me, but I suspected it had more to do with keeping me close so I couldn't suddenly bail on him. Not that I would have; it wasn't his fault he didn't remember me. It wasn't *his* fault we were in this mess.

We trudged along the road as the dingy afternoon darkened to twilight and then to night. The rain was so heavy we could see no more than a few feet ahead; I doubted this would hinder Persephone much in her search for us – I'd never heard of black magic and witchcraft being dependent upon the weather.

When we came to a hamlet, just one tiny shop-cum-off-licence and two or three farms, I shouted, 'We can't keep walking all night!' The rain was coming down so hard and the wind was so strong I doubted he'd heard me, but I was wrong.

He stopped and put his mouth to my ear so I could hear: 'This is unnatural weather. She is calling upon the elements.'

I swiped my sopping hair from my face. 'She's *causing* this?'

He looked up at the sky and nodded. 'She uses darkness.'

I'd grown to understand daemons and their world, but this black magic was something else entirely. That I was using some unknown power of my own which I didn't really understand wasn't making me feel any better – but the dark side of me was craving a confrontation with Persephone: she had tried to take Jinx from me and given half a chance, I would take her down.

My kickass bravado lasted about fifteen minutes as I fantasised sending her flying across rooms and into brick walls until she flopped unconscious to the ground – but then my little inner voice pointed out that although it was possible I *could* do this, I didn't actually know *how*. When the moment came I might well be full of fury and revenge, only to find my inner daemon refused to come out to play.

We came to a huge sign announcing Farm for Sale by Auction, and I pulled Jinx's sleeve to get his attention. Moving in close so I could make him hear me over the storm, I cried, 'It's worth a try.'

He didn't respond but let me lead him down the lane. I hoped there'd be at least an empty barn; somehow we had to get out of the torrential rain.

Muddy rivers gushed down the gullies on either side of the narrow road, and in a couple of places we had to wade through rainwater surging up past our ankles. The sky above us crashed and banged, zigzags of white light flashing bright enough to illuminate the countryside. Jinx was right: this wasn't natural weather. *Who on earth was Persephone?*

The farm was in complete darkness and as soon as we stepped through the gate and into the yard I could see the place was derelict: the farmhouse windows were smashed and the door kicked in, and I had a moment of anger at people who could so willingly destroy the property of others for no real reason other than just because they could.

I had a quick look inside, but the floor above had collapsed into the hallway and water was running in a steady stream down the walls. I led Jinx towards the cowshed looming out of the darkness instead, but that had fared no better: someone had tried to burn it down and it stank of wet bonfire. The concrete floor was littered with half-burned wood and straw. I was beginning to think we had wasted our time, and the thought of the return trudge along the lane – when a moment ago I'd had hopes of finding shelter – had my spirits dropping again. But we were free, and I wasn't about to give up. We would find somewhere.

We plodded past a couple more ruined buildings and I was wondering whether I should go back and investigate the rest of the ruined farmhouse when Jinx suddenly picked up his pace and took the lead, moving through a gap in a broken fence into yet another open field.

He kept walking, and I squinted past him through the driving rain to see what had piqued his interest, but nothing was obvious. Then ahead, I saw a grey shadow taking shape: a stable block. We weren't walking through a field but a paddock, and I could just about make out the remains of a couple of jumps and other paraphernalia surrounding us like the skeletons of long-dead beasts.

The local yobs apparently hadn't made it this far. I hurried to catch up with Jinx and was by his side when he pushed open the door.

I lit one of my precious candles so we could look around. The people who'd lived here had taken their horses seriously: backing onto the stable block was a tack room and an inside exercise arena. The aromas of hay and horse manure still tainted the air, but it was dry and several degrees warmer than outside. Even so, I was shivering with cold. Bugger the risk of burning the place down; I was going to try and make a fire.

I scraped together a pile of straw and when I went in search of something I could use for firewood I found a stack of painted wooden poles and some broken fencing panels that had once been used for jumps. After Jinx's short burst of enthusiasm, he had shut down again. He slumped back against the tack-room wall and stared into space as I lit the fire and then looked around for anything that might be useful. Horse blankets would have been good – though I realised that was probably too much to ask – because we really needed to get out of our wet clothes so they could dry out a bit.

I made a rough and ready clothes horse out of some of the poles and stripped off my jacket and jumper and hung them up in front of the fire. I even managed to persuade Jinx to give me his coat, and when I turned back after hanging it up to dry I found he had pulled off his boots and was taking down his trousers.

'Okayyy,' I said, taking them from him, then thought, *What the hell!* and took off my own boots and jeans, although I did keep my underwear on.

Without his coat I could see other scars marking his body that hadn't been there before. Like the bullet wounds, they were fast disappearing, but the evidence of his torture was clearly visible. I clenched my teeth and went to gather some hay from the stalls. I *would* make Amaliel pay, but now was not the time to let my anger get the better of me. I focused instead on piling up the hay for us to sit on. It was a bit prickly, and it stuck to our wet skin, but it was far better than sitting on cold concrete. I dropped down next to Jinx – close but not too close. We should probably be sharing body heat, but given the circumstances, I wasn't at all sure that would be a good idea. My Jinx wouldn't have been able to let this opportunity pass us by; he would have had me wrapped within his arms in moments and be kissing me senseless.

I sat there staring into the flames and wondered where Jamie and the others were, and why Kayla hadn't found me yet. Now I had the time to think about it, I realised that was weird: *where was she?*

Exhaustion finally took its toll and I slipped into the dark.

I woke from a nightmare, my eyes heavy. Judging by the fire, I must have been asleep for only a few minutes; even so, a maroon arm was around my shoulders and my cheek was resting against his chest. I don't know if he realised I was awake, but he pulled me closer, and the warmth of his skin against mine felt so good I didn't try to pull away. I closed my eyes again and drifted off.

In my dream I was being buried alive. I could feel the weight of the earth crushing down on my chest as I struggled against it – then my head hit concrete and I was awake, and a pair of maroon hands were clamped around my throat.

Jinx lifted himself up so he was astride my waist, his fingers pressing harder and harder. My lungs screamed for breath – my windpipe was being crushed and darkness was rapidly enveloping me. I pummelled his chest with my fists, fast losing any strength I once had. My head hit the ground again in an explosion of stars and it dawned on me that I really was about to die. *Jinx was going to kill me.*

No! I screamed inside my head. *No!* It was *not* going to end like this! I made a fist and for the second time in as many days, punched him as hard as I could in the groin – he didn't have the protection of his leather trousers this time, which made my pathetic blow effective enough to make him gasp and let go – unfortunately, it also reminded him that he was naked, and I was pinned beneath him.

He took hold of my chin with one hand and forced my head back so I was looking up at him as he snarled down at me. His other hand grabbed the front of my bra.

'No,' I gasped at him, 'Jinx, don't do this! *Don't do this*—' My throat felt like it was red-raw, but if I didn't speak, he wouldn't hear me. '*Jinx!*' And I slapped him as hard as I could across the side of his face.

I don't think he even felt it. He glared down at me as he lowered his head towards mine until his hair was cocooning both our faces in a veil of black. I closed my eyes. I didn't want to see him when he was like this. His lips crushed against mine, and I knew if I survived the night, I would have bruises on my chin where he was holding it so tight.

I lay still, saving my strength for when it mattered. I'd let him have his kiss, but I'd fight him for the rest. He lifted his head slightly, but I kept my eyes screwed shut. His lips touched mine again, but this time they were soft and gentle. The fingers gripping my chin relaxed and his thumb swept up to caress my cheek. Then his arms were around me, pulling me up against him and holding me tightly to his chest. He was still astride me, but he'd dropped back so he was straddling my legs.

He caressed my hair, he kissed my cheek. He pressed his face into the crook of my neck and his shoulders began to heave.

'Jinx?' I whispered.

'Forgive,' he said against my neck, his voice a harsh whisper, 'forgive me. I thought you were her. I thought . . .'

I stroked his hair and cupped the back of his head. 'Do you remember my name?'

'I will. Promise, I will.'

I let my head rest against his. 'What happened?'

'She . . . she tries to fill my head—' And he shuddered and pressed a palm against his temple. 'Hurts . . . *hurts*.'

I wrapped my arms around him and cradled him to me as he began to rock back and forth. 'Hurts so much.'

His head slipped down to rest against my breasts as I held him. He groaned again, but there was nothing I could do to help, just hold him tight. My hand slipped down from his hair to stroke his skin and my fingertips found raised ridges of puckered flesh across his shoulders and running in lines down his back; his beautiful, finely sculpted back. I could have cried. The daemon inside me added her anger and outrage to mine.

In my mind I heard a voice that sounded remarkably like mine say, 'She's going to die.'

I took Jinx's damp coat down and wrapped it around the pair of us and eventually he slept. I didn't – I couldn't. I needed to be awake, in case she tried any more of her freaky mind games on him.

His sleep wasn't peaceful; he twitched and groaned for hours, but when I stroked his back or hair it calmed him. Why didn't she come? Jinx had told me she could find us, but maybe it was just his mind or his soul she could find . . . Jamie had told me the Blue Fire would bind Jinx to this world, and the ritual had bound him to either Persephone or Amaliel – or even both of the twisted psychos – but maybe they couldn't find his physical body.

I hoped that was the case, because otherwise we were likely to have a whole load of Sicarii descending on us anytime soon.

Jinx began to mutter and moan again. He was still asleep, but he was getting really agitated, and this time my touch was doing nothing to placate him. He started to shake – and then he went rigid and his eyes snapped open – blank eyes, but not for long. They lit up with an inner glow, not his familiar golden glow within the green but the dark, scarlet shimmer of someone else controlling him.

His lips curled into a nasty sneer. 'So, what are you going to do now?' he said. His lips were moving, the vocal cords and mouth were his, but the voice wasn't.

I stared into Persephone's eyes and forced a bitchy smile onto my lips. 'I'm here – you're not.'

The smile faltered, ever so slightly. 'He will kill you. I will make him choke the life out of you.'

'Really?' I said, getting to my feet. 'You tried that once before, but as you can see, I'm still here. Oh, and *you're not*.'

She glared up at me through his eyes. 'He's going to kill you,' she repeated.

'No, he isn't,' I said, praying to whatever gods might be listening that I was right. 'If anyone kills me, it will be you. He doesn't know what he's doing. So if I die' – I gave a nonchalant shrug – 'it won't be his fault, and he'll know it in his heart.'

His lips curled into a sneer. 'I knew you would be weak.'

'I pretty much guessed you'd be a bitch.'

'Why he should care so much for . . .?' She obviously realised she'd been about to say it out loud and his lips closed into a thin line. Jinx got to his feet and glowered at me. 'He's going to bring you to me, and when he does I'm going to make him take you apart, bit by bit. I'll make his hands do the work, and all the time he will know exactly what he's doing and he won't be able to stop himself. Let's see if your final words to him will be those of forgiveness.'

Bitch. 'You know what?'

Jinx frowned at me.

'You're as boring as you are unpleasant.' My inner daemon gave a little wriggle, like she was shaping up for a fight, and I hoped that meant she was about to give me a hand. I forced my lips into a feline smile and held my hand out to my Deathbringer. 'Jinx – tell her to go. You really don't want her in your head right now.'

His green and golden eyes flamed, as did the ring on my outstretched hand; although I didn't have time to give that much thought as he strode towards me. She was still inside him. She raised his hand and it drew back in a fist, and I forced myself not to flinch away.

'Jinx,' I whispered, raising my other hand as if welcoming him into my arms, really hoping he would still be able to hear me. 'Jinx—' And my outstretched hands began to glow with a soft light, bathing the whole of my body in it.

Jinx stopped dead, his eyes growing wide, no doubt mirroring Persephone's surprise. 'Anything you can do . . .' I said, and the light spread across to Jinx and enveloped him in its radiance.

He snarled and fell to one knee, and when he looked up, she was gone.

'Lucky I have you,' he said. 'You're a lucky lady.'

I took him by both hands and pulled him to his feet. 'I am *your* lucky lady,' I told him and he stepped into my arms and I hugged him to me.

He fell asleep with his head on my shoulder again. I pulled his coat up to cover us and pondered on our dilemma. Jamie had told me that as the Guardian, he policed the interactions between the Under- and Overlands, and that he had been led to me that first time by all the daemonic activity that had suddenly sprung up around me. If this was the case, why weren't he and his Guardian mates crawling all over this place? Between Persephone and me, we must have caused enough activity for *someone* to notice.

And Kayla was very conspicuous by her absence. She had told me she could find me anywhere; that she'd always be drawn to me – and yet here we were, and she wasn't. She might already be dead, but if she could be trapped by the Blue Fire, she could also be encased in one of Amaliel's phials – and if that happened, I didn't know if I could get her out again.

Jinx moaned softly in his sleep and snuggled closer. He rested his left hand on my right shoulder and I kissed the top of his head and pulled the coat a bit snugger – and in doing so, I noticed the ring on my finger, gleaming in the light from the fire. There was no gold and red flame in its centre like I'd seen before, and surely if it was likely to catch the light in such a way, it would be now, as we lay bathed in flickering firelight. It was strange.

I studied it for a little longer, then I wondered what the time was. It felt like it must be two or three in the morning, so we had three or four hours before it got light ... we should really get on the move again before then, but I had no idea where we should go.

We couldn't go to our friends for help, as they'd no doubt be surrounded by Guardians, and our forty-eight hours' grace had definitely run out. We couldn't go back to the Underlands – mainly because I didn't know how to get there on my own. No one had ever thought to tell me how it worked, and I wasn't sure Jinx would remember. I wasn't even sure he knew who and what he was; he certainly hadn't recognised his own name. And added to all that was the knowledge he could turn on me at any moment. It was such a bloody mess.

Jinx let out another low moan and began to twitch against me. I stroked his hair and murmured softly to him, 'Hush now. Everything's all right.'

It didn't have the desired effect and I knew this probably meant Persephone was having another go at him.

He sat up with a jerk, his breathing harsh and rapid, as if he'd woken from a bad dream, and sat there panting and staring into space while I stroked his arm, hoping it was having a calming effect.

Then he looked down at me and said, 'Kayla says to tell you hello—' and slumped back onto the hay, pressing his fists into his screwed-up eyes.

Fifteen

It was as if every time Persephone entered his head, a little bit more of him was chipped away. For a short time, I'd thought my Jinx had almost come back to me; sadly, judging by the way he was acting since he'd woken, he'd gone again.

She was clearly making him suffer: he shuddered periodically, and kept pressing his hands to his temples. I tried talking to him, but couldn't get a word from him. If she was doing it to confuse and disorientate him, she was succeeding very nicely.

Why she would do this when her objective was for me to give myself up to her to save Kayla, I had no idea – perhaps it was to punish me?

It was no good; I had little choice now. I would have to find Jamie and try to convince him that Jinx was no risk to the Overlands while he was in our hands. Of course, if he had a nightmare and tried to strangle me again, that would put paid to that argument – and if Jamie or the Guardians didn't kill him, Shenanigans or Pyrites would.

Part of me wanted to go and find Amaliel and Persephone – the nasty, vengeful part. I wanted to see both of them dragged down to Hell, or wherever the place might be that truly evil people were carted off to. Nothing would have pleased me more than to see the pair of them surrounded by those chattering, slithering dark nasties and being carried off into the nightmarish place where they lived.

But first I badly wanted to kick her shapely derrière.

'Come on,' I said, and took Jinx by the arm and pulled him to his feet.

'Dark,' he said, hugging himself.

'Didn't we agree it was better to travel when it's dark?'

He didn't reply, but squeezed his eyes shut and winced.

'Is she still hurting you?'

He gave the tiniest of nods.

'Will it be better when it gets light?'

'Not so easy for her,' he whispered.

He looked so miserable, and I wished with all my heart that there was something I could do to help him, but any powers I had were for helping the dead . . . or were they? I'd freed both Kayla and Jinx from the Blue Fire; maybe I *could* free him from her control. I felt like I was clutching at straws; surely if I could, I'd have broken her hold over him when I'd released him that first time?

'Well, it's worth a try.' I stood up straight, closed my eyes and concentrated, but my inner daemon remained silent. I focused on Jinx, and imagined surrounding him in golden light. *Nothing.* I stretched out my hands towards him, praying for a little inspiration. *Still nothing.*

It was no good. It had been worth a pop, but now we needed to get moving. But I had no idea where we should go — and did it really matter if we waited until it got light? Then again, maybe once she had connected to him, she could get clues from inside his head, find where we were hiding out?

That spurred me on. 'Come on. If she finds us here, we're done for.'

Jinx drew himself up straight, took a deep breath and gave another small nod. He tried to hand me his coat. 'Cold,' he said.

'I have a jacket, and besides' — I gestured to his body — 'it's probably best we keep you covered up as much as possible.'

He chuckled; it might have been a small one, but that laugh lifted my spirits. 'You too,' he said, and the twinkle in his eyes might not have been quite so bright as it used to be, but there was still a twinkle.

When I looked down, my hands were glowing daemon-rose, and when I tried to make myself change back into my human disguise I just couldn't do it. 'We're not going to get far looking like this,' I told him.

He pulled on the coat and then took my hand. 'Does it matter?'

'Jinx, I have to get you home.'

'You know how?'

'Do you?'

His smile disappeared. 'No.'

'So we keep moving until we think of a plan.'

'Or she captures us.'

I looked up at him as we walked out into the paddock and started towards the farmyard and the road beyond. 'It's not just Persephone and Amaliel we have to worry about.' I didn't think there was much point in me keeping this from him. 'Persephone wants to use you to—'

'Hurt people – I know this.'

'*Human* people.'

'I will not.'

'Jinx, you attacked me.'

His shoulders slumped. 'I thought you were her.'

I lifted his hand to my cheek, then pressed his fingers against my lips. 'There are some more of our kind, daemonkind, who are here in the Overlands. They also want to find you.'

His expression grew resigned and he started to walk again. 'They do not want to save me.' It wasn't a question.

'No,' I agreed.

'Then lucky I'm with you.'

'I guess.'

It was no longer raining, and I was hoping that was because Persephone had worn herself out. All this mind-control and calling upon the powers of nature must be exhausting – which set me thinking once again about who she was. Humans couldn't do this sort of thing, not even high priestesses of Satanic covens. It just wasn't possible.

'Jinx, you said Persephone wasn't of this world – who is she? *What* is she?'

'Like us. She conjures Blue Fire,' he said and we started walking again.

'Jamie said there have been humans who could do this.'

'Jamie?'

'The Guardian.'

Jinx didn't appear any the wiser. 'He's wrong.' He paused for a moment. 'Who's Kayla?'

'My friend.'

'Persephone has her.'

'I can't understand how. I helped her escape the Blue Fire once before.'

'Once bound by its magic it's easier to be captured again. It lingers.'

'I have to save her.'

'Then we should find Persephone.'

'Yeah, right; so she can use you to kill millions.'

'She wanted death – maybe I should give it to her.' This time when he smiled it was a full-on Jinx smile. 'Give her taste of own medicine.'

We trudged on until we reached the lane, thankfully no longer under water, and then onto the road. It was still dark, though probably not for much longer; the birds were already beginning to stir in the trees.

I pondered on what Jinx had told me. His idea of attacking her before she had a chance to attack us might have cheered him up, but it scared the proverbial shit out of me.

As we walked, every now and then I gave him a surreptitious glance. He wasn't wincing and grimacing so often, and he'd lost that vacant look, which had to be good.

An owl hooted in the distance and there was a rustling in the trees ahead. Jinx stopped dead in his tracks. 'How long until dawn?'

'Not very, I wouldn't have thought. The birds are waking—'

Jinx was turning in a circle, his eyes searching the sky. 'Not only birds,' he said. 'We need to find shelter.'

He grabbed hold of my hand and began to run, pulling me along beside him.

'What's wrong?' I panted.

'Not just birds,' he repeated.

The foliage on either side of the road began to shiver and shake, and at first I thought maybe Persephone was playing with the elements again. Unfortunately for us, she'd come up with another way to torment us, which could only mean she knew where we were.

There was a whooshing sound, and when I looked back over my shoulder, the canopies of the trees behind us exploded up into the sky, turning it black as thousands of creatures erupted outwards into the air and swept towards us in a chattering wave.

The one glance was enough. With my eyes fixed ahead, I clung onto Jinx's hand for dear life and *ran*. The road was deserted – it wasn't much more than a country lane closed in on either side by trees and hedgerow, so we were trapped inside a narrow channel.

The sound of fluttering wings grew louder; they were almost upon us. *They're only bats*, I kept telling myself, *they can't possibly hurt us*. Then one faster than the others hit me on the shoulder, which made me stumble. They may have been tiny, but even the smallest and lightest of creatures are dangerous when travelling at speed. Then another hit me, and another.

We are so fucked, I thought as several hit me all at once, sending me staggering.

Jinx threw his arm around my shoulders and pushed us to the ground. He lay over me, covering our heads with his coat, but even so, I could feel the creatures dive-bombing us, their delicate bones shattering as they hit our backs until the weight of their dead bodies weighed down upon us. Then a crow let out a raucous cry, and another answered, their strident squawking overriding the bats' high-pitched squeaking.

'Stay still,' he said against my ear as the bombardment changed and heavier bodies started raining down; now I could feel claws digging into my legs and short, sharp nips as beaks pecked at me. Jinx had us cocooned within his coat, but how long would it hold out beneath their relentless onslaught? My ears rang with their cries, and I felt something hot and wet running down my right calf. Jinx crawled on top of me; trying to protect me.

In a moment of clarity amongst the chaos I realised Persephone had found us and was pinning us down until she could get here — we had to do something, but if we tried to stand, we'd be overwhelmed by sheer numbers.

Then I felt something tapping away against the crown of my head, even through the coat — at first it was like an irritating drumbeat, but within seconds it had become painful as the beak pecked through the leather. Jinx hugged me closer; if I was in pain, I knew he must *really* be suffering.

All I could hear was the crows; I couldn't even hear my own breathing. We were beleaguered, with no way of escape. I wriggled my arm from underneath me and searched for Jinx's free hand. Our fingers touched and I felt him stretch to press his fingertips against mine.

'I love you,' I whispered, doubting he could hear, but feeling the need to actually say the words. If Persephone took us, I would never have another chance.

'And I—'

But he didn't finish what he was about to say, because there was a roar above us that made the ground shudder, followed by the panicked flapping of wings; the squawking became shrill cawing and then there was silence, apart from the thudding of more bodies falling like huge hailstones.

My heart soared: I'd recognise that roar anywhere.

There was a nudge at my head, someone trying to lift the coat, and the acrid smell of burning reached my nose, then it was overwhelmed by the familiar smell of liquorice as a long, rough tongue swiped the side of my face.

'Pyrites!' I cried and struggled to crawl out from beneath the body pressing me into the earth.

Jinx lifted himself up and I heard a muffled, 'Urgh.' Pyrites' tongue had obviously found my Deathbringer too.

'Stupid sod,' I heard him say; the first time he'd sounded anything like my old Jinx since I'd found him, and I managed a quick look back at him as I got up onto my knees before Pyrites tried to wash my face off. Jinx's expression was one of puzzlement and I heard him mutter, 'Where did that come from?'

We were surrounded by the dead bodies of bats and birds; some of the crows still had wisps of smoke floating up from their burned feathers.

'Pyrites, can you take us away from here?'

He got down on his stomach and batted his eyelids at me.

'Come on,' I said, taking Jinx by the arm and pulling him towards my drakon.

Jinx hung back.

'What?'

Jinx frowned at me.

'Don't you remember Pyrites?'

His forehead creased with concentration. 'I . . . I remember . . .' His shoulders slumped. 'It's gone.'

I laid my palm on his chest. 'It will come back.'

'I hope so,' he said, and he sounded so dejected that it almost broke my heart.

I stroked his cheek. 'If it doesn't, we'll just have to make you new memories,' I told him. 'Good memories.'

His lips twitched into a small smile. 'If they're of times spent with you, you'll have no complaint from me.'

'I should hope not,' I replied as he helped me up onto Pyrites and clambered on behind me. After a moment he wrapped his arms around my waist.

'This is nice also,' he whispered in my ear.

As soon as we were settled, Pyrites began to grow, but he stopped before he reached his full size – he knew he needed to be as inconspicuous as possible. Jamie had made it quite clear that a drakon flying around in the human land was not a good idea, but right now we didn't have any choice. We were only a few miles from Gatwick Airport, probably smack- bang in the middle of the flight path, so I really hoped it was early enough that there wouldn't be too much air traffic yet. I could just imagine the news coverage if we were spotted by someone on a plane.

Pyrites flapped over the hedge and into the adjoining field, giving himself a bit of room to manoeuvre, and then we were off – and not a moment too soon, because I spotted the lights of three vehicles hurtling along the narrow lane below us.

'Good boy,' I said, patting Pyrites' neck, and was rewarded with a purr.

Jinx rested his chin on my shoulder so he would be heard above the wind whistling past us. 'Would it not be a good idea for us to follow the vehicles? They may well lead us to Persephone and Amaliel.'

He was right: if we knew where they were hiding out, we could rescue Kayla and thwart Amaliel's ambitions. As for Persephone, if she was daemonkind, she had no business in this world either, so we would somehow have to send her back, or destroy her. Or maybe we could leave that to the Guardians – after all, wasn't that their job?

I leaned forward to call to Pyrites, 'Take us down.' My drakon puffed smoke, but did as he was told. As soon as we landed, he shrank so we could jump down, and then we huddled together while I explained what I thought we should do.

'There's nowhere we can go where we'll be safe,' I told them, 'so at least if we know where Amaliel and Persephone are holed up, we can take the battle to them.'

Pyrites puffed more smoke.

'What's the matter, lad?'

He gave Jinx a sideways look.

'Who sent you to find us? Was it Shenanigans?'

Pyrites bobbed his head.

'Does Jamie know?'

Pyrites gave a snort and rolled his eyes.

'He doesn't?'

Pyrites shook his head, but he didn't look very happy about it.

'You do know why he mustn't know?'

Pyrites gave Jinx another look, nodded and to my surprise pushed his head under Jinx's hand.

'He's on your side,' I told Jinx.

Jinx gave me a wry smile. 'No, he's on *your* side. If that means helping me, he'll do it.'

Pyrites bobbed his head in acknowledgement.

There wasn't much more to be said. We climbed back on Pyrites and he took to the skies. The cars had stopped in the middle of the lane, so we kept our distance – it was getting lighter quickly now, and we didn't want anyone looking up and seeing us outlined against the sky, or hearing the beat of powerful wings.

They didn't hang around for long, so Pyrites only needed to circle overhead a couple of times. They drove slowly until they found somewhere to turn around, then they set off at a foolhardy speed – but why should they worry? Unless the vehicle burst into flames, a car crash in this world was unlikely to hurt them; it was the unlucky humans who would be the losers in any collision. For a moment I considered how easy it would be for Pyrites to fly down and roast them – but he couldn't. They had Kayla.

Pyrites flew along behind them; not so low that he could be seen from the cars but not so high we were likely to be noticed by air traffic control – I hoped.

Once out of the lane they headed across country. I was thankful they kept away from the motorway, where flying low might be one distraction too many for any eagle-eyed drivers – a pile-up on the M23 was the last thing I wanted. They were heading towards the coast, in the general direction of Brighton, although I doubted that their hideout would be in the busy seaside town. As if to prove me right, the convoy below us soon turned inland.

Jinx leaned forward, his lips brushing my ear. 'You think you're such a clever little girl, don't you?' he whispered – but it wasn't him.

His arms, that had felt so comforting wrapped around me, tightened until it was painful to breathe. With one hand I tried to prise his arms away from my body. The other was busy holding on to Pyrites.

'Jinx,' I gasped, 'try and fight her.'

'Why should he fight me?' she asked and Jinx nipped my ear-lobe between his teeth. 'Especially when he knows what fun we're going to have with you.' Then he nipped me again, harder.

I tried to pull away, but he hugged me even tighter.

'Now, little bitch, you're to sit very still – don't even think about alerting your pet – if you do, not only will the Deathbringer bite off your ear, but I will see to it that several armed missiles are fired directly into his belly. I suspect not even a Jewelled Drakon could survive that.'

I relaxed back against Jinx. It was all I could do.

'Now, follow the vehicles and when they stop, get your pet beastie to land in the garden behind the house.' Jinx nipped my ear again. 'Understand?'

'Yes,' I said.

'Do you?' He bit my earlobe so hard he must have drawn blood.

'Yes!' I said through gritted teeth.

'Good. And Soulseer.' She paused. 'Don't try any tricks. If you do, I will hurt everyone you care for so very badly that you'll never sleep again without hearing their screams.'

Jinx suddenly slumped against me, and I had to hang onto his arm to stop him falling. When he regained consciousness, the lights were on, but nobody was home.

Persephone thought she was clever, but if she'd any sense at all, she would have waited until we'd almost reached our destination before pulling that little stunt. As it turned out, I had some time to push aside my panic and plan.

I knew for certain that Jinx and I would be taken prisoner, but I wasn't about to let her capture Pyrites – and if he could get away, he could alert Shenanigans and lead him to where we were. Of course, that meant Jamie and his Guardians were likely to get this information too, but it had to be done: loyal as he was, Shenanigans wouldn't risk me for Jinx, and neither would Pyrites.

I had been so sure Jinx was beginning to break free of Persephone. Now my naïve optimism was probably going to get us killed, or at the least, seriously hurt. She obviously had something nasty planned for me.

At last the vehicles pulled into a long winding drive leading up to yet another massive house with two wings that gave it an H shape, and a terrace overlooking a huge lake at the back. Being a Satanist was obviously very lucrative.

I left it to the last minute before leaning forward to give Pyrites his instructions, hoping Jinx couldn't overhear me.

'Pyrites, I know you won't like this, but you must do exactly as I say. Do you understand?' He puffed out dark grey smoke and his ears flicked back. 'As soon as we land, shrink to the size of a bird and get out of there. I need you to find the others and bring them as soon as you can. Preferably not Jamie and his Guardians, but if you can't lose him, so be it. Understand?'

He gave another puff, but it was black smoke – but that was all the time I had, as Jinx grabbed my arm and pulled me back.

'You wouldn't be up to something would you?' she asked, and I finally accepted I really might have lost Jinx for ever. If that was the case, there was no way I'd be able to protect him from Jamie and his angel army.

A little part of me withered and died.

Sixteen

Pyrites wasn't stupid; he landed on the far side of the lake and was away so quickly she and her people had no chance whatsoever of catching him. Feral Jinx was back; he grabbed my arm and started marching me around the edge of the lake towards the house as a Land Rover came bouncing across the grass towards us; *she* wasn't in it, but the hired help were. A human was driving, with a Sicarii in the passenger seat and two disciples in the back.

The two from the back piled out and Jinx got in of his own free will – although I suppose that was a bad choice of words: he had no free will any more, and when she wasn't inside his head, he was little more than a beast – how the hell had that happened again? I supposed a mind could only take so much tampering.

My heart was breaking. Even if Jamie and the others arrived in time to save me, Jinx was doomed, and if so, any future relationship with Jamie was too. I knew he had to do his duty – but I didn't have to like it, and I doubted I could live with it.

No one said anything, no sneered threats; nothing. The two disciples crammed in on either side of us were stone-faced, and once inside the car kept their eyes fixed on a point straight ahead. Even the grey-robed Sicarii sat there in silence.

The very human driver glanced at us in the rear-view mirror a couple of times and it was clear he didn't want to be there either. My curiosity was piqued: surely the Sicarii should be jubilant? They had the Deathbringer – a creature who could provide them with thousands of souls at the click of his fingers – back under their control. Yet the brooding silence told another story.

'So,' I said, deciding to test the water, perhaps even cause a little bit of mischief, 'how is it now Amaliel *and* Persephone are calling the shots?'

I felt the minion beside me stiffen. The wide eyes of the human reflected in the mirror were scared. He was not some fanatical Satanist, or if he had been, the allure had worn off. None of them replied.

'What are their plans? World domination? I don't suppose Persephone's interested in collecting souls – slaves maybe, but souls?' I wrinkled my nose. 'Nah, I doubt it.'

'Be silent, woman,' the Sicarii in the front said.

'I must admit I'm rather surprised Amaliel has taken on a partner – I mean, him being such a control freak himself.'

'I said, *be silent.*'

The disciple next to me shifted in his seat, but when I looked at him, he kept his reptilian snout and crocodile eyes straight ahead.

Jinx's hand dropped onto my knee and squeezed, but his expression was still angry. What the hell did that mean?

The car skidded to a halt at the back of the house, the two minions clambered out and Lizard Man grabbed me by the arm. As he half-dragged me from the car, Jinx slid out behind me, took hold of my other arm and snarled at the daemon, 'She's *mine.*'

Lizard Man flinched away from me as though I'd burned him.

The Sicarii led us silently up the stone steps to the patio behind the house and in through the open French windows. It was noticeable that the two minions following us were keeping their distance: what the hell was going on? I heard the Land Rover drive off. I suspected that given the choice, the driver would be heading for the main gate, and out. Morale was clearly not high within Team Persephone.

The minions closed the doors behind us while the Sicarii stopped in the centre of the high-ceilinged room and turned to face us. While we waited for our hosts, I examined the room. The walls were hung with paintings of someone's long-dead obviously human ancestors, so I doubted they were anything to do with our hostess. The men were all rosy-cheeked, with heavy jowls and white powdered wigs; the porcelain-skinned women were all encased in tight-fitting bodices – probably the cause of their pale complexions, as I imagined they'd found it hard to breathe corseted within stiff whalebone.

Delicate, highly ornate furniture was placed tastefully around the room. It was a set piece: for show only; I thought the owner would no doubt have the vapours should someone actually sit on the chairs, or play the harpsichord.

The gold- and cream-lacquered door opened, and Persephone was preceded into the room by Joseph and another – the unfortunate Gabriel's replacement? Joseph gave me a perfect, white-toothed smile; that he was so comfortable in such dangerous company really made me wonder at his sanity.

Persephone was dressed in a knee-length, closely fitting purple lace dress, accessorised with a black patent leather belt and matching stilettos. She entered the room with an over-the-top catwalk strut. If she was daemon, she was keeping her real self under wraps.

'Jinx, darling,' she said, holding out a slender, bejewelled hand to him. 'I am so glad you've returned to us.'

He gave her a dirty look.

'Now, now, don't be like that.' She strode across the carpet, reached out and flicked aside his coat with her forefinger. 'All healed up, I'm glad to see.'

She looked at me, and her smile became slightly fixed. 'Though you haven't killed *her* yet.'

I gave her my best hundred-megawatt smile and rested my hand on Jinx's arm. 'Why would he, when we've been having so much fun?'

Her nostrils flared and I was pleased to see she had to fight to keep the smile on her face. 'Believe me when I tell you the fun for you has only just begun. If I leave him to his own devices you will be nothing more than a pile of bloody, steaming meat.'

I looked down at myself and then back at her. 'Yet here I am, safe and sound.'

'But not for much longer.'

'We'll see.'

She turned her attention back to Jinx and laid her palm on his naked chest. His fingers tightened on my arm. 'Let's take you upstairs for a wash and brush-up.' His grip became painful.

She gestured at me with her head. 'Take her downstairs,' she told the two minions. 'I'll be down to deal with her later.'

'No,' Jinx said.

Persephone arched an eyebrow. 'No?'

'She's mine.'

Persephone began to laugh. 'Jinx, darling, you appear to be under the misguided impression you have a say in anything.' She moved in closer and whispered in his ear, loud enough for me to hear, 'But you don't – my will is your will.' She took a step back and reached out to press the tip of her right forefinger against the centre of his brow.

His hand jerked from my arm as his features contorted with pain, lips pressing tightly together like he was trying to hold in a scream.

'On your knees,' she said, her eyes glittering and her teeth parting slightly, showing a pointed pink tongue.

Jinx groaned.

'I said, *on your knees.*'

With a grimace, he dropped down onto one knee and then the other. His head fell forward and she took a step closer to him, lifted her pointed shoe and pressed the sole against his crotch.

'You, my darling, are going to come upstairs with me and I'm going to show you what it's like to really fuck.'

Jinx trembled, again reminding me of a frightened colt, panicked and scared, but unable to bolt to safety. She moved her foot, placing the thin stiletto in his groin, and pressed it hard enough against the leather that it made an indentation; it must have been painful.

'You've made your point,' I said.

She smiled. 'No, I don't think I have.' And she pressed the heel in even harder, making me wince.

'What is it with you?' I looked her up and down. 'I would ask if you'd had a troubled childhood, but that wouldn't be any excuse: I had a crap life as a kid and I'm not even close to you on the psycho-bitch Richter scale.'

She laughed, though it was forced. 'Mock as much as you like. You'll soon be wishing you had treated me with respect – not that it would have made the slightest difference. I'm going to gradually strip away the veneer until you are little more than a wild beast willing to do *anything* to make the pain stop. I did it to the Deathbringer; it will be the simplest of things to do it to you: you'll know nothing but pain – mind-numbing, blistering agony.'

My heart was racing, and I fought to stop myself shaking: she'd done this to Jinx so I knew I stood no chance, but I was damned if I'd give her the satisfaction of seeing that I was almost shitting myself. 'Are you so sure that he's yours?' I asked calmly. 'Are you so sure that when the chips are down, he won't choose to save me?'

'He will do as he's told.'

I took a deep breath, and hoping my legs would support me, I moved forward to stand beside my Deathbringer. I put my hand on his head. 'Do you really think so?' I asked.

'At my say-so he will take you apart—'

'We'll see,' I said, and I caressed his hair for what I thought would probably be the last time. I could posture as much as I wanted, but if he was truly hers, I was so fucked I might as well slit my own wrists and save myself the pain to come. At least it was a plan.

She gave me a narrow-eyed look, then lifted her chin and her lips raise slightly in her condescending smile. 'He is mine, and when I send him down to you, he will prove it.'

His head moved ever so slightly, pushing against my hand, just like Pyrites did when he wanted comfort, and I pressed down and let my fingers massage his crown.

'Well,' I said, 'there is one difference between the two of us – I love Jinx with all my heart, whereas you only care about how powerful he can make you.'

She actually threw back her head and laughed out loud at that.

'Stupid, stupid, *stupid* little girl. It's your love for him that will be his ultimate downfall: when he holds your cold, dead body in his hands and realises he has destroyed you, he will lose whatever will he might have had left. At that moment he will be mine for ever.'

'Or he might just destroy the creature who took me away from him,' I pointed out helpfully.

Her smile faltered again, so briefly I doubted she even knew it. 'Take her down,' she ordered, and the minions grabbed me and dragged me away before I had one last chance to whisper to Jinx how much I loved him. I hoped he knew that, but he was so messed up by her mind control that I wasn't sure he knew much of anything. The last thing I saw as they pulled me, struggling, away, was her laying her hand on his head where mine had so briefly rested. His shoulders were slumped and his head was bowed. I looked back at him for as long as I was able, hoping he would look up, give me some sort of sign that I hadn't lost him for ever.

I was disappointed.

I would have laughed, if my situation hadn't been so dire. The cellar where they imprisoned me was as much a set piece as the room upstairs: almost a replica of the cell where Amaliel had kept me before taking off the tip of my little finger. Just the thought of it made me ball my hand into a tight fist.

They manacled me to the wall and left me to contemplate the assortment of vicious-looking implements spread out on a wooden bench a few feet away. Some I remembered from my stay in Amaliel's care; the others were bright and shiny-new, and far too modern to have come from the Underlands – in fact, I'm pretty sure several came straight out of Dexter's kit. I wondered whether Amaliel had taken up watching satellite TV during his exile in the Overlands – though I doubted any perverse or disgusting torture thought up by Hollywood could teach him anything.

Rather bizarrely, there was a crystal bowl at one end of the table, together with a matching decanter. I got as close to the table as the chains would allow to take a look. They were actually quite nice pieces, incongruous next to the various instruments of suffering – if there had been goblets, I'd have thought Amaliel used them to torment his captives when they would do anything for a taste of cool, fresh water – but this was probably too subtle for Amaliel; he was more of your down and dirty torturer.

I sank to the floor, which was cold and hard, but the least of my worries. Psycho Bitch hadn't mentioned Kayla, and I hadn't asked, not wanting to give Persephone the satisfaction of being able to gloat even more than she was already. Perhaps she'd been lying about Kayla to entice me here? Unlikely . . .

I leaned back against the wall and did the only thing I could do. I waited.

Part of me wanted to wait for ever. I didn't want to be tortured and I didn't want to die horribly, and I especially didn't want to die at Jinx's hands. But I also wanted it to all be over – at least I wouldn't be sitting in a cold cell imagining everything she might be doing to Jinx. I most certainly didn't want to imagine them together, naked and sweaty and entangled in sheets. I imagined she'd like it rough. I didn't want to think he might be enjoying it.

No – *no*. He was gentle and tender, and he loved me. He loved *me*.

Then the door began to creak open and for a split-second I wished he had enjoyed being with her a little bit more, keeping her busy just a little longer – but yet again I was disappointed. It wasn't Persephone, but a figure swathed in black: my old pal Amaliel. He closed the door and stood there staring at me, studying me in silence, his eyes burning.

I didn't bother to get up, but returned the stare.

'I assume your drakon has gone for reinforcements,' he said at last. 'It's becoming extremely tedious having to continually relocate.'

Relocate? He was certainly picking up the local lingo.

'Persephone didn't give me the impression she was going anywhere soon.'

He gave one of his disgusting phlegmy laughs. 'She's getting ready to leave as we speak.'

'What?' I couldn't hide my surprise and fear – if she left with Jinx, I might never find him again.

'You surely don't think she's stupid enough to stay and wait for the Guardians?' He glided towards the bench. 'Unfortunately, I haven't the time to deal with you in the manner I would have wished.' His hand hovered over the array of instruments as I fought to keep my expression calm and my teeth from chattering. 'The Sicarii are all for your prolonged ritual slaughter, so your private demise will make me extremely unpopular – but to be honest, the Sicarii are becoming tiresome beyond belief.'

'But they're your followers.'

He gave a dismissive wave of the hand. 'They were useful once, but since you proved that the living could not go into the afterlife and safely return, they have become – well, shall we say, surplus to requirements.'

'You mean the collecting of souls has become pointless?'

'To me, yes, though it is and will always be the Sicarii way. No, there were murmurings of discontent at the direction in which I was taking them, which I managed to overcome with promises that here in the Overlands, the Deathbringer would give them *millions* of souls: that way, humans would flock to join the cult, rather than die. The Sicarii would reign supreme in a way that would never have been possible in the Underlands.'

'So it *is* all about power and world domination,' I sneered. 'God, you're like some bloody comic-book villain.'

'You appear to have forgotten that this "comic-book villain", whatever that means, is holding your life in his hands.'

He was right; I had. Briefly.

'Unfortunately, Persephone's and my joint objectives have clashed with theirs, and once again there are Sicarii jostling to oust me,' he explained as his forefinger tapped first one and then another of the implements lying on the bench. *See? Just like a comic-book villain to explain his dastardly plan*, I thought. He lifted a rusty pair of long-handled pincers and an image I had once seen of a similar utensil being used to remove a victim's tongue floated into my head. Instinctively I clamped my teeth and lips tightly shut and wished I'd done so a lot earlier; preferably before I'd insulted him.

Still holding the pincers he lifted another object to show me. It looked like a pair of metal false teeth. 'This is an interesting little apparatus.' He turned it in the light, studying it. 'It is fitted into the mouth of a habitual liar, a nag, rumourmonger, you get the picture? Then' – he tapped the handle fitted onto one side with the pincers – 'this is turned until the mouth is forced open as wide as it can get. After an hour or so, as you can imagine, the pain is excruciating. However, it doesn't stop there: the screw is turned again and again until the miscreant's jaws are literally cracked apart.' He had another merry gurgle. 'Sadly, I haven't got a few hours to kill.' He dropped it back on the table.

He glided over to stand before me. 'It's a shame. I've been so looking forward to this . . . I'd thought up a very special death – maybe not quite as painful, and probably quicker, but you would die in terror, your fear so great it would be *palpable*.'

I frowned up at him, teeth still clamped shut.

'Instead, I am going to have to make it quick. Such a waste. But first, I have something to show you.' He reached inside his robe and pulled out a chain on which hung a small glowing tube of blue light. 'Do you know what this is?'

I shook my head.

He gave another of his disgusting gurgles, his eyes gleaming red. 'In this crystal I have captured the soul of your sister Kayla. She will remain imprisoned for ever – unless the phial is broken, when she will disperse into the ether as a nothingness, a nonentity, forever lost. Her spirit will perish. There will be nothing anyone can do to save her.'

I studied the pendant, trying to keep my face blank. This was one of the four pieces of jewellery Kubeck's uncle had made: four crystal phials held in four gold baskets on four gold chains.

He dropped the crystal back inside his robe. 'I have had to change my plans. I had intended to have the full set: Kayla, you and her idiot father Baltheza – you, however, thwarted my original plan, so now it will have to be just you and Kayla.'

'You're vile.'

'So I've been told,' he said and turned back to the table to peruse his diabolical instruments. He dropped the pincers and his hand moved, tapping first one, then another with his fingertip. For someone in a hurry, he was taking his time – and he could have all the time in the world, as far as I was concerned. His hand rested on the handle of a long serrated blade. Maybe if I could keep him talking for long enough, Jamie would arrive in time to save me. I didn't like my chances, but if it meant a swift death rather than a painful one, it was something.

'So who was the fourth crystal for?' I asked. I wanted to show him I knew something he didn't think I did.

His hand tightened around the blade's handle and he slowly raised his head to stare at me, his eyes glowing red. 'Fourth?' he said eventually.

'You had four made: one for Kayla, one for me, one for Baltheza – so who was the fourth one for?'

He studied me in silence, twisting the evil-looking blade in his bony fingers. 'I always knew it was a mistake arresting the jeweller for treason. I should have disposed of him.'

'Of course, then there's the original crystal,' I went on. 'The one you had made for "a special lady".'

Amaliel strode towards me, grabbed my arm, hauled me to my feet and glowered down at me. 'Do you know what? I've a good mind to take you with us.' His chest sounded like a bubbling saucepan as he drew in a deep breath. 'Do you know why?'

I shook my head, terrified, but at the same time curious. What had made him so angry?

'Because I want to see you suffer. I want to see your despair when your lover walks this world, leaving death in his wake. I want to see your heartbreak when you watch me smash your sister's phial into a thousand pieces. I want to see you burning inside the Blue Fire. And I want to think of your soul writhing in torment within a crystal bauble hanging around my neck every single day.' He gave me a vicious shake that rattled my teeth, then threw me against the wall hard enough to knock the breath out of me. 'Fortunate for you that I can't.'

'The first crystal—' I gasped '—the first crystal – who was it for?' Judging by his reaction it was important, worth risking his anger to get the answer.

His hand went inside his robe and this time when it reappeared an amethyst crystal dangled from his fingers, glowing and flaring in the torchlight.

'You ask – but are you sure you really want to know?' He held the crystal about six inches from my nose. 'Are you?'

I lifted my hand to touch it, and the stone in the ring on my finger suddenly sparked red fire from within its depths. He snatched the crystal back from me and enfolded it in his fist. 'You wear her ring!' he said, his voice accusatory.

I froze as the realisation of what he'd just said hit me. At last I knew what had happened to my mother.

He turned back to the table in a flurry of black, clearly agitated that he'd betrayed his secret. Baltheza had hinted that Amaliel had somehow convinced him to have Veronica executed and he'd ever since regretted it – he'd probably regret it even more if he knew what had become of her.

When Amaliel swung back around to face me, he was holding the serrated blade in his right hand and a steel hook attached to a leather strap in his left.

'I am going to make you wish that you'd never been born,' he spat.

'But not now, I'm afraid,' a voice said apologetically, and when I managed to drag my eyes away from the seriously scary-looking apparatus hanging from Amaliel's outstretched hand, I saw Joseph standing in the doorway.

Amaliel spun around. 'Who do you think you are to tell me what I can and can't—!'

Joseph held up a hand, halting Amaliel mid-flow. 'Don't shoot the messenger! The Guardians are but a few minutes away. If we don't leave now it'll be game over.'

'This isn't a game.'

Joseph shrugged. 'If you're going to kill her then just get on with it.'

Amaliel threw the hook onto the table with such force that several instruments clattered to the ground, then he was coming at me, the serrated blade raised to head-height.

I moved as fast as I could, throwing myself as far away from him as the chains would allow, but it was no good: I was about to die and I couldn't do a damn thing about it.

Amaliel started to laugh. 'Not so brave now, unlucky Lucky de Salle.'

I could feel a scream building up in my throat. He was right, I wasn't feeling brave at all. He swung the blade at my head, and I dropped to my knees, throwing up my hands in front of my face and praying somehow the manacles and chain would offer some protection.

'Joseph, where the fuck are you?' Persephone shrieked from upstairs, just as the blade glanced off the chain, sending sparks flying.

Amaliel snarled and drew back his arm again—

'Joseph! Amaliel! The Guardians will be here any minute!'

'You've just run out of time,' Joseph said. 'Come on.'

'She has to die,' Amaliel said.

'Joseph,' she shrieked again, and Amaliel snarled furiously and grabbed me by the wrist. He pulled me to my feet and in a deft movement, let go of my wrist and gripped me around the throat before holding the blade so it was hovering above my right eye.

'Joseph!'

'Does that woman never shut up?' Amaliel muttered over his shoulder and I heard a snort of laughter from behind him.

The serrated blade filled my vision. I was going to die.

'*But not today*,' a voice whispered in my head, as though it had suddenly occurred to my inner daemon that I needed a bit of help, and I clenched my hands together and struck out at Amaliel's arm, knocking it aside.

'Bitch!' he spat as I started struggling in his grasp, kicking out at him as hard as I could – then I started to feel warm, and I didn't need to glance down at myself to know I was shimmering golden.

'What the f—?' Joseph muttered.

Amaliel abruptly let go of my throat and just as suddenly, dropped the knife: the blade was glowing red, clearly too hot to handle. He couldn't touch me while I was like this.

I grinned and tried to advance on him, but the chains held me back.

He took a step away from me, his red eyes flaring, and as he did, I caught a glimpse of something glistening on the sleeve of his robe, as though it was traced with golden thread, then it was gone. I must have imagined it.

Joseph hurried forward and grabbed Amaliel by the arm. 'Leave her,' he said, pulling him towards the door. 'Leave her before it's too late.'

Amaliel hissed. 'Next time. Next time, Soulseer. Next time you die.'

'Yeah, yeah, yeah,' Joseph said, still tugging at his arm. 'But there won't be a next time if I don't get your skinny ass out of here now.'

Amaliel spun around and pushed past Joseph, ready to sweep out of the door – but at the last moment he stopped, glided back to the table and snatched up the crystal bowl and decanter. And despite all the other craziness spinning around in my head, I couldn't help but think it weird that Amaliel was somehow emotionally connected to a couple of pieces of homeware. Joseph moved aside to let him pass, then stood for a moment looking at me.

'My, my, my, aren't you full of surprises,' he said with a pleasant smile.

I kept quiet.

'I'm beginning to understand why Amaliel is so desperate to get you out of the way.' Then he laughed. 'Be seeing you, Lucky.' He went to leave, then turned back to me, his smile gone. 'Don't underestimate them,' he said. 'They have every intention of ruling this world and they'll play dirty to do it. Can you do that? Can you play dirty?'

He looked me straight in the eyes for several seconds before giving a small nod, then leaving without another word.

I stared after him, nonplussed. *What was that all about?* Then I sat back down on the floor and waited. My guards would be here soon and in the meantime, I had plans to make. As well as Kayla's phial, I would also have to take my mother's from Amaliel – she might not have been much of a parent to me, but I doubted she'd had much choice in the matter. I wondered whether she'd left my father and me under her own volition, or whether she'd been snatched away by Baltheza, or even Amaliel? There had to be some reason why he kept her spirit in a phial hanging from a chain about his neck.

I stretched out my foot, and slowly, carefully, managed to drag back the blade Amaliel had dropped until my grasping fingers closed around the hilt. I was working on the chain holding the manacles to the wall when a door slammed back on its hinges and feet pounded on stone stairs; my heart did a little flip as Jamie appeared, framed within the doorway.

He stood there for a split-second and in that moment, several emotions passed across his face: relief, concern, and the one that made my battered heart beat a little faster: *love.* I might not be able to trust him completely in some things, but when it came to how he felt for me, that was something I couldn't doubt.

He leaped across the room and dropped to his knees, pulling me into his arms and hugging me so tightly I could barely breathe. 'I've been so worried about you,' he murmured, and then released me slightly so he could look at me. 'Are you all right? Are you hurt? Did Jinx hurt you? If he did—'

I pressed my fingers against his lips. 'Yes, no and no. Jinx would never hurt me,' I told him, pushing the memory of his hands around my throat from my mind. Jamie didn't need to know about that.

He looked into my eyes, and then he was kissing me and I felt so safe within his arms that I never wanted him to let me go. It was always like this: they both made me feel this way, which was why I needed *both* of my men, together.

There was a cough from across the room: two daemons who looked like angels and could have easily been Jamie's brothers were standing at the door.

'The Deathbringer isn't here,' one said.

'Does the woman know where he is?' the other asked.

The woman? 'I wouldn't tell you if I did,' I muttered under my breath so they wouldn't hear, although Jamie did.

'What about the Sicarii? Do they know anything?' Jamie asked the Guardians.

'As good as nothing – they say Amaliel and the woman Persephone abandoned them.'

Jamie hopped up onto his feet. 'Are there any pliers?' he asked, moving over to the bench.

'James,' one angel said, 'it might be better if she remains restrained? Release the chains from the wall, but perhaps keep her hands manacled—'

'What—?' I scrambled to my feet.

'Some say she cannot be considered a friendly influence,' the other said, completely ignoring me.

'You cannot be serious?' I glared at the two angels, then noticed Jamie had stopped frowning at them and was now studying me. 'Jamie, if you even *think* about leaving me chained up, I will never speak to you again. I mean it – *never*!'

'Lucky, you have to understand—'

'No,' I interrupted, 'no, I *don't*. Jinx has done *nothing* wrong – he is the *victim* here. You're all treating him as if he's the villain – and now me by association? Honestly?'

Jamie turned back to the bench and as he picked up a tool the second angel walked over. 'Let me.'

'You keep your feathery little arse away from me!' I glowered at him.

'Charles and Peter have your best interests at heart,' Jamie started, but I was already shaking my head furiously.

'Like fuck they do—'

'Excuse me,' a voice said, and Kerfuffle barged his way between the two angels and came trotting over to me. 'Mistress, we've been so worried.'

'I'm fine,' I told him, 'at least I will be, once someone takes these off.' I lifted my wrists to show him the manacles.

He waddled over to the bench and picked up a pair of cutters.

'Ah, Kerfuffle is it?' Charles took a step towards us, raising a hand.

'*Mr* Kerfuffle to you,' my diminutive guard grumbled without turning.

'I think it had been decided that it would be for the best if the woman remained restrained for the time being—'

Kerfuffle turned around, hands on hips. 'Decided by *whom*?'

'Ah—' Charles glanced at Jamie, who put his hand over his mouth; I could see he was trying very hard not to laugh. I was glad *he* found it funny; *I* was about ready to kill someone.

Kerfuffle obviously felt the same. 'This *lady* is the Soulseer, and a *royal* princess. She is also my mistress and I am not about to leave her chained up on the say-so of a little dipshit like you.'

'Well, I say,' Charles said, 'there's no need to be so rude—'

'Rude? I'll give you *rude*,' Kerfuffle started squaring up to them, and it was fortunate for all concerned that Shenanigans, the voice of reason amongst my guards, appeared at the door.

'Mistress!' His face lit up with a relieved, goofy grin as he hurried to my side. He tutted when he saw the manacles and took the cutters from Kerfuffle, who was still eyeing up Jamie's pals. 'Let's get these off of you, Mistress.'

'Thank you,' I said, giving Charles and Peter a triumphant smile.

'James?' Peter said.

'Keeping her chained up will make this situation even worse than it already is,' Jamie told him. 'Come . . .' and he drew them outside the door. Their whispered conversation was doing nothing for my temper.

Jamie returned, but fortunately, his feathered friends did not. I scowled at him.

'They're just being a bit over-enthusiastic,' he said.

'*Over-enthusiastic?* They wanted to keep me chained up! What was that all about?'

Kerfuffle and Shenanigans exchanged glances, then kept their eyes down as they worked on getting those damned manacles off me.

'They think you are more on Jinx's side than ours.'

'Jamie! This shouldn't about *sides* – you know that! Jinx needs our help. You should see the state of him. He's confused, doesn't recognise me – he's even forgotten his name.'

'But Lucky, that's the problem,' Jamie tried to explain. 'If he isn't in control of himself, he's a danger to humanity – and, dare I say it, to you and me and the rest of the Underlands.'

'Jinx would *never* hurt me,' I said as Shenanigans cut through the second manacle and carefully took it from my wrist.

'Really?' Jamie's eyes narrowed as he clocked the bruises around my neck. 'Then tell me how you got those.'

Both Shenanigans and Kerfuffle looked at my throat and Kerfuffle sucked in a breath. 'Not good, not good,' he muttered.

'Amaliel grabbed me—'

'Maybe he did, but I can see old bruises beneath the red,' Jamie interrupted. 'Jinx did this to you.'

I tried to make excuses, to explain: 'He didn't know what he was doing – as soon as he realised, he was distraught.'

'Don't you see?' Jamie said. 'This is exactly what we mean: if he was out of control enough to try and choke the life out of you, the woman he loves, do you think he'll care what he does to a million strangers?'

'He thought I was Persephone – and yes,' I told him stubbornly, 'yes, he will.'

'You're not fooling anyone. You know I'm right.'

'Jamie, if you *saw* him – if you saw what *they've* done to him – you'd want to help him. You'd want to save him too; I know you would.'

He reached out and ran his fingers down my cheek, indecision written all over his face, then gave a resigned sigh. 'I want to save him, Lucky, but . . . what do you want me to do?'

'Let me try and find him – let me try and bring him back.'

'Can we go somewhere and talk about this?'

This was better than I'd expected, but Shenanigans and Kerfuffle both looked worried.

'Wouldn't it be better if—?' Shenanigans started, but Jamie silenced him with a gesture.

'Come on,' he said, and putting his arm around my shoulders, guided me out of the room and up the stairs.

As we passed the fancy room where I'd first entered, I saw the Sicarii and their brown-robed disciples kneeling on the floor in a line, hands on their heads, while several angel-winged daemons pointed very un-angelic crossbows at them. I spotted Charles and Peter, in conversation with two others; all four gave Jamie and me pointed looks as we passed them.

Jamie led me into a small anteroom and as soon as he'd pulled the door shut he tried to pull me into his arms – but I was having none of it. If it hadn't been for Kerfuffle and Shenanigans, I wasn't at all sure I wouldn't still be chained up.

I backed away, glaring at him. His shoulders slumped and I could see the very real regret in his eyes. 'Amaliel has Kayla and my mother,' I said.

'Your *mother*?' Jamie ran his hand through his curls. 'Your mother's been dead for twenty years or more . . .'

'Dead, but not at peace.' I explained about the crystals, and Amaliel's thwarted plans for Baltheza and me.

'Do you know where they've gone?'

I shook my head. 'But they're planning something big; I know that much. Let me find them—'

'You'll never find them on your own.'

'I have to try,' I said, 'and you either help me, or you don't.' Looking at Jamie's troubled expression, I asked, 'What is it?'

'I have orders to take you back to the Underlands . . .'

'Orders from whom?' I asked and the image of the golden-haired woman sprang into my mind. 'Who was the woman back at the other mansion?'

'You saw her?' he asked, sounding surprised.

'Just before Jinx grabbed me.'

'She is the Keeper. There are those who oversee both our lands; Jinx and I are their emissaries, either to correct the balance, or to police the interactions between the worlds.'

I gave a nod. He'd told me that before.

'Well, she is our conduit: she communicates their will, and we act on it.'

'And she has told you these *very important people*,' I said sarcastically, 'have ordered you to bring me back?'

He did have the good grace to look a little embarrassed about it. 'I'm afraid so.'

'Well, they can whistle,' I told him. 'I'm not theirs to command.'

'You're the Soulseer—'

'And until a few months ago they knew *nothing* about me – or if they did, they chose to ignore me. So frankly, I don't care what they say or what they want. I'm not going anywhere without Jinx and there's nothing you or anyone else can do about it.' The last of any warm, cuddly feelings I had for Jamie had drained away.

'Lucky, I'm not the enemy,' he said, reaching out to touch my face.

I stepped away.

'Lucky, listen to me. I said I would help you and I *will* . . . I know the three of us are meant to be. I know without Jinx, we'll be broken, a piece of us missing. So I'll do whatever it takes, even if it means—' He broke off, pulled himself up very straight and forced his lips into a tight smile.

'Means *what*?'

'Nothing,' he said, but before I could question him further, there was a rap on the door.

'Guardian, a moment, if you will,' someone called.

Jamie took my hand and raised it to his lips. 'Whatever I say and do out there, remember I love you, and I will keep my promise to you.' He pressed his lips against my fingers. 'Come on.'

I wasn't surprised to find Pinky and Perky waiting outside with those smug angelic expressions on their too-pretty faces.

'One of the prisoners has told us something you should hear,' Charlie-boy said.

Jamie kept hold of my hand, obviously not caring one jot what they thought, and led me back into the room where they were keeping the Sicarii. My guard were standing beside the door, and it was clear from their body language that they were as pissed off as I was.

Kerfuffle was glaring at the Sicarii or the angels, or maybe even both. Shenanigans' thick lips were curled down in an uncharacteristic scowl. Vaybian was leaning against the wall, his arms crossed, gazing at both angels and Sicarii with arrogant distaste. Even Kubeck was frowning, and Pyrites was puffing dark smoke.

I caught Shenanigans' eye as we passed and mouthed, 'What?'

He glanced at an angel standing in front of one of the kneeling Sicarii; the two angels on either side had crossbows pointing at the Sicarii's head.

I wondered what on earth had been going on.

As we approached, the angel facing the Sicarii said, 'James, this one has told us something very interesting.' He prodded his prisoner. 'Tell the Guardian what you told me.'

The Sicarii clutched his hands together. 'I beg clemency.'

Jamie's thumb was caressing mine as though he never wanted to let me go, even at a time like this. 'What mercy did you show any of your victims? What mercy did you show the humans back at the church?'

'It was the woman Persephone – she sacrificed the girl, she had the humans murdered, not us – not the Sicarii.'

'Tell me what you know, and I'll relay your cooperation to those who will make the final decision.'

The Sicarii looked over his shoulder at the other grey-robed daemons and they bowed their heads. He returned his attention to Jamie. 'They are going to the capital, where the Deathbringer will bring forth the first of the Devastations: apocalyptic events of such monumental proportions that the entire human race will bend the knee to Amaliel and Persephone. Humans will see them as acts of their God or his nemesis, the Fallen One.' The Sicarii laughed, a truly horrid sound. 'Plague and pestilence will be followed by other natural and unnatural calamities, each one worse than the last.'

'And the first will be?' Jamie was gripping my hand tightly.

The creature laughed again. 'Do you think they would have left us behind if we had been privy to such information?'

Jamie stared down at him.

'James?' the angel asked.

'Take them back home for trial. We will continue the search for Amaliel and the Deathbringer.'

'I will pass that news on.'

'You do that, Pasqual,' Jamie said, and the edge to his voice told me this daemon was no friend.

'And the woman?'

'The *Soulseer* will stay with me.'

'Your orders were—'

'I know very well what my orders are, but I must speak with her, as she too has information – disturbing information.'

Pasqual didn't bother to stop his lips twisting into a sneer. 'And what "news" could be so important that you would not do as you have been bidden?'

Pretty Peter and Charlie-boy gave little gasps of outrage behind me and one exclaimed, 'Pasqual! You question the Guardian's motives?'

'She is not in chains. She holds his hand – and may I venture, his heart – in her very tight grip, so yes, I do.'

'Bloody upstart,' Kerfuffle muttered.

'Think what you like,' Jamie said, 'but I will question her, and she will not return to the Underlands until I have.'

Pasqual bobbed his head. 'I will see this message is also passed on.'

'You do that,' Jamie said, and after giving my hand a final squeeze, he turned around and told Charlie-boy, 'Take Lucky and her guards somewhere safe to wait for me. I'll be there shortly.'

Charlie-boy and Pretty Peter bowed in acquiescence and as they gestured for me to go with them, Jamie moved in close and whispered to me, 'I trust them to keep you safe. They are my most loyal Guardians.'

'Really? They wanted to leave me chained up—'

He grinned. 'I often have the same thought.'

'I thought Jinx was the only one of you into bondage?' I mumbled, slightly bewildered by this turn of events.

'I hate to disillusion you, but Jinx and I have the same taste in many things, you being a case in point.'

Jamie's angels led us to a large sitting room furnished with several leather couches and deep, wide armchairs, and a fire roaring in the grate. This room, unlike the last, was for living in. Even the landscape paintings on the walls were welcoming.

Kerfuffle very pointedly pushed the door shut before Peter and Charles could follow us in, and I walked over to the far side of the room so we could talk without being overheard.

'We have to get away from here,' I told them.

'It's going to be difficult giving the Guardians the slip,' Shenanigans said.

'Jamie has promised to help us.'

Kerfuffle's marshmallow face creased into a frown so deep it looked like it must hurt and the room fell into an uncomfortable silence. Vaybian looked around, then snorted in disgust as no one spoke. 'That could be very bad news for Jamie,' he said.

I remembered the sadness in Jamie's eyes as he'd said he would help me . . . I *knew* there was something he wasn't telling me. 'Go on.'

'He' would not want you to know this, but you must: the Guardian answers to the Veteribus. If he fails in his duties to them – if he disobeys a *direct* order – they will take his wings.'

Shit! The thought of Jamie losing his wings was so terrible that I was suddenly finding it hard to think straight. That he would risk himself in such a way for me and for *Jinx*? That meant he must love me more than I'd ever thought. He might have deceived me and manipulated me – but never for his own personal gain; I could see that now. But could I *trust* him, knowing that he could pull his mesmerising trick on me at any point?

I looked up to find all eyes upon me.

I would have to deal with one thing at a time. 'So we'll have to find a way for me to escape without Jamie being involved – and we need to make absolutely certain there's no way he could possibly be blamed for my actions.'

'It won't be easy – those who wanted to keep you under lock and key will be as attentive as prison guards,' Kubeck said.

'Bloody Guardians,' Kerfuffle mumbled. 'They've always had a very high opinion of themselves.'

Pyrites hopped up onto the couch next to me and laid his head on my lap.

'Hush,' said Shenanigans just as I was about to ask about the Keeper, and the door opened a crack and Charles popped his head around. 'Apologies for the interruption, but James said you might want to come and see this.'

In yet another sitting room we found six or seven more angels standing in a semi-circle, looking up at a huge plasma screen. As we walked in, a female news reporter was saying, '—scenes coming to you from across the river from the Palace of Westminster' – and sure enough, there were shots of Big Ben and the Houses of Parliament. Then the cameraman focused on the Thames.

'It's begun,' Vaybian said grimly.

The images of the River Thames as it meandered through the city were shocking – I'd heard the Bible stories, of course, but to actually *see* it ... This wasn't a scene from a Hollywood movie depicting a river in a far-off land, this was the Thames. True, it still passed the same old landmarks – the Eye, the Houses of Parliament, London Bridge, the Tower – but today there was a striking difference. Today its waters were the colour of arterial blood. It was as if London was bleeding out from its very heart.

Seventeen

When the news report finished, we started back to our living room – but we had walked just a few steps when we heard raised voices, Pasqual's the loudest.

'What is it with him?' I asked our escort.

'He has ideas above his station,' Peter replied.

'He wants the Guardian's position,' Charles added, 'and if he gets it, may the spirits help us all.'

'He's not very popular, then?'

'He has his following,' Peter said.

'Most of us see the link between James, the Deathbringer and the Soulseer as a good thing; a positive force for the future. Some don't.'

'Oh,' I said, still none the wiser.

Peter fell in step beside me and moved closer. 'It is rumoured that some of the Veteribus see the Trinity as a threat.'

'That's only speculation,' Charles added.

'Who exactly are the Veteribus?' I asked.

'It is they whom we serve,' he said, leaning forward to open the door for me. 'It is they who protect the three realms.'

'Thanks,' I said – and stopped dead. '*Three* realms?'

'The Underlands, the Overlands, and the Hereafter.'

He gestured for me to enter, and I went to stand by the fire while the rest of my guards trooped in. Once the door closed behind them, they clustered around me.

'Peter just told me the Veteribus govern the three realms,' I started. 'Does anyone know who or what they actually are?'

'They are—' Kerfuffle began, but Shenanigans shushed him again.

'For goodness' sake,' Vaybian sneered, 'they can't hear you.'

'I wouldn't be so sure,' Shenanigans said, 'not when the Guardians are just next door.'

'They are all-seeing and all-knowing,' Kubeck said.

Vaybian rolled his eyes. 'If that truly were the case, they would have seen the Deathbringer abducted and would have known who had done it, and we'd all be sitting safely sipping ale in the Drakon's Rest.'

'He has a point,' Kubeck said after a pause.

'But who are they?' I asked. 'And where do they live?'

Kerfuffle tried to explain. 'They don't exactly *live* anywhere. The Veteribus are ethereal beings. Their voice – the Keeper – resides in the Crystal Mountains—'

'—where Pyrites comes from?'

'More or less. Pyrites lives in the Icedfire Mountains, which surround the Crystal Mountains. The High Gardens, or Askala, is high up in the Crystal Mountains – it's what humans would call a temple.'

'It's meant to be the most beautiful place in the whole of the three realms,' Shenanigans said dreamily.

'Quite so,' Kerfuffle said, clearly not as impressed as his huge friend. 'High Gardens is home to the Keeper and her twelve attendants, and it is she who communicates with the Veteribus.'

'In other words, she's the one giving the Guardian and Deathbringer their orders.' I looked around at my friends. 'Jamie said they don't communicate directly – so what was she doing here?'

Kerfuffle shrugged. 'That's a question you would have to ask the Guardian.'

'But the long and the short of it is that the Guardian and Deathbringer answer to the Veteribus, and it is they who keep the order of things,' Vaybian said. Then, almost as an afterthought, he added, 'Although they might have known the Deathbringer's real name . . .'

'He's right,' Kubeck said in a low voice, moving in closer, 'who else but the Veteribus would know the Deathbringer's daemon name? And yet *Amaliel* knew it . . .'

Oh God, I thought, *do we have another enemy? A traitor in the ranks of the Veteribus?*

'I hope for all our sakes I'm wrong but there is a strong whiff of treachery about this,' Vaybian said. 'Whether it's the Guardians or their masters, I'm not at all sure. For the moment I suggest we trust no one but each other.'

None of them looked happy about it, but all my guards nodded in agreement.

'For all of that, we have more immediate things to worry about,' Kerfuffle said, 'like getting out of here and finding the Deathbringer.'

'And we have to act now,' Shenanigans said. 'The river is just the start; things will probably escalate from here on in.'

'What do you think will be next?' I asked.

'Let's hope it's something else that isn't life-threatening.'

'If it truly is blood flowing through the city it will become so within days,' Kubeck said. 'It will putrefy . . .'

'So it will be a plague next, caused by the blood, rather than Jinx?' I asked.

'No,' Kubeck said, his brow creased in concentration, 'the people of your world would expect disease from a river full of rotting blood. Amaliel wants humanity crawling at his feet. He wants to be seen as all-powerful, so he will do something more creative: something unnatural, apocalyptic.'

It was fast becoming apparent that Kubeck really wasn't a lowly serf: he had an education way over and above how to make trinkets for the nobility.

'I flew into this place, so I guess I can fly right out,' I told them, and Pyrites paddled his front claws against my thigh like a cat, making a purring sound from deep inside his chest.

'You can't do this on your own, Mistress,' Shenanigans said.

'I won't be on my own: I'll have Pyrites.'

'I'm coming with you,' Vaybian said, and it didn't sound like a suggestion.

Kerfuffle put his hands on his hips and glared up at the green daemon. 'Why you? Mr Shenanigans and I have been Mistress Lucky's guards right from the start – and she knows exactly where *our* loyalties lie. With you, I'm not so sure.'

'Amaliel has my lady trapped inside some crystal bauble hanging about his neck. I will slice his head from his shoulders and set her free.'

'He has a point,' Shenanigans told his friend.

Kerfuffle's scowl softened a tad. ''tis true, but the Lady Kayla is dead and my mistress is not. If you go with her, you make sure it stays that way.'

'I will guard my lady's sister with my life: I swear it.'

'After today's events, I suspect the Guardians will be leaving for the capital before long,' Kubeck interrupted.

'Then I'll just hope that while they're squabbling I get a bit of a head-start.'

'You'll have to get past those two first,' Kerfuffle said, looking at the door, behind which Charlie-boy and Pretty Peter waited.

'Maybe,' I said. I strode across to the window and pulled the curtain to one side to get a better look. No double-glazing here, just old-fashioned wooden sash windows – and most importantly, they'd been renovated, not painted shut.

I reached up and twisted the catch. 'Here, let me help,' Kubeck said, twisting the stiff catch until it opened, then sliding up the bottom window as quietly as he could. He stuck his head outside and peered all around before announcing, 'The way is clear.'

'Some guards they are,' Kerfuffle grumbled.

'Well, let's be thankful for it.' Shenanigans helped Vaybian climb outside.

'The Guardian might have had us put in a room from which we could escape unseen by unfriendly eyes.' Kubeck suggested.

'True,' Kerfuffle conceded, and I really hoped this wouldn't occur to the other Guardians.

Shenanigans took my hand and helped me climb out onto the ledge. As Vaybian lifted me down, Kerfuffle looked worried. 'You should take another of us with you.'

'No, I want you all here to keep an eye on Jamie and make sure he doesn't get himself into any kind of trouble.'

'Do you still have your communication device?'

I shook my head. 'Jinx decided we'd be better off without it.'

Kerfuffle rummaged in his pocket, pulled out his mobile and reached through the window. 'Here, take this – then you can at least keep in touch and tell us where you are.'

I gave him a smile as I pocketed the phone. 'Take care, all of you.'

'You too, Mistress,' they chorused as Pyrites flew up onto the window frame, hopped to the ground and began to grow. When he was big enough for the two of us, he sank to his stomach so we could climb up onto his back.

'Try not to be seen,' Kerfuffle said. 'The river turning to blood is one thing, but seeing two daemons flying over the countryside on a drakon will definitely cause a hullaballoo.'

'Or maybe even a kerfuffle,' I said.

My little daemon friend's cheeks flushed red. 'And possibly that,' he admitted.

Pyrites was up in the air almost as soon as we'd clambered aboard, and he appeared to know exactly where he was going.

'He can smell the blood,' Vaybian shouted in my ear, as if reading my mind.

It was all very well us setting off for London, but I had no idea where to begin searching for Jinx. From what I'd been told about him, I supposed he would actually be walking the streets with death and destruction following behind him – if we had watched the news for long enough, would we would have seen him perched on a rooftop somewhere, looking down upon his work? He might even have been standing on one of the bridges as he had conjured up Amaliel's first 'Devastation'.

Pyrites was a nippy little bugger, Jinx always says, so it wasn't long before we caught sight of the city skyline. I resisted the urge to keep looking back over my shoulder; Vaybian would quickly let me know if any Guardians were in hot pursuit. As we got closer, Pyrites took us up higher; it was an overcast day, so he tried to keep us within the low cloud, though it was pretty damp and uncomfortable.

The Thames, when we reached it, was worse than I could ever have imagined. The river was flowing still, but large numbers of dead fish were floating on the crimson surface, and it stank – not rotten, not yet, but the metallic, coppery smell of fresh blood.

Vaybian leaned close into me so I could hear and asked, 'What now?'

'I think we'll have to risk being seen. From up here we can at least spot Jinx.'

'They might have gone into hiding pending his next performance.'

'Do you think Amaliel will leave it that long?'

'I don't— What in the name of—?' He pointed, and I didn't need to squint into the distance to see a tide of black hurtling through the sky towards us.

'What the f—?'

Amaliel knew I'd be coming. He'd got Jinx to send the second 'Devastation' to meet me.

Within moments we were in the midst of a sky full of chattering black locusts, and it was terrifying. I flattened myself on Pyrites' back and Vaybian covered me with his body as the creatures swarmed about us, the whirring sound of their beating wings building into a crescendo. We were colliding at speed, but it wouldn't have mattered, if only there hadn't been so damn *many* of them; it was beginning to hurt – but Pyrites didn't mind one bit. He was snapping at the creatures, having a fine old feast, and using the cover of the insects to fly lower – no one was going to see us through the black cloud, even if there'd been anyone left on the streets – I suspected most people would have run for cover the moment the locusts came into sight.

It was impossible to see in front of us – but as I pulled my head back down after trying, I caught a glitter of light: my ring was glowing again – and this time I knew it wasn't my imagination, or just a reflection of candle or firelight, for the stone was glowing a bright emerald with a spark of burning red deep in its centre.

The beast inside my head who had been quiet for a long time now gave a little twitch, as if still half asleep and batting away an annoying bug. Then it gave a wriggle; if she was waking, trouble was coming, and I doubted it was of the flying kind. This made me much more vigilant and I tried to sit up a bit. The sky was still full of the creatures, but they were no longer a dense black mass; they were gradually thinning out. And then ahead of me I saw him. Straight ahead of us striding across London Bridge was the Deathbringer.

Of course I would find him here, heading for a place he knew well. Just across the river was the Monument, commemorating the Great Fire of London, which had started only yards away – ignited by Jinx's passing, or so I'd been told.

I patted Pyrites on the neck. 'Take us down.'

Pyrites swooped and came around so he'd land halfway across the bridge and facing Jinx. The creature inside my head flexed her muscles – I was glad she was confident, as I was more than a little afraid. The road was littered with dead bugs and cars, their windscreens smeared with insect blood: there'd been a pile-up on the northbound carriageway. This was where things might get tricky: the cars were still occupied and as the swarm of locusts began to dissipate, drivers and passengers who had been huddled down in their seats were starting to sit up. What they would see now was a dragon and two very strange-looking people coming at them from one direction, and a tall, maroon, horned man with long, flowing, almost-black hair, looking every inch like the devil or one of his minions, coming from the other.

White faces pressed against the windows, eyes and mouths opened wide. It would be only a few moments before shock was overcome by curiosity and mobile phones and cameras would appear. Vaybian changed instantly, and I followed suit. I didn't need to say anything to Pyrites; a Jack Russell was already trotting along beside me, snapping at the occasional low-flying locust. That left just one more problem . . .

Jinx was stalking towards us, his coat flapping out behind him, making him look like one of his ravens. I heard a caw from above us, then another from behind, and when Jinx held out a hand, one glossy black bird alighted on his fingers and others swooped from the sky; some hopped along on the pavement behind him; others landed on the railings beside us. Within moments he was being followed by a sea of black, his coat flowing out behind him like a Goth's living bridal train.

'I'm beginning to think that what we look like isn't going to make a lot of difference.'

Vaybian sucked in breath through his teeth. 'Nor I.'

I remembered what it had felt like when the crows had attacked Jinx and me; his coat had offered us some protection, but it hadn't taken them long to peck through. If these birds attacked, Vaybian and I would very quickly be pecked to bits.

Pyrites gave a growl, and a head pushed up beneath my hand. He had transformed himself into a mastiff. 'Good boy,' I whispered, caressing his ears.

When Jinx was four or five yards away, he stopped and we did too. His forehead creased into a frown as he looked at me. *Was there any recognition?* I wasn't sure. He did look a little puzzled. Then his lips twisted into a snarl. 'Out of my way, woman.'

What was it with everyone calling me 'woman'?

I crossed my arms. 'I can't do that.'

He lifted his right hand to stroke the feathers of the bird perched on his left. 'I have an army of followers. You have but one daemon – and not a very prepossessing one at that.'

'If you want to see your little friends vaporised by a sheet of flame, bring it on,' I said, caressing Pyrites' head.

Jinx's eyes narrowed. 'Get out of my way.'

'No.'

He scowled at me.

'Haven't you done enough?'

'I haven't even started.'

'To achieve what?'

Confusion passed across his face. 'I . . .' Then it was gone and the snarly expression returned.

I knew Jinx was just a tool – Amaliel and Persephone didn't control death; that was the prerogative of the Deathbringer . . . could there possibly be enough of *my* Jinx left to keep fighting them?

I told Vaybian to stay where he was, held out my hand and started to walk towards Jinx – and he began to stride towards me, until we were close enough to touch. I stopped; he took that one step more and a memory skittered through my head of an attic room full of autumn gloom; of another dangerous daemon moving closer and closer to me . . . I could almost smell the scent of lavender.

I shook the thought away, it wasn't helpful.

The puzzled expression had returned to Jinx's face. The raven perched on his wrist gave a squawk and fluttered away as Jinx grimaced and pressed his hand against his temple.

I took a step closer and as I reached out to him – he was in pain and I wanted to stop it – the stone in the ring on my finger flared and the creature inside my head snarled. I wished I knew what it meant.

'Jinx,' I said, 'fight her.'

He groaned again, and staggered slightly. I went to steady him and then his arms were wrapped around me tight and he hissed against my ear, 'Gotcha.'

I began to struggle, but he was too strong for me. I heard Vaybian cry out, and the birds surrounding Jinx erupted into the air in a raucous cloud of black flapping wings.

'Jinx!' I screamed at him. 'Fight her, *fight her*—'

He began to laugh, but it wasn't him, not really.

Eighteen

If anyone was shouting, they were drowned out by the cries of thousands of ravens, and all I could see of Vaybian was a mass of black flapping wings. Then a different noise pierced the cacophony: a helicopter was coming towards us.

I was hoping it was a news team, or maybe even the police, Heaven help me – but I wasn't holding my breath. Persephone apparently had unlimited resources at her disposal, so a helicopter was certainly within her reach.

The birds swarmed away from us, forming a barrier between me and Vaybian and Pyrites. At any moment I expected a stream of flame as Pyrites tried to clear away the birds, but I was more concerned about the rope ladder being lowered from the chopper now hovering above us.

I began to struggle, yelling to make myself heard, 'Jinx! For fuck's sake, fight her!' I managed to free an arm and smacked him as hard as I could around the face.

He snarled at me, grabbed me by the wrist, and slapped me back, so hard I swear my feet left the ground.

'You are going to be *so* sorry you did that,' I screamed at Psycho Bitch.

Jinx grabbed hold of the ladder and I pummelled him with my fists, kicking him and trying to knee him in the groin, but it did no good whatsoever. We were airborne.

'If you struggle, you will fall,' he snarled in my ear.

'Then,' I hissed back, 'I will fall.' And I raked my fingernails down the side of his face; my ring flared and the creature inside my head roared encouragement.

Jinx's eyelids fluttered shut and when they opened for a moment

I could see sheer panic – then his lips moved. 'You!' he said, and he rested his forehead against mine, his horns brushing my hair.

'Jinx, we can't let them take us.'

He glanced down at water thick with blood flowing below us. I really didn't want to end up swimming in that disgusting mess, but better that than being taken. Jinx let go of the ladder and we were falling. I couldn't stop myself screaming – then I clamped my eyes and mouth shut and prayed that the force of hitting the water wouldn't knock us out cold. At least it wouldn't kill us, and even as I thought that, I felt myself change.

Jinx was still holding me as we hit the surface feet-first and plunged down and down. It wasn't as cold as I'd expected; I found myself wondering if the blood had warmed it.

As soon as we stopped sinking, Jinx shrugged off his coat and began to swim, one arm wrapped around my waist – but not upwards, as I'd expected. I took a chance and opened my eyes; down here, deep beneath the surface, the water was coloured a rich scarlet, but it wasn't pure blood, more like several hundred someones had bled out into it.

I began to swim with Jinx, hoping he knew what he was doing. I was grateful he kept hold of me – if he'd let go, I doubted I'd ever find him again in this murk.

I thought my lungs were likely to burst as Jinx finally struck upwards. It was darker here, and I realised he'd brought us up under the bridge, where we couldn't be seen from above, a good way from the northern bank.

I could still hear the cries of birds above us, and the *whomp, whomp, whomp* of helicopter blades – they must have come around to find us. I wondered if Vaybian and Pyrites had seen us drop into the river through the mass of birds; I just had to hope they'd got safely off the bridge and let Shenanigans know what had happened.

Jinx didn't let go of me until we reached one of the walls supporting the bridge, and we hung there, treading water and gasping for breath.

'We wait,' he said.

'Here?'

'If you want to live. They want to kill you—' He stopped. Grimacing, he raised his hand to his temple. I made a grab for him, but he began to struggle, trying to escape the pain.

'Jinx, let me help you,' I said, but he thrashed away from me and cried out, then disappeared beneath the surface.

I began to panic: he'd been right next to me – and now he was gone? 'Jinx!' I upended myself and dived down, searching for him, but in the red soup shadowed by the bridge I couldn't see a thing. I bobbed to the surface and took a couple of breaths, then dived deeper, but I still couldn't see him. I screamed his name under the water, and then thrashed to the surface, where I coughed and spluttered, trying to spit out the vile liquid, even as I looked around, hoping against hope I would see him bob to the surface. It couldn't end like this; it just *couldn't*.

When I'd got my breath back I dived back down, letting my weight take me deeper, fighting against my own natural buoyancy to force myself downwards to the river bottom – but there was nothing. My panic was fast turning to despair: *he was gone*. He could have been hanging there a foot away and I couldn't have seen him. He might have taken that last breath, sucking in water until his lungs were full, and even now be sinking into a blood-infused watery grave . . .

I stopped swimming and hung there for one last moment before I started to slowly float back up, admitting to myself that I really had lost him.

Then out of the corner of my eye I saw something dark – I needed air, but if I went up to breathe, I might never find that shadowy outline again. I started to swim towards it, and spotted a maroon hand – I propelled myself forward and grabbed hold of it, then made for the surface, pulling him along behind me.

We were still under the bridge, but we'd drifted a good few yards from the concrete supports; I thanked our lucky stars that neither of us had been caught in the Thames' dangerous currents.

I pulled Jinx onto his back. His eyes were closed and his skin had a slightly purplish hue. He looked . . .

No, he was the Deathbringer, *he didn't die*. He *couldn't* die.

I needed to do CPR – but I needed a solid surface beneath us. So if I couldn't do chest compressions, at least I could force air into his lungs. Treading water, keeping us afloat, I opened his mouth, pressed my lips against his and breathed out, once, twice, three times, then so many I lost count. I spread my hand over his chest and the ring on my finger flared. The creature inside my head cried out, and I almost broke down.

The ring flaring must mean something – but it didn't matter, not now. All that mattered was that Jinx—

'Don't leave me,' I whispered, and pressed my lips against his one more time, forcing as much of me into him as I could.

It didn't work.

I stroked the cheek that still bore the scratch marks where I'd raked it with my fingernails, and the human part of me began to cry. I felt like letting myself sink down into the river's murky embrace – but no, I had to be strong. Amaliel still had Kayla, and I had to find a way of getting her back, and my mother too.

I cupped Jinx's chin with my hand and on my back, dragging him with me, began to swim to shore.

I kept close to the bridge, not that it mattered any more, and when I got to the final support I took a breather, clinging to it while I studied the bank. I kept one hand under Jinx's head to keep it above water, but I guess that didn't matter much either.

I spotted a flight of steps on the left; I'd make for that. I closed my eyes and breathed deeply, suddenly feeling bone-weary, like all my energy had been leeched from within me. I felt myself change back to human.

I put my hand under Jinx's chin once again, lay back into the water and pulled his head up so it rested on my chest, preparing for that last lap—

—and icy fingers grasped my wrist, the shock sending me floundering. In a frenzy of bubbles I sank beneath the surface before managing to right myself and get my head above water. I gasped for air as I swiped sodden hair from my eyes. My right wrist was still encircled in an iron grip.

'You,' he said, as if surprised to see me. '*You.*'

'Yes, it's me.' And I started crying, and this time I couldn't do anything to stop the tears.

Jinx let go of my wrist to run his fingers down my cheek. 'Don't cry,' he said. 'Please don't cry.'

'I thought you were dead—'

His lips curled into a smile. 'And now so do they.'

I stared at him for a moment trying to take it in. '*What?*'

He cupped his hand to his ear and looked up, as if telling me to listen, and when I twisted my head and stared up at the bridge above us I realised I could no longer hear the sound of rotor blades, or the cawing of a thousand birds.

'Persephone thinks you're dead?'

'She does.'

'But the Deathbringer can't die—'

'Yet you thought I was dead.'

'You were pretending?'

'I was disconnecting myself.'

'You can do that?' I wasn't sure whether to punch him or kiss him.

'It would appear so. I didn't know until it came to it, or I would have done it earlier.' He looked at the riverbank. 'Come on,' he said and began to swim for shore, keeping under the bridge for as long as he could.

'We need to get out of these clothes,' I said as we climbed up onto the Embankment. 'Apart from being wet, they stink.'

'The least of our problems I'm sure.'

'Jinx,' I said suddenly, 'do you remember me? Do you remember who you are?'

He took my hand when we reached the top of the steps. We were on a long walkway – if it hadn't been for the locusts, it would doubtless have been crowded with people going about their daily business. Lucky for us it wasn't, but I doubted this would last for long; now the bugs had gone Heaven knew where, the people would quickly return – tourist or local, I was betting everyone would want to take a look at the Thames the colour of blood. Even if it did smell pretty vile.

'I have been here before,' Jinx said, looking around and totally ignoring my question. 'I can feel it – although I recognise none of this.'

'When you were last in London this bridge wasn't here. The old bridge was about a hundred feet upstream and probably quite different. I think it's changed a couple of times since the Great Fire.'

As we started to walk along the Embankment I thought we must have looked a very odd pair to anyone who might be looking out of their windows. We were soaking wet, our clothes stained red with blood, and the man gripping onto my hand so tightly was bare-chested and maroon, with long black hair and rather cute little dark maroon horns peeping out just above his hairline. It was a shame he'd lost his coat; it had at least made his strange body colour not quite so obvious. Then of course there was his tail.

As we passed a block of offices I looked up and as quickly looked away again, keeping my head down. As I thought, the windows were quickly filling with people pointing their mobiles at us: within thirty seconds images of Jinx and me would be going viral. The wicked part of me was tempted to change into my daemon self – that would really give them something to chew on – but one of us looking like a comic-book character was quite enough.

I rummaged in the pocket of my jacket for the mobile Kerfuffle had given me. I wasn't holding out much hope that it'd be working after its soaking, but thought I should give it a try. Sadly, it was completely dead – I doubted even a techie genius would be able to get the thing working again. I stuffed it back in my pocket; maybe it was covered by my credit card insurance.

Then I wondered what on earth I was thinking.

'We really should get away from here,' I told Jinx, and the words were hardly out of my mouth before I heard sirens in the distance and the thumping of rotor blades. 'Come on.' I tugged on his hand, drew him down a side road and started to run.

'Where are we going?'

'Anywhere but here.'

'But why?'

'Because we don't want to get ourselves arrested.'

'We have done nothing wrong.'

'I'm not sure about the legality of bringing down plagues of locusts and ravens upon London, but I'm sure there must be some sort of bylaw – and as for polluting the River Thames with blood' – I blew out through pursed lips – 'they'll probably throw away the key.'

I know sarcasm is the lowest form of wit, but I was at a very low ebb.

He frowned at me, obviously thinking the same. 'The blood is dispersing.'

'I thought it might be.'

'The locusts have gone.'

'Somewhere.'

'And the ravens have returned to the skies.'

'Whose side are they on, yours or Persephone's?'

'The ravens are mine – crows, not so much; they are the lesser bird.'

I dragged him along the road by the hand as the sound of sirens got louder and the helicopter drew closer. I hoped it wasn't Persephone, back for another go – although I supposed we could hitch a ride until we were out of trouble with the police.

We were coming up to a junction when a police car swerved around the corner with a squeal of tyres and slithered to a standstill, shortly followed by two more.

'Shit!' I skidded to a stop and glanced back over my shoulder to see two motorcycles with blue lights flashing appearing at the end of the road, blocking the other exit.

Policemen jumped out of the cars ahead and one shouted, 'Stop right where you are!' His electronic megaphone made him sound like a Dalek. 'Hands on your head and on your knees!'

'I kneel for no man,' Jinx said, going all haughty.

'I think we might have to,' I said.

'This is your final warning: put your hands on your heads and give yourselves up.'

'If you have some kind of trick up your sleeve to get us out of this mess, now would be a good time,' I said.

He gave me a puzzled look. 'I am wearing no sleeves.'

'Jinx,' I said, before we had a repeat of last time, 'we need to get out of here without getting shot or arrested.'

He raised my hand to his lips. 'Your wish is my command, my lady.'

Still holding my hand he took a step forward, threw back his head and with his free arm outstretched, he cried, '*Omnes dormieris!*' His voice echoed through the street and then there was silence all around us. I could still hear the sounds of the city up ahead, but not a thing stirred in the immediate vicinity.

Policemen locked in time crouched behind cars or stood mid-step, rifles in hands. The motorcycle cops had frozen mid-dismount. I looked up at the windows of the buildings above us; the onlookers were the same, standing motionless, some with mobile phones glued to their ears, some pointing them down at us, no doubt videoing the excitement going on below to Tweet or post to YouTube, Instagram and Facebook.

Jinx gave me a self-satisfied smile. 'Good enough, milady?'

'Great! At least you've remembered something useful,' I said, tugging on his hand. 'Come on, let's go before they wake up.'

We ran past the police cars, around the corner and onto the main road. Cars were driving by and pedestrians were beginning to venture out, but as soon as they saw us coming they darted back inside shops or offices to get out of our way. I caught a glimpse of our reflections and I could see why: Jinx, with his long hair plastered to his head, looked like some very horrible demon from an old Japanese painting, and even my human self looked as scary as hell covered in drying bloody water.

'Jinx, could you at least try to look human?'

'You think it would help?'

I took another quick glance at myself in a window. 'Probably not,' I admitted with a sigh.

At this rate everyone within sight would be ringing 999 before we'd even moved a hundred yards – and sure enough, I soon heard the high-pitched scream of more sirens heading our way.

'Come on,' I said, dragging him into the next doorway. I pushed open the heavy glass door and the woman behind the reception desk glanced up with a welcoming smile – which immediately turned to a grimace of horror as she grabbed for the phone.

'Jinx,' I hissed, 'do something.'

'*Omnes dormieris*,' he said, and the woman froze.

'Will everyone in this building be out for the count?'

'Probably; certainly this floor and the next.'

'We need to find the bathrooms.'

'You intend to take a bath?'

'No, I intend to wash some of this crud out of my hair and off my face, and if we can find a coat for you to wear, that would be good too.'

'This is your plan?'

'It's the best I can do for the moment, but if you have any better ideas please feel free to share them,' I snapped.

He gave me another of his puzzled looks. 'Are you for some reason vexed with me?'

I rubbed the bridge of my nose between forefinger and thumb. 'It's not you; I'm pretty much angry with everyone at the moment.'

I took him through a door which opened onto a stairwell going up and down. I doubted there'd be much for us in the basement, but upstairs there would be a loo somewhere, and maybe even a cloakroom; we really needed to nick a couple of coats.

Some god or other must have been smiling on us for once. We

found the bathrooms, and this turned out to be a particularly swanky office, because they included a shower cubicle.

'Right – you get in the shower and I'll find us some dry clothes,' I told him.

I think he was about to argue, then he thought better of it. 'Will you be joining me?'

Had it been *my* Jinx, the old Jinx asking, my stomach would have given a little flip, but his expression was so guileless I assumed he was just asking the question.

'In a mo,' I said.

'Don't take too long,' he said, making me think again, but when I glanced back, he was busy pulling off his boots.

I hurried out into the hallway and started opening doors and peering into each room. In the last office I got lucky: a young woman with glasses perched on the end of her nose was sitting at a desk, one hand poised over her keyboard, the other grasping a coffee mug. She looked to be about my size – and even better, hanging from the handle of a cupboard behind her were a couple of dry-cleaning bags.

'Sorry,' I said, snagging the top bag off the door and hoping it wasn't a favourite outfit.

I'd really lucked out for once: it was a skirt and jacket; if the lapels weren't cut too low I might even get away without wearing a shirt underneath.

I pulled open the other bag and grinned. 'Well, hello!' It was a man's suit, though hopefully not her boss', otherwise she'd be looking for a new job pretty soon.

I had a quick look at her shoes to see if they'd fit, but they had six-inch heels and, as I really didn't fancy breaking my neck, I let her keep them. I was surprised at how felonious I was becoming. Kayla used to call me 'Little Miss Goody Two Shoes', but it looked like when the chips were down, I wasn't quite so good as either of us thought.

I hurried back to the bathroom and was greeted by hot steam coming out from the shower cubicle. I quickly stripped off, rinsed my boots inside and out and propped them upside-down in a sink, then did the same to Jinx's. I pulled a load of paper towels from the dispenser and put them in a pile just outside the cubicle, ready for when we got out – perhaps not ideal, but better than nothing.

It didn't look like Jinx was coming out anytime soon, so I opened the door a crack. For a moment all I could see was steam, but when it cleared a bit he was standing with his back to me, hands pressed against the tiles, the water pounding directly onto his head. The scars across his shoulders and back were fading at last; when I had first touched them they had been puckered ridges and now they were dark pink lines. I wondered if this might mean her power over him was fading too. I hoped so.

I tentatively reached out and ran my finger across where two lines met and I felt his body go rigid. His head whipped around, his expression softening when he saw it was me. He slowly turned to face me and reached out to touch my face. My breath caught in the back of my throat. Despite his earlier guileless expression I knew exactly what was on his mind – *did this mean my Jinx was coming back to me?* It was for this reason I couldn't deny him, I told myself, but it was a lie. I wanted him so badly; I wanted him to be mine again.

'My lady,' he said, sliding his hand around the back of my neck and drawing me to him.

His other arm snaked around my waist and his lips pressed against my throat and my chin and then my cheek and when they finally kissed mine I wondered how many times a woman could have that 'first' time with the same man.

Then he lifted me up and everything else that was going on – all the bad stuff – was swept away and all that mattered was the touch of his skin against mine and his lips against my lips and my body sinking onto his. I couldn't let myself think that this could be the last time. If I did I thought I might just die.

Nineteen

Except for the long leather coat, I'd never known Jinx to wear anything other than boots and leather trousers, so seeing him in a dark grey suit was odd. As well as the jacket, there was a pale grey shirt and a navy and grey tie wrapped around the neck of the coathanger.

The suit was a tad big around the waist and hips, but once the belt had been pulled in a couple of notches it didn't look too bad beneath the jacket – though judging by Jinx's expression he didn't think the same.

The woman whose clothes I'd appropriated was bigger in the bust than me, but the suit didn't look too bad, especially with her pretty white camisole peeking out between the lapels of the buttoned-up navy jacket. My biker boots didn't do much for the whole ensemble, but it was way better than being wet and stinking.

Jinx was still frowning at his reflection in the mirror. 'I do not like this.'

'Do you want to walk around in soaking wet clothes all day?' I started to plait his long locks.

'I really do not care.'

'Dressed like this, we'll be a little less conspicuous – and if you could try to pass for human, that would be good too.'

'I don't know how.'

'You can't remember?'

He continued to stare at himself.

'I had to try and remember what I looked like before I became my daemon self, but I suppose as you've never been anything but a daemon that wouldn't apply.'

'You know me well?'

'I don't make a habit of sharing showers with men I don't.'

He didn't crack a smile. 'Good.'

This was going to be very interesting when we got back to the Underlands – *if* we got back . . . If Jinx didn't regain his memory, I had no idea what he'd make of Jamie. But I had plenty of other things to keep me occupied; that would have to wait.

'Come on. Time to go.'

He took one last look in the mirror. 'I really do not like,' he said as he followed me out into the hallway.

I smiled. He looked gorgeous, actually.

Back on the street we hurried along with our heads down, hoping no one would pay us much attention. There were people about now, but everyone was in such a hurry that if they did notice Jinx, they'd already moved on before anything registered.

'Where are we going?' he asked.

'We're heading back to the Thames. I must try and find Pyrites,' I explained. He was our only hope of getting back to the others, and I was worried about him – and even, somewhat to my surprise, Vaybian.

When we reached the Thames I could see Jinx was right: the blood was dissipating. If Persephone and Amaliel had been aiming for full-on Biblical Devastations, they must be disappointed; this would be yesterday's news in a few hours, forgotten in a week.

We walked along the Embankment until the buildings gave way to a little piece of green within the city. The Victoria Embankment Gardens were just what we needed; the trees would hide us from view from above.

Then I came to a halt. Three men were walking towards us, and they might have been dressed like businessmen, but with or without wings, I knew angels when I saw them.

I swung Jinx around and we started back the way we'd come, but there were two men in black suits, followed by another three in jeans and trainers, and they were all making straight for us. These five were all human, and Joseph was leading them; that was the giveaway that they were the enemy.

How on earth had they found us? Or had they been following each other and we'd stumbled into the middle of whatever was going on? The river was on the other side of the road, so the park was our best bet – except for a low wall topped with railings barring us from entry.

'We need to get in there,' I told Jinx.

He didn't ask why; even if he hadn't recognised the Guardians, he certainly knew Joseph and his colleagues. He swung me up into his arms and with a single bound was up and over the railings. As soon as we touched the ground he dropped me back down, took my hand and we were off and running and I thanked any gods who might have been listening that I hadn't purloined the woman's high-heeled shoes.

I hoped the Guardians would be more interested in the Satanists than us, but I doubted it would take them long to polish off five humans, even of the Satanic variety – then I heard automatic gunfire . . . the Guardians might not be our friends, but they were the good guys, and I really didn't like the idea of them being all shot up.

Then my common sense kicked in: there was nothing I could do to help them, so I should keep running – but running to *where*? We had nowhere to go, and we couldn't just keep running for ever.

Desperation bubbled up inside me, and if it hadn't been for Jinx's tight grip on my hand, I might have faltered. Then up ahead, I saw Vaybian, striding towards us with a Jack Russell trotting along at his side. I'd never have believed I'd be so pleased to see him. He started to lift a hand in greeting, and paused as his attention shifted to something going on behind us.

His lips moved, and Pyrites appeared in all his Jewelled Drakon glory.

'Are you mad?' I muttered, but after risking a look behind me, decided on balance he probably wasn't.

There were now at least eight men running after us, none of whom were Guardians, and several were carrying the type of weapons you normally only see in movies or war-zones.

Vaybian jumped onto Pyrites and reached out a hand to pull me aboard, then Jinx clambered up behind me.

'Let's go!' Vaybian cried and, with a flap of Pyrites' mighty wings, we were airborne, leaving our pursuers behind.

'Tell him not to go too high,' I shouted to Vaybian. 'We have to keep below radar.' Then I remembered none of them would know what radar was. Still, Pyrites did as he was told.

Of course, flying low to avoid being picked up by air-traffic control meant we were in full view of anyone below who happened to be looking up, or out of the windows of any of the dozens of skyscrapers surrounding us. The streets had been empty only an hour ago, but now it was back to business as usual. It would take just one to look up and cry out and that would be that: a dragon would have been officially seen flying over the streets of the capital.

'It's a shame we haven't got a cloak of invisibility,' I muttered to myself.

Surprisingly, we made it almost as far as the Houses of Parliament without being spotted, but of course people were staring up at Big Ben or the Palace of Westminster or some other bloody building. A shout went up and when I dared to look down, it was onto a sea of open-mouthed faces peering up at us, and a cacophony of frantically clicking and whirring cameras and mobiles. YouTube was going to be inundated.

At least Vaybian wasn't green, and I too was in my human form – that my skirt had ridden up almost to my waist and I had a maroon-skinned horned daemon wearing a very nice suit clinging to me was the downside. I was thankful he'd kept his tail hidden from view – he'd stuffed it down one leg of his trousers, although he'd not been at all happy about it. Sitting on Pyrites was probably making him pretty uncomfortable.

'The Guardian is not going to be happy,' Vaybian said, leaning back.

'I don't expect he will,' I said. I *really* hoped he wasn't in trouble with anyone.

Pyrites flew along the river and took us down to land in the first expanse of green he could find, one of the Royal Parks. As soon as his feet touched the ground he began to shrink and within moments we were standing astride a Jack Russell. I scooped him up in my arms and gave him a hug and was rewarded with an enthusiastic licking.

'Is he all right?' Vaybian asked, giving Jinx a pointed look.

'He doesn't remember who he is, or we are, but apart from that I think so.'

Jinx frowned at Vaybian. 'Who is he?'

'He's a friend,' I said.

'I'm not sure I like you,' he told Vaybian.

'Do I look as though I care?' Vaybian said with one of his arrogant looks.

Jinx glowered at him.

'Will you both stop it?' I said. I really didn't need two petulant daemons to deal with, not just at that moment. 'We need to find Amaliel.'

'Maybe you should have let them take you up into the skies with their mechanical beast,' Vaybian said.

'Yeah, right. I want to find them and rescue Kayla, not need rescuing myself. Anyway, I'd rather not become part of Amaliel's jewellery collection.'

'A fair point,' Vaybian said, 'but we will never find them if we keep running away.'

Which was also a fair point.

'I know where they are,' Jinx said.

Vaybian and I both stared at him. 'You do?' I asked.

'Yes. The woman has a residence not far from here.'

'She does?'

'Why would I lie about such a thing?'

'I wasn't doubting you, Jinx, I was just surprised.'

'Could you take us there?' Vaybian asked.

Jinx gave him one of his arrogant looks. 'I don't want to take *you* anywhere.'

'Jinx, for goodness' sake! We have to find Amaliel and Persephone and rescue Kayla.'

'Who did you say Kayla is?'

'My sister and my friend,' I said. This was like pulling teeth.

'Does *he* have to come with us?' Jinx asked, jerking his head in Vaybian's direction.

'He's Kayla's partner, so yes.'

'Partner?'

'Boyfriend, lover, betrothed.'

'Is that what we are?' he asked.

'Yes,' I said, and he smiled.

'Then I shall take you there, though to be close to that woman is something I would rather forego.'

'You can leave Psycho Bitch to me,' I said. There really was a different side to me, and I'd never even suspected: not only could I steal if I had to, but it turned out, I could also bear an enormous grudge against anyone who tried to hurt those I cared about.

'Should I phone the Guardian and tell him you are safe?' Vaybian asked.

I shook my head. 'I don't want to get him into trouble.'

'Then I shall text Shenanigans.'

We'd shown everyone how to use mobile phones, but for Vaybian to say he would text Shenanigans so offhandedly when only a day or so ago he had found cars, refrigerators and electric lights unsettling made me feel like I was in the Twilight Zone.

'What is this "Tecs"?' Jinx asked.

'It's "texting" and it's what I was doing on my mobile when you very kindly threw it away.'

His face cleared. 'Ah: Tecs is sending messages.'

We started walking, but as Jinx was still maroon and had horns I didn't see how we were going to get very far without getting ourselves into trouble of some description.

'Apparently we have been on the television,' Vaybian said, looking up from his mobile.

'I thought we might.'

'And three Guardians have been injured.'

'Are they all right?'

'Yes; Shenanigans says their pride was more hurt than their bodies, although there was a lot of blood.' He paused a moment, eyes fixed on the screen. 'He says the Guardians are looking for large open areas where a drakon could land.'

'Wonderful. So they could be here any minute?'

'Apparently so,' Vaybian said, tapping off and sliding his phone into his back pocket. 'It would help if the Deathbringer would at least try to blend in.'

'He says he doesn't know how.'

'Nor did I, until I tried,' Vaybian grumbled.

'Jinx, please, try to look human?' I asked him again.

'I don't *want* to look human.'

'Please – for me.'

He cocked his head to one side. 'It would please you if I had the appearance of a human?'

'Jinx, I love you just the way you are, but in this world you stand out like a . . . like a . . . Well, you just stand out, and we can't let the Guardians or Persephone's men catch us.'

'All right, I will try.' He stopped walking and closed his eyes. His forehead creased in concentration. He stood like that for quite some time, then opened one eye.

'Have I changed?'

'No,' Vaybian and I chorused with varying degrees of frustration.

He closed the eye, pressed his palms together, raised them to his lips, then bowed his head as though he was praying. The air around him rippled, sending out shockwaves a lot more powerful than when any of my guard had changed, and it belatedly occurred to me that this probably wasn't a good idea; it was exactly the type of disruption that would lead the Guardians straight to us. But by then it was too late.

Even though he was standing only a few feet away, for a moment

I could see only his outline – then there was a rush as the air came back in and I felt a sucking sensation pulling me towards him. It stopped as abruptly as it began.

Vaybian gave a gasp, and Pyrites made a weird mewling noise. Jinx had changed.

Oh yes, he'd changed all right.

I've been lost for words a time or two, but for the first time in my life I was totally speechless.

'Jinx, when I said change, I sort of meant into a human version of yourself,' I stammered.

'There is no such thing.'

I exchanged a look with Vaybian, who was clearly as gob-smacked as me. 'At least it will cause some confusion when we find Amaliel's hideout.'

'Who for?' I looked Jinx up and down, feeling distinctly odd.

'You said I was to change into human form and I have. This' – he gestured down at himself – 'will ease our way into the woman's den.'

'It was bad enough when you opened your mouth and Psycho Bitch spoke, but this is something else.'

Vaybian circled Jinx and began to laugh. 'You make a very good woman, Deathbringer.'

I felt a little sick: he'd become human all right – but he'd become *Persephone*.

'In this form, the Deathbringer may well be able to get us close enough to rescue my lady,' Vaybian said, 'maybe even without the need for us to enter.'

'And how would we know if it was her or Jinx who came out?' I asked.

'We'll have a secret sign,' Vaybian suggested. 'Though I recom-mend we get moving: the Guardians were already seeking us; the power of the Deathbringer's transformation will lead them straight here.'

As we hurried through the park, I had to suppress a slightly hysterical giggle. Jinx might have been the absolute image of Persephone, but he was striding along like Jinx, and in high heels, which was no mean feat.

As soon as we were back on the street I started looking for a taxi, then I stopped abruptly. 'I don't suppose you know the address?' I asked Jinx.

'I will know it when I see it.'

So a taxi was out of the question. 'So which way?'

He pointed a long painted nail, and I knew London well enough to recognise we were headed in the general direction of Belgravia. I hurried them across the road and into a side street, hoping the Guardians wouldn't risk taking to the air to find us.

Jinx strode along as if he knew exactly where he was going – and I noticed glumly that he was coping with high heels better than I ever had. Which set me to wondering . . . I immediately pushed the thought aside. Nah – there was no way Jinx was a cross dresser. I doubted whether daemons even knew what it meant.

It wasn't long before Jinx slowed and took hold of my arm. 'That is the place,' he said, pointing to a beautiful four-storey Georgian mansion.

'Wow!' I muttered. 'I knew she was rich, but . . .'

The house must have been worth *millions*. A limousine was parked out front in a residents' parking bay – how much did that permit cost her a year? Why this woman dabbled in the occult I couldn't fathom. And something else puzzled me: her connection with Amaliel. I wasn't sure who was using whom, but Amaliel had clearly come to the Overlands as her partner-in-crime.

'What now?' Vaybian asked.

I studied the front of the house. Just like the Sussex mansion there were discreet cameras trained on the front door and at either end of the building. Persephone probably had good reason to have twenty-four-hour security staff, so there was a good chance they were continually monitored.

'Shall I attempt entry?' Jinx asked.

'You can hardly go and ring the front door bell – Psycho Bitch would have her own key.'

'No key,' Jinx said.

'No?'

He shook his head. 'Numbers.' He mimed stabbing a code into a keypad.

'I don't suppose . . .?'

He grinned at me, which was rather disconcerting, as it was with Persephone's face. '6666.'

'At least she's predictable.'

Both Jinx and Vaybian gave me puzzled frowns – Jamie was interested in human theology, but Vaybian didn't have a clue and Jinx wouldn't remember if he had known to start with.

'Do you think we could do that?' Vaybian said, gesturing with his head at Jinx.

'What, change into Persephone?'

He rolled his eyes. 'No – but make ourselves look like someone else?'

'I really have no idea.'

Vaybian closed his eyes, his brow creasing in concentration, muttering, 'If a damned drakon can do it, so can I.'

That was a point: if Pyrites could change into any kind of dog, and even a bird – why couldn't daemons look like other daemons? Too late, I remembered the Guardians would sense the magic and cried out, 'No!'

But it was done: the air shimmered for a moment more, there was the same weird sucking sensation as when Jinx had changed, Vaybian's image blurred and flickered – and then Joseph was standing there.

'Wow,' I said, 'just look at you!'

'We know Joseph is currently out, so my entering shouldn't cause a problem.'

'He could have come back,' I said, indicating the limo.

'I doubt this Persephone woman suffers failure with kind words and jugs of ale,' Vaybian said. 'If I were him, I wouldn't return until I had found what I'd been sent for. Therefore, I will return with you and Persephone's lookalike, and hope she isn't the first person we encounter.'

'If she is, you have my leave to kill her.'

'The Guardian said we weren't to harm humans—'

'She's no human,' Jinx snarled.

'Are you sure?'

'She conjures Blue Fire and . . .' He hesitated, then murmured, 'I have been closer to her than I care for.'

I didn't want to know what he meant by that, although my overactive imagination was having a field day. I hated her more than enough already; I didn't need more reasons.

'Are you free of her?' Vaybian asked. 'If we enter the drakon's den, will she be able to break down your defences? If so, it is better that you stay here.'

'I have been entombed in Blue Fire once, so it will make it easier for her to imprison me again,' he conceded. 'Hopefully we will find Amaliel first and take what is yours before she is alerted to our presence.'

'Can I make a suggestion?' They both turned to me, Jinx with a slightly puzzled expression, Vaybian's more expectant. 'Why doesn't Jinx change back into himself, then there is no chance of Persephone bumping into her doppelgänger and Vaybian can say he's captured me and Jinx is back on side?'

Jinx rested his chin on his fist; a familiar gesture which just looked weird done by Persephone. 'I do not like looking like this,' he admitted. 'It feels too . . . *intimate*.'

'I must admit just looking at him gives me the creeps,' Vaybian said.

'Looking at *her* gives me the creeps!'

Jinx didn't wait for any more discussion; the air shimmered and my Deathbringer was back. The suit was gone; he was wearing his trademark black leather trousers and boots, and he'd replaced the long leather coat with another, this one soft and supple, and not pecked into a holey mess by crows.

He breathed in deeply. 'Better.'

'You like the coat?'

He cocked his head to one side, 'You do not?'

'Yes, I suppose so.' It did suit him, but it also made him look a little scary, especially with his hair hanging loose, and that make me wonder how much of him still belonged to Persephone.

'You do not appear sure.'

'I—'

'If you want her to believe I am still hers, I must look the part.'

He was right, of course, but it didn't mean I had to like it.

'What if Joseph turns up while we're in there?' I wondered.

'We kill him,' Jinx said.

'He's a human,' Vaybian reminded him.

Jinx turned his glowing eyes on Vaybian, his expression dark. 'If he were a human, he would deserve to be crushed like an insect beneath the heel of my boot for what he and his mistress intend for this world. As he is not, he will get what he deserves.'

'Joseph isn't human?' I asked.

I had been quite sure that he was. If I was wrong, he had somehow managed to hide his daemon self beneath a very substantial façade – but then, hadn't I done the same thing most of my life? Were they like me, or were they born to this world to live like sleepers, undercover and waiting for the time they were to be awakened by their handler? Maybe while humans were worrying about foreign sleeper spy cells, we had something much worse lying in wait.

'Soulseer,' Vaybian said, shaking me out of my reverie, 'if we're to make a move we should make it now. The longer we wait the better the chance of us being discovered, either by the Guardians out here, or upon the return of the real Joseph in there.'

'Right,' I said, taking a deep breath and pulling myself up to my full five foot five, 'let's go.'

Jinx took hold of one arm and Vaybian took hold of the other and they marched me across the road to the house, leaving Pyrites to keep guard and alert us if the real Joseph should return. We'd texted Shenanigans so he knew where we were; if anything happened to us, we hoped the cavalry would arrive shortly. And even if they didn't, the Guardians would be drawn towards Jinx and Vaybian's earlier displays of power.

'Torch the limo if you have to,' I told Pyrites. 'Though if you do, get out of the way fast: it'll explode – but at least we'll hear it inside.' He shrank to the size of a bird and perched up in a nearby tree. I didn't like leaving him, but we would be better served with him as a lookout than inside with us. Besides, I didn't want Persephone getting her evil claws in another of my friends.

By the time we'd reached the door I was pretty sure it was only Jinx and Vaybian holding me that was stopping my knees from giving way. I was beyond scared – but I had to *help* Kayla and my mother. I cheered myself up with the thought that I would hopefully get to see the smug smile wiped off of Persephone's very red lips.

Vaybian tapped in the code, pushed the door and in we walked, as easy as that.

The entrance hall was dominated by a huge staircase with ornate banisters leading up to a landing going off to the left and right. Thick carpet patterned in red and gold covered the floor and stairs and paintings in ostentatious, gold-lacquered frames covered the off-white walls.

Small pieces of antique furniture were strategically placed at either side of the two doors leading off from the hall: dainty occasional tables and fancy cabinets on which stood porcelain Japanese vases full of sweet-scented flowers. Like her beautiful painted face, it was all for show, just like her other lairs.

'Which way?' Vaybian hissed.

Jinx pointed and led us back behind the stairs. Of course – another bloody basement. It was Amaliel we were after, and where else would he be except down underground, hiding in the dark like the rodent he was.

Jinx yanked open the door and let go of my arm to step onto the staircase. Vaybian gestured for me to go next and he followed on behind. Despite our differences, I felt that much safer knowing he was at my back.

A bulb enclosed in a thick glass wall light glowed overly white at the top of the stairs, and there was another at the bottom; that illumination led me to believe there was someone waiting for us down there – whether they were expecting us or not was a different matter.

Then a little flame of doubt bloomed in my chest. Jinx might still be in her thrall; this might all be part of the game. The words he was speaking could be *her* words; the gestures he made *her* gestures. He could be leading us to our doom.

At the bottom of the stairs was a solid, heavy door, a fire-door, maybe. Jinx took hold of the handle and turned it. The door swung open on well-oiled hinges, not making a sound. He stepped inside, with us right behind him. I paused on the brink, but it was too late now: if this was a trap, Vaybian and I had fallen for it hook, line and sinker.

Blue light flowed through the open doorway and I wondered which poor soul was now captured within its fiery grasp. Then I saw – and for the second time in as many hours I was left speechless.

It was the bokor encased in blue flickering light, his rigid body twisting and twitching, his mouth stretched wide in a silent scream. Amaliel, standing to one side, his back to the door – his back to *us* – gazed up at him as he hissed, 'Know now who wields the real power!'

We moved into the room, Jinx on one side of me, Vaybian to my other, but although I didn't think we'd made any noise, Amaliel must have sensed he had an audience, for he spun around to face us, his eyes flared and he took a step back.

'Well, well, well. It appears there's no honour among psychos either,' I said. I couldn't quite believe that at last we had him just where we wanted him: cornered like the rat he was.

He took another step back so he was standing just behind the writing bokor. I wondered what he'd done to so piss Amaliel off when the two of them had been in cahoots for *years*.

Amaliel's eyes went to Jinx and he recoiled, gasping, 'Keep him away from me—'

When I looked at Jinx, I could understand why; he'd gone all feral again – and Vaybian's expression wasn't much better.

'Let me go,' Amaliel said, a wheedling tone in his voice.

Was he mad? 'And why should I do that?'

'I have something you want.' Amaliel groped around inside his robes and pulled out two crystals hanging on the chains about his neck.

'And if I let you go, will you give them to me?'

'Yes—'

'You cross your revolting black heart and hope to die disgustingly and painfully?'

'I . . . promise.'

Jinx made a snarly sound in the back of his throat; he obviously gave the same weight as me to any promise Amaliel might give.

I crossed my arms and stared straight into his terrible eyes. 'I don't trust you.'

'Nor I you.'

'Then we have a problem.'

He rattled the crystals together. 'I will smash them.'

I stared at him some more. We both knew I didn't have much choice, but I wasn't about to show him that I was fazed. 'Take them from around your neck and hold them out in your hand.'

'And you will let me leave?'

'If you hand them to me.'

'You can't trust him to do what's right,' Vaybian whispered in my ear.

I glanced his way and our eyes met. 'If I'm to save Kayla, I've no choice. Get ready to make a grab for them.'

Amaliel had unclasped the chains from around his neck and was holding them in his bony fingers, the phials clinking against each other as they dangled. Vaybian took a step towards him and Amaliel snatched his hand back and clasped it against his chest.

'We had a deal, Amaliel.'

'You have said you'll let me go – but will he?' Amaliel pointed a skeletal finger at Jinx.

'If you don't hand the Soulseer the phials, it will be *me* you will have to worry about,' Vaybian snarled.

'This is not helping,' I murmured. I wondered what Amaliel was thinking about 'Joseph' switching teams; he'd not commented . . . I took a step towards Amaliel and when he took a step back I smiled. 'You're not *scared* of me, are you?'

'Of *you*?' If he was aiming for defiance in his voice, he failed miserably.

I started to laugh. 'I don't believe it. You are! You're scared of me.'

'Don't be ridiculous – why should I be scared of you?'

'Well, if you don't hand me the crystals right now you'll pretty soon find out.' I stretched out my hand, and when he took another step back, the phials still clutched to his chest, I said, 'Amaliel, I'm beginning to lose patience.'

'If you stand over there' – he pointed to the far corner – 'I will place the crystals there' – he pointed to the middle of the floor, next to where the bokor continued to burn – 'then you will let me leave.'

'Right, so you can slam the door shut behind you and lock us in? I don't think so,' I said, folding my arms.

'You will soon be released – the Guardians are no doubt on their wa—' But he was interrupted not by angelic-looking daemons but by an enormous *boom!* from up above. The room shook and puffs of dust started floating down from the ceiling.

Our eyes went to the doorway – the car had exploded, which meant Persephone was back – and that was all Amaliel needed.

'Catch them if you can!' he cried, and as he leaped for the door he flung the crystals towards the far corner.

Vaybian threw himself across the room, his fingers outstretched, and I had just started after him a fraction of a second slower, when a strong hand grabbed my wrist and held me back.

'*Omnia statur!*' Jinx said – and *everything* went still. This wasn't like before; then, just the living had frozen in time. Here I could see the clouds of dust hovering above us, Amaliel was frozen in the doorway and Vaybian was sprawled out in midair, his fingers not quite reaching the crystals. *He had missed them.* The amethyst crystal had just hit the wall, the tip had shattered and the golden basket in which the crystal rested was glowing red and melting.

Jinx let go of my wrist and strode over to where the undamaged crystal had stopped mid-flight. He wrapped the chain around his fingers and it fell limply into his hand. When he lifted the crystal up to the light, a deep blue glow pulsed from within. It was Kayla's crystal.

I couldn't remember my mother and my heart ached for her. She was well and truly lost to me, for ever. But now wasn't the time to grieve; that would have to come later.

A small smile lifted the corner of Jinx's lips as he dropped the crystal into his top pocket. I was about to object, then thought better of it: he had saved her, not me and not Vaybian, so I guess that gave him the right to keep her safe now.

He glanced Vaybian's way and with a look of disgust placed the tip of his forefinger on the back of his head. Vaybian fell in a sprawl to the ground with an undignified yelp and instantly changed to daemon. He crawled up onto his knees, looking this way and that, then saw the crystal shattering against the wall and his face contorted into an expression of outright misery. 'Kayla?' he whispered. 'My princess? *My princess—?*'

'It's okay, she's safe,' I told him. 'Jinx saved her.'

'Can I see?' he asked, looking from me to Jinx.

'No,' Jinx said, and touched the amethyst crystal, which continued its flight into the wall and exploded into dust.

'Was there not some way—?'

Jinx shook his head as the golden cage and chain flowed to

the floor and melted into a liquid pool. 'It was too late for her –
hopefully, seeing this will make Amaliel think both crystals
were destroyed.'

A door slammed upstairs, followed by raised voices and the
sound of pounding feet.

'Idiots!' a female voice shrieked. '*Bloody idiots!*'

'They must still be inside,' a calm male voice with a slight
American drawl replied. Joseph.

Persephone was far from calm. 'Find them! Find them, find
them, *find them!*'

Jinx stalked to the door and grabbed hold of Amaliel's arm.
Reanimating him, he dragged him back into the room, growling
from the corner of his mouth, 'Be still!' as Amaliel tried to pull
away. 'Be still, or you will not see a second more.'

Amaliel stopped struggling, but held himself as far away from
my death daemon as he could.

'We fight?' Vaybian asked.

'We *barter*,' Jinx said.

'Barter?' I asked.

'For your freedom.'

'I'm not the important one, Jinx,' I told him. 'If they have you,
they have the means to destroy this world.'

He gave me a sideways glance. 'To me you are important.'

'You can't even remember my name!'

'I will, I know this. In my last moments I will.'

I didn't understand what he meant, but he was scaring me.
Then several people in suits were at the door. They stepped inside
and parted like an honour guard as Persephone appeared, closely
followed by Joseph.

Her petulant pout was replaced by a crafty feline smile when
she saw Jinx, and her smile increased a tad more as her eyes wandered over Vaybian – then her gaze shifted to me and her nose
wrinkled.

'Why on earth is she still around?' she asked Jinx.

Jinx scowled at her. 'She is mine.'

'There you go again,' she said, 'thinking you have a say in anything. When will you learn?'

Her attention returned to Amaliel and the bokor and she tapped
a pointed red fingernail against her lips, a gesture that weirdly
brought Kayla to mind. 'And please let go of him, Jinx,' she said,
indicating Amaliel. 'He is not *your* enemy.' She took a couple of
steps forward to stand right in front of Amaliel, and I noticed
Joseph keeping very close to her right shoulder. 'Have you finished with Gaston?' she asked, gesturing towards the bokor.

'I was interrupted, but yes – for now.'

'You'd better release him – we need to go.'

'Why bother?' Joseph said. 'He won't be good for anything now.'

'He's a lot tougher than you think.'

Joseph shrugged, clearly not convinced.

Amaliel raised the flat of his hand toward the pulsating column
of fire and muttered something I couldn't understand. For a
moment the fire burned bright, then it darkened to violet, there
was a pressure on my eardrums and the flame vanished, leaving
tendrils of smoke and a smell like a blown-out candle. The bokor
remained rigid for a fraction of a second, then fell to his knees,
clutching at his throat and struggling to breathe.

'I hope you've learned your lesson,' Persephone said, slipping
her arm through Amaliel's as she looked down on the kneeling man.

'Remember, child, who I am – remember what I have done for
you,' the bokor gasped. His rich voice now had the rasp of a man
who had gargled with razorblades.

It was like flicking a switch. Persephone's disdainful look
turned into rage as she snatched her arm from Amaliel's and towered over the bokor. To his credit he didn't flinch as she screamed,
'*Done for me? What exactly have you "done for me"?*'

'I took care—'

Persephone raised her hand. 'Don't you dare! Don't you dare
say it, because it would be a lie.'

'I—'

'No!' Her lips twisted into a nasty smirk. 'Jinx, darling, time to show me what a good boy you are.'

He put his fist to his temple as she crooned, 'Jinx, why fight me? You'd feel so much better if you just let go.'

His fist dropped to his side and his eyes narrowed.

'Kill him,' she said. 'Make him really burn.'

Vaybian and I both took an involuntary step back; being close to a burning black magician wasn't our idea of fun.

'Persephone, you don't—' Amaliel warned.

She spun around to face him, her beautiful face contorting in a rage bordering on madness – no, strike the 'bordering'. Psycho Bitch had jumped right off that cliff.

'Who do you think you are to tell me what to do?' she shrieked, spittle spraying from her lips as she bared her teeth.

Joseph laid a hand on her shoulder, but she shrugged it off.

'I am not one of your fucking little *acolytes*!'

'You will treat me with respect,' Amaliel said, and she must have been crazy not to hear the warning in his voice.

'Respect? Treat you with *respect*? Why should I? Why the *fuck* should I?'

'Persephone—' I heard Joseph whisper and he leaned in close to murmur something in her ear.

'I am your father,' Amaliel said, so softly that I thought for a moment I must have misheard him.

I looked from her to Amaliel and back again. *Amaliel was her father?*

Persephone stood there glaring at him, her bosom heaving, then her head snapped around, her temper suddenly focusing on me. 'And she' – Persephone pointed her finger at me – 'is my sister, but that's not going to stop me killing her, is it?'

My mouth dropped open. *Sister?*

Persephone gave me a faux-shocked look. 'Oh, sweetie – didn't you know?'

'He is *not* my father,' I snapped.

'No, sadly for you, he isn't,' Psycho Bitch said, 'but the

loose-knickered Veronica was my mother as well as yours, so, like it or not, we are related, which is another extremely good reason to see you a rotting corpse. So, Jinx, if you would do the honours? You can start with him,' she said, turning back to the bokor.

'Ah, Persephone,' Joseph said, putting his arm around her shoulders, 'do you really think that's such a good idea?'

She frowned, still glaring at me, and asked him, 'Why wouldn't it be?'

'Don't get me wrong; I'm looking forward to seeing him gone as much as you are – but burning him to death here in central London? Making a burned-out car disappear is one thing . . .' He glanced at me and added, 'Nice trick blowing up the car by the way.'

I gave a nonchalant shrug in response, my mind in turmoil. *Sister?*

'But turning him into a fireball will probably take this house and half the neighbourhood with it. And he does have his uses.'

Persephone tapped her finger against his cheek. 'I knew there was a reason for keeping you around apart from your very pretty face.' She turned to face me. 'I will lock them down here until we're ready to leave.' She rested her head on Joseph's shoulder. 'I'll ponder upon what to do with our African friend and in the meantime think up something exciting for her.'

'You will leave *her* to me,' Amaliel said.

This time she did hear the warning, and a slight frown clouded her forehead. 'I'm sorry. I was angry; I was—'

Amaliel raised a hand, stopping her mid-flow. 'No matter. But you must learn you cannot have everything your own way.'

She lowered her eyes, suddenly the penitent child. 'I know.'

'Come, we have work to do.' Then he glanced around and his eyes lit upon the crystal dust and puddle of gold. He stared at them for a moment. 'A pity,' he said, his eyes shifting to me. 'I was so looking forward to having a full set.' And the penny dropped; I knew exactly who the final crystal was for. Persephone obviously had her uses for now, but when she was no longer needed . . .

His revelation had obviously gone clean over her head. Blissfully unaware of Amaliel's future plans for her, Persephone was acting as if nothing had happened between her and her equally psychotic father. She strutted to the door, then stopped and ordered, 'Come, Jinx. I have plans for you.'

Jinx didn't move.

'Be a good boy and don't be difficult.'

He still didn't move.

'A bullet through the brain will kill one of your kind, will it not?' She waved in Vaybian's direction. 'That one's of no importance. Kill him.'

One of the men by the door stepped towards Vaybian, gun in hand, until Jinx moved between them and the human recoiled.

'Jinx, do *not* try my patience,' Persephone said.

He put his hands on his hips and pulled his coat tight, and his tail snuck out of the vent at the back and jiggled at me: that was enough for me to know he was not under her sway, so I would have to trust him to get Vaybian and me out of this mess.

His hand dropped to his sides and he hung his head; without looking back he followed Persephone from the room and her men filed out behind them. Joseph was one of the last to go. He gave me an almost friendly smile, then stepped outside and closed the door, sliding the bolt with a solid thud, locking us in with the bokor.

Twenty

Vaybian and I sat down in one corner, the bokor in another. We didn't speak – I didn't want him hearing our plans. I slept a bit, waking a couple of times to find my head resting against Vaybian's shoulder. I tried not to think about what Persephone was doing to Jinx. I wondered where the others were; they were taking an awfully long time to get here . . . And I began to fret about Pyrites, all alone out there. I hoped he had found somewhere safe to hide.

Then the door opened and Joseph led in a posse of goons and gestured for us to get up and go with them. There was no point refusing, not when Psycho Bitch had made it quite clear Vaybian was expendable, so I followed the rest of them up to the front door and into the second of three limos idling in the street. There was no evidence of an exploded car to be seen. Psycho Bitch was lounging across the back seat of the first car, with Jinx pressed up against the opposite window, as far away from her as he could possibly get. As I was pushed inside, Vaybian and the bokor were marched along the pavement to the third, where Amaliel was waiting. Two of the hired help slid in, one either side me so I was sandwiched between them.

Amaliel might have been scared of me, but it was clear these two certainly weren't. Perhaps they were too stupid – though not so stupid that they didn't have holstered guns inside their jackets. I thought they were both human, although I was beginning to doubt my ability to tell; I had been so sure Persephone and Joseph were from this world.

'A bullet through the head will kill your kind,' she had said – perhaps she was in denial? Or more likely she just thought herself better than the rest of us. But she had said she was *my sister* – and that meant my mother must have had sex with Amaliel! *How could she?* And was that why he'd kept her trapped in the crystal? Perhaps it was unrequited love. Sadly, I would never find out what had really happened.

I rubbed the bridge of my nose – I was beginning to feel rather queasy. 'Could you open the window a bit?' I asked.

The two goons ignored me.

'If you don't want me throwing up all over you, I suggest you do as I ask.'

'Daemons don't throw up,' one of them said. He looked as if he'd gone a few rounds with Mike Tyson; his nose had been broken one too many times and the ear closest to me was all knobbly.

'How do you know?' I asked.

'Of course they don't.'

'Why not?'

'Well—'

I heaved an exaggerated sigh and tried the other one. He wasn't as big as Boxer Boy but he still had a hard, chiselled look. He was greying at the temples and his fair hair had been clipped short in a bristle-cut. His light tan accentuated the moon-shaped scar beneath his right eye and the pitted flesh across his cheeks I suspected was more likely caused by shrapnel than a teenaged skin condition. Ex-military, I guessed, and probably the more intelligent of the two men.

'Look, I really do need some fresh air,' I repeated.

'Tough,' Blondie sneered.

'Willing to risk that I'm not one of those daemons who puke up molten lava?'

Blondie laughed, but his boxer friend didn't appear too sure. 'Can they do that?'

'She's messing with your head.'

'If you don't open the window a crack you'll be finding out pretty soon.' Although I was actually beginning to feel a little better, messing with their heads sounded like a fun idea. 'There's a daemon at court whose urine is so strong it burns holes in material. His party piece is to piss his initials into the flagstones outside the inn,' I told them. 'Then there's another one who regurgitates his food like a fly – we always have to remember to give him a porcelain plate, otherwise his dinner burns all the way through the table.'

'You're kidding!' said Boxer Boy.

'She's pulling your chain.'

'It wouldn't hurt to open the window a crack.'

Blondie chuckled. 'If it makes you happier, but she's not gonna puke, and if she does it's not gonna be molten lava.'

'Still . . .' My pugilistic friend wound down the window a couple of inches and I favoured him with a smile.

'Thank you.'

I took a couple of deep breaths, leaned back into the leather seat and closed my eyes, wondering where we were going. Would Persephone dare to return to the mansion in Sussex? Or had she yet another hideaway?

The car started to slow and we pulled to a stop. I opened my eyes. We had apparently stopped for fuel, as had Persephone's car. The third limo had pulled over to one side and was waiting for us.

'I suppose getting out to stretch my legs would be out of the question?'

They didn't dignify that with a reply.

While our driver was filling up, Joseph came strolling over to have a word with him, and when he'd finished, he opened the front door and leaned in.

'Everything all right back there?'

They both gave grunts.

'Good,' he said and started to withdraw.

'Joseph,' I said, and he stopped and leaned back in. 'Where are you taking us?'

'Somewhere private.'

'They will find us – the Guardians will find us.'

'You'd better hope they don't,' he drawled, 'because if they do, their priority won't be us, it'll be your ex-boyfriend.'

'Ex?'

'I think he's had a change of – well, shall we say *heart* ?'

'Yeah, right.'

'Why do you think I'm out here? It's certainly not to take the air.' He gave me a grin. 'You know what they say about two being company.'

'Funnily enough, no,' I said, forcing my lips into a smile. 'Jinx, Jamie and I never found three to be a crowd.'

'Good point. I'll mention that to Persephone; perhaps she'll invite your Guardian to join them.'

I suspected my smile was more of a grimace.

He laughed, showing those very white teeth, then he winked, backed out of the car and strode away. Had Jinx succumbed to Persephone? I should never have let him anywhere near them again; I should have run with him, and kept on running until he was out of their reach – but then what would have happened to Kayla? *Christ, Jinx had Kayla!*

I shut my eyes and tried to stop the thoughts; if I didn't, they'd drive me mad with worry.

Then the driver climbed in and we were off again. After a few miles I dragged open my eyes; I was exhausted, and in danger of nodding off. We were travelling at a fair lick, the countryside passing in a blur. I kept an eye out for road signs, trying to get an idea of where we were going, although what good it would do me, I had no idea.

Our car was now last in the cavalcade, but I was still wedged between two gun-toting guards with not even a glimmer of a plan in my head. We slowed as we approached a roundabout and the first car peeled off to the left. The second had to wait for on-coming traffic and as it too went left, we crawled forward and waited for a couple of more cars coming from the right.

There was a thump on the top of the roof and the car swayed slightly.

'What the fuck?' Blondie said.

The driver leaned forward with his head turned to one side, as if trying to look out of his windscreen at the roof, which was pretty dumb – but then, he probably wasn't employed for his brains.

'I think something hit the roof,' Boxer Boy said, and wound down his window a bit more, then he undid his seatbelt and leaned out.

'Bonner, get back in here and shut the window.'

Bonner glanced back. 'But—'

'I said *shut the fucking window*.'

Bonner turned back, grumbling – then there was a *whoosh*ing sound and he was gone.

Blondie instantly reached for his gun, shouting to the driver, 'Step on it!'

The driver slammed his foot down on the accelerator and we shot forward into the path of traffic; I heard blasting horns and squealing tyres, then we were careering around the roundabout, the car fishtailing as we swung to the left.

'Where the fuck's Bonner?' the driver shouted.

'How the fuck should I know? He was here one minute and then he was gone.' Blondie pointed his gun at me, and at the open window.

There was another thud on the roof, this time hard enough to make the car swerve.

'What was that?' The driver's wide scared eyes were reflected in the rear-view mirror.

'Shut the window,' Blondie said to me, his gun still pointed at it.

'You shut the window,' I said.

He moved the gun a fraction so the barrel was in line with my head. 'I said: shut the fucking window.'

My brain was on high-alert and shouting, *Gun! Gun! Gun!* but I fought it down. 'There's no need to be rude,' I shouted back. 'Anyway, you shut the window. You've got a button your side, haven't you?'

He frowned at me, and as he turned in his seat to fiddle with the switch in the door panel I quickly undid my seatbelt and slid across the seat to where Bonner had been sitting. My hair went whipping out of the window as I pressed myself against the door.

'Hey! What're you doing? Get back over here——'

'You said to close the window,' I said, pushing myself up against it.

'Get back here. *Now!*'

He lifted his gun again, his anger palpable, and for a moment I thought he was actually going to shoot me, then he started groping for the release button for his seat belt. I leaned back, my head out of the window, and then something grabbed me under my arms and I was hauled out through the window and hoisted up into the sky.

I heard the car squeal to a halt below me, but it was too late; I was flying across fields then over a line of trees, laughing as I went. 'Yes! Go, Pyrites!' I cried, and he puffed a plume of white smoke in response.

About a mile away from the road he lowered me down and immediately shrank to the size of a pony, and I flung my arms around him the moment I could and covered him with kisses. Heaven alone knew what anyone on the road behind us had thought – but right then I didn't care; my drakon had saved me yet again, and he deserved all the praise in the world. Then something occurred to me.

'Did Jamie send you?'

Pyrites rolled his eyes and snorted. Obviously not. Jamie had made his feelings quite clear about my drakon taking to wing in the Overlands.

'Will you be in trouble?'

He snorted again, flared his nostrils and gave a rumble in his chest. So I guess he didn't really care. Now all we had to do was get Jinx and Vaybian back – oh, and Kayla. But how?

I thought about following the cars, but that hadn't gone too well last time . . . In the end I realised I had no choice; I'd have to re-group with my guard and hope we could lose the Guardians and get to Jinx before they did. If only I'd been able to work out where Persephone was going, but unfortunately, she hadn't left any loose ends or clues for me to follow . . .

I began to smile . . . actually, she had.

Boxer Boy hadn't got very far; he wasn't dressed for trudging through fields at the best of times, and after all Persephone's stormy weather, they were *very* muddy. As soon as he saw us coming, he dropped to the ground, his arms wrapped around his head. What good he thought that would do, I had no idea. We landed a few yards away and walked over to stand directly in front of him. He lifted himself up briefly to peer out at us from between his arms, and upon seeing Pyrites, curled into a tighter ball.

'Bonner, we're not going to hurt you,' I started.

He somehow managed to huddle even smaller.

'Unless, of course, you don't tell me what I want to know.'

'Go away,' he mumbled.

'I'm not going anywhere until you and I have a little chat.'

'No.'

'Do you know what my drakon is capable of?' I asked, laying my hand on Pyrites' flank. 'It is said his fire can get to 2000 degrees or more. That's centigrade, *obviously*. So he could roast you in an instant or, if he wanted to dial it back, just give you a *very* painful burn. And I do *not* have time to waste.'

Bonner whimpered, and if it hadn't been for the urgency of the situation I might have felt mean. As it was, I did feel mean, but not in a sympathetic way: I wanted to hurt someone – Persephone – very badly, and I would do whatever it took to make sure I had the opportunity.

'Pyrites,' I said, 'get ready to roast—'

'No!' Bonner cried. 'What do you want? I'll tell you whatever you need to know.'

'Where is Persephone going?'

'Naples,' he said. 'She's got a Learjet to take the daemon to Naples.'

'*Naples*? Why Naples?'

'I don't know, *please*, I don't know—'

He was just the hired help; I doubted she'd have told him her dastardly plans. I didn't like the sound of them being in Naples, though – then a memory skittered through my head. I hadn't been long in the Underlands, and Jamie had been taking me to find my final guard. When I'd asked why he and the others were uneasy, he had stopped mid-stride. 'You're about to meet one seriously dangerous individual,' he'd told me. 'He's a bringer of death – literally. Where he walks, death and disaster follow. When he travelled across Europe the Black Death was not far behind him; when he passed through the streets of London the Great Fire kindled; when he left the city of Pompeii it was consumed by molten rock.'

Pompeii had been destroyed when Mount Vesuvius erupted, burying the city under tons of ash. And Vesuvius was still active, and just a short distance along the coast from Naples.

'Oh crap,' I muttered. 'Come on, Pyrites, let's go!'

We left Bonner in the field and went in search of an airfield in the general direction of where the cars had been taking me. I was hoping they hadn't left the country yet, but it was a forlorn hope.

It took far too long to spot the airfield, and when we did, there were no planes standing on the tarmac. *Bugger*, I thought, but I got Pyrites to take us down anyway. If Amaliel and Persephone were really taking Jinx to Naples, we were in so much trouble I hardly dared think about it. I had no choice: I had to find my guard, but they could be anywhere by now. I wondered for a moment if I tried to change, whether using that power would bring the Guardians, and therefore Jamie, running . . . except that several times we'd used huge amounts of power and the Guardians had been conspicuous by their absence – why was that? That was a question for another time; I had more important things to worry about – like an erupting volcano.

But as we landed, I noticed a very welcome sight: travelling swiftly across the airfield was my guards' red vehicle. I jumped off Pyrites and waited.

It came to a halt, the driver's door swung open and Jamie jumped out. He took a step towards me – and then stopped; the relieved smile slid from his face upon seeing my guarded expression. It was so good to see him, and it would have been so easy to walk straight into his arms – but there were so many things between us, the risk of him losing his wings by helping me being one of them. No matter my feelings, it was better I kept my distance.

'How did you find me?' I said at last.

'You've been on television,' he replied.

'And on these electronic devices,' Kerfuffle added, waving an iPad at me.

I wasn't surprised; the internet was everywhere these days.

'It should be a bloody mess,' Jamie said, 'but as usual, what the newspapers don't know, they make up. The favourite explanation so far is that it's all a big publicity stunt by some unknown group of environmentalists.'

'How do they explain Pyrites?'

'CGI, mirrors and holograms. The Prime Minster has stated categorically that a dragon has not been flying over London and the Home Counties.'

I couldn't help but smile. It was so typical of this world.

'Where's Vaybian?'

'Persephone has him, and Jinx.'

'Guardian,' a voice called, and I looked over my shoulder to see Pasqual, followed by Charles and Peter.

Jamie turned away as though he hadn't heard, and I was almost immediately surrounded by my guards, who subtly moved me out of Pasqual's earshot.

'Don't worry,' Jamie whispered, 'Charles and Peter will detain him.' I could see Pasqual trying to get away from them to make his way over to us, but the two angels were having none of it.

'I told you they're as loyal to me as they come,' Jamie whispered, seeing me watching them.

I looked up into his eyes and came straight to the point. 'We have one huge, bloody great problem' – my guards all snapped to attention, eyes on me – 'and maybe it's better you don't know.'

'Let me be the judge of that.'

He was right; whether he helped me or not would be his decision, and anyway, I *needed* his help. I couldn't do this alone. 'I don't think Persephone is particularly keen on the biblical approach any more – she's going straight for the apocalyptic. She's flying him to Naples.'

I heard Shenanigans suck in breath and Kerfuffle muttered, 'Not good, not good.'

Jamie ran his hand through his curls and gazed at Pasqual, who was still being delayed by the two other angels. 'You realise how serious this is? There are whole communities living around the base of Vesuvius and up onto its slopes. If it should suddenly erupt, it could kill millions.'

'Three million,' Shenanigans butted in, holding up the iPad.

'Fuck it,' I said.

Jamie put his hands on my shoulders. 'How was Jinx when you last saw him?'

'He knew what he was doing. I think he was putting on an act for her.'

'You think?'

'Yes,' I said, my voice determined.

'Has she said where he is?' Pasqual asked from behind me, making me jump.

I swung around, but he was too busy glowering at Jamie to notice. Charles and Peter hovered anxiously behind him, their ever-present angelic smiles slipping a bit.

'We have another problem to deal with,' Jamie told him, and gestured for Pasqual to move away from us.

As they walked off Jamie's expression was unreadable. What was he going to tell Pasqual? What did I want him to tell Pasqual? Did I really want him to risk his wings for Jinx? I didn't know any of the answers.

Neither did I have the time to dwell on it; as soon as Jamie had led Pasqual out of earshot my guards and the two angels circled around me.

'Mistress, we must get to Naples.'

Pyrites pushed his head up under my hand, purring at me.

'It's too far, boy; and you wouldn't be able to carry all of us.' Besides, a drakon crossing the border would most certainly have them scrambling their Eurofighters.

'There must be a way,' Charles said.

I thought for a moment. 'Why can't we do what Amaliel did? Why can't we hop back into the Underlands and then out again, but in Naples?'

'Because our kind will be waiting for you,' Peter said with an apologetic smile.

'But if we did it really quickly, how would they find us?'

'The journey between the worlds may feel like moments, but it takes longer than it appears. The surge of power from within the Overlands would alert them and they would follow its progress to the spot where you are likely to appear.'

'Thank you for the warning, Peter – you and Charles might want to turn away now. I don't want you to risk your wings.'

They both gave grateful smiles and stepped away, although I noticed they took up positions as though they were still guarding us.

I turned back to my guard. 'There's also the problem of us only being able to travel through a few at a time.'

'Only from the Underlands to the Overlands – going home is a different thing altogether,' Kerfuffle said.

'Then what if we each go to a different place?' Kubeck suggested. 'The Guardians must be stretched pretty thin if they're guarding the Sicarii back in the Underlands and three of them are here.'

'I don't know how to do it,' I said. *And how would we fight Persephone with only one of us?*

'We will show you, Mistress,' Shenanigans said.

'One of us should travel with Mistress Lucky,' Kubeck added. 'If she is to go to Naples, we can't leave her alone until we find our way back to her.'

'If you, Shenanigans and Pyrites all appear at different locations, I can travel with Mistress Lucky to Naples,' Kerfuffle said.

'That's settled then?' I asked. My guard nodded and I took a deep breath and gave them a shaky smile: we finally had some sort of strategy.

While Jamie was keeping Pasqual occupied I quickly changed, thankful I'd thought to throw some spare clothes into my bag in the back of the van. The purloined skirt had become extremely irksome; I was well and truly fed up with flashing my knickers every time I climbed on or off Pyrites, or did anything else even vaguely more active than walking.

As soon as I was back in jeans, we all sloped off in different directions, counting seconds as we went. Kubeck was to go first; twenty seconds later Shenanigans would send Pyrites back, then after another twenty seconds he'd go back himself. After another twenty seconds Kerfuffle and I would leave, and if there was trouble, he would send me on my way to Naples while fighting off any Guardians who might try and stop us. He would follow on later, if he could.

Kerfuffle opened the van door and inside, there was emptiness. I took a final glance at Jamie, who was still keeping Pasqual occupied. I smiled; perhaps I could trust him in some things. Kerfuffle stepped up and into the doorframe and reached back, holding out his hand. I took his soft, warm palm in mine and stepped inside—

—and we were gone.

We fell, but a few moments before we landed it felt as if we were buoyed up on a cushion of air, and we landed in an upright position, hitting the ground feet-first.

We were in a cave; one I recognised from what felt like a long time ago. It was the cave I'd hidden in when we had first gone on the run from Amaliel.

'In here!' I heard a voice call from outside.

'Bollocks, the Guardians have found us already,' Kerfuffle said. 'Quick, this way—'

He led me to the small cave where I'd found food and a box of blankets last time I'd been here with Pyrites. 'Quick,' he said, 'through there.'

As I dropped to my knees I glanced back over my shoulder. 'Aren't you—?'

But I never got to ask the question because Kerfuffle was already waddling away to put himself between me and the two Guardians who had stepped inside the cave.

'Move aside,' one said.

'Make me,' Kerfuffle growled, and as I dropped through the hole into pitch-black dark, I heard the sound of fighting. As I hurtled through the air, I prayed I would end up where I needed to be; I pictured Mount Vesuvius as it had appeared on Google; if they weren't there yet, they would be soon enough.

Or would they? Jamie had told me that when Jinx had left Pompeii, it had been consumed by molten rock – so would he actually be *on* Vesuvius? What if he wasn't? In my mind I could see him stalking Mediterranean streets wearing that damn leather coat.

Then I began to slow and was buffeted about for a moment before my feet hit the ground.

'Well, hello,' a voice I knew said. 'How nice of you to join us.'

Twenty-One

That I wasn't on the rocky slopes of Mount Vesuvius was immediately obvious. I was standing on white marble tiles in a large, airy room reminiscent of the considerably smaller villa Jinx, Jamie and I had been staying in before this whole nightmare had begun.

Persephone was elegantly arranged on a chaise longue, dressed – or no, *arrayed* – in a silk embroidered dressing gown, a crystal flute in hand. Amaliel was standing beside her, gazing at me with hot-red eyes. Jinx was crouching at the end of the chaise longue by her feet.

'Interesting little trick,' she said. 'You must explain to me how you do that.'

Amaliel gave one of his gurgling laughs. 'Had she any control or idea of what she was doing, do you think she would have come here?'

'I don't know – you tell me.'

'I suspect it is her connection to the Deathbringer.'

'She no longer has any connection to the Deathbringer,' Persephone spat.

'There must be, otherwise she wouldn't have been drawn here. There is no other way she could have found this place.'

Persephone gave a petulant snort and took a swig of her drink.

I made myself look at Jinx, though I was scared at what I might see in his eyes. He stared back at me, his green and gold eyes glowing and his lips curled into a snarly smile, although he didn't look angry; it was more like he was pleased to see me in some dark and possibly nasty way. I tried not to read too much into it; everyone was playing games.

Persephone took a sip from her glass. She regarded me over its rim. 'I'm glad you're here. You've arrived just in time to see the next stage of our plan to bring your pathetic little human world to its knees.'

'You think it'll be that easy?'

'I know it will.'

'Humans are used to catastrophes befalling them; to them such calamities are what they call "acts of God". They happen all the time.'

'Of course, they're used to a catastrophic event maybe once or twice a year, but not once or twice a month, or a week, or maybe even every day.'

I fought to keep my voice calm and measured, which was difficult when I could see images of dying children flicking through my head like some ghastly newsreel. 'Why would you want to do this? What possible satisfaction would you get from causing such misery?'

'You said it yourself,' Amaliel said.

'I did?'

'"Acts of God", you called them, and we will be those gods. Your people will bend the knee to us, or they will suffer the consequences.'

'Really?' I forced my lips into a quizzical smile. The pair of them really were stark staring bonkers – but then, I supposed most megalomaniac mass-murderers were somewhere on the psychotic scale.

'Humans have always needed gods,' Persephone said. 'Throughout their history they have worshipped and prayed to all manner of creatures, even though they can't see them or touch them. This time they will have gods who will stand before them and answer them. Once they have seen and felt our power, they will flock to us and venerate us in their billions.'

As she spoke, with each sentence her voice got a tad louder, a bit more strident. In a moment of sheer psychobabble I could see her in my head, marching around with a small black moustache glued to her top lip and making dramatic arm gestures and I began to giggle. I tried to stifle it, but I couldn't.

Persephone's eyes narrowed. 'You think this is *funny*? You think this is a joke?'

'No,' I said, 'how could I possibly find two people as sick as you are funny? That you two losers actually believe humans will worship you is, however, hilarious.'

'I hope you find it all so amusing when you are staked out on the mountainside waiting to be consumed by molten rock. I doubt you will die laughing.'

Amaliel glided forward a few steps and held out a hand, gesturing that she should stop her tirade. 'Where is the Guardian?'

'Forget the bloody Guardian,' Persephone said. 'He didn't catch up with us before and he won't be able to find us now.'

He whirled around to face her, and as he towered over her, a flicker of fear passed across her face, so fleetingly that it was possible that I'd imagined it – but I didn't think I had.

She gave another huff. 'Just get on with it.'

'The Guardian,' he said, returning his attention to me. 'Is he on his way?'

'Where's Vaybian?' I countered.

'He's somewhere safe.'

'Let me see him.'

'You will soon enough,' Persephone said. She stretched and got to her feet in one fluid movement. 'Well, as she's here and her Guardian lover isn't, I think we can assume she has come alone.'

'Lover?' I heard Jinx mutter.

Persephone reached out and ran her knuckles across Jinx's cheek. This time he didn't flinch away. 'Don't you remember?' she said to him, then laughed; a tinkling laugh that would have sounded really pretty if it hadn't been so cruel. 'Of course you don't. How could you?' She took another sip from her glass then rested it against her lips, painting the rim with blood-red lipstick. 'You, she and the Guardian were apparently quite the *ménage à trois*.'

She rested her head on his shoulder and slowly, insultingly, looked me up and down. 'Who would have thought it? Maybe you take after dear Mama more than I thought.'

Jinx was looking at me in an angry, feral way when I heard a door open behind me, and I turned sideways, keeping one eye on Persephone and Amaliel, to see three men walk into the room: two came to a halt on either side of me and the third stood beside Persephone.

'You were right,' Joseph told her. 'You said she'd come.'

'Of course she came. She still has this misguided idea that she'll somehow take the Deathbringer from me.'

He folded his arms and gave me a quizzical look. 'Do you really believe that?'

Persephone moved a little closer to him and squeezed her arm through his. 'And you said Veronica had loose knickers,' I muttered under my breath.

She gave another of her tinkling laughs, which weren't lovely at all; in fact, they were really becoming quite annoying.

'Joseph is a very dear friend,' she said.

Yes, I got that much.

'Now,' she said, 'we have a very busy day ahead of us tomorrow so I suggest we get some rest.'

'I think to wait until tomorrow would be a mistake,' Joseph started, but Persephone lifted a finger to his lips to hush him.

'We will go ahead as planned,' she said grandly.

Joseph glanced her way. 'If she's here, the Guardians won't be far behind. Not to mention her personal guards, which include a pretty impressive dragon.'

'I think Persephone has hit the nail on the head; the Soulseer appears to have come alone in a pathetic attempt to save the Death-bringer, and if that is the case, there is no need to worry about the Guardians,' Amaliel said. 'They will have been successfully mis-directed for the time being.'

I wondered exactly what he meant by that.

Persephone tapped the rim of the flute against her lips and glanced Amaliel's way. 'Anyway, Daddy and I don't want people to die in their beds – where's the fun in that? We want them to see the flames shooting up into the sky, it turning black with rock and ash. We want to see them running, trying to find an escape when there is none.'

'You truly are one very sick woman,' I said.

'And you will soon be a very dead one.'

'So will you – you just don't know it yet.'

'Save the dramatics; they won't save you.' She waved her hand and the men flanking me grabbed my arms, although she must have known human men couldn't hold me if I didn't want them to.

'And before you even think of giving either of these gentlemen any trouble, remember, we have your sister's lover. You hurt them, and he will pay in blood.'

'Like father, like daughter,' I said, as I let them lead me away. I glanced at Jinx to see his eyes were following me. His expression was very dark indeed. My breath caught in my throat as Persephone drew him up and reached out to run her fingers down his cheek, then stepped in close for a kiss.

There was no shudder this time; no drawing away. He pulled her into his arms in an almost savage movement and kissed her hard.

I was locked in a small square cellar underneath the villa. The walls and floor were lined with rough-cut marble slabs that were more of a dirty yellow than those above. At the top of one wall there was a narrow barred window, which I assumed was more for air circulation than anything else, as it would have taken someone the height of Shenanigans to be able to peer out.

The good news was that it became clear Persephone and Amaliel weren't going to take Joseph's advice, for it grew dark outside without anyone coming to get me. All I could do was hope the others found us in time – if they were okay. As for the Guardians . . . I didn't like the sound of Amaliel's comment about them at all.

I took a turn round the room, examining the door and walls, but they were pretty solid; even in my daemon form I wouldn't be able to break down the door. Eventually, I sat down – and with nothing to do but sit and contemplate my fate, I had plenty of time to worry.

Were my guards all right? When I'd left Kerfuffle, he'd been fighting off two Guardians – I really hoped he had given up as soon as I'd left, but knowing him, he wouldn't have: he was far too feisty for his own good at times.

Then there was Jamie: what was he doing? Was he in trouble because of Jinx or me? The thought that they could take his wings for helping us was too terrible for words; I had to force myself to stop thinking about it.

The hours rolled on and sleep eluded me. It was cold and the floor was hard and I was wound up so tight I felt like something inside me was going to go ping. I tried not to think about Jinx and Persephone together, or to dwell on the scene that had played out as I'd left the room. *It was an act*, I told myself. It had to be an act. The thought that maybe it wasn't made my heart ache.

I counted the minutes and waited.

A couple of times I heard movement out in the hallway: a weird shuffling sound, and soft moaning, and I hoped Amaliel wasn't torturing Vaybian. I stood next to the door to listen, but it went quiet. Then I remembered the bokor; it was entirely possible he was residing in the cellars as well. That was more likely – I was certain Vaybian would never allow himself to moan, even if terribly tortured.

I was sitting against the door and my eyes were finally beginning to droop shut when there was a scrabbling on the other side. My first thought was rats, as it sounded a bit like claws on wood – but it was coming from halfway up the door. Then the handle began to move up and down, first a couple of times, then in a more frantic rattle: someone was trying to get in. Had Vaybian escaped? I got to my feet.

'Vaybian?' I whispered.

The rattling stopped abruptly and I pressed my ear right against the wood. I opened my mouth to whisper his name again when a weird crooning sound came from the other side. 'Luuckkyy! Luuckkyy!'

I froze, and my heart almost stopped as I remembered the strange hunchbacked figure stalking me through the woods. *What was this thing?* I felt myself change.

'Luuckkyy!' it cried again, and I sank to the floor, my back against the door. If the creature did try to break in, I had to be stronger than it – whatever it was, I was certain I didn't want it anywhere near me. There was something *rotten* about it.

After an age during which I hardly dared breathe, it rattled the door handle one more time, then with a pitiful moan, it took off along the corridor. I held my breath, listening hard as the dragging feet receded, and didn't breathe again until I heard the door at the top of the stairs swing shut with a solid *thump*.

Dawn came with the sound of birdsong and a sliver of grey light seeping through the small slit of a window. Gradually the villa and the surrounding area began to come alive. The tinkling of bells and the bleating of sheep or goats in a field nearby would have, on any other day, made me smile. I could hear the cry of seagulls, which wasn't much of a surprise as Naples sits on the western coast of Italy – and only five or six miles from Mount Vesuvius.

I got up and started to pace. Where were they all? My guard, the Guardians—? Where was *Jamie*? If they didn't get here in time, millions of people could die, maybe even the entire population of Naples and the other villages surrounding the volcano.

In a moment of clarity it finally hit me: I couldn't risk the lives of three million people in the hope that Jinx wouldn't do Persephone and Amaliel's bidding. I couldn't risk even one innocent person. I had let my love for Jinx blind me.

If Jamie and the Guardians didn't get here in time I would have no choice. If it couldn't be proven beyond all doubt that Jinx wasn't under Persephone's control, I would have to stop him.

Twenty-Two

When they came for me I was sitting with my back to the wall, facing the door. I'd been hoping it would be the two humans – I would have tried not to kill either of them, but they had a choice in what they were doing, and weighed against the lives of three million innocents, I think I could have lived with *my* choice.

The two humans did come, but they were armed, and Joseph was with them. Jinx was not.

'I would ask you if you slept well, but I'm pretty sure I'd know what the answer would be,' Joseph said as he stepped into my prison. He gave me a friendly smile, reached inside his jacket and turned his back on me – and there were two short, sharp *pops* and the two humans crumpled to their knees, their shirts rapidly turning crimson.

I pressed myself up against the wall. 'What—? Why—? I—'

Joseph turned back to me still smiling. 'You want to stop this, don't you?'

'I—'

He reached out his hand to me. 'Come on, we haven't much time.' When I didn't move he leaned forward and grabbed me by the arm. 'Look, I'll help you as much as I can, but let's get this very clear right now, I'm not about to die for you, or any of the other poor bastards Persephone intends to annihilate. So if you want even half a chance of saving them, you have to move. *Now!*'

If there was even a small possibility, I had to take it. I let Joseph lead me out of the room and we hurried along the corridor and up a flight of stairs at the back of the villa. He opened a door and poked his head out, then pulled me along after him.

'Why are you helping me?' I asked as we crossed a courtyard, me trotting to keep up with him.

'I like it in the Overlands. I've got a good life here – I'm special to these people, someone to be feared, and in some cases, venerated.'

'If you were a god you'd be even more special.'

'That's just it, I wouldn't be; I'd be one of Persephone's fucking minions.' His lips twisted into a grimace. 'We had a good thing going until her fucking whack-job of a father turned up. She was always borderline insane, but now she's . . . well, she's impossible.'

We entered a small walled garden, the air scented with rich flowers, and I wished I had more time to appreciate it. I also wished it wasn't up to me to save the world – I'd've loved to be sitting on the stone bench under the orange trees in the centre of the garden, breathing in the heady perfumes with not a care or worry. Instead, I had more cares and worries than any person should have to shoulder alone: three million of them, give or take.

Outside the garden was a narrow dirt track bordered by olive groves on either side.

'Where are you taking me?'

'Not far now.'

After a few yards he pulled me off the road and into the trees where a small, beaten-up red car was parked. One tyre was almost flat and the exhaust was tied up with string, barely missing the ground. 'In just under an hour Persephone is going to take your Deathbringer by helicopter up to the top of Vesuvius. It's still early, so it's not yet packed with holiday makers. She'll wait while he does whatever it is he needs to do to get the party started and then whisk him away before the damn thing blows. You need to get there first to stop him.'

'Won't she realise you helped me?'

'I'll tell her you shot the guards and put the gun to my head and made me go with you, but I managed to escape.'

'Where did I get the gun from?'

'You took us by surprise, attacking the first guard as he walked through the door and taking his gun.' He pulled the gun out of his pocket and handed it to me. 'It has four rounds left – use them wisely.' He opened the car door.

I looked at him and then the car. 'You're expecting me to drive *that*? It's a wreck.'

'If you don't, approximately three million people will die. Want that on your conscience because you didn't want to drive a fucking car?'

He was right. Anyway what was I afraid of? Driving the damn car wasn't likely to get me killed. Hanging around outside Villa Persephone probably would.

'All right,' I said, getting in. 'Which way do I go?'

'Drive to the end of the lane and turn left, then left again at the next turning. The track will lead you out onto a main road where you turn right. Keep following that road until you see the signs directing you up the mountain.'

I grabbed the door handle and slammed the door shut. 'Tell me something,' I said, leaning out of the open window. 'Do you really think she has enough control over him for this to happen?'

He stared at me for a few seconds before answering quietly, 'You didn't see what they put him through.' He looked away for a moment. 'I know you think he won't be able to go through with it – you hope that the daemon you love is still in there somewhere – but I'd be lying if I told you I thought that was true. He might try fighting her; he might even know what he's doing and not want to do it, but when she gives him the order he won't be able to help himself.' He stepped back from the car. 'If you really love him – if you *truly* love him – then I feel sorry for you, because this is just the beginning. If you don't stop him today, next time it won't be just a region she gets him to wipe out. Next time it'll be a whole country.'

And with that cheery news I turned on the ignition, put my foot on the accelerator and bumped my way out onto the lane. When I looked in my rear-view mirror I could see Joseph standing in the middle of the dusty lane, watching me drive away.

Before I went to the Underlands I'd always hated driving – even a short trip to the nearest shopping centre would end with my fingers set into rigid claws. This time was different; the only thing running through my mind was that I was on my way to kill one of the men I loved. I couldn't even think about what would happen if I failed to stop him.

Finding the main road was as easy as Joseph had said, and there were plenty of signposts directing me to *Parco Nazionale del Vesuvio*.

Although it was early, there were already cars in front of me making their way through the hairpin bends on the twisty road to the top. One thing was for sure: Jinx and I were going to have an audience, whatever happened. I passed a couple of buses already disgorging their T-shirt and shorts-wearing passengers.

As I drove, now passing souvenir stalls piled high with T-shirts and *Monte Vesuvio* memorabilia, I kept checking the clock on the dashboard. The minutes were speeding by and I was beginning to wonder whether I was going to make it in time, but just a few yards on, I came to a red-painted snackbar and shop and swung my car into the car park.

I climbed out of the car and locked it – judging by the state of it, I doubted it would get stolen, but I didn't really want to have to walk all the way down the mountain if the worst should happen. Then it occurred to me that if the worst did happen, I wouldn't be walking anywhere.

I followed the tourists to some wooden kiosks up ahead and then realised I had no money to pay for the parking, or get a ticket to the crater, where I assumed I needed to be, so I turned away and wandered back the way I'd come, trying to look nonchalant. I had no watch, so no way of telling the time without the clock in the car, but I couldn't have long. I'd have to be a little creative. I noticed a couple of passers-by giving me odd looks as I strolled past them; I suspected I probably looked as guilty as sin. Then I saw a woman grab hold of her small daughter's chubby little hand and pull her close to her side as she passed me and I realised that with everything else that was happening, I had clean forgotten I was still in my daemon guise.

I slipped behind a car and changed – I needed to be inconspicuous if I were to get onto the mountain, and if nothing else, the Guardians might feel the power-surge and know I was here. I found the quietest place I could, hopped over the safety railings and made my way down to the crater's edge. No one started shouting or asking what I was doing, so I just kept going until I joined the official pathway below.

It was hot and it was dusty. Even through my biker boots the soles of my feet felt over-warm from the heat coming off the mountain. All over the place I could see wisps of vapour rising up out of the ground. Sadly, I didn't think it would take much to get this baby going.

Then I heard the sound of rotor blades and when I looked up into the perfect blue sky, shading my eyes with my hand, I could see in the distance a small black dot coming towards me.

Showtime.

As the helicopter got closer, people started stepping up to the rails to see it – although why they should have been interested in an approaching chopper when there was such a spectacular view in front of them, I had no idea. I wanted to shout at them to run for their lives, but I didn't. It was too late for that now.

The helicopter dropped out of view not far from where I was standing.

I started to run towards that spot just as it reappeared over the crater's edge. I looked up, straight into Persephone's eyes, and she began to laugh. Amaliel was sitting beside her and I guessed he was laughing too. I choked back my anger and carried on running. I would kill Psycho Bitch if it was the last thing I ever did – but first I had to find Jinx.

Had they dropped him just below the crater's rim?

I turned the corner, and there he was, climbing up over the railings and onto the path. I slowed to a trot and then to a walk, and as I felt my anger rippling outwards, I changed back into daemon form. The people on the path beyond Jinx followed him, eyes wide – then they saw me.

One man put his arm around his wife's shoulders; another

woman crossed herself. They knew something bad was about to happen.

I walked towards him, my hand delving into my pocket and resting on the gun. Would I use it? *Could* I use it? My heart was racing, adrenalin pumping through my body. I still wasn't certain that I could.

He walked towards me, his hair hanging over his face so I couldn't see his expression, but when he was a few feet away he stopped and looked up. I wasn't sure I liked what I saw. His forehead was creased into deep lines and his eyes glittered.

'Why are you here?' he asked.

'I came to find you.'

'You shouldn't be in this place.'

'Neither should you.'

He grimaced and pressed his palm against his right temple.

'Jinx,' I said, holding out my hand to him, too late realising it was my right hand; the hand I needed to use the gun.

He took a step towards me, then another. I looked up at the helicopter circling the mountain, but they were too far away for me to see their faces.

Jinx reached out and touched my cheek. 'I will remember your name,' he said. 'I know now that you are important to me.'

'As you are to me.'

He winced again. 'The She-Devil,' he whispered, his face contorted in pain, 'she tortures me.'

'Don't let her make you do this.' I reached up and ran my fingers down the side of his face.

There was a sound like rock cracking and I heard gasps from people on the path. I glanced towards the crater. A large plume of steam spurted out of the rock.

'How many?'

'How many what?'

'How many humans here?'

I had to gulp back the sob I could feel building up in my throat. I had a very bad feeling I knew where his mind was going.

There was another crack, and I could see something red oozing out of the crater's centre.

'How many?' he asked again, still wincing.

'Around three million,' I told him.

'So many?'

I nodded. I had no words.

There was a strong smell of burning rock and the temperature began to climb. Jinx's eyes went to the crater where I could see liquid fire was gradually rising up from the bottom.

Then a movement behind him drew my attention: three figures alighted on the path and he must have seen my expression for he spun around to face Jamie, Charles and Peter. Jamie was empty-handed, but both Charles and Peter held crossbows.

'Jinx, let us help you.' I rested my hand on his shoulder.

'Move away from him, Miss,' Peter said.

'No,' I said and despite telling myself that if it came to it I would kill Jinx myself rather than let him cause the deaths of millions, I stepped in front of him, shielding him from the crossbows.

'They will shoot through you if they have to,' Jamie said, his expression full of anguish. 'Please get out of the way.'

'No,' I told him. 'Give me a chance.'

'I have my duty. I am the Guardian.'

'Guardian?' I heard Jinx say and he grabbed hold of my arm and pushed me out of the way. 'You are the Guardian?'

'Yes,' Jamie said, his shoulders going back and his chin tilting upwards.

Jinx scowled at me. '*He* is your other lover?'

'His name is Jamie, and he's your *friend*,' I said, stressing the word.

'You love her?' Jinx asked.

'With all my heart.'

Jinx gave a small nod and turned his back on Jamie and those two very dangerous-looking crossbows.

Jinx cupped my face in his hands. 'I think, if we had had time, you could have saved me,' he said, 'but we have no time.' As if to prove his point there was a rushing sound and another spout of steam covered the rising lava with smoke, making the crater look like a pool of storm clouds.

'Jinx?'

His lips pressed against mine, softly, and then he pulled away. 'I love you, my lucky, lucky lady.' And then he vaulted over the fence and started running down the bank of the crater.

'No,' I screamed. '*No!*' and would have bounded after him, but I was suddenly surrounded with feathers as Peter and Charles grappled with me, pulling me back. Then I saw Jamie running; he jumped the fence and took off, swooping down the crater after him.

For a moment the smoke cleared and I saw Jinx turn back. 'Lucinda!' he cried, a triumphant smile on his face, 'Your name is Lucinda!' Then he spun around, ran and launched himself forward into the crater, arms outspread. For a moment, as he hung in the air, he looked very much like one of his ravens in flight.

I saw a flash of white feathers as Jamie swooped down, disappearing into the smoke behind him, and as the two angels dragged me back, a plume of flame shot up out of the centre of the volcano to screams from the people about us.

'No!' As I started to fight the two angels, crying, '*Jamie! Jinx!*' the creature within my head threw back her head and shrieked in pain and sorrow.

The sky that had been so blue turned purple then black as dark clouds raced across the sky, and it began to rain: big, fat, unnatural drops of rain like the tears I wished I could cry. Within seconds my hair was plastered to my face, but I continued to stare at the crater, hoping they would come out, but they were gone: I *knew* they were gone. And if Jinx was gone, Kayla was gone too. And now I began to sob: the dry, tearless sobs of a daemon, and then above the roar of the storm I heard rotor blades . . .

The pilot was having trouble controlling the helicopter; I could see it bucking and rolling as it was buffeted by the storm. My eyes narrowed and my inner daemon flexed her muscles. It had turned as black as night and I could barely see for the clouds of smoke being thrown up from the crater, but I could still hear.

I felt a pressure building up inside my head, then a gust of wind cleared the mist for a split-second and I could see the helicopter. It was directly in front of us.

I smiled.

'Don't do it,' Peter warned. 'If you kill a human—'

I peered through the mist until another gust cleared it away and I could see Persephone's eyes were wide and panicked: she understood that her immortality was about to be wrenched from her grasp. Amaliel sat rigid beside her, but it was the man flying the craft, doing a heroic job of keeping it aloft, that I was interested in. Could I snuff out his life?

Of course I could!

—and then he looked up from his instrument panel. *Joseph* was flying the machine.

The fight drained out of me. I couldn't kill Joseph; he might not be one of the good guys, but he had helped me escape. And if I hadn't been there to greet Jinx, maybe he wouldn't have been able to stop himself from doing Persephone's bidding.

I closed my eyes and took a deep breath. As the rain began to ease I opened them again to see the sky was beginning to clear and the helicopter was disappearing from view.

Twenty-Three

Peter and Charles reverted to men in black suits, rather incongruous for a mountainside, but I don't think they were thinking straight either. Peter walked me down the slope, a bit away from the gathering crowd, and we found Kerfuffle making his way up. Charles drew him to one side and after some murmuring my little daemon guard came and sat down on the grass next to me and patted my hand. He didn't say a word, and I didn't want him to. He was there and he cared. That was enough.

I wanted to search for Psycho Bitch and Amaliel, but Pasqual, my least favourite angel – who noticeably turned up after all the hard work had been done – made it clear that I should let the professionals deal with them, not that they'd done such a good job so far, always turning up when the trouble was over.

Pasqual was an arrogant dick, and so full of himself that even in my distressed state I wanted to punch him. As I watched him strutting around giving orders, telling *his* troops how they were going to deal with 'the situation' I got more and more upset, and Kerfuffle was so bristling with rage I thought he was going to leap up off the grass and throttle the little prick.

'Let me get you away from all this, Mistress,' he said, just as I was in real danger of either breaking down or blowing a gasket, but I shook my head. I needed to know what they were doing about finding Amaliel and Persephone.

As grief washed over me in waves, it was followed by darker, baser feelings: I *really* wanted to hurt someone, but as satisfying as it would have been to punch Pasqual in the face, I knew it wasn't him I really wanted to hurt.

In my head I kept seeing Persephone stroking Jinx's hair, touching his face. I saw him shivering at her touch – and I saw him snogging her face off. I saw him . . . I saw him launching himself into the volcano, and my angel following.

Why weren't the Guardians searching for Amaliel and Persephone?

I couldn't bear the inactivity; I had to do something, anything. 'Kerfuffle, I need to go,' I whispered. 'There's something I need to do and I'm quite sure they'll try and stop me.'

He looked up at me, his expression understanding. 'Maybe it's something I should also be stopping you from doing.'

'I need to do this, Kerfuffle. I *have* to . . .'

He patted my hand. 'I know.' He scrambled to his feet. 'I'll get you a head-start, but I can't let you risk your life, so I'll be right behind you.'

'Thank you,' I started, but he was already stomping up the slope to where Pasqual was still giving it large. As soon as Kerfuffle reached the top I jumped to my feet and began to stride towards the car park. I heard raised voices, and couldn't resist peeking back, only to see Kerfuffle swinging a punch at Pasqual. I began to run.

When I reached the car park I slowed to a walk. It was busier now, with laughing, chattering tourists milling about everywhere. Small groups of people were talking in hushed tones, and more than once I caught the words *Diavolo* and *Angeli* as I passed – they must have seen everything . . .

The battered little red car was right where I left it, and as I strode towards it, the tourists quickly moved out of my way, several crossing themselves. Being a strange colour was probably enough to make most nervous, but I imagined my expression was pretty dark, too. Jamie had always said my face was an open book.

My drive down Vesuvius passed in a blur. All I could see was Jinx and Jamie disappearing into a pool of smoke, which made me think of the three of us at play in the lake, with Pyrites warming the water and turning it into steamy clouds – and my already broken heart was in danger of shattering.

I focused on turning my sadness into anger; until I had my revenge I would not grieve.

Never had I driven so fast or so recklessly. Amaliel and Persephone might have risked returning to the villa but they wouldn't be there for long, and I couldn't lose them now. I dumped the car where I'd found it and set off running along the dusty lane. This time there was no thought of sitting to enjoy the aroma of the orange blossom or to admire the beautiful flowers in the walled garden. I was on a mission.

When I reached the back door it was slightly ajar. I pressed myself against the wall and edged close, and I heard the drag of a boot against marble, then I caught a whiff of something familiar and deeply unpleasant. I shuddered: it was the odour of the creature – the same smell that had been in Philip's apartment.

'Do hurry up,' I heard Amaliel say. 'We haven't got all day.'

I peered inside just in time to see a robed figure disappear down the stairs to the cellar. As I pushed the door open and slipped inside I was tempted to follow Amaliel, knowing I'd probably find Vaybian down there, but as I reached the stairs I heard a tinkling laugh from further along the corridor. *Persephone.*

I didn't hesitate. I was going to kill that bitch if it was the last thing I ever did. I ran down the hall and pushed the door open. Persephone was seated on a long couch while Joseph stood across the room, leaning against the mantelpiece of a huge marble fireplace. If they were surprised to see me, they didn't show it – but I felt as if all the breath had been knocked out of me.

Jinx was on one knee, his head bowed as she petted his hair with long pale fingers tipped with glossy blood-red nails. Jamie was standing opposite me, his usually immaculate snow-white feathers dishevelled and blackened with soot. Four of Persephone's goons were crowded around him with guns drawn; one had the muzzle pressed to Jamie's right temple, another to the back of his head.

'How nice of you to join us,' Persephone said, and Joseph laughed.

I couldn't quite get my head around the scene – I'd been so certain they were dead. I'd seen them die.

Jamie eyes met mine. 'Save yourself,' he mouthed.

My eyes returned to Jinx; I'd thought he was free of her – how wrong could I have been? She ran her fingers through his hair and touched his face, and he rubbed against her like a cat.

Something inside me froze, and I felt worse than when I'd thought he was dead.

'Now, what should we do with you two?' Persephone said, smiling from me to Jamie and back again. *Evil, conniving bitch*. My feelings were obviously written all over my face, for she began to laugh. 'Poor little Lucky. How long will it take you to understand that *I* am the one with the power? *I* am the one who owns his soul?'

She caressed his head and he kissed her fingers. 'Now, Guardian, you have a choice: you can join me willingly or I can let Daddy dearest play with you for a while before I make you mine by force. To be quite truthful, I think you will be the easier nut to crack. Your inherent goodness makes you weak.' She fondled Jinx's hair some more. 'The Deathbringer has the shadows of death staining his soul – that made him a real challenge, but you can see I managed it anyway. Why put yourself through all that?'

'I would rather die,' Jamie said.

She gave him a bitchy smile. 'There is always that option, of course, but it would be such a waste' – she turned to glare at me – 'but then again, maybe not, when Daddy has been so looking forward to getting his hands on your Guardian. It will give him such pleasure to make you watch as he takes him apart piece by piece, extremity by extremity.'

'You are vile,' I spat at her.

She laughed that tinkling laugh of hers. 'Actually, as it happens, I have a better idea.' She paused, tapping her finger against hers lips, then nodded towards Jamie. 'Take him downstairs. Daddy can start getting him ready for me.'

'You can try,' Jamie said, flexing his muscles, and two more guns swung upwards to point at his head.

'What good will you be to her or me with your brains splattered all over my very expensive carpet?' She strode over to me, grabbed hold of my arm and pulled me to the sofa, then rested a hand on Jinx's head. The nails of her other hand bit into my upper arm.

'Now, Jinx my dear, I want you to show everyone what a good little boy you are.' She smiled as Jinx climbed to his feet. 'Kill her.'

Jamie went to step towards me, but the butt of a gun hit him on the temple and another smacked him across the back of the head. 'Down on your knees,' one of the goons said.

'Jinx,' Jamie said, 'don't do it. Fight her – *fight her.*'

Jinx stared at him for a moment, his expression unmoved, then his eyes returned to Persephone. 'You ordered that I turn the river to blood, and I did. You ordered that I bring down a plague of locusts, and I did. You ordered me to cause molten rock to spew forth from this world's core—'

'And you failed me,' she whispered. 'Don't fail me again, because if you do I will have to think up a special punishment for you.' Reaching up, she caressed his cheek. 'And you wouldn't like that.'

'*Omnes dormieris,*' he whispered.

'What?' she asked.

My heart jumped for joy: *he was my Jinx.* She'd thought she was so clever, but she had played straight into his hands. She'd been touching him and holding onto my arm when he'd uttered his words of magic and now everyone in the room except us was frozen in time and Jinx had her right where he wanted her. He smiled his dangerous smile as he grabbed hold of the wrist of the hand that was touching his face.

'What do you think you're doing?' she asked, letting go of me to try and prise his fingers from her arm. 'Joseph—! Bruno—!'

'There will be no help to be had from those quarters,' he said, gesturing to the men surrounding my angel, all frozen in a bizarre tableau.

'Let go of me now, or I'll make you really sorry.'

'Once, not so very long ago, you ordered me to make her rot,' Jinx said.

My mouth went dry. Was he mine after all? The expression on his face scared me; that look usually preceded violence.

'Yes, I did, my darling. Will you do it for me? Will you do it for me now?'

'Did you know that when someone calls upon a daemon and orders him to take a life, the life of he who calls becomes forfeit if the order cannot be fulfilled?'

'Then *fulfil* it, Jinx! There she stands. Kill her – take her life.'

Jinx very slowly shook his head, 'I cannot.'

'Why ever not?' she said, pouting at him.

'By taking her life I would be destroying two others whose lives you did not bid me to destroy; therefore, I am unable to fulfil your demand.' He grabbed her other arm and stared down at her. 'You ordered me make her rot, and rot you shall, in her stead,' he said.

Her expression went from angry to confused to scared in the blink of an eye.

'Let go of me, let go of me now!' she cried, then she looked down at the wrist he was holding and began to scream.

I almost joined her. From beneath his fingers black lines were tracing their way up her arm, leaving behind flesh that was fast mottling and blackening. The air shimmered around her, and she finally dropped her human guise.

She took after our mother more than she did Amaliel: like Kayla, snakes wove in and out of her hair, which was an aubergine colour, similar to mine. Her eyes were so dark they looked black, and the skin that had not yet began to putrefy was a shimmering lilac. But as soon as the tendrils of black reached her neck, they blossomed like ink dropped into a bowl of water. Her body was rotting before my eyes – and still she screamed.

The blackness was creeping up her face when she finally gave one enormous wrench and staggered away – then her screams turned into high-pitched shrieks for her arm remained in Jinx's grasp, leaking gore onto her expensive carpet.

She staggered around the room looking for help where there was none. Then her eyes alighted on me and she tottered towards me, her remaining arm outstretched as though imploring me – but her expression said something entirely different and I was in no doubt that if she could reach me, she would try to kill me, even as she breathed her last.

I backed away. The flesh was already beginning to rot from her fingers, ivory bone peeking through the tips. Her lips had cracked and receded, exposing pointed teeth and white jawbone. Her cheeks sank in and the skin across her cheekbones split as her shrieks became gurgling sobs. Black tar oozed from her mouth and down her chin.

Her snakes fell limp, withered and dropped from her head, along with her lank hair, leaving a fast-mouldering scalp that was little more than dry flaps of skin attached to a yellowing skull. And just when I didn't think it could get any worse, one of her eyes flopped out onto her cheek and ran like a glutinous tear down what was left of her face.

With a bestial wail her legs gave way beneath her and she fell down onto her knees and remaining hand – but even so, she carried on trying to reach me, dragging herself across the floor in a lopsided crawl. It was horrifying to see, but even as I edged away I was unable to tear my eyes from her, watching her decomposition in terrible, fascinated horror.

Finally her bones could support her no more and she fell flat onto her face, what was left of her body collapsing in on itself. Then with a cry that was more of a sigh, she was gone – but it still wasn't the end: her yellowing bones grew darker until they were a dirty brown and began to crack and split. The back of her skull caved in, and within moments her bones had disintegrated to dust.

All that was left of Persephone was a dress and some discarded jewellery amongst ash.

I turned away, struggling to get my stomach under control. Waves of relief, followed by nausea swept through me: it was done. She was gone. And although I'd loathed her and wanted her dead, this was a far worse fate than I would have wished upon anybody.

'It is what she wanted for you,' Jinx said, as though reading my mind. 'Do not for one moment think that she didn't get what she deserved.'

He stretched out his hand to me and I stared at it for a moment, then took it and let him pull me into his arms.

'I thought you were dead,' I whispered against his chest.

I felt his lips on the back of my head. 'I'm sorry, but we hoped if we struck out against Amaliel and Persephone before anyone realised we were alive we'd have more chance of success. Of course we should have realised you'd come here—'

'You *planned* this?'

'We improvised.'

'Hadn't you better bring Jamie back?' I said, glancing across at my other lover, who was frozen, still surrounded by Persephone's four henchmen and Joseph.

Jinx smiled down at me, the corners of his eyes crinkling. 'I suppose so, though a little more time to ourselves would be nice. But we have yet to find Amaliel.'

'I'd almost forgotten about him,' I said.

'Well, I have not.' And from the rapid change of his expression, I had a feeling that when Jinx got his hands on Amaliel, Persephone would look like she had got off lightly.

Jinx gave me a swift peck on the lips and released me to stride over to Jamie. He pressed a fingertip against Jamie's forehead and my angel's eyes fluttered and he looked around him, a frown clouding his face.

'What in the name of—?'

'There was a chance you were going to get yourself shot, so I had to slow things down a bit,' Jinx said.

'Persephone?'

Jamie followed Jinx's eyes as he looked at the pile of clothes and ash on the floor. He took in the sight for a moment, then he nodded once and moved on. 'Where's Amaliel?'

'Downstairs,' Jinx said. 'I think we should take care of him now; Persephone didn't have a quiet death.'

'What about Joseph and the others?' I asked.

'I should kill him,' Jinx said, pointing at Joseph.

'No,' I said, laying my hand on his arm. 'If it hadn't been for Joseph, I wouldn't have got to Vesuvius in time to stop you.'

'Then I shall leave them,' Jinx said, and headed for the door. 'They'll awake in an hour or so. For now, I suggest we hurry.'

We ran to the basement and found Vaybian in the storeroom next to where I'd been imprisoned. He looked up in weary resignation when we unlocked the door, but managed a smile when he realised it was us.

'Amaliel?' he asked.

'Down here somewhere,' I answered. 'We must hurry.'

We moved on, but something else had been left behind: the lingering smell of putrefaction.

'Death is here,' Jinx said, but there was a puzzled expression clouding his face.

'What is it?' I asked.

His brow creased in concentration. 'I . . .' He let out an exasperated sigh. 'I remember something, but . . . No . . . No, it's gone.'

The stench got worse the further along the corridor we went, and as we came to the last room, we discovered Amaliel's parting gift. A wide smear of crimson decorating the far wall led us to the bloodied, crumpled figure slumped behind another of Amaliel's wooden benches strewn with diabolical instruments.

The bokor hadn't died well. The back of his head was slick with blood and crushed from where it had been smashed against the wall. Impossibly large eyes bulged from the sockets and tight maroon lips were drawn back in a rigor grimace of fear and pain. Thick gouts of blood ran from between his teeth, which had bitten through his fast purpling tongue. I turned away and something else caught my attention.

'What on earth—?' Directly opposite me was a wet patch splattered across the wall. I walked over to take a look and something crunched beneath my feet. Shattered glass? I crouched down. No, not glass: crystal. I scanned the floor until I found a piece large enough to examine. I picked it up, turning it in my fingers.

'What've you found?' Jamie asked.

I stood up, examining the fragment. 'Amaliel had a crystal bowl – he took it from the mansion where you found me. I thought it meant something to him, but obviously not, if he smashed it.'

Jamie took the glass from me and then looked up at the wall. His face creased into a grim smile. 'Amaliel obviously received some bad news before he left,' he said.

I looked at him blankly, and then a memory floated into my head: Kerfuffle standing on a chair in my kitchen peering down into my best crystal bowl, talking to Kayla, who had returned to the daemon world. 'Amaliel was communicating with someone in the Underlands?'

Jamie and Jinx exchanged a glance. 'Yes,' Jamie said, 'but the important question is, with whom?'

As Jamie theorised, I studied the chamber – then I noticed something moving out of the corner of my eye and I spun around, my heart in my mouth, hardly daring to look. But it was just shadows, that was all. My shoulders sagged with relief. Then I looked again.

'What is it?' asked Jinx.

'The shadows,' I said, 'they're moving.' I stepped towards them and they began to intensify. 'Look,' I said, pointing – and a hand shot out from the darkness and grabbed hold of my wrist.

I screamed and started to struggle, but I was being dragged inexorably towards the pool of black that was dancing and swirling as if alive. I heard Jamie shout, 'Lucky!' – then the room disappeared and I was falling . . .

When I eventually came to a stop it was no surprise to find myself held in Amaliel's bony grasp, and I knew exactly where we were: probably the last place my men would look for me. We were back in the second Sicarii stronghold, a subterranean labyrinth carved into the rock below a cursed, blackened wasteland. The place brought back horribly painful memories: this was where Kayla had died.

Amaliel started to drag me across the cavern towards the dais at its centre. Although I struggled, my wrist could have been enclosed in an iron bracelet, so strong was his grip.

Then from behind me I heard a cry. 'Luuckky!' And the stench of rotting flesh washed over me. 'Luuckky!' It lurched closer. 'Luuckkyyyyyy.' Then it let out a plaintive cry.

The sound was so heartrending that I forgot the horror and looked closer. How come it could say my name?

'Luuckky,' it cried again as he stumbled one more step.

Then I got it.

The creature that once had been Philip Conrad limped towards me in a lopsided kind of stagger. The memory of the fire-door swinging closed and the strange smell in Philip's apartment skittered through my brain. Was that why the Sicarii had been at Philip's flat? Maybe he had given them the slip and they had been trying to find him?

'Luuckky,' he repeated, and lurched towards me.

For a moment I was mesmerised by the horror he'd become. I'd seen terrible things in the Underlands, but this living, breathing man now reduced to a shambling reanimate was far more shocking than anything I could have imagined. The once-handsome man I remembered had been replaced by an abomination: a rotting caricature of his former self. Rancid yellow parchment-thin skin inscribed with lines of purple stretched impossibly tight across his bony skull. His cheeks had hollowed into blackening caverns. Jaundiced eyes peered out at me from sunken, bruised sockets. His professionally tousled hair clung limply to his cranium in lank, oily clumps, and dirty, broken fingernails tipped the clawed fingers outstretched towards me.

'Philip?' I whispered.

Amaliel let out a gurgling laugh. 'I see you have finally worked it out.' Then he resumed dragging me towards the dais at the centre of the cave, Philip shuffling along behind.

'Why did you do this to him?'

Amaliel's glowing eyes didn't even glance his way. 'It was an experiment: Persephone's voodoo friend said it could be done, but I didn't believe him. Turned out he was more powerful than I guessed. Quite remarkable for a human, actually, but he had ideas above his station. He thought only he could control Philip, having been the one who created him . . . I decided to prove to him that Philip was just as much mine as he was his. Quite spectacularly, as it happened.'

When we reached the dais he dragged me up the steps, slipped a cable-tie around my wrist and locked me to one of the rings embedded into the stone altar. A cable-tie, for Heaven's sake! I strained against the plastic for a moment, but it was pointless; there was a reason law enforcement agencies used this method to restrain people.

Amaliel took a step away from me, gurgling happily to himself as he slipped his hand inside his robe and pulled out a very sharp-looking knife that glinted red in the glow from the brazier. I backed as far away from him as the cable-tie would allow. I'd seen how ruthlessly he'd cut Kayla's throat: one quick slice and it was all over. Was that how it was going to be for me: a caress of a blade just beneath my chin followed by my life's blood pouring down my chest?

I was never going to have the chance to say goodbye to my friends. I was never going to tell Jamie and Jinx how very much I loved them one last time. It couldn't end like this . . .

Amaliel must have been able to guess what I was thinking as he laughed some more. Jamie was right – I would never make a poker player. 'Ironic, isn't it?' he said. 'If you hadn't been such a good little Soulseer and set free all the spirits my Sicarii friends had collected here, you might still have stood a chance.'

I frowned at him. 'How do you mean?'

'The creatures you called upon to take the Sicarii down into the depths of darkness? They would have taken me if they'd had the opportunity.'

Philip scrambled up onto the dais to stand by Amaliel's side. 'Luuckky,' he said, and Amaliel cast him an irritated look.

'I was going to kill you quickly, like I did your sister, but on reflection, I'd rather you suffered for a *very* long time.'

'Luuckky,' Philip moaned.

'Oh, do shut up,' Amaliel said. 'You're becoming tedious in the extreme.'

Philip groaned, and there was something so pathetic about the sound that I forced myself to tear my attention away from the knife that was filling my vision and our eyes met. He made a strange mewing sound and looked down at himself, making a weird gesture like he was telling me to look too. And then I understood. Oh my God, he *knew* what he'd become – there was still something of the Philip I'd once known trapped within that decaying corpse.

'Philip, why don't you show me what a good boy you can be? If you do, I might just get you that new body you've been hankering for.'

'You can do that?' I asked, trying to think fast; I didn't like where this was leading one little bit. 'I'd've thought you'd need the bokor for that.'

Amaliel gave a hiss; I'd obviously hit a nerve. 'You know *nothing*.'

'I shouldn't imagine that it's that easy transferring a soul from one body to another.'

He shoved the knife through his belt and reached into his robe and when his hand reappeared, dangling from his fingers was another of his gold chains. He lifted it up so I could see the ornate golden basket and its contents sparkling in the lamplight. The deep purple crystal was slightly larger than the others and had intricate designs engraved into the stone. It was truly beautiful. I was beginning to get the feeling that Amaliel had been very clever indeed.

'It's not much different to imprisoning souls within a crystal phial – not much difference at all.'

My mouth went dry, but I had to ask. 'Who . . .?'

'You surely didn't think I would part with her so easily when I had spare phials to hand?'

'My *mother*?'

He ran a finger down the length of the phial in an almost tender motion. 'Did you know that once Baltheza and I were the best of friends?' He looked away from the crystal and directly at me. 'No, of course you wouldn't.' He tucked the crystal back inside his robe. 'When Veronica first came to court, not long after Baltheza wedded her sister, I couldn't take my eyes off her. She was the most beautiful creature I had ever seen.' He gave a snort. 'I made the mistake of telling this to my *best friend*, and of course, that was it. Baltheza had to have her.'

'You loved my mother?' I said in disbelief.

'I *wanted* your mother – an entirely different thing altogether.'

'I . . .'

'That would have been the end of it, but he couldn't just *have* her. He *taunted* me with her – *she* taunted me – and thereby their fates were sealed.' He drew in a deep, gurgling breath. 'Then you turned up and wrecked my plans. No matter; you will be joining Veronica shortly, although not before you've suffered a truly painful death.'

My mind was spinning; my mother wasn't yet lost to me! But any relief was short-lived, for Amaliel was moving towards me, pulling the knife from his belt and raising it up so it glinted in the torchlight. I couldn't help but flinch away from him and he gurgled as he lowered the knife. 'No, that would be too easy. I think I'll let Philip play with you for a while. He quite likes getting bloody. He's developed rather a penchant for fresh meat.'

Philip made a strange mewling sound and I saw something in his eyes that made me wonder. He didn't appear at all happy with his lot, that was for sure, but neither would I if I'd been condemned to inhabiting a fast-decaying body. I mean, what would happen when all the flesh was gone? Would he still be wandering around sightless, voiceless and deaf? An animated skeleton clattering around aimlessly, but still knowing what it was? Oh God, poor Philip – not even he deserved that.

'Luuckky,' he said again.

'Yes, yes, yes,' Amaliel said, 'it's Lucky, and in a minute you'll get to play with her.' He turned his attention back to me. 'He has his uses. Unfortunately, he's reached the stage where there's no delaying the decaying process. Gaston said if we'd had him embalmed upon death he would have lasted considerably longer. As it is, I'll be glad when the flesh has left his bones and he no longer stinks so.'

I swallowed back bile and it took me two attempts to ask, 'What happens then? Will he still . . .?' I couldn't bring myself to say, 'Will he still be alive?' as he was as dead as dead could be – anyone could see that. I suppose, 'Will he still be?' was actually the question I was trying to ask.

'I'm not absolutely sure,' Amaliel admitted, 'but it will be interesting to see. Once I know, I might consider making an army of these creatures. Now I have the knowledge – another reason I no longer needed Gaston – it will be the simplest of things to do. It would be certainly less wasteful than the Sicarii way. Imagine it: an army of the dead invading your world. I could win the war by the fear they'd instil alone.'

Philip made another of those pathetic mewling sounds and when I looked at him, he was clenching and unclenching his blackened fists. There was a flicker of something within his eyes that might have been anger.

'So you see,' Amaliel continued, 'whatever happens, you really have to go. What good is an army of the dead when it takes just one stupid girl to release their souls into the afterlife?'

Philip's head swung around to look at Amaliel.

'Now, enough chatter. Philip, be a good fellow and make Miss de Salle's last moments as bloody and painful as you can. I want to hear her screaming for mercy before you've done with her.'

Philip looked me directly in the eyes. 'Doooo iiitt,' he said.

'Yes, yes, yes,' Amaliel sneered, 'that's what I said. Just get on with it.'

Philip shuffled closer, lifting his hands and flexing his fingers as he did. 'Doooo iitttt,' he said, and as his fingers closed around

Amaliel's neck, I realised he was speaking to me. He wanted to be set free – he didn't care if he was to be taken down into some terrible place; he just wanted this nightmare existence over.

Somehow Amaliel managed to twist around to face Philip. I knew how strong he was, and they were now locked in a terrible struggle. Unfortunately, I had a feeling it was one Amaliel would win – Philip in death was strong, but he was literally falling apart. Amaliel tore at Philip's face, ripping flesh from bone, then he began to tear at Philip's throat, and the hands that were gripped around his own neck.

'Dooo iiitttt,' Philip cried, and I closed my eyes and visualised the doorway opening . . .

Almost immediately, the atmosphere within the cavern changed, and when I opened my eyes, I looked down at the glowing ring upon my finger.

Amaliel realised what was happening and with a roar, gave Philip an almighty shove, sending him tumbling from the dais and onto the rock below. 'What's happening?' he demanded, his head whipping from side to side. 'What are you doing?'

Across the cavern the air was shimmering. A tear appeared very quickly, as if those waiting on the other side knew there was no time to waste.

Amaliel stalked across the platform and grabbed hold of my wrist. 'What trickery are you calling upon?'

'Trickery?' I asked.

'I know you are doing something! Tell me what, or I will slit your throat this very instant.'

'Noooo!' Philip wailed as he tried to clamber to his feet.

'Amaliel,' a voice called. 'Amaliel—' Then another called his name, and another.

He let out a hiss and raised both hands to his head, pressing his fists against where I assumed his ears would be.

I'm not sure what he was hearing, but I doubted it was the same as me. The voices sounded wonderful, and had I been free, I would have found myself drawn towards them.

But Amaliel was bent almost double, his claw-like hands clutching at his head. His knife clattered to the floor and I stretched out my hand towards it, but my fingers couldn't quite reach. I got to my feet and stretched out a foot. The tip of my boot skimmed the handle, but it wasn't enough.

Philip was trying to clamber back up onto the dais, but he was having trouble, and when he finally did manage to drag himself up over the edge, I could see why: his right leg was bent at a very odd angle and a shaft of white bone was poking through. Even so damaged, he started crawling across the rock.

The golden light began to dim as the angelic voices and the tinkling laughter faded into a discordant cacophony that really grated on my nerves – then it stopped abruptly.

Silence reigned. A cold breeze caressed my skin and the lamps around the walls began to flicker and die. The tear in the fabric between this world and the hereafter blackened and twisted at the edges like burning paper; the inner light changed from gold to red, purple to black. Amaliel slowly straightened, his hands dropping down away from his head. He turned full circle, not even hesitating as his gaze passed across the gateway. The inky black void began to pulsate like a heart beating; I could almost believe I could hear its steady *thump*. Then I realised I could: a steady beat of a heart or a drum began to intensify until the whole of the cavern echoed to its hammering.

Amaliel could hear it too; I was sure he could. While he was distracted I tried to reach the knife, but each time my toe touched the handle it spun a little further away.

The pounding had grown so loud I could scarcely think straight. My only solace was that Amaliel was having just as much difficulty as he turned this way and that, his fists once more pressed against his head.

I tried one last time to reach the knife, pulling against the cable so hard that it was cutting into my wrist and I could feel the sting as it broke the surface of my skin. My toe caught the edge of the knife and this time I managed to flip it towards me.

Amaliel couldn't have heard the clatter as it bounced across the stone – I certainly couldn't, not over the beat of what sounded like a hundred hearts – but something alerted him to what I was doing as he suddenly bounded across the dais and snatched the knife up from the floor.

'Bitch!' he shrieked.

I backed away as he stalked towards me, his bone-white hand raised, the knife glinting in the meagre light. I lifted my own arm up in the forlorn hope that it might protect my face – then the ring on my finger glowed, there was an almighty crack and Amaliel flew backwards across the dais and landed in a crumpled heap.

The heartbeat stopped abruptly.

Again there was silence, except for the pounding of my own heart and Amaliel's gurgling breathing as he staggered to his feet. '*Bitch!*' he repeated.

As he took his first step there was a gruesome slurping sound from across the chamber and over his shoulder I saw something move. I squinted into the dark, and he glanced back. Something had emerged from the black pulsating membrane and was flowing across the floor like an oil-spill – then it solidified as it rolled into a ball, and in a blink of an eye the ball had elongated upwards into a pillar. Arms erupted from its sides and the bottom split open, forming long, gangly legs and giving it the look of some horribly distorted shadow. Before the figure was fully formed another glutinous mess broke away from the membrane, then another, and another.

Amaliel returned his attention to me, unaware of what was happening behind him. 'I have had enough of your parlour tricks,' he said, 'and your interference.'

The figures began to rise up as he strode towards me, but they were like newborns taking their first steps: they were slow and shaky. He raised his right hand up above his head. 'You will not escape me this time.' And he was right; the black creatures would never reach me in time. He loomed over me, eyes glowing as he drew back his hand – and then he was spinning away from me,

locked in battle once again with the creature that had once been
Philip. How he'd managed to get up and balance on one leg I had
no idea, but although he was falling all over the place as he fought
to cling onto Amaliel, he wasn't giving up. He knew what he was
doing: he was giving me time – giving the creatures from beyond
the veil time.

While Philip held Amaliel with one hand, he battered at
his head with the other, clawing at the cowl covering his face.
Amaliel struggled, returning blow for blow, hissing and gurgling
as he fought to release his arm from Philip's grasp – then he tried a
different tack, grabbing hold of the fingers clenched around his
arm and peeling them back, ignoring the crack of snapping bone.
Philip was still fighting, but it was a losing battle, and with a final
crack of splintering bone, Amaliel was free.

Philip crashed to the floor, his broken leg collapsing beneath
him, and Amaliel lifted his arm in triumph, the knife aimed at
Philip's upturned face.

The blow never fell. Black slime wrapped itself around
Amaliel's hand, rapidly consuming his arm, and he began to
scream, a high-pitched screech that really hurt my ears. More
creatures swarmed across the chamber to surround him, and
strangely enough, the mass parted to stream either side of Philip,
leaving him where he had fallen. They had only one target, it
appeared, and that was Amaliel.

The creatures scooped him up and lifted his struggling body
above their heads, then carried him back towards the cavernous black
hole from whence they came. The more he fought, the more he sank
into them. They wrapped themselves around his extremities, and
then his body, until he was as much a figure made of tar as they were.

When they reached the entrance to their world, the membrane
stretched out towards them and sucked them back in until they
and Amaliel disappeared into the shimmering mess with a final
sucking slurp. Amaliel was gone – and so was my mother.

The doorway pulsated and surged for a few moments more, and
then, with a slap, it disappeared – and Philip and I were all alone.

Most of the lamps had blown out and there was very little light in the chamber, except for that from the brazier, which was fast burning to ashes. I really didn't want to find myself sitting in the chamber alone with Philip when all the lights finally went out.

'Noooo,' Philip cried, and he began to crawl across the dais towards me.

I was confused. *Why hadn't they taken him?* Was this to be his lot? I didn't know what to say; I didn't know what to do.

'Helllpp meeee.'

'Philip, I—'

But the chamber began to fill with light, and where before there had been the dark, unwelcoming place to where Amaliel had been taken, now a golden light began to seep out across the floor, and Philip turned towards it. 'Luuckky?'

I was nonplussed – I had been so sure he was destined for the other place . . . but golden figures filled the entrance to the other side and the tinkling, happy voices I'd heard before began to call to him. But he needed to be set free from his decaying body and I didn't know the words.

'Luuckky?'

'I don't know how,' I whispered. He had saved me, but I didn't know how to save him.

'Luuckky!'

Think, Lucky, think, I told myself.

The voices that had been calling Philip's name began to cry, 'Soulseer, Soulseer . . .'

Philip began to crawl towards the light, his broken bones scraping against the stone, and I really hoped he couldn't feel the agonising pain. 'Please, release this man,' I whispered. 'Please set him free.' The ring on my finger flared and I was bathed in warm light.

Philip crawled a few feet more, then with a moan his limbs gave away beneath him and he collapsed into a lifeless heap. The voices fell silent, then there was a shimmer above where he'd fallen and a wispy figure rose up and gradually took shape until the immaculate and handsome man I'd first met floated above his decaying carcase.

Philip looked back at me. 'Why?' he asked.

I wasn't sure what to say. 'I don't know,' I said. 'I guess maybe they think you suffered enough – or it could be that when it really mattered, you did what was right.'

His shoulders slumped and he bowed his head. 'I'm sorry,' he said. 'I am truly sorry.'

And I believed him, and clearly they did too, for the voices began to sing again, and when he walked into the light he was surrounded by glowing figures, welcoming him. I saw him turn and raise a hand in farewell and then he was gone and the doorway slowly closed, and with it went most of the light.

All I had to see by were the dying embers of one of the braziers and a solitary torch at the far end of the cavern. Unfortunately, I was still tied to the altar, and the knife had fallen off the side of the platform.

I was trapped.

I sat back down on the floor and started to try and gnaw away at the plastic. It was at an impossibly awkward angle, which didn't help, and was so tight it was digging into my wrist, making my fingers numb. I reckoned I could probably chew my way through eventually, but after only a few minutes my teeth were hurting and my jaw was aching.

I lost all track of time as I focused on getting free; I didn't dare let myself think of my mother – to have had her snatched away from me once again was just too hard.

I might have been chewing at the damn tie for ten minutes, twenty minutes or even an hour; the only thing I was certain of was that it was getting darker, and if I didn't free myself soon I was going to have to find my way out in the pitch-black.

Eventually it occurred to me that I'd probably have a better chance of escaping if I gnawed away at my own flesh. I eyed up my wrist in the gloom, but I couldn't. A little voice inside my head said, '*Then you're going to die here alone in the dark.*' I closed my eyes and took a couple of deep breaths.

'Come on, Lucky. You can do this. You *can* do this,' I told myself, and lowered my mouth to my wrist.

'Lucky? Are you there?'

Had I heard a voice calling? I sat up straight, ears straining — was I imagining things?

'Lucky?'

With a shout I got up onto my knees. There across the cavern were two figures I loved so very much.

'Over here,' I called, and within a couple of ticks I was free.

'How did you know where to find me?' I asked.

'There was a surge of power. We knew it had to be you,' Jamie said.

And suddenly I was caught up in a threesome hug that was bordering on painful, so tightly were they holding onto me, but I didn't care: I was alive and in their arms and there was no place I'd rather be.

Twenty-Four

We went back to my cottage, and as I packed things up and collected the few bits and pieces I'd really missed while in the Underlands, the boys watched the news coverage of the incident at Mount Vesuvius, which was certainly causing a lot of debate.

Video footage was played over and over again while various 'experts' dissected it, piece by piece. The Italian authorities were going along the same line as the British government had over the River Thames affair, all agreeing it was a stunt by environmentalists, trying to make their point . . . not that anyone knew quite *which* point.

But the bystanders who were interviewed were having none of it, and I stopped what I was doing to watch this. The woman I'd seen cross herself told the reporters and anyone else who would listen that they had all been saved by three of God's heavenly angels, and the Angel Gabriel himself had chased Satan back into the fiery pit.

The authorities closed ranks, and that would probably have been that, except someone dragged a couple of geologists out of their academic lairs, and that made the whole thing blow up again. They were adamant volcanoes didn't erupt that way; there had been no seismic activity recorded before or after the event. They had studied all the video footage available, and what they had seen was *impossible*; volcanoes didn't suddenly start to erupt and then abruptly stop in such a way.

The conspiracy theorists said it was a hoax by the Catholic Church and the world leaders stuck staunchly with the environmental terrorism story, but the people who were on Vesuvius that day, who saw it happen first hand, refused to be swayed.

'If you'd been there, you'd understand,' a young man said. 'You could feel their power. You could feel something miraculous was about to happen.'

My Jinx, the old Jinx, would have found it all hilariously funny. The Jinx I had brought back from Naples watched it with grim concentration.

We arrived back in the Underlands in a night-darkened yard surrounded by flickering lamplight somewhere near Baltheza's court.

'We'll join the others here,' Jamie whispered. 'I don't want to meet the rest of the Guardians until we're ready, so we must lie low.'

'Jamie, about the Guardians—' But I was interrupted by a door slamming and the sound of boots on cobblestones echoing through the quiet night. A moment later I heard Shenanigans shout out somewhere very close by, and as I turned my head to look back, Pasqual stepped from the shadows. His smile was one of triumph as he raised a crossbow, took aim and fired it directly at me.

Jinx shouted, 'No!' and pulled me to one side as someone else barged me in the shoulder, sending me flying. There was a thud and a groan, and then I was lying on the ground, Vaybian sprawled across me. Something hot and wet was seeping through my T-shirt.

I screamed, 'Vaybian!' and looked up to see Pasqual reloading his weapon, his face dark with anger.

He lifted it again and took aim.

'You sanctimonious arsehole,' I shrieked, and my inner daemon obviously agreed, because when I threw up my hand my mother's ring began to glow, my body shuddered and the air pulsed outwards, throwing Pasqual backwards and smashing him against the inn's wall. The crossbow misfired, sending the bolt shooting into the air over our heads as Pasqual slid down the stonework, leaving a bloody trail behind him. I didn't care if he was dead or not; I was only concerned about the green daemon lying across my legs.

Jinx rolled Vaybian carefully onto his back and we both kneeled beside him. The bolt had pierced the left-hand side of his chest and blood was pumping out of him at an alarming rate. I looked across at Jinx. 'Is there nothing we can do?'

He shook his head. 'Death waits by his shoulder.'

Vaybian's eyes flickered open. 'My lady Kayla,' he gasped, 'may I see her – one more time?'

Jinx reached into his pocket and pulled out the phial. He lifted Vaybian's hand and wrapped his fingers around the chain, holding it up so the dying daemon could see the blue crystal.

Vaybian smiled. 'My lady,' he whispered.

'Release her,' Jamie said, dropping down beside me.

'I don't know that I can—'

'He's dying, Lucky. You must try.'

I looked down at my hands and concentrated, trying to repeat the feeling I'd had when I'd released Kayla from the Blue Fire, hoping being trapped in the blue crystal might be similar. Nothing happened for a few seconds, then I felt my body growing warm and when I looked up I could see myself reflected in Jinx's eyes: a glowing creature with a golden light flowing from her skin.

The light enveloped us and the crystal began to whirl around and around on its chain, and as it spun it began to blaze with a light so white its image was imprinted on my retinas even when I closed my eyes. The crystal stopped, then began to spin back the other way.

'Kayla,' I whispered. 'Kayla—' and with a flash the crystal exploded into a cloud of sparkling fairy dust that swirled up into the night above us and started spinning into a column of glistening particles that gradually flowed together, forming a tall, feminine figure.

'Kayla . . .' Vaybian was smiling, but his voice was growing weak. 'My Lady.'

And then she was there. Jinx and Jamie stood, making room for her to kneel at her lover's side.

'Vaybian,' she said, and rested her hand on his, even though he surely couldn't have felt it.

'My Kayla – together again, at last.' He smiled up at her and she leaned down to kiss his lips. When she pulled away from him he looked the happiest I'd ever seen him, though the light was already dying from his eyes. There was a shimmer of emerald above him, and—

—he was gone.

Kayla looked up at me, her misery palpable.

'Lucky, it's time to let her go,' Jamie murmured.

'Kayla—'

But before I could say another word, the air grew heavy, the lamps around the courtyard flickered and a small pinprick of light appeared in the corner. It grew into a slit, light pouring from it.

I heard gasps; when I looked around the courtyard, it was suddenly filled with daemons. I was surrounded by my guard, all with weapons drawn, who were separating me from a line of Guardians also bearing arms. Notably, Peter and Charles were standing shoulder to shoulder with my friends.

From the Guardians' expressions I thought it unlikely they were about to start a fight. They too could see the light, and the emotions crossing their faces ranged from fear to joy to awe. I wondered how they could all see it – then I heard Jinx chanting, and I understood: Amaliel had cursed Kayla to hold her within the crystal; I had set her free from her prison and now Jinx was setting her free from the curse.

Kayla stared towards the light, then back to me, indecision written all over her face. 'Lucky, I can't—'

'You must,' I said. 'You owe it to Vaybian – more importantly, you owe it to yourself.'

'Oh, my darling,' she said, and rested her cheek against mine for a moment before kissing me. It might have been imagination or wishful thinking but I felt her lips against mine. 'Keep her safe,' she said, turning to Jinx and Jamie.

'We will,' Jamie said. 'I swear it.'

'And I,' Jinx agreed.

The courtyard was now alight with the golden glow and we could hear the laughter and singing. Golden figures stood in the opening, waiting for Kayla to cross, and amongst them I saw a figure I knew, who called out, 'Kayla!'

When she saw him her face lit up into a smile.

'It's time,' I told her. 'Go to him.'

She ran her fingers across my cheek. 'You won't forget me.'

'Never,' I said. 'I love you.' I had to force back the sobs. There would be time later; I didn't want to give her any excuse to stay. She had given up so much for me, and so had Vaybian. It was their turn to be happy.

'Goodbye, my darling,' Kayla said. 'I'll love you always.'

Her fingers trailed down my arm and I lifted my hand, wishing I could feel her skin against mine just one more time. Her fingertips finally slipped off mine and she glided towards the light. She hesitated just outside the opening, closing her eyes and bathing in the golden rays. She had never looked more beautiful.

She stepped into the light and golden arms stretched out to welcome her. The singing became louder and the laughing more joyous as Kayla walked into Vaybian's embrace, then she turned and looked at me. She gave me one last smile and mouthed, 'I love you.' The light flared for a moment more, then the tear began to close until it was little more than a black line seeping gold, then the light was gone and the line drew into itself until it vanished, leaving me to mourn not only for Kayla, but for the mother I'd never had a chance to know.

Unfortunately there were some who had other ideas. Pasqual was not dead. As the horrible little turd scrabbled across the yard to try and retrieve his crossbow, Kubeck grabbed him by the wings and hauled him off the ground.

'And where do you think you're going?'

'Put me down—!' He screamed. 'Put me down this instant! I am *the* Guardian – you go against the Veteribus if you go against me!'

'You are not the Guardian to us,' I said, and the rest of my daemon guard drew close, flanking me.

'Or me,' said Jinx. 'Only the true Guardian is part of the Trinity, and I can tell you one thing for certain: it's not you.'

The rest of the Guardians exchanged anxious looks, and I could see their problem: what they had been told was not necessarily the truth.

'I was always led to believe that the Guardian was born, not made by giving a daemon a title,' Charles said, nailing his colours firmly to the mast.

'The Veteribus—' Pasqual began to shout.

'The Veteribus say quite a few things,' Jinx said, his eyes glowing in the lamplight, 'but I for one shan't be quite so willing to take their utterings at face-value.'

'*You* have been sentenced to death,' Pasqual said.

'By whom?'

Pasqual licked his lips and didn't look quite so sure of himself.

'And what of my fine feathered friend?' Jinx asked.

'The Keeper has told us the Veteribus are calling him a traitor,' Peter said, with an apologetic grimace at Jamie.

'And the Soulseer?'

'A fraud,' Charles said.

'And what do you gentlemen say to that?' Jinx asked, his eyes resting on each of the angels in turn before finally looking directly at Pasqual.

'They were mistaken,' one of the angels said in a hushed voice, and there were other murmured *yesses*: hard to deny that after what they'd just witnessed.

'They lied,' Jinx said. 'They out and out *lied*.'

I didn't care. I had lost Kayla for ever. My heart was aching and nothing much else really mattered.

Then Jamie rested a hand on my shoulder and Jinx slipped his arm around my waist and I realised that, actually, yes, there were other things that mattered very much – like making sure my Guardian kept his wings, my Deathbringer kept his life and I kept my men.

Persephone hadn't succeeded in taking them from me, Amaliel hadn't managed to take them from me and I was damn sure no tribunal of so-called 'ethereal beings' was going to either.

I took a deep breath, pulled back my shoulders and tilted back my chin. *No one* was going to take them from me.

Twenty-Five

We returned to the royal palace, where we knew we'd be safe – which struck me as somewhat ironic, given my history with the building and its occupants. Its chambers and dark corridors were filled with so many memories, and on the way to present ourselves to Baltheza, more than once I thought I caught a glimpse of Kayla out of the corner of my eye, but when I turned around, she wasn't there. Of course she couldn't be – she was gone, and I would never forgive Pasqual for the part he had played in that.

Lord Baltheza hadn't taken very kindly to Pasqual trying to shoot me, and as a result, he was now residing in the Chambers of Rectification. Baltheza had also ordered the remaining Guardians to tell the Veteribus that their 'chosen' Guardian was under arrest for treason – and that he would be very angry if he discovered they had issued the order for my assassination.

'Let them stick that in their craws and choke on it,' he said grimly.

But I had other things to worry about. The relationship Jamie, Jinx and I had was special, but I wasn't sure things would ever be the same. Occasionally the old Jinx peeped out, but several times I'd seen him watching Jamie with a strange expression on his face, and as we made the long walk through the palace corridors from Baltheza's chambers I could see it again. My heart grew heavier with each step and my nerves began to jangle, and by the time Jamie opened the door and ushered me into my chambers, I was so cranked up I felt physically sick.

If Jamie had noticed Jinx's expression, he didn't let it bother him. He led me across the room to the sofa by the fire and pulled me down beside him. Jinx followed us in, but stopped by the door as if unsure he was welcome, until Jamie beckoned him over with a smile.

He stalked over and dropped down onto the floor by my feet, resting his arm on the couch and his head on his arm, looking up at us.

'What I don't understand is why Pasqual tried to kill you,' Jamie said.

'Did Charles or Peter know?'

'They knew he was going to try and *arrest* us, take us back to Askala – but kill you?' Jamie ran his hand through his hair. 'I think that came as a surprise to everyone.'

I thought on this for a bit. 'Arrest us for what?' I asked eventually.

'Charles and Peter didn't know, and Pasqual told them to mind their own business – that's why they came looking for us.'

This was all doing my head in. 'Do we think Pasqual was acting on his own initiative?'

Jamie wrinkled his nose. 'I don't think he's got the brains, but he's always been ambitious, and some of the Veteribus have clearly taken a shine to him – probably because he'll do whatever they might say without question, while I will not.'

We sat thinking about this for a bit, until Jamie said at last, 'I guess the main thing is we're all here, alive and well, and *that* is cause for celebration.'

'And that's what we should do,' I said, and before he could say another word I pressed my fingers against his lips. 'Tonight we celebrate the three of us being together again.'

That brought a smile to his face.

I had been all for christening the rug in front of the fire, but it would have meant making the fire up and getting it going, and who had time for that?

I was still worried about how Jinx was going to react to Jamie in our weird three-way relationship, especially when Jamie got up and took me by the hand to lead me towards the bed, for Jinx had stayed kneeling by the couch – until I held out my other hand to him, when he smiled, and followed willingly.

He let Jamie undress me, and I missed his teasing, but once we'd leaped onto the huge bed and I started running my hands across his broad chest and playing with his cute little horns, he happily joined in the touching and kissing until the three of us were romping the way we used to . . . well, nearly.

I'm not sure how much Jinx remembered, but there were moments when he looked like he'd had an inkling of how things had been between us before – he didn't laugh, not the way he used to, which made me sad – but when he did crack a smile it was so warming, like the rays from the two suns beaming down on me.

And when we had finished making love, his expression was one of contentment as he flopped back on the pillows, his eyes already drooping shut.

'That went better than expected,' Jamie whispered in my ear and I realised I wasn't the only one worried that our happy little threesome might not work the way it had before.

Later – *much* later – we inevitably returned to the subject of Pasqual and the involvement of the Veteribus in my attempted assassination.

'Perhaps I should travel to Askala?' Jamie suggested.

'No!' I said, alarmed at the thought of him leaving me.

'Lucky, it's not something we can just ignore.'

'Not if they're complicit in your attempted murder.' Jinx's expression was very dark indeed.

We lapsed into silence.

Of course, now I had this conspiracy theory rattling around in my brain I was seeing dark shadows everywhere – I even started to wonder whether Amaliel had been working with – or for – the Veteribus . . . but that was just plain stupid, wasn't it?

'What's going on inside that head of yours?' Jamie asked as he climbed up back onto the bed, a pitcher of wine in his hand.

I dived right in. 'Is it possible that Pasqual could have been carrying out the Veteribus' orders instead of acting on his own initiative?' Then I remembered what I'd been about to tell Jamie just before Pasqual tried to kill me. 'There's something else I forgot in the excitement.'

Jamie passed me a glass of wine and poured more for Jinx and himself. 'Go on.'

'When Joseph raised concerns about waiting to blow up Vesuvius, Amaliel said something about the Guardians not being a problem as they'd been "successfully misdirected" – that sounds to me like there's a traitor, either amongst the Guardians or the Veteribus.'

Jamie's smile slipped away. 'I hope it isn't so, but the more I think about it, the more I wonder, and the more I wonder, the more the simplest of past words spoken or snippets of conversation or tone of voice have taken on significance.'

Jinx shifted up the bed and plumped up a pillow to shove behind my back. 'Like what?' he asked.

'I'd not noticed at the time, but of late I realise I've been somewhat sidelined. There've been occasions when I was told my involvement in the affairs of the Overlands wasn't needed – even a couple of times when I was actively discouraged from doing anything.' His thoughtful frown darkened.

'What?' I asked.

'The moment you were born, a shockwave passed from your world into ours; that's how we knew a daemon child of considerable significance had been born in the Overlands. I was all ready to cross over to find you, but Pasqual was sent instead.'

'And he was unsuccessful.'

'Your mother shielded you from us – and the next time you came to our attention must have been when she was taken back to the Underlands and you were unprotected, and once again, Pasqual was sent when it should have been me. But Kayla got to you first, and now I'm beginning to think it was just as well.'

'You think he would have killed me?'

Neither Jinx nor Jamie had to say a word.

Jamie jumped off the bed, grabbed his trousers and started to get dressed. 'I'm going down to have a chat with my old friend Pasqual.'

Jinx's eyes narrowed and he too started to dress as Jamie said to him, 'You may want to join me.'

'As will I,' I said firmly.

Jamie took my hand and played with my fingers a moment. 'Very well,' he said.

'But know that we'll do whatever is necessary,' Jinx said, without even a hint of apology.

I took Jinx's hand and squeezed both their fingers. 'We're in this together.'

Jamie looked at me, his blue eyes staring into mine until the world around me disappeared. 'I love you so very much,' he whispered, raising my hand to his lips and kissing it.

The descent into the depths of the palace's torture chambers was just as dark, dank and scary as I remembered. Amaliel may have been long gone but his presence lingered, and so did the stench of suffering and decay. When we reached the corridor at the bottom of the first flight of stairs I almost expected him to glide out of one of the cells, his fiery eyes burning from within his hooded robe.

It was late and the daemons who worked down there had knocked off for the day, leaving two guards on duty in the main chamber, next to a blazing brazier which might have been glowing red but was doing nothing to ease the chill pervading the place. They looked up from their game of cards.

'We want to see Pasqual,' Jinx said.

One guard pushed several coins into the centre of the table to join a fair-sized pot. The other peered down at his cards for a moment as if checking to make sure they hadn't changed, then he too upped his stake.

'He's a right popular inmate this evening,' the first guard said at last. Even sitting down he was a big daemon; he had a huge craggy face textured like a walnut shell, and of similar colour. His hair was hidden by his shiny leather helmet.

'Popular?' Jamie asked sharply.

'You're the second party to visit in less than half an hour.'

'Twenty minutes,' the other lisped, 'if that.' This one might be slight of frame, but if I'd had to make a choice of who I'd favour in a brawl, my money would have been on the smaller guard: a forked tongue flickered out over the sharp fangs curving down over his bottom lip and long, blade-like talons tipped each of his scaly fingers. I hadn't a clue how he held his cards; I guessed it needed a lot of practice.

'Who came to see him?' Jamie asked.

The two guards exchanged a glance, then began to frown. 'I . . .' The big one rubbed his chin. 'Now you ask, I'm not sure.'

Fang-Face wasn't any the wiser either. 'I remember them coming and asking for the key, and they couldn't have been long, because the next thing I remember is—' He didn't finish but threw down his cards and jumped to his feet, knocking back his chair.

'Oh shit,' Jinx muttered, and he and Jamie were off along the corridor with the small guard chasing after them.

I followed on at a more sedate pace. I had a horrible feeling hurrying wouldn't make a blind bit of difference.

Jamie urged the guard to get a move on as he fumbled with the key in the lock and then the door was flung back on its hinges, hitting the stone wall with a bang that echoed throughout the underground passageways.

Jinx and Jamie started roundly swearing and crouched down next to Pasqual's body, examining him with expressions of grim distaste.

I didn't need to ask if he was really dead. His once white feathers were awash with jade.

Jamie looked up at me. 'Someone didn't want him talking to us.'

'Who would do this?' I asked.

Jinx rested his chin on his fist as he stared down at the dead daemon. 'Someone powerful.'

We left the two guards standing over the late, departed Pasqual and scratching their heads. Neither could remember anything about the person or persons who had visited their prisoner: Walnut Head was adamant there had been only one, Fang-Face was sure it was three, dressed in black robes; Walnut Head said his daemon had been in some sort of uniform. The only thing they both agreed on was that it had been no more than half an hour before we'd arrived, calculated by the number of hands they'd played.

'Of course, if they'd both been mesmerised it could have been an hour, maybe two,' Jinx said as we climbed the stairs.

'What sort of daemon can mesmerise another?' I asked.

Jamie and Jinx exchanged a grim look. 'A Guardian,' Jinx said.

'Or the Deathbringer,' Jamie added.

After some discussion we decided telling Baltheza his prisoner had been murdered in his cell could wait until morning. No good would come of waking him with such news.

'Do you really think it was a Guardian who killed Pasqual?' I asked, too ramped up to settle as my men climbed into bed beside me.

'Well, it wasn't me,' Jinx said, 'so it's the only possibility.'

'They would kill one of their own?'

'Some of them were willing enough to let Jamie forfeit his wings,' Jinx pointed out.

'No,' Jamie said, 'most of them are good, solid daemons who believe in what they do.'

'*Most*, but not all,' Jinx noted. 'If it had been you in that cell and you had received such a visitation, I'd have bet on it being Pasqual who'd carried out the deed.'

Jamie leaned back against the headboard. 'I'm with you on that one. He always had an agenda.'

'And look where it's got him – although the manner of his death was strange.' Jinx snuggled down the bed until his head was resting on my hip. 'A thin blade shoved up beneath the ribs at such an angle? That means the killer got up really close and personal.'

'Almost as if he and his killer were embracing,' Jamie agreed.

'How awful,' I said.

'Now say that like you mean it,' Jinx said.

'I do. It's awful.'

'Hmm.' Jinx rubbed his head against me. 'I think if James had lost his wings you would have knifed Pasqual in the ribs without a second thought.'

'Jinx!' Jamie's expression was horrified.

I was about to deny it, but then I thought about it for a moment or two. Could I kill someone so brutally? I might like to think not, but if I was *really* angry, I had a feeling Jinx was right: I probably could.

'Lucky?'

'To be totally honest, there have been times over the past few weeks when I think I might have killed for either of you – I'm not proud of the dark thoughts I've had recently, but if anyone should hurt you or try and take you away from me' – I gave them both a crooked smile – 'I'm very much afraid I would do *whatever* it took.'

'That's my girl,' Jinx said, and as his head disappeared under the blanket, any retort I might have been about to make instantly fled from my mind.

I heard Jamie chuckle, and then I was lost – this time in a *very* good place.

Baltheza had already been informed of Pasqual's demise by the time we were up and about and in a show of his complete indifference, had gone off hunting.

My guards were pretty subdued over breakfast. They might not have really liked Vaybian overmuch, but his death had still cast a shadow over their usual cheerful outlook on life, and hearing of Pasqual's unfortunate end was doing nothing to lighten their moods.

'I would say good riddance to bad rubbish,' Kerfuffle said, 'but I have a feeling in my bones that this is not a good thing.'

'That a Guardian or the Veteribus could be implicated in Pasqual's death is definitely not a good thing,' Kubeck agreed. 'In fact, it is probably the worst possible of scenarios.'

Jinx filled his plate from the breakfast table and gestured with his head to my empty dish. 'Aren't you eating?'

I looked at the platters piled high with bacon and eggs and other assorted breakfast foods and shook my head. Even the smell was making me feel a little queasy.

'You should eat something,' Jamie said.

'I think I'd probably throw up if I did.'

Jamie glanced my way. 'Aren't you feeling well?'

'It's nothing. I'm just a bit down, is all.'

Jinx popped a piece of bacon into his mouth, and as he chewed, a contented smile lit up his face. 'I'd forgotten this,' he said.

'What?' Kerfuffle asked.

'Bacon, eggs, us all eating breakfast together.'

Kerfuffle's glower softened. 'Having meals together like this are the best times of the day.'

Shenanigans smiled one of his goofy smiles. 'It's like we're all family.'

Jinx piled some more food on his plate. 'Family?' He thought on it for a bit. 'I like that. Family's good.'

That afternoon a small funeral service was held for Vaybian – and a little surprisingly, as he'd made it clear he had never liked the daemon, Baltheza decreed that Vaybian should be interred in the royal mausoleum with Kayla. 'He guarded her body in life – it is only right that he guards it in death,' he said, and closed the subject.

I was invited to dine with him in his private quarters and, as there was no longer any danger from him, Jamie and Jinx hadn't joined us, which was a first.

'So, what are the Guardian and Deathbringer going to do about Pasqual?' Baltheza asked after I explained what had happened while we were in the Overlands.

'I really don't know,' I admitted.

'I must admit to being puzzled by recent developments.' He sat back in his chair and considered me over steepled fingers. 'And this attempt on your life? I cannot understand that at all.'

'None of us can—'

He carried on as though I hadn't spoken. 'It is also very strange to me that the instigator of all this intrigue – the unknown entity with whom Amaliel was communicating – remains at large and is being generally ignored.' He fixed me with another of his steely-eyed stares. 'It is all most odd.'

I wondered whether I should tell him what had become of my mother, but decided there wasn't any point: at best he'd feel guilty and at worst he'd feel nothing at all, and I'd rather live with the illusion that he'd once cared for her. If what Amaliel had said was true, she was probably just a pawn in another of his games – I hoped it wasn't so but . . . There was something I did want to ask Baltheza, and I was wondering how to broach the subject when he brought it up himself.

'I'm pleased you have taken to wearing your mother's ring,' he said.

'It's beautiful,' I told him, lifting my hand and letting the torchlight play on the stone.

'I had it specially made for her.'

'Really?'

Topping up my goblet of wine and pouring one for himself, he said, 'After Kayla was born, things were a little difficult between my wife Marla and Veronica, as you might imagine, and at one time I feared for your mother's life.'

'You thought Marla would—?' I hesitated, not sure this was something I wanted to put into words.

Baltheza stared at me over the top of his goblet and I wondered if I had already gone too far, but then he smiled. 'They might have been sisters but there was no love lost between them, and Marla was more than capable of that, so I had the ring made for Veronica as a modicum of protection. The stone is the finest drakon glass.'

'Drakon glass?'

'A very rare product of a drakon's fire: legend has it that such stones have magical protective powers and can ward against poison and dark magic, amongst other things.' He chuckled. 'Perhaps if I'd had such a trinket made for myself, Amaliel wouldn't have been so successful with poisoning me.'

I glanced down at my hand, thinking maybe the stone's protective powers were more than a legend – and that maybe he really had cared for my mother after all.

As soon as it was polite, I excused myself – Baltheza had been far better company than I'd imagined, but his disquiet over the situation Jamie, Jinx and I found ourselves in made me suddenly anxious to return to my men. That Baltheza insisted two of his guards accompany me didn't do anything to help my stress levels.

Twenty-Six

When I reached my room it was empty, which was strange – where was everyone? I couldn't remember ever being totally alone while residing in the palace, and even though Baltheza was now saner than he had been and unlikely to have me assassinated, there was this whole new potential danger. Maybe Jinx and Jamie were next door with the rest of my guards?

I looked around, about to make for the door, when I spotted something on the pillow: a folded sheet of parchment. That was odd too – why would they leave me a note? Usually they left messages with one of the others.

I sat on the edge of the bed and read the message scrawled in large looping swirls of black ink:

> Lucky, we have been called to Askala.
> Will be back before you know it. J and J

It was short and to the point, and I was pretty sure neither Jamie nor Jinx had written it. Jamie wrote in small, neat script; the letters on this note were large and untidy. I could imagine that Jinx might write like this, but he would have addressed it to Lucinda. He hardly ever called me Lucky – and he certainly wouldn't do so in a letter.

No, neither of them had written this note – and anyway, they wouldn't have left me alone and unprotected; at the very least they'd have made sure one of my guards was here waiting for me, or more likely, all of them.

I had to find Shenanigans, Kerfuffle and Kubeck. I scrambled off of the bed and stalked across the room to my dressing room, already fiddling with the buttons down the back of my court dress as I went. The sooner I was out of this damned thing and back into my own clothes the better.

I stripped off the dress, sending several of the buttons pinging across the room, and reached for my jeans. As soon as I'd dressed, I hurried next door, but I hesitated outside my guards' chamber, not sure whether I should knock or not. I'd just decided I should when I started to wonder why Kerfuffle wasn't already opening the door – he usually knew when someone was outside before they'd even made their presence known.

I knocked: three short, sharp raps of the knuckles against the hard wood, and waited. There was no answer, so I knocked again and waited. Still no answer? Maybe they'd got bored with waiting – maybe they had gone to the inn . . . Or maybe something had happened to them.

My heart thumping, I slowly turned the ringed handle and pushed the door open.

All sorts of visions passed through my head before I had the courage to step inside: I imagined my guards all sprawled out across the floor, their throats cut. I saw them sitting in a circle around their platters, heads lolling forward as if asleep, but actually poisoned by the wine. If I'd waited any longer I'd have had my over-active imagination seeing even worse, so I stepped inside the room.

It was empty.

They were at the inn – they had to be.

'Mistress Lucky?' The voice behind me made me jump, but to my relief when I turned, Kubeck was standing in the doorway. 'Sorry, did I alarm you?' he asked, seeing my expression.

'It's all right. I just wondered where everyone was.'

He grinned. 'Shenanigans and Kerfuffle are with their lady-loves at the inn and Pyrites is off hunting – and I have just returned from visiting my Uncle Davna to tell him the news of the Chief Corrector's demise.'

'Is he well?'

Kubeck waggled his hand from side to side. 'He still mourns his son, but knowing the daemon who took Simion from him is no more has eased his pain.'

I gestured for him to follow me back to my own chamber. 'Where are the Guardian and Deathbringer?' he asked, looking around the empty room.

I crossed to the bed, picked up the note and passed it to him. 'What do you make of that?'

As he read the message his forehead creased into a puzzled frown. 'They wouldn't just leave like this.'

'I didn't think so either.'

'Just after you left for dinner with Lord Baltheza they told us quite plainly that we should ensure you're never left unattended until we've solved the puzzle of your attempted murder.'

'And yet they've gone,' I said.

He handed me back the note. 'You think this is a forgery?'

I looked back down at the over-the-top, untidy scrawl. 'Yes,' I said and dropped the note back on the bed. 'How far is this Askala place?'

'Pyrites could probably get us there in a few hours.'

'Too long,' I said. 'I think we'd better find the others.'

'With your leave, I'll go and get some weapons,' Kubeck said. 'I'll be but a moment.'

Weapons would be good.

He added, 'But I suggest you lock the door until I return.' And with a little bow of the head he hurried off.

I followed him across the room to do as he'd suggested; I had been so sure that now Amaliel was gone I'd be safe in the palace, but if my guards were worried, I should be too. I turned the key in the lock and as an afterthought drew the bolts at the bottom and top of the door.

'My, my, my,' a voice said, 'you are taking your security seriously.'

I spun around to see a woman I had never seen before standing in the doorway to my bathroom. For a moment I was dumbstruck – was there a secret passage leading into my bathroom? Then I remembered the figure pushing me down beneath the bathwater, the figure I was now pretty sure had been Philip. So there *must* be a secret passageway.

As the woman stepped into my chamber, alarm bells immediately started going off in my head. This woman was dangerous; I was sure of it.

She was almost completely black – not chocolate, not ebony, but the blackest black you could possibly imagine; almost like a picture in negative. Her black hair fell in waves which disappeared under her cloak, beneath which she was wearing close-fitting leather body armour that on anyone else would have probably looked ridiculous; on her it was both incredibly sexy and very commanding.

The two horns that peeked out just above her hairline were glossy, twisted points that could have been carved out of coal. Her skin was like normal everyday skin, but totally dark, like she'd been dipped in matt black paint. Her lips were black, her eyebrows were black and when she smiled at me I could see her teeth and even the inside of her mouth were black. The only parts of her that weren't were her eyes, and even they had not a hint of white. They were burnished copper orbs with vertical slits for pupils like a cat's.

'How . . .?'

'I have been sent by the Guardian to escort you to Askala,' she said.

'Why didn't he come himself?'

'He is otherwise engaged,' she said.

There was a knock on the door and I heard Kubeck call to me. I turned – and the woman was suddenly between me and the door. I took a step back, amazed by her speed.

'I wouldn't answer that if I were you.'

'Why ever not? Kubeck is one of my guards.'

'James said I was to tell you to trust no one, not even your guards. He believes one of those close to you is in collusion with the enemy.'

'Right. And why on earth should I trust you? I don't even know you.'

'I was told you would probably be difficult,' she said, grabbing hold of my arm.

'Let go of me,' I snapped, but when I tried to shrug her off her leather-clad fingers tightened, digging painfully into my upper arm.

'Mistress Lucky!' I heard Kubeck call through the door as the mystery woman dragged me struggling and kicking towards the black hole that had once been my bathroom.

'Do behave,' she said as I grabbed hold of the doorframe with my free hand.

'Help!' I screamed as she wacked me across the knuckles with the hilt of a dagger that had appeared in her fist, then she pulled me through the portal and I was in pitch-blackness and falling.

We stopped briefly, almost as if we were in an elevator or turning a corner, before falling again, and when we eventually arrived at our destination, although I was furious at the way I'd been treated, I also began to feel a little foolish. We had landed in a pink and gold marble courtyard surrounded on all four sides by a building that looked very much like a temple – if I'd ever wondered how Askala would look, this probably would have been it.

The woman let go of my arm. 'This way,' she said, and I had little alternative but to follow her. She walked ahead to a white-and gold-painted door leading into a long wide corridor of more pink and gold marble. To our left, long open windows overlooked a lantern-lit gardens. At any other time I would have wanted to stop and look, but I had only one thing on my mind: making sure my two men were safe and well.

At the end of the corridor we went through a large hall of yet more pink and gold marble with tall marble pillars flanking the windows and doorways. Carved marble tiles, the only decoration, bordered the floor and ceiling.

'Almost there,' the woman said as we stopped outside yet another door and she rapped firmly, three times.

'Come in,' a female voice called and the woman opened the door and gestured that I should enter first.

I heard the door close behind me, and when I looked back the woman was gone.

I wasn't quite sure what to expect, other than the room would be of pink and gold marble; at least I wasn't disappointed in that. At the far end of the chamber was a woman dressed in white, standing by a large picture window with her back towards me. After a couple of moments she turned to greet me and somehow I wasn't at all surprised to recognise her: the woman I'd seen with Jamie – the Keeper.

'Welcome, Soulseer,' she said. 'I am delighted to meet you at last.'

'Really? Then why the heavy-handed approach? You could have just sent me an invitation to come and visit.'

She laughed. 'And where would the fun have been in that?'

I had to force myself not to scowl at her; she was one of the good guys, after all – right? I fought back my bad humour and tried to relax. 'Where are Jamie and Jinx?'

'You'll see them shortly. I just wanted to get to know you – to find out if everything that's being said about you is true.'

'Like what?'

She strolled over to a small table, picked up a golden decanter and poured red wine into two gold goblets. She handed me one before returning to stand by the window. I joined her.

The window looked out over a sheer drop, with clouds lapping around the mountain face a hundred feet below; it gave the illusion that we were surrounded by a steaming ocean, which immediately brought to mind images of Jamie, Jinx and Pyrites at play in the lake; a happy time that felt like a lifetime ago.

She gazed at me over the rim of her goblet as I took a sip of the wine and looked back at the clouds resting in the purple moon-lit sky.

'You're not at all what I imagined.'

I gave a humourless laugh. 'What you see is what you get.'

'There are some who say you are a fraud.'

'A fraud of what?'

'That you cannot possibly be the Soulseer of legend.'

'I've never heard the legend, so I wouldn't know.'

'James believes you are the Soulseer.'

'And what does Jinx say?'

'Ah, the Deathbringer.' Her lips curled into a feline smile. 'He is still not quite himself, but if nothing else is true, he would still rather die than see any harm come to you.'

She gestured that I move closer to the window, but I was as close as I wanted to be; even with the mountainside below obscured by clouds, the drop was too deep for my liking.

'When I need to think I stand here and look out across the sky. It helps me clear my mind.'

'It is beautiful.'

'Like being in what humans call Heaven?'

'I guess.'

She linked her arm through mine and drew me so close to the window that my knees were touching the wall and my hip the window ledge and I felt the first flicker of real fear. I tried to pull away from her, but her arm was wedging mine tightly against her body.

'I sometimes wonder what it would be like to dive down into the clouds,' she said. 'They look like they go on for ever and ever.'

I took a step back and yanked my arm from hers, spilling some of my wine down the front of my white T-shirt. 'What do you want, other than to scare the crap out of me?'

'You are immortal – why should you fear me?'

'I'm pretty sure even an immortal wouldn't survive a head-dive out of your window,' I pointed out, 'and anyway, I'm half-human.'

'If you truly are the Soulseer, you are as immortal as the Guardian and Deathbringer.'

'Why does it matter so much to everyone?' I asked, suddenly irritated. 'I see the dead – big deal. I always have, and I suspect I always will.'

'But you don't just *see* the dead, do you? You can open the door to the hereafter.'

'Only to let the dead move on.'

She stared at me for a moment. 'Let me get you some more wine,' she said, taking my goblet and strolling over to the small table to top up our drinks. I used the opportunity to move away from the window. I felt all goose-bumpy, and when I looked down at my arms I noticed a couple of gold threads hanging from the sleeve of my T-shirt.

Gold thread? That meant something. I tried to remember, but before it came to me the Keeper interrupted by holding out my replenished goblet, and the thought was gone.

I didn't really want it, but I took it from her anyway, too late realising the trembling of my hand was more than a little obvious.

'You're a woman of passion,' she said.

I didn't reply. I was finding it hard to think straight.

'And you care very passionately about both the Guardian and Deathbringer, do you not?'

'Yes.' My voice was not much more than a whisper as my irritation drained away, to be replaced by a bone-weary lethargy.

'How much do you care? Would you do anything to save them if they were in danger?'

'Yes.'

She took hold of my chin and lifted my head so I was looking directly into her eyes, until they were all I could see.

'Would you die to save them?'

'Hmm.'

'You would?'

'Hmm.'

She put her arm around my shoulders and guided me back to the window. I stumbled, and she held me upright. What was the matter with me that I felt so exhausted?

'Doesn't it look beautiful?' She gestured down at the clouds. 'It would be so quick, so easy – you wouldn't feel a thing, and you'd die knowing you had freed your lovers.'

'Freed them from what?' I said, or at least, I think I did; I was beginning to feel very odd indeed.

'All you have to do is climb out onto the ledge and jump,' she said, and somehow I was standing on the window ledge with the Keeper by my side.

'Giddy,' I said, and could feel myself swaying. 'So giddy.'

'Why don't you beat your wings and fly?' she suggested.

Wings? Was I an angel now? I felt her palm on the small of my back. *Something was wrong.* I knew something was wrong. I turned to face her and she smiled.

'Goodbye, Soulseer,' she said, and she pushed me.

Chapter Twenty-Seven

I teetered on the brink – if she had had any sense at all, she would have pushed me really hard, but she hadn't, and as I began to fall, I did what any normal person would do: I grabbed out for the nearest object – and that was the Keeper.

I clung onto her wrist for grim death as my feet skidded from under me and I hung out above the void. She tried to prise my fingers loose, but that was her undoing, because I was at least thinking clearly enough to be certain that if I was going, she was coming with me. She staggered, then almost righted herself – until the weight of my body pitched her forward, and with a shriek she plunged over the side and we were both falling.

She screamed all the way down, but I spread out my arms and legs like a skydiver and closed my eyes – I didn't want to see the ground coming before I hit it. Actually, I was feeling quite nice; I just wished she'd shut up. All that screaming – how undignified was that?

I wished Jamie was here. Maybe he could teach me to fly. No, I needed wings. I giggled. I could do with some now. I could do with . . . ah, so tired.

Then she stopped screaming and I thought, *I can sleep now.*

I woke up in a strange room, although the ceiling spinning around above me was of pink and gold marble, which I thought I recognised, but my poor thumping head made it difficult to think. I closed my eyes, but that didn't help; I felt like I was spread-eagled across a merry-go-round on speed. My stomach began to churn and there was a roaring in my ears, and just when I thought I was about to throw up darkness took me.

When I finally came to again I was still in the same room,

though thankfully the ceiling was no longer rotating. The bed was warm and comfy, and although there was the memory of an ache behind my eyes I felt a hell of a lot better than I had before.

I could hear the gentle burr of snoring and when I struggled to sit up I found my legs pinned down by my sleeping drakon. Pyrites shifted a bit as I pulled myself up the bed, then he opened an eye and, seeing I was awake, scrambled up beside me to give my cheek a lick of hello.

'Mistress Lucky?' Kubeck appeared above me.

'Where am I?' I asked.

'We're in Askala,' he told me. 'How are you feeling?'

'A bit woozy,' I said, pushing myself up into a sitting position. 'What happened?'

'I think it better that the Guardian and Deathbringer explain. They know the whole story.'

'Jamie and Jinx are here?'

He gave a bob of the head. 'They'll be back shortly, once the tribunal has reached its verdict.'

'Tribunal? *Verdict?*' I started imagining all sorts of things, like Jamie and Jinx wrapped in chains. 'But they haven't done anything wrong—'

'No, no, Mistress. You misunderstand me – they're awaiting the verdict and sentencing of the woman they call the Keeper.'

I sank back against the pillows. 'The Keeper,' I murmured to myself and it all began to come back. My stomach gave an unpleasant lurch and for a moment I felt like I was falling again, even though I knew I was safe in bed. 'She tried to kill me.' My voice was shaking.

Kubeck pulled up a stool to sit closer to the bed. 'If we'd arrived a moment later it would have been too late,' he said. 'We heard a scream as we reached the door to the Keeper's chamber. Fortunately, the woman didn't stop screaming as she fell, otherwise—' He sucked in breath through his teeth. 'As it was, the Guardian and Pyrites reached the pair of you only just in time.'

For the next few hours Kubeck fussed over me, making sure I

had plenty to drink and trying to entice me to eat some fruit or the dainty little pastries he had purloined from somewhere or other, but I wasn't a very good patient; I couldn't settle. He'd assured me that Jinx and Jamie weren't in trouble, but I couldn't quite believe it, and until my two men were back with me I wouldn't be happy.

At last the door opened and Jamie came striding through, Jinx right behind him. Their expressions were so serious I immediately thought the worst, then the relief in their smiles as they saw me told me that at least one of the reasons for their dour expressions was their worry for me. They both started to talk at once.

'—are you—?'

'—you all right—?'

'—we were so worried—'

'—we thought we'd lost you—'

'—we so nearly didn't get to you in time—'

'I'm fine,' I told them as they dropped down to sit either side of me. Jamie hugged me to him, and Jinx took hold of my hand, caressing my fingers with his. 'At least, I am now. I was worried about you, too – *but what the hell happened?*'

Then the whole story came tumbling out, Jinx interjecting from time to time, his expression grim, as Jamie explained, 'It must have been just before you arrived back from dinner with Baltheza. There was a surge of power from somewhere beneath the palace.' He gave a wry smile. 'Do you know, for a few seconds I actually thought that maybe Amaliel had somehow come back. Stupid really, but I did wonder.'

'As did I,' Jinx added. 'I'd put nothing past that creature.'

'When we investigated the labyrinth of corridors of Amaliel's domain, we found an open door to a secret passage leading to a flight of stairs – we'd just started up them when there was another rush of energy, from right above us,' Jamie went on. 'You can imagine what we thought when we got to the top and found we were in your bathroom. It didn't help that we could hear Kubeck out in the corridor battering against the door trying to get in. We really did fear the worst.'

'Then Kubeck showed us the note, which immediately brought us to Askala,' Jinx said.

'Fortunately for Isla—' Jamie stopped when I looked blank, then explained, 'The Keeper, her name's Isla, anyway, lucky for her, Pyrites returned from his hunting just as we were setting off. It was he who had saved her – although I'm not sure how happy she'll be about that now she's been arrested and charged with trying to kill you, amongst other crimes.'

'But why did she want me dead?' I asked.

Jamie and Jinx exchanged a look and my angel's face flushed a deep rose. 'She's been questioned at length, but she refuses to say anything other than everything she has done has been for the good of Askala.'

I studied Jamie's glowing face and the penny dropped. 'She fancies you,' I said. The way she had touched his arm and the expression on her face when I saw them together should have been a big enough clue.

'Well, one of the few pieces of information she volunteered was that she thought you were a bad influence on me,' he admitted. 'She also says she acted alone, but that doesn't ring true.'

'*None* of it makes any sense,' Jinx said.

'Did she admit to being in cahoots with Amaliel?' I asked.

Jamie shook his head.

'Or Pasqual?'

'No,' Jamie said.

'And who was the bitch in black?'

Jamie and Jinx both frowned at me. 'Bitch in black?' Jamie asked.

I told them about the woman who had brought me to Askala. 'The first surge of power you felt must have been when she arrived and the second when she left with me.' Then something else occurred to me. 'How did she know about the secret passageway into my bathroom?'

We sat in silence pondering on that one. How had she known? Unless she was no stranger to the hidden ways that riddled the palace . . .

Jamie went very still for a moment, then he ran a finger along my wrist. 'This woman in black – what did she say? Did she give any clue as to who she was?'

'Not really, just that you'd sent her to bring me to Askala – that you'd said I was to trust no one, not even my guard. She was *really* fast – and very strong. Then she dragged me into a black hole and the next minute I was in Askala and she was ushering me into the Keeper's lair.'

'I have heard rumours of a daemon such as she,' Jamie said eventually, his voice low, 'but I'd thought it just a story to frighten small children.'

'The Shadow?' Kubeck whispered.

Jamie's lips pressed into a thin line.

'Rumour or not, we now know the Keeper wasn't acting alone,' Jinx said, 'and that makes me wonder about what we discussed before.'

I suddenly remembered something else. 'Isla was the one communicating with Amaliel, and she must have visited him in the Overlands at least once.'

'What makes you say that?' Jamie said.

'There were long golden strands of hair on Amaliel's robe – at first I thought they were golden threads, then just before she pushed me out of the window I found some on my T-shirt.'

'This could explain something that's been bothering me,' Jamie said. 'You and Jinx were using power all over the place when you were in the Overlands, but half the time we either didn't feel it, or when we did, it was almost as though it was distorted. The rest of my Guardians went off on several wild goose chases, only to find that you weren't where they'd been led to believe.'

'She could do that?' I asked. 'She could mask our use of power?'

Jamie's expression became ultra-grim. 'Not without help.'

'Which brings us back to the Veteribus,' Jinx said.

Kubeck had been sitting quietly on his stool, listening, but before we could say any more he moved closer and whispered, 'Not here.'

'You don't think—?' I started, but he put his forefinger to his lips.

'I think it's time we took Lucinda home,' Jinx said.

'Are you feeling well enough?' Jamie asked, studying my face.

'I'll feel a lot better once we're out of here,' I told him. As beautiful as Askala was, I didn't ever want to see the place again.

We decided to use conventional methods of transport; they might be speedy, but I still didn't much care for the jumping through black holes method. Anyway, Jinx wanted to be reunited with Bob and I'd never seen the huge creature look so cheerful as when he descended from the sky to see Jinx there waiting for him; there was a definite spring in his step as he trotted to my Deathbringer's side to nuzzle at his neck. Kubeck and I rode on Pyrites and Jamie used wing power.

Everyone was smiling as we set off for home.

As we were traversing the Icedfire Mountains which surrounded Askala, Pyrites' birthplace, we saw several drakons from a distance, and a couple more snoozing on the mountainside below us, but I was rather disappointed that none came up close.

'These days they're not over-fond of daemonkind,' Kubeck explained and Pyrites puffed grey smoke. This was another question for my angel, I guessed, as no one could doubt Pyrites' love for me.

It was only once we'd left the mountains behind that Jamie gestured for us to land and we resumed our previous conversation where we'd left off. I sank down onto the grass, still feeling a little light-headed, with Jamie beside me and Jinx sitting cross-legged opposite. Kubeck and Pyrites joined us, forming a circle, while Bob wandered around munching contentedly on the leafy vegetation surrounding us.

'I know you probably don't want to hear this,' Kubeck said, 'but I think you're right – there is more to this than Amaliel and the Keeper working together to subjugate the Overlands.'

We all looked thoughtful, then Jinx said, 'I think what we have here is two people with totally different and yet linked agendas banding together.'

'How do you mean?' Jamie asked.

'The Trinity,' I said.

'Pardon?'

'She told you I was a bad influence,' I said. 'What if this is what it's all about? We know Amaliel tried to find me as soon as I was born, and at the same time Pasqual was sent to kill me, we think.'

'Amaliel wanted power, and he didn't much care which one of us he used to get it,' Jinx said.

'Isla, on the other hand, wanted me dead, because for some reason she believes the three of us together – the Trinity – are a threat.'

'And what better way to destroy the Trinity than by helping Amaliel bind the Deathbringer to bring death to millions in the Overlands,' Kubeck said. 'The Deathbringer would be for ever bound, Amaliel would in the meantime attempt to kill the Soulseer and trap her soul in one of his little trinkets and the Guardian would lose his wings if he helped his friend or lose the Soulseer's affection if he didn't.'

'But why should it matter to Isla?'

'Power,' Kubeck said.

'But she has no power,' Jamie said.

'Who gives you and the Deathbringer their orders?' Kubeck said.

'The Keeper is the voice of the Veteribus,' Jamie said.

'But who's to say when she speaks it's their words she's using?' I asked. 'You're always telling me how power corrupts—'

'No,' Jamie said, 'I don't believe it.'

'Jamie, she tried to kill me!'

'I know that! What I mean is, I don't believe she did this without the help of someone other than Amaliel and this mystery woman. For one thing, she would only have known Jinx's daemonic name if someone had told her – and second, she simply wouldn't have the capability of blocking the resonance of the use of daemonic power in the Overlands.'

'You do know there's only one explanation?' Jinx said. My angel looked extremely uncomfortable, but Jinx's expression was one of disgust.

'But what can we do?' I asked.

'Nothing,' Jamie said, his shoulders slumping. 'We can do nothing.'

'Except hope that either we're wrong, or the Veteribus will come to the same conclusion and be on the lookout for a dark soul within their ranks.' There was a long, uneasy silence as we all thought on this.

'What will happen to Isla now?' I eventually asked.

'She will be punished – but whatever her punishment, it will not be enough,' Jinx said.

'Do you know what it will be?' I asked Jamie.

'No,' he said very quietly, 'it hasn't yet been decided.'

Twenty-Eight

After dropping Kubeck off at his uncle's shop we went straight back to our villa by the lake to finish the holiday which had been so rudely interrupted. Jinx sent a raven to let Shenanigans and Kerfuffle know we were all well; they were to join us in a few days.

I was still a bit jittery and out of sorts, and I drifted listlessly around the villa. Whatever drug the Keeper had given me certainly hung around.

We'd only been back at our retreat for a couple of days when we had unexpected visitors. Pyrites and I were coming back from a stroll along the beach when in the distance I saw Jamie and Jinx on the verandah in front of the villa, locked in conversation with two Guardians. It didn't look as if there was a lot of laughter going on.

Then one of the Guardians leaned forward and handed Jamie a small box or package. A few more words were spoken, the Guardians both bowed their heads, then they backed away a few steps before taking off into the skies.

Jamie and Jinx stood there watching them fly away, and then Jamie looked down at the package. His lips moved, and Jinx rested one hand on my angel's shoulder. I began to hurry; something had happened and I doubted from their body language that it was anything good. I was still a few yards away when Jinx caught sight of me. He murmured something to Jamie and they both came down off the verandah and walked to join me.

'We've had a visitation,' Jinx said.

'I saw. What did they want?'

Jamie looked down at his hand. 'They brought something for you,' he said and unclenched his fingers to show me.

On his palm sat a small, finely engraved gold box. 'For me?' Jamie grimaced. 'Why do I get the impression that you're not very happy about this?'

'It's not how I feel that matters.'

'I don't follow you.'

Jinx took my hand and led me to the verandah. He sat, and pulled me down onto the step beside him. Jamie arranged himself on my other side, took hold of my hand and began to stroke my thumb with his: a familiar gesture; one he used when trying to give me comfort – or when trying to find some of his own.

'What *is* it?' I asked.

Jamie held out the box again. 'The Veteribus have appointed a new Keeper, and Isla's punishment has been carried out. Officially, Isla was a co-conspirator with Amaliel in a plot against us.'

'And *un*officially?'

'Assurances have been given that if a member of the tribune was involved, they too will be found and brought to justice.'

'So, what's in the box?'

Jamie lifted my hand to his lips and after a brief kiss looked into my eyes, his expression sad. 'It has always been the way with the Veteribus that the punishment should fit the crime.' He let go of my hand to prise the lid from the box. 'Isla was imprisoned within Blue Fire while the court deliberated on her ultimate punishment.' Within the box were a couple of curls of golden hair. 'She had no wings to be taken from her, so her head was shaved.' I peered at the shining locks; now I could see something else, nestled within. 'Her ultimate punishment was not just death, but that her soul should be imprisoned within a crystal phial, as yours would have been, had Amaliel had his way.'

With my fingertip I brushed away the hair to reveal a dark blue crystal that glowed at its centre with celestial light.

'She is now yours, to do with what you will.'

For a moment I stared at the crystal, horrified at what had become of the woman. This truly was a fate worse than death. Then I flicked a curl of gold back over the phial and closed the lid.

I supposed they could have thrown her off the cliff – but maybe they did, before entrapping her soul.

'Take it away,' I said. 'I can't bear to look at it.'

It vanished into Jamie's pocket.

Dinner would have probably been a sober occasion if I'd let it, but I'd had enough sadness and worry to last me a lifetime. We were here, we were alive and our enemies were gone; at least those we knew of. Jamie cooked and Jinx kept us supplied with wine, and when Pyrites wasn't capering around my feet he was flying rings about my head or sitting on my lap licking my face or my hand at every opportunity.

It was a real shame that I couldn't do justice to the wonderful meal Jamie had prepared. It looked amazing, but the smell, which should have set my mouth watering, just made me feel plain ill. I surreptitiously fed lumps off my plate to Pyrites, but I don't think I was fooling anyone.

Jamie dropped his cutlery onto his plate and leaned back in his chair with a contented sigh while Jinx poured us all more wine.

'Will we ever find out if one of the Veteribus was in collusion with Amaliel?' I asked. 'I mean if one of them was . . .' I hesitated, not wanting to put my fear into words.

'They might try and strike against one or all of us again,' Jinx filled in the gap.

I nodded and put my knife and fork down, my appetite completely gone.

'Are you all right?' Jamie asked. 'You haven't eaten much.'

I looked down at the remains of my meal and suddenly felt a bit nauseous. 'I'm just tired, I guess.'

He didn't appear so sure. 'You're rather pale.'

Jinx dropped the chicken leg he'd been gnawing and wiped his mouth with the back of his hand. 'I suppose it's to be expected.'

Jamie frowned at him across the table. 'What is?'

'Lucinda being a bit peaky.'

'Peaky?'

'Umm,' Jinx said, taking a swig of wine.

'Jinx, what are you talking about?' Jamie asked in exasperation.

'You know – mothers-to-be.'

'*Lucky's pregnant?*'

'Twins,' Jinx said.

'How can you possibly know that?' I asked.

'The difference between life and death is a mere heartbeat: I can sense the beginning of new life just as I can feel it ebbing.'

I glanced down at my very flat stomach and then at Jinx. 'I can't be.'

'Why?'

'I . . . How on earth did this happen?'

Jinx gave a snort, then started to laugh so hard I thought he was probably going to piss himself.

I could feel my cheeks heating up as I realised what I'd said, so I told them I wanted a bath and spent far longer in it than was strictly necessary. I really needed some time alone to think. My head was all over the place and I wasn't sure whether to laugh or cry. I really wished I had Kayla to talk to now, and my mother. It would have been nice to have a mother to talk to about something like this.

Was I *really* going to have twins? Would Jinx lie about such a thing? Everything was spinning around in my head when suddenly I recalled a snippet of conversation between Jinx and Persephone that made me feel giddy.

He'd said, 'Did you know that when someone calls upon a daemon and orders him to take a life, that the life of he who calls becomes forfeit if the order cannot be fulfilled?'

'Then fulfil it. There she stands. Kill her – take her life.'

'I cannot.'

'Why ever not?'

'By taking her life I would be destroying two others whose lives you did not bid me to destroy; therefore, I am unable to fulfil your demand.'

I realised I'd never know if he would have killed her if he hadn't known I was pregnant – I wanted to believe it would always have been her rather than me, but that wasn't something I could ponder for too long; it's the sort of thing that would have driven me mad. And when all was said and done, I was alive and she wasn't.

I went to join them on the beach, still thinking about the new lives inside me.

'Are you not happy?' Jinx asked, brushing my hair back from around my face so he could look into my eyes.

'I . . . I really don't know. It's a shock. I've never given it any thought before.'

Jamie went very quiet, and it didn't take much to know what he was thinking about; I was wondering the same: I was pregnant – but by whom? Jinx hadn't actually said, although he had implied it could be him – and he did appear very pleased with himself. That in its own way was good; he'd finally got back his smile – maybe it wasn't the same Devil-may-care grin he used to have, but the slightly forbidding look that had almost permanently marred his face since I'd found him again had gone.

Unfortunately, Jamie's smile had sort of disappeared.

Jinx went and got the flagon of wine and three goblets. 'To toast the expectant mother,' he explained as he handed out the goblets.

'Not for me,' I said, covering mine with my hand.

'Why ever not?' he asked, sinking down onto the sand beside me.

'Alcohol is bad for unborn babies.'

'Lucky, you're a *daemon* – your babies will be just fine,' Jamie said, taking the offered goblet.

'Are you sure?'

'Absolutely.'

I accepted a small measure, but I still wasn't convinced.

'To the five of us,' Jinx said, raising his goblet.

'To the five of us,' Jamie and I chorused, and my hand automatically went to my stomach.

'You are going to be a good mother,' Jinx said, looking at my hand on my tummy.

'I hope so.'

'Just as the lad and I are going to be good fathers.'

Jamie's eyes jerked up to meet Jinx's. '*Fathers?*'

Jinx grinned at him, and Jamie's lips slowly curled up into a smile, his eyes crinkling at the corners.

'We're *both* to be fathers?'

Jinx gave a bob of the head. 'One winged baby, one horned and tailed.'

'Boys?'

'Ah ah, if I told you that, where would be the surprise?'

'As long as they're healthy I don't care,' I said, grinning from ear to ear. I wasn't at all sure I was ready to be a mother, but Jamie and Jinx would be the best of fathers.

We finished the bottle of wine while the sun set over the lake and the amethyst waters changed to deep purple to black.

'Come on,' Jinx said, hopping to his feet and reaching down for my hand.

Jamie also stood and did the same, and I smiled up at the pair of them, took each of their hands and let them pull me up. Jamie put his arm around my shoulders and Jinx slipped his around my waist as they led me back inside.

'I think we should celebrate,' Jinx said.

'I think I've had enough wine,' I said.

'Who said anything about wine?' Jinx kicked open the bedroom door with a nudge of his toe and gave me an exaggerated wink.

'You, sir, are incorrigible,' I told him.

'And you are adorable,' he said, kissing me on the nose and then pulling me from Jamie's arms to swing me around and round and drop me onto the bed.

'Good enough to eat,' Jamie said.

'That, brother, would be a waste.'

And they sank down on the bed beside me and we set about celebrating, all thought of death and assassination attempts forgotten – at least for the time being.

★

As the first rays of dawn filtered in through the shutters, casting soft shimmering lines of pink across the bed, I lay awake. Jamie was spooning my back, his right wing as usual spread out over us like a protective feathered blanket. Jinx lay on his back, eyes closed with a small smile curling his lips, thinking similar thoughts to mine, I suspected.

The lovemaking between the three of us had been unexpectedly tender, and at times so sweet it had almost hurt. Every now and then, one of my lovers laid their palm upon my stomach, their smiles of happiness bringing a lump to my throat. But there was still that one elephant in the room, and if I were to ask the question I had promised myself I never would, it had to be now. If I were to ever get a truly honest answer, at least one I could believe, it would be now.

'Jinx . . .'

'Umm.'

'Are you awake?'

'Umm.'

I took a deep breath, not sure how quite to carry on. He opened one eye, looked at me for a moment, then closed it again.

'No,' he said.

'No?'

'Nothing and no one in this world or any other could ever make me do something so terrible to you.' He smiled up at me, his eyes still closed. 'I will love you until the end of days and I promise I will always keep you and our children safe, my lucky lady.'

'And so will I,' Jamie murmured in my ear, and nuzzled my neck.

I closed my eyes, happier than I could've ever imagined. I believed both my men with every inch of my heart. More importantly, I think my inner daemon did too, for when I dozed off into sleep, I'm pretty sure she was smiling.

The End

Acknowledgements

Taking those first few steps as a writer once you've managed to secure a publishing deal is not quite what you might expect – in fact, after the initial euphoria, it can be totally bewildering and sometimes bloody terrifying. I was lucky – joining Jo Fletcher Books as an author was like becoming part of a family. The other authors enthusiastically welcomed me into the fold and offered their encouragement and advice when at times I must have looked like a rabbit in the headlights. In no particular order I would like to thank Naomi Foyle, Stephanie Saulter, Tom Fletcher, David Towsey, Stephen Jones, Snorri Kristjansson and Sebastien de Castell.

Thanks for your support, guys.

The other members of the family and working behind the scenes at Team JFB are Sam Bradbury and Olivia Mead and I would like to say thank you to these ladies for looking after me on a day-to-day basis – not an easy task, I'm sure!

I would also like to thank my editor and partner-in-crime, the lovely Nicola Budd, who took every step of this exciting journey with me. It really was a joint effort.

Lastly, I would like to thank the amazing Jo Fletcher who, I'm quite sure, thinks of her authors and their creations as her children. Maybe it's just me, but when presented with my draft manuscripts, Jo somehow has the knack of patiently asking questions that have my ideas spinning off into all sorts of unexpected directions making my stories all the richer and me, I hope, a better writer.

Thanks, Jo.

Sue Tingey is the author of the fantasy romance series The Soulseer Chronicles and lives with her husband in East Grinstead, West Sussex.

She spent twenty-eight years working for a major bank and after taking voluntary redundancy in 2001, spent another fourteen or so years working as a practice manager for an arboricultural consultancy. She has now given up the day job to allegedly spend more time with her husband; he however has noticed that an awful lot more writing appears to be going on.

Sue admits that storytelling is her obsession and was thrilled when she was offered a three-book deal by Jo Fletcher Books in 2014.

You can learn more about Sue on her website www.suetingey.co.uk or contact her on Twitter @suetingey